Dragonsight

Paul Collins was born in England, raised in New Zealand and moved to Australia in 1972. In 1975 he launched *Void*, a science fiction magazine.

In 1978, Paul moved from magazine to book publishing, with a series of original Australian science fiction and fantasy novels and anthologies. During this time he published Australia's first heroic fantasy novels.

He sold his first professional fantasy story in 1977 to the United States magazine *Weirdbook*. The best of his short stories have been collected in *The Government in Exile* (1994). A later collection, *Stalking Midnight*, was published by cosmos.com.

His first fantasy novel for younger readers was *The Wizard's Torment*. Paul then edited the young adult anthology *Dream Weavers*, Australia's first heroic fantasy anthology. This was followed by *Fantastic Worlds*, and *Tales from the Wasteland*.

Together with Michael Pryor, Paul is the co-editor of the highly successful fantasy series, *The Quentaris Chronicles*; he has also contributed to the series as an author. Paul's recent works include *The Jelindel Chronicles*, *The Earthborn War* trilogy and *The World of Grrym* trilogy in collaboration with Danny Willis.

Paul has been the recipient of several awards, notably the inaugural Peter McNamara, the Aurealis, and the William Atheling. He has been short-listed for many others, including the Aurealis and Ditmar awards.

Paul served time in the commandos, has a black belt in both tae kwon do and ju jitsu, he was a kickboxer, and trained with the Los Angeles Hell Drivers.

Visit him at *www.paulcollins.com.au* and *www.quentaris.com*

Also by Paul Collins

Dragonlinks

Dragonfang

Wardragon

Swords of Quentaris

Slaves of Quentaris

Dragonlords of Quentaris

Princess of Shadows

The Forgotten Prince

Vampires of Quentaris

The Spell of Undoing

The Slightly Skewed Life of Toby Chrysler

Allira's Gift (with Danny Willis)

Lords of Quibbitt (with Danny Willis)

Morgassa's Folly (with Danny Willis)

The Wizard's Torment

Cyberskin

The Earthborn

The Skyborn

The Hiveborn

Sneila

Metaworlds (ed)

Dream Weavers (ed)

Fantastic Worlds (ed)

The MUP Encyclopaedia of Australian Science Fiction and Fantasy (ed)

Dragonsight

BOOK THREE IN THE JELINDEL CHRONICLES

Paul Collins

FORD ST

Published by Ford Street Publishing, an imprint of
Hybrid Publishers, PO Box 52, Ormond VIC 3204

Melbourne Victoria Australia

Text © Paul Collins 2005
4 6 8 10 9 7 5 3

First published 2005
National Library of Australia
Cataloguing-in-Publication entry

Author: Collins, Paul 1954–
Title: Dragonsight /
Paul Collins

ISBN: 9781921665073 (pbk.)
Target Audience: Fantasy – Juvenile fiction
Dewey Number: A823.3

Cover design: Grant Gittus
Map: Marc McBride

Contents

Q'zar
Mordicar
Sezel
BRAVENHUR
Hazaria
BRAVENHURST R.
Tanglewood
Forest
PASSEN
PASSENDOF
Chasmgyle
Obly
Dren
Tol
Valley of Cl
TANGLESEA
OCEAN
ALGON MTS.
BALTOR
Zaria
H
SKELT
Marisa Riv
Dragonfrost
D'loom
GARRICAL MTS
Blacklight Castle
D
BARRIER R.
Yul
Altimak
KAPLUS IS.
HAMA

EQUATOR
HAZGAR MTS.
Ogven
Serpentire River
River
SERPENTIRE
Centravian
UNISSERA
BAY OF SAMILE
ARCADIA
NERRISSI
DELBRIAS
HAMATRIOL
LYCELLIA
GRATZ
Ishluk

Prologue

The monk was deep in contemplation inside the cave mouth when the world began to change. At first the sound was far off, a rumble of distant thunder. Yet it was a vibration that seemed to emanate from the air and ground alike.

The holy hermit stirred, sensing that something was wrong. He gazed about, blinking away all things otherworldly from his eyes. His meagre possessions – a sheepskin rug, a carrying bag, a pot, a kettle, a small sack of food, and his magical talisman – were where they should have been.

He turned to look outside. What he saw made him scramble arthritically to his feet. He hurried to the ledge projecting from the mountainside and looked out over Dragonfrost: a vast plateau of crumbling rock and blasting sand storms in the Garrical Mountains. It was devoid of life, scoured clean by the howling winds that had blown unceasingly for thousands of years, eating away stone and rock like rivers of acid.

A shadow had fallen across Dragonfrost, and from its depths

a maelstrom was blowing, the beginnings of a vast, churning tornado. Inside the shadow a great rain of stones and boulders, some as big as houses, and twisting ropes of dirt, fell to earth. The ground erupted in a frenzy of explosions as the boulders rained down, forming craters in the plateau and throwing up enormous swathes of sand and pulverised rock.

The hermit's gaze shifted to the sky, searching among the ragged clouds for the source of the attack, but his eyes were rheumy with age. He squinted, trying to make out shapes that were neither cloud nor imagination.

The sound that had awoken him increased to a throaty roar, as if some beast of unimaginable girth had awoken in the depths of the earth, seeking release. Then he glimpsed it. Something dark and irregular in the cloud-torn sky; the roar increased till it hurt the old hermit's ears.

When he saw the cause of the mayhem, he fell to his knees, awed. It filled the sky as far as the eye could see.

Another world had come to Q'zar. Perhaps it was Reculemoon or Blanchmoon. Or maybe one of the planets, fallen from its lofty orbit, thrown afar by an angry god; perhaps this was the End of Time spoken of in the old myths. The Judgement. The Great Accounting.

Still the other world fell slowly from the sky. The hermit scrambled for his talisman and muttered charms of ward and safety, and one or two of propitiation, just in case.

The thunderclaps continued, as though mighty mountains were being ground together, or continents torn apart. The noise buried itself in the old man's bones, threatening to shatter them. Indeed, the hermit's teeth were chattering, but whether from the trembling ground or from fear, he could not tell.

The falling world had reached the hermit's eye level. He gazed in wonder at the ragged base, from which boulders and rocks and great torrents of dirt still poured like a tumultuous waterfall. In a moment that too had dropped beneath his high-flung eyrie. Next came vast walls of stone, rising for thousands of feet, before levelling off.

Finally, the new world was lodged deep into the earth below him and he gazed down upon it in disbelief. From his lofty perch he could see it laid out, though the farther side – more than eighty miles away – was lost in a haze: the new world was a vast irregular ovoid, surrounded by sheer barrier mountains within which were many narrow winding canyons, leading towards a gigantic crater some fifty miles across. In the middle of the crater rose a single sharp pinnacle of dark basalt, easily five thousand feet high.

Perched precariously atop the rocky finger was a forbidding castle, ringed by battlements and festooned with jutting towers and keeps.

The hermit frowned, squinting harder. Around the pinnacle, darting and weaving in the air like a swarm of gnats, were myriad creatures, little more than specks from where he stood. He decided that they looked like hundreds of tiny sparks of fire.

The new world made contact with Q'zar. The sound was ear-shattering. Instantly, enormous dust clouds spurted into the air and rose up on all sides, cloaking it from view, before rushing outwards with thunderous ferocity.

The hermit paled. He knew that when the walls of sand hit, anything in their path would be blasted out of existence. He stumbled into his cave, gathering handy possessions in haste.

The cave led deeper into the mountain, and on through to the other side via narrow fissures. He knew he had to bury himself as deep as possible before the scouring sandstorm arrived; worse, he knew even as he shoved his pot and kettle in the sack that a wave of grit was rushing inexorably towards him, hurtling through the air like a tidal wave.

In all, he had a few minutes. That was all. But he must live; he must carry the message to the world. He believed now that he had been chosen. He must warn the people of all lands that the ancient prophecy had come true.

The dragons had returned to Q'zar.

Chapter 1

AMBUSHED

Some two hundred miles to the west of Dragonfrost, D'loom, the chief seaport of Skelt, had experienced a kind of rebirth. In both tavern and royal court it was hotly debated whether this was a cause for celebration or curses. In the days since the Preceptor's armies had been broken and scattered, the lands had fallen into anarchy. The ancient roads, once protected by royal decree backed up by garrisons of soldiers, were now largely abandoned to brigands, hunting unwary victims.

Navigating the sea lanes had become as precarious, yet D'loom had prospered. When pirates returned to wreak havoc on the trading ships, they had chosen the port of D'loom as their headquarters, giving the city and its ships a type of immunity. Naturally this immunity came at a price, or more accurately, a percentage.

The son of the former king knew a good thing when it clutched him by the throat and held a dagger to his heart. He offered the pirates haven, and a tenth of all taxes. Because even ordinary pickpockets and second-storey thieves thought twice before risking the wrath of the pirates, a kind of law and order had descended on D'loom. The port city actually prospered, while other cities fell into decline.

Jelindel dek Mediesar was a young woman whose face was etched by fine lines, proof that she had endured war, terror, and generally dangerous living. She was sitting in a tavern, thinking about D'loom's sudden prosperity, and how some occupations flourish no matter what the circumstances. She was an archmage-warrior, an occupation unique for a woman. To add to her achievements, she was also an intelligent archmage-warrior, and this gave her considerable advantage over the competition.

Daretor, a rather introspective master swordsman, lounged beside her. Through a series of misfortunes, he had run foul of a former companion called Zimak, a thief. Daretor currently inhabited Zimak's diminutive body, while Zimak strode inside Daretor's magnificently muscled frame. Many months had passed since the body-swap. Fortunately for Daretor, Zimak's body had been amicable to hard work and exercise. Now feeling more comfortable in Zimak's body, the swordsman nonetheless suffered spells of depression whenever he pondered the fate of his own body in the hands of the mead-guzzling Zimak.

A grizzled, gaunt man sat before the pair, dickering for their services. His name was Theroc, and he was from Yuledan. He claimed the town was under attack by aerial beasts that came at night, plucking citizens from the streets. The town, already plundered regularly by brigands from the nearby mountains, was on the point of collapse. None dared leave their homes, for fear of the airborne predators that came at night, and the brigands that came by day. Fear was stamped across Theroc's features. His eyes darted at any noise and he would not sit with his back to window or door.

'We will pay you whatever you ask,' he was saying, 'if only you come quickly. If not, I fear Yuledan will have only ghosts for citizens.'

Daretor leaned forward, staring at the ground. 'You say nobody has seen these beasts?' he said, concentrating on Theroc's words rather than his face.

'I say none has seen them and lived,' Theroc replied. 'Here, this is half of what we can pay.'

He pushed a heavy pouch across the table; it clinked with the dull sound of gold oriels.

Daretor hefted it, then peered inside. He nodded at Jelindel.

'Expect us in three days,' she said.

Theroc sighed with relief. 'I will send a message,' he said, seizing Jelindel's hand and kissing it fervently before rising.

Theroc nodded awkwardly at Daretor. Jelindel noted that as he left the tavern he glanced nervously skyward before hurrying along the street. He ran doubled over, shoulders hunched, as if fearing an attack from above.

Jelindel grinned at Daretor, tapping the bag of gold coins. 'This and its companion could keep us in comfort for some time,' she commented.

'Have you any idea what the sky beasts might be?' he asked.

'No, but things that fly are very vulnerable. They must be light if they are to fly. Consequently, they can't have heavy scales, and will be easily wounded. From all accounts, you had no problems with the bat-wing warriors in the Forest of Castles.'

'That said, the Preceptor's deadmoon assassins very nearly killed you,' Daretor pointed out.

'But I am still alive, and they are not. If it flies, it can be easily hurt.'

Jelindel watched Daretor for a time. He seemed more introspective than usual.

'You're thinking about the fliers from the Forest of Castles,' she stated, rather than asked.

Daretor sucked noisily at a sliver of meat caught between his teeth. 'Their wing devices could but carry their own weight. They could never have snatched up victims and flown off with them.'

Jelindel tucked the purse safely away. 'Well, it looks as though we're still partners. Your vow to hang up your sword and join a monastery was short-lived.'

Daretor snorted. 'I said nothing about joining a monastery. Besides, why should I be a scholar when I have you to do the thinking?'

'Good point, Daretor darling. Keep that thought and we'll live happily ever after.'

An hour later they were strolling up Fish Street, aiming to book passage for themselves and three horses on one of the great caravans that provided the only safe long-distance transportation for passengers and cargo. The sheer size of the caravans deterred any attacking force smaller than an army.

They spent the rest of the day gathering supplies. That night they took a comfortable room so that they might have their last good sleep for what would probably be a very long time. Despite the comfortable bed and clean sheets, Jelindel had trouble sleeping.

'Do you remember what I said on the battlefield after the Preceptor's army fell?' she asked Daretor softly.

'Go to sleep.'

'Did I say that?'

Daretor stirred, thinking back. 'Um . . . you foresaw that anarchy would return to the world. Stands to reason. Remove the means to enforce law and order, and you can kiss law and order goodbye.'

'I also said that we would have a part to play,' said Jelindel. 'A thousand years of darkness lies ahead.'

'A thousand years,' muttered Daretor. 'Why is it always a thousand years? Why not nine hundred and a score years, or eleven hundred?'

'I am having a premonition about all this, Daretor. In some way that I can't yet fathom, we're involved. Our obnoxious ex-comrade Zimak too, I think, wherever he is. I have a feeling that this work in Yuledan will start us on that road.'

'Don't mention that thieving wastrel,' Daretor grumbled. 'Why do your premonitions always come just as I am trying to get to sleep?' he wondered. 'Why not in the morning?'

The next day they arrived early at the caravan grounds. The number of pack animals alone exceeded two thousand, and they were to be escorted by a force the size of a small army. By mutual agreement, Jelindel and Daretor were part of this force.

'They should be paying us,' muttered Daretor, as they rode out of the city, 'not us them.'

They were already covered in dust, and the pace was very slow.

'We are paying to have the protection of the caravan's sheer size,' Jelindel pointed out.

A customs officer rode past. 'May your journey be prosperous!' he called out cheerily.

'There speaks a man who is not going on the journey, yet will grow prosperous on our departure,' said Daretor.

By late afternoon D'loom was a smudge on the horizon. The caravan was well organised and run with efficiency, but this did not stop Daretor and Jelindel from being covered in dust, chilled by the wind, and abused by the marshal riders.

'Do you know that I have not had a single thought of ambush all day?' Jelindel asked.

'I, on the other hand, have thought of nothing but dust that smells of horse and camel manure,' replied Daretor.

'Why have we never travelled this way before?' Jelindel wanted to know.

'It's called poverty,' Daretor said. 'P.O.V.E.R.T.Y. People who have no money suffer from it. They have adventures involving ambushes because lone travellers on the open road are easy targets.'

'Well, we're not poor anymore and I say this is definitely the way to travel. It's like being in a large travelling town.'

'Especially for first-class travellers, who get the wagons with dust mesh screens.'

'Most especially first class. The largest wagons even have privies.'

'It would seem you can take the girl out of the countess but not the countess out of the girl.'

Jelindel ignored the remark. 'It's sort of romantic, don't you think?'

'Romantic?' Daretor asked. His mind went slightly blank at the thought.

'Yes, romantic. It's something we should try once in a while.'

'You're deliberately annoying me because I wanted a good night's sleep before the journey.'

'Not true!' Jelindel snapped, and turned her back.

❖

Caravans are very much like moving towns. By day they are a long, thin line. By night they are a small, compact settlement with markets, defences, homes, workshops, and even taverns. With the caravan stopped for the night, Jelindel toured the market to see what was on offer. Amid the exotic drinks, foods, trinkets, amulets, herbal powders, and weapons, she found a book stall. Few people paid much attention to the stall and its owner, and Jelindel soon learned that the man could not read. Someone had apparently marked the books according to what they thought their value ought to be, but whoever it was did not know much about literature. Significant books with no pictures were reasonably priced, while simple books with nice pictures and good leather covers were expensive. There were books about dark magic with forbidding covers; one in particular was so horrible that it drew Jelindel's eye. She picked it up reluctantly. It was about Golgora, the paraworld of eternal punishment. 'The Place of the Damned,' she said, shuddering. She dropped the book back on the pile, childhood nightmares unpleasantly rising within her. She moved quickly to a stack of geographical books. They seemed safer. One of these took her fancy, and she bought it. The price was low because it contained maps instead of pictures.

Jelindel took the book to her tent, and began poring over it by the light of a candle. Candles were expensive on a caravan because they took up weight that might otherwise be occupied by spices.

Over the course of the next two hours Jelindel merged with the book, peering at the intricate maps, and reading the histories that accompanied each place name. It brought back memories of her childhood home, before it was stormed by the Preceptor's lindrak assassins. She could not bear to think of her slaughtered family. In those far-off days she had loved maps; the larger and more exotic the better. For hours she would study them, tracing out roads and ancient highways that linked now vanished towns and kingdoms, creating her own imaginary kingdoms and visualising them in her mind.

Daretor returned from sentry duty at the perimeter of the encamped caravan. 'You're burning a candle?' he exclaimed.

'All the better to see by,' replied Jelindel.

'But don't you know how much they cost?'

'Well, yes, I paid for it after all.'

'But you could read by sunlight.'

'No I couldn't. I'm riding a horse between dawn and dusk, and I'm supposed to be watching out for danger as well.'

'Well, have you eaten yet? I'm hungry.'

As it happened, Jelindel had forgotten about dinner. They stepped out of the tent, carrying their packs for security. As they did, a thin man moved swiftly away in the direction of the market. Jelindel had the distinct impression that he had been eavesdropping outside the tent.

'What do you think you're doing?' Jelindel demanded, but the man had already vanished into the crowd.

Daretor looked at her, puzzled. He hadn't noticed anything. 'Something the matter?' he asked.

'Nothing,' she said, putting an arm around him. 'Nothing at all. Let's go and buy some overpriced food and drink.'

The area near the food stalls had become a type of open-air tavern. The caravan master sat at the centre of a circle of several dozen people, holding court like a minor monarch. Jelindel and Daretor listened as they ate dinner, which consisted of various odd looking scraps wrapped in stale flatbread.

'I come from a long line of sailors,' the caravan master was saying, 'going back eight generations, but in me it nearly came to a halt because – and I am ashamed to admit it . . . ' he roared with laughter, 'that no sooner am I upon the water, no matter how calm it may be, than I am bent over the railing being sick. Nothing to be done about it. Nothing at all. So here I am. Captain of a ship of camels and horses that sails a different sea, one that is mercifully without the slip and sway that so unmans my poor landlubber's stomach.'

'You can't be ridin' a camel!' someone called, and everyone laughed.

Also gathered around were a number of merchants travelling to Hez'ar in Baltoria, and some farming representatives returning to the great forests east of Passendof, beyond the Serpentire River. There was also a scattering of noblemen and their families and a mage or two. That, in itself, was odd. Mages tended not to travel, except in times of extreme danger.

Jelindel and Daretor knew no one on the journey, though some of the travellers had heard of the famed fighting duo. Certainly the two mages, under contract to a town in Unissera, had heard of the Archmage Jelindel dek Mediesar. Jelindel quickly became the centre of attention, but she was not the type who liked to boast and be admired. She made it her business to vanish as soon as she could. Sometime later, Daretor found her back in their tent, lying on her unrolled bedding, too tired to even undress.

'I love travelling,' she said to Daretor as he began to remove his boots. 'I just hate the crowds that go with caravans. If we had a rich patron, we could circumnavigate all Q'zar in our very own caravan. We would employ twenty elite lancers to deter brigands, and visit at our leisure every state on the continent.'

'Why?'

'To bring the maps of my dreams to life.'

Daretor shrugged. 'If you like,' he said, 'but we had better find that patron soon. The days are getting darker and troubles brew like plagues. You heard the captain say they've had to change the routes and shorten the overall journey. Many lands have fallen on bad times, and even worse rulers. You yourself have predicted that things will get worse.'

'Why is it when one tyrant falls, twenty rise to take his place?' Jelindel sighed. 'And caravans will be the first casualties. Provinces and shires will withdraw into themselves, becoming suspicious of strangers. A darkness of the mind will descend on all humanity . . . '

'There you go again.'

Jelindel laughed. 'I'm just pandering to your spirit for adventure.'

Sounds of commotion came from the distance, men shouting, and the clash of steel.

'Never fails,' muttered Daretor. 'Get my second boot off and the fighting starts.'

'It begins,' said Jelindel. 'Our rest is over.'

'What do you mean? It's probably just some drunken camel drivers.'

'I think the peril of Yuledan has come to us before we can come to it.'

'We're many leagues and days from Yuledan.'

'Nevertheless, it comes for us. I can feel it. Quick. Get your boots back on and fetch your sword. I don't know what comes, only that it does.'

The sound of fighting grew closer. Jelindel and Daretor had just emerged from the tent when a company of foot soldiers appeared from amid their neighbours' tents. Daretor instantly recognised the device on their leather surcoats: a flaming-red dragon's-head motif on a field of black. They were being attacked by soldiers from the Tower Inviolate. But that was impossible!

Daretor dropped into a fighting stance, his mind in fighting mode, while Jelindel stood ready with an enchantment on her lips. Before either of them could react, someone tossed a handful of yellow gems into a nearby campfire. The crystals exploded in a soundless rush of air and coruscating light. Then Daretor and Jelindel knew no more.

Jelindel was the first to recover. She stirred and opened one eye, knitting her brows as she tried to remember what had happened. Objects loomed in front of her and it was another minute or two before her vision cleared. She was in a hold, probably aboard a ship. The muffled hissing of the wind, the creaking of leather, the swaying of the floor, confirmed her worst suspicions. Although there was something not quite right.

Salt.

There was no smell of the sea, no sound of gulls, and certainly not the ever-present salt spray. A nearby groan distracted her; Jelindel turned to find Daretor gazing at her. His hands and feet were bound, although hers were not. There were, however, ligature marks on her wrists and ankles; she *had* been tied, but could not remember anything.

'Where are we?' Daretor asked, perplexed.

'In a lot of trouble?' suggested Jelindel.

'Well, I would be a lot happier if I were in a lot of trouble and had my hands and legs free.'

She untied his wrists and rubbed them to restore the circulation, then he untied his own ankles.

'We're on a ship,' Jelindel said. 'But something's not right.'

Daretor knuckled the stinging sensation from his eyes. The

yellow gems seemed to have affected him in ways they had not Jelindel.

'We're not on a ship,' he said. 'Not, at least, a ship of the sea or land.'

'What do you mean?'

'We're on the back of a flying creature,' he told her, wincing as the blood pumped back into his feet. 'I think it's a dragon.'

Daretor's tone chilled Jelindel. 'You're serious?' she asked.

'It fits, doesn't it? Aerial beasts in Yuledan, gouts of fire. Besides, I recognised the livery of our attackers at the caravan. They must be from the Tower Inviolate.'

'But that's on another paraworld.'

'I know,' Daretor said. 'But if we were able to travel there, then what's to stop them from coming here?'

Jelindel seemed distracted for a moment. 'Nothing, I suppose. But it's unlikely that they would come all this way to retrieve an escaped gladiator.'

'Agreed,' said Daretor, shrugging. 'But why else come for us?'

'I don't know,' Jelindel said, biting her lip. 'I guess we will find out soon enough.'

Daretor blinked away the pain roaring behind his eyes. His vision had become blurred by a red haze. 'What did they do to us back there?'

Jelindel moved closer to him. 'Are you all right?'

Daretor drew a ragged breath. 'If feeling as though I've drunk a squad of lancers under the table can be deemed as all right, I guess I am,' he groaned.

'That's all right, then.' Jelindel ran her fingers through his hair, concentrating. Bit by bit she drew writhing energy from his scalp, wincing as she absorbed it. When she could stand the pain no longer, she flicked the build up from her fingers.

'It's easing,' he said.

Jelindel devoted part of her attention to dispelling Daretor's psychic hangover and another to finding out what might have happened at the caravan.

'Ordinarily I could have shielded us from their magic,' she said at last. 'But it was very strong – I suspect it was ancient magic. Dragon magic, which is said to be the most powerful of all.'

'I've had enough of dragons,' Daretor said. 'Hundreds of the horrors. Intelligent, too.'

Soon, Daretor was able to stand and move about. They crossed to a viewing plate, and Daretor's suspicions proved correct. Patches of cloud whipped past. The land was far below. Once, they ploughed through a skein of jet-black magalels, scattering them left and right, leaving them squawking in their wake.

Without warning, the door to the cargo hold opened. A man entered while two guards stood inside the opening, warily alert. The man bowed curtly. He had a sharp face, hawkish from some angles. His thick brows met in the middle, over intelligent eyes. An air about him indicated that he was no underling. He seemed malevolent, despite his seeming politeness.

A wolf badly disguised as a sheep, thought Daretor, not bothering to assess the possibility of escape while up so very high.

The man seemed to read Daretor's mind. 'Where would you go?' he asked. 'Unless you can fly? My name is Rakeem. I am vizier to his Majesty, King Amida, whose hospitality you have already been privileged to experience.' He gazed at Daretor, who shrugged.

'What do you want with us?' Jelindel asked. 'You don't seem to want us dead.'

Rakeem switched his attention to her.

'You know what we want.'

'Actually we don't,' said Jelindel, with the confidence of someone who has nothing to lose. 'I assume you are from a paraworld, the very paraworld where my friend Daretor was marooned in times past.'

'Innocence does not become you, Archmage, but I shall speak our intentions plainly if you want it that way. We are seeking a powerful talisman that was stolen the same night your friend here, along with his accomplice, escaped from our domain. We want it back.'

'We stole nothing!' Daretor said heatedly.

'Do not insult my intelligence,' Rakeem said. 'Did you not also steal one of our dragons? I would hardly call that "nothing".'

Daretor glared back. Jelindel scratched her head.

'Steal is putting it a bit strongly,' Daretor said. 'We'd been unlawfully and unjustly imprisoned, and sentenced to die in your barbaric games. Escaping on one of your own dragons was only fair. Speaking for myself, I took no talisman.'

'Perhaps.'

'What did it look like?' Jelindel asked, gesturing for Daretor to keep silent.

Rakeem seemed surprised at the question. 'It is a strange artefact, brought perhaps from an unknown paraworld long ago. It is made of something called red jade – a rarity everywhere. A thousand years ago it was fashioned into the shape of a dragon heart, and ever since it has pulsed as if filled with a dragon's life's blood.'

'We did not steal it,' Daretor repeated, 'although we might have if given a chance.'

Rakeem scowled. He walked to the door and turned to face them again. 'It is the dragonsight. My king wants it back, even at the price of destroying your world to get it.'

'That's a high price to pay,' said Daretor.

'That is of little consequence. He doesn't live here, does he?' said Rakeem.

'Why is the dragonsight so valuable?' asked Jelindel.

'If you had it, I would not dare tell you. If you do not, it is none of your business.'

He strode out the door, followed by his men-at-arms. The door slammed shut, and a heavy bolt shot home.

Jelindel breathed out. 'Charming,' she said. Daretor snorted in amusement. 'Perhaps you should tell me more about this world before we land. Am I liable to need a crash course as a *female* gladiator?'

'No need to worry there,' Daretor said, smiling wanly. 'You would acquit yourself well enough.'

'Well enough to do what? Stay alive for thirty seconds? Come now, tell me everything.'

Daretor told her the story in more detail. Nearly a year earlier, he and their former companion, Zimak, had been marooned on another paraworld. They had materialised thousands of feet above ground. As they hurtled to inevitable death, they were netted by a flight of dragonriders and carried to the Tower Inviolate. Here they were recruited as gladiators, for the amusement of the locals. With the help of a slave called Osric and his dragon S'cressling, they had escaped. Eventually they had returned to Q'zar. Osric went back to his own people with the stolen dragon, hoping to breed healthy dragons and build an army of airborne creatures that might rival the dark dominion of King Amida.

Jelindel pondered the story. 'Something doesn't quite make sense,' she said.

'How so? I think it's a good story and it's true.'

'They must think you have hidden the dragonsight on their paraworld, otherwise they wouldn't be taking you back to their world. You don't have it in your coin purse, after all.'

Daretor shrugged. 'You could be right. If we had stolen it, it would be the logical thing to do, in case we were caught before returning to Q'zar.'

'Did you hide it?'

'No!' snapped Daretor.

'All right, all right. I shall assume that you are telling the truth, which might not be a very sensible thing to do. But let us assume it anyway. That leaves Zimak. Surely they must also be seeking him?'

Daretor's face hardened. 'Let them find him. It's nature's way of punishing him for all that dissolute living. Good-for-nothing, overgrown braggart.'

'Darling mine, if ever you're to swap bodies, then you had best hope nothing untoward happens to him. Now where was I? Zimak was last seen heading towards Fa'red's castle in Skelt. What reason could he have, do you suppose, for seeking an audience with his bitterest enemy?'

'And ours.'

'Maybe he wants to swap recipes.' Jelindel ventured, scratching her head.

'More likely tales of his amorous conquests,' Daretor said with a sneer.

'Now, now . . . No, I'm thinking he might have the dragonsight. Obviously it's a potent icon, otherwise this King Amida wouldn't be going to so much trouble to bring you to book.'

'Zimak . . .' Daretor left the name dangling.

The dragon lurched, banking steeply; they were flung off their feet and rolled across the floor till they crashed against the wall. They climbed cautiously to their feet and peered out the porthole when the floor corrected itself.

They were passing through a mountainous region, negotiating a high pass between peaks.

'I wonder where we're heading,' Jelindel mused. 'They must have powerful magic to bring a beast of this size through a portal between paraworlds.'

'Beasts,' said Daretor, reminding her of the mission to Yuledan. 'Theroc spoke of the night *swarming* with aerial creatures.'

'If these are the same dragons,' Jelindel said.

The dragon emerged from a bank of grey cloud. Ahead were the foothills of the northern slopes of the Garrical Mountains. Instead of a great empty basin where Dragonfrost should have been, there rose a sheer rocky wall at least five thousand feet, its uppermost peaks cloaked in cloud.

Jelindel was dumbfounded.

'Sort of vaguely not of our world,' she said, confused. 'I think . . . this is not possible.'

'It's the Tower Inviolate,' Daretor said.

She stared at him. 'That's in the other paraworld.'

'Well it's here now,' Daretor said, wide-eyed.

The truth dawned on Jelindel. 'Is this the mountain shield wall that you told me about? The one that surrounds the crater in which stands the Tower Inviolate?'

Daretor nodded, too pensive to comment.

'Don't you see what this means?'

Daretor didn't turn. 'No, I don't. To me it looks like they've brought their entire domain through the portal.'

'That's exactly what they seem to have done,' Jelindel said.

'But no magic could achieve such a thing. Could it?'

'I'm open to suggestions.' Jelindel shook her head, still gazing at the massive wall. 'With such magic, they could do much, much worse. Nobody on this world could hope to stop them. Then again, they might come in peace, and achieve greatness.'

The dragon dived into one of the canyons, the sheer walls of which were barely wider than the beast's powerfully beating wing tips. The flight through the canyon was frightening but also exhilarating, though neither Jelindel nor Daretor were in any mood to appreciate it.

'This is definitely some powerful magic of the ancients,' said Jelindel.

The dragon flew from the inner canyon opening out over a vast crater some five miles across. At the centre of the crater rose the Tower Inviolate. The scale of the magic used to transport such a huge object from one paraworld to another stupefied Jelindel. Power to do that simply did not exist. And then another thought occurred to her.

'I have remembered something from the writings of an oracle,' she said. 'An ancient prophecy that claims that one day the dragons of Q'zar are destined to return.'

'Of Q'zar?

'There once were dragons on Q'zar. You've heard the fairy tales, the curses – remember I showed you and Zimak the fossilised remains of one such beast in the Valley of Clouds. Places such as Dragonfrost, which till now has lain empty . . . it makes me wonder if this is where they originally dwelt. Maybe this entire massif was originally from Q'zar. From this very spot. Maybe it has finally found its way back home.'

'Why and how?' asked Daretor, dreading the obvious answers.

'Why? Who knows? How? Well, because you and Zimak showed them the way.'

Daretor drew a deep breath before replying. 'Are you saying it's my fault?'

Jelindel shook her head. 'This isn't about whose fault it is, Daretor. Perhaps you acted as a beacon. A candle can't help but attract moths.'

'These dragons are a little larger than moths.'

'True, but what matters is how are we going to deal with them. Are they here as friends or foes?'

'Something must have made them leave in the first place,' Daretor reasoned.

'Good point.'

'And that something can be found again.'

'Where?' asked Jelindel.

'I didn't say I knew everything.'

Jelindel thought for a time.

'It was thousands of years ago. Some scholars say the dragons' land sank beneath the sea, and yet others say that a terrible foe came through the portal from another paraworld. Seashells have been found in the middle of Dragonfrost, and in other unlikely places.'

'Perhaps we'll soon learn the truth,' Daretor said, eyeing the dark tower that was growing closer with every moment. Dozens of dragons, all bearing passengers, swarmed about the castle and the huge roosting holes.

Below, the floor of Dragonfrost appeared a dry dusty desert, networked by a maze of thin ravines that covered the floor like the wrinkles on the face of an ancient crone.

The dragon landed heavily in one of the roosting holes, and Jelindel and Daretor were once again flung to the floor. At the same moment the door opened and the guards hurried in, seemingly used to the swaying of the deck. They snapped shackles on both prisoners.

Jelindel and Daretor were escorted to the main deck. From there they were taken over a gangplank to a ledge halfway up the roost wall. Then they were led along a dark tunnel.

'I never wanted to see this place again,' muttered Daretor.

After several winding passageways, lit by little more than smoking tallow torches, they emerged in a grand chamber that rose in shallow tiers – like high steps – to a central stage or lounging area. King Amida and his courtiers held court here, and suffered whatever entertainments were brought before them.

The prisoners were dragged before King Amida and forced to their knees. Rakeem appeared from another entrance, followed by several lackeys. He had found the time to change into courtly robes, and looked as if he had been anointed with oils. His skin gleamed in the lamplight.

The king, resplendent in fine robes and regalia, stared disapprovingly at Jelindel and Daretor. 'You have found them,' he said, beaming at Rakeem. 'Tell me about the girl.'

Rakeem inclined his head in abeyance. 'She is the man's mate. I deemed it wise to bring her also, as she may know something of the dragonsight. She will, in any case, provide the other with incentive to speak truthfully.'

'As always, Rakeem, you see all the ways. You are not unlike the dragonsight itself, I think.' The king chuckled and Rakeem bowed humbly. The king stared at Daretor fixedly.

'Where is it?' he demanded. 'Where is my talisman, you wretched thief?'

Daretor kept his eyes downcast, trying to efface himself as far as his pride would allow. 'Is it permitted to speak to the king?' he asked.

'It is. Speak. And none of your barbarian lies.'

'Your Majesty, your esteemed vizier has explained the nature of the thing that you seek, but I do not have it. I did not steal this talisman nor have I ever laid hands upon it. I am a warrior and a man of honour. I have spoken the truth.'

The king contemplated Daretor's words.

'I remember your deeds in the arena, Q'zaran,' he said. 'I know you as the gladiator that felled the mantid. Yet it stands that when you escaped from the citadel so too did the dragon-sight go missing. Such a coincidence suggests its own answer.'

'Sire, it may be that my former companion, whose honour is less than desirous, may have stolen the object that you seek,' Daretor said. 'If that were so, he would not have told me about it, but hoped to sell it for his own gain.'

The king laughed. 'That is exactly what he said about you.'

Zimak stepped out from behind a hanging tapestry, a spear point encouraging him to move along. He was scowling.

'Zimak,' said Jelindel, genuinely surprised. Daretor struggled against his manacles. The sight of his once bronzed and toned body now turned to flab dismayed and angered him.

'Well, thief and betrayer,' he growled. 'Now we know how we were found. What profit have you negotiated for handing us over?'

'None,' said Zimak. 'I am a . . . er . . . guest of King Amida, like you. I was deep in some negotiations in Skelt when these fine people located me.'

'Deep in the process of selling us out to Fa'red, I'll wager,' Daretor shouted. 'Or selling something that doesn't belong to you.'

The king watched the exchange, enjoying the display as though it were a pantomime. He clapped his hands. 'Enough,' he announced. 'Take them away, Rakeem. Test them. The Sacred One will know the truth.'

Guards hurried forth and grabbed Jelindel and Daretor. They bustled them from the audience chamber and raced along dark corridors, through several chambers in which industrious men and women were hard at work, to a jutting inner buttress in which a door was outlined.

One of the guards tugged at a rope and a distant bell sounded. A moment later it was followed by a harsh grinding noise.

A clattering sound came from behind the door. The guards pulled it open, revealing a small enclosed chamber with no door or window. Jelindel and Daretor assumed this was their prison cell, but the guards pushed inside with them and closed the door. One of the guards tugged on a rope which again caused a bell of a different tone to sound.

Without warning the room lurched then dropped downwards, as if it were falling into a hole in the ground. Jelindel and Daretor clutched each other as the primitive elevator descended.

The guards laughed at the fright on their faces. One explained how the elevator worked: a series of ropes and pulleys, operated by slaves in the depths of the castle. They winched the hanging cabin up and down the vertical tunnel, as required.

'It is a wonder,' Jelindel said sincerely.

The cage stopped and they were ushered into a chamber with a deep fissure in the floor. Jelindel suspected that lava flowed inside it. The air was oppressively hot, wafting up and carrying the reek of brimstone.

The sweating guards led Jelindel and Daretor towards a dark shapeless mound sitting on a kind of rocky island where the magma fissure split in two before rejoining again. The prisoners crossed a small stone bridge to the island.

Rakeem appeared from the other side, his face expressionless. He crossed another bridge and gestured for the prisoners to kneel. An intensity behind his eyes caused Jelindel to frown.

'You are in the presence of the Sacred One,' Rakeem softly intoned, as if he were in the holiest of churches. 'Here you will speak the truth, for nought else can be heard in this place.'

The dark mound stirred. A huge sinuous shape uncoiled and lifted a gaunt serpentine head to gaze at them with a yellow cat's eye the size of a dinner plate. The other eye socket hung limp and shrouded by loose skin. It was an ancient and withered dragon. Bat-like leathery skin hung from his frame like a quilt. Where once scales would have shone in myriad colours, they now hung dark and dank as their surroundings.

'Who comes?' asked a deep sibilant voice. The dragon took a deep breath, struggling for the strength to speak. 'Who comes to trouble me?'

'It is I, Sacred One,' said Rakeem. The dragon's eye narrowed, peering at the vizier. Rakeem took an involuntary step back as if the weight of this gaze was too much to bear. 'It is Rakeem – the king's adviser.'

The ancient dragon pondered the statement and a slow chuckle rumbled from his heaving stomach. 'That is nothing to me,' he wheezed. 'The king of men is still a man and he and all his descendants will be dust before I breathe my last. Why do you disturb my slumber?'

Rakeem seemed affronted by the speech, but betrayed not an ounce of verbal disapproval. 'Sacred One, we have need of the truthsense. We believe these prisoners stole the dragonsight.'

The dragon's head swivelled and the piercing yellow eye stared into Jelindel and Daretor. The creature's breath rattled, a long juddering sound that reminded Jelindel of a lowering drawbridge.

Although Jelindel had time to cast a stronger barrier between herself and the dragon, the beast's gaze bored straight through it. She felt a profound lethargy come over her.

'Did you take the dragonsight?' the old dragon asked.

They both answered that they did not. 'Know you who did?' Again they answered in the negative. The dragon considered this, or maybe – as Jelindel came to believe – it used the moment to probe deeper into their beings.

The dragon's breath grew laboured. 'Have you experience of finding that which is lost?' the Sacred One asked.

'We have,' Jelindel said. Daretor nodded in agreement. Jelindel later said that she sensed a deep sadness behind the dragon's words.

'Then I bid you find the dragonsight and restore it to its . . . proper place. Go now. Let me return to my Dreaming.'

The ancient dragon's head sagged; the eye closed, extinguishing the remarkable lantern. Jelindel and Daretor jerked as if waking from a dream. They looked at the dragon in wonder. The only sign of life was his deep rumbling breath.

Rakeem ordered the guards to remove the prisoners. He seemed only too happy to leave the slumbering giant to his sleep.

Chapter 2

DEADLY PHILTRE

They were thrown into a room that, despite its purpose, turned out to be a well-furnished prison cell. The iron-bound door was bolted and every window was barred. Nor were they alone. Zimak was lounging on a couch with his feet up, as if waiting for them. Another man was asleep on a nearby mattress.

'Hie,' Zimak said. 'At least the old guy knows honest faces when he sees them.'

Daretor made to stride across and grab him, but Jelindel restrained him.

'What punishment is this?' Daretor demanded. 'What have I done to deserve being locked up with a traitor?'

Zimak shifted sulkily. 'Give me a break, Daretor. That's not fair.'

'You stole my body,' Daretor thundered.

'To save your life,' Zimak shot back.

Jelindel pulled harder on Daretor's arm. 'Let's keep to the matter at hand. We should hear Zimak's story first,' she said.

Daretor snorted. 'Why not? After all, a rat's a rat until proven otherwise.'

'Exactly my sentiments,' said Zimak, sitting up. 'Besides, I'm no traitor, and I don't even like cheese.'

'Do you deny telling them where to find us?' Daretor demanded.

Zimak fidgeted. He looked at Daretor, then at Jelindel. 'No,' he said, 'and yes.'

Daretor turned to Jelindel. 'His brain is addled.'

'My brain is no more addled than yours, Daretor,' Zimak countered, gaining confidence from Jelindel's patience. 'I was taken before the Sacred One, as you were. He asked me many questions, some concerning you and your whereabouts, and much else besides. Rakeem wanted me to tell him as much as I know about our world's history, as well.'

'That would have been a short conversation,' Daretor said.

Jelindel squeezed Daretor's shoulder. 'When were you taken, Zimak?'

'Several weeks ago. They tracked us to Q'zar, then kidnapped me back to their paraworld. In so doing they discovered that this is where they hailed from, thousands of years ago.'

'I was right,' Jelindel breathed. 'These *are* the dragons of Q'zar or at least their descendants.'

'So you see, I had no more say in the matter than you. Nobody can lie to the Sacred One. It simply isn't possible, as you might have noticed.'

Daretor grunted a reply that Zimak couldn't make out. 'I'll take that as an abject apology.'

'You little skink rat,' Daretor exploded, lunging forward.

Zimak stifled a yawn, confident that Jelindel would restrain the swordsman. She did.

'We know for a fact that you presented yourself before Fa'red,' Daretor grated. 'If not to join forces with him, then what?'

Zimak shook his head in apparent shock. 'You do me a disservice, Daretor.' He looked at Jelindel. 'I would have expected more from you, after all we've been through.'

Jelindel tightened her grip on Daretor's arm. 'Spare us the theatrics, Zimak,' she said.

'How else could I have found you? Q'zar is a big place. I would have grown old searching. No, I needed help. How better to achieve my ends than to pretend to throw my lot in with one of the most powerful men around?'

'Perhaps we didn't want you to find us,' Daretor said pointedly.

'Last *I* heard, you ungrateful barbarian, you wanted your body back.' Zimak shifted wearily on the seat. 'Yours is fine when it comes to cracking heads, but for the most part, it goes to fat too easily.'

Daretor's eyes blazed. He leapt forward, dragging Jelindel behind him. They tumbled on to the seat, with Jelindel pinning Daretor down.

Zimak had barely shoved off from the seat before the pair crashed on to it.

'That's a fine way to show your appreciation for all I've done,' Zimak panted, unused to sudden movement.

'You planned to kill Prince Ulad and swap our bodies from the start,' Daretor raged. 'You and that wench Andzu.'

Zimak pulled his head back as though slapped. 'Actually, she was Princess Andrella from Bazite. You think you've been hard done by. Look at her. She wound up in Premiel's wasted body with dozens of voices screaming in her mind for revenge. To top that, she was slashed to death while giving me time to free you. Think of others for once in your life, Daretor.'

'I'll kill him!' Daretor swore. He struggled, but somehow Jelindel managed to subdue him.

'The Sacred One,' Jelindel said, diverting Daretor's rage. 'Speak now or I'll let Daretor go.'

'Gah, what an abomination,' Zimak spat. 'What did the old clown say this time?'

Calling the Sacred One an 'old clown' seemed sacrilegious. 'He wants us to find the dragonsight,' Jelindel said. 'I imagine there are the usual inducements.'

Zimak nodded. 'Like, they'll cut off our orchids if we don't?'

'I imagine that's pretty close,' Jelindel said. 'At least in your case. Now, before we go any further, did you or did you not steal the relic?'

'For the last time –'

'It was around King Amida's neck,' Daretor interrupted. 'The day we fought the mantid in the arena. You pointed it out to me.'

'Looking and stealing are two different things,' Zimak said, wagging a finger. 'Besides, when did I get a chance to steal anything? You were with me the whole time.'

'You could have snuck off when I was sleeping,' Daretor said.

'That's preposterous,' Zimak said. 'I'd need to be super human to get out of the slave pen, break into the king's chamber, steal the dragonsight, and return to the pen unseen.'

'We *were* super human on that paraworld,' Daretor reminded him.

'I didn't even know that the bauble was worth anything,' Zimak said. He flapped his hands in exasperation. 'We've been framed, pure and simple, you great big lummox!'

Before Daretor could point out that it was now he, Zimak, who was the 'great big lummox', Jelindel flicked a glance at the sleeping man. 'Who's he?'

Zimak seemed surprised. 'You don't know?' He crossed to the sleeper and shook his shoulder. 'Wakey, wakey! We've got visitors.'

The man sat up. Dazed, he turned to face the others.

Daretor cried out, amazed. 'Osric? Is it really you?'

Daretor grabbed Osric by the shoulders and embraced him. 'Tell us everything that happened after we escaped the tower. By White Quell you must have a story to tell!' He stepped back before the Bazitian could gather his wits. 'You look unwell,' Daretor added, as an aside.

'It is also good to see you, my friend,' Osric said. 'First, you must know that time does not flow the same on the different paraworlds. In my world some ten years have passed since last we saw each other. In that time, much has happened. I reached my people and, as you foresaw, I became a hero, returning with a fertile red female dragon. We chose our best male to breed with her and in no time we had a clutch of powerful dragonlings, more than sixty in the first laying alone. It was a wonderful time. We raised the dragons as equals, as they are meant to be, not under the domination of a vain tyrant and a cruel vizier. The dragons respected this and grew in freedom, in a way that the king's dragons did not. By the start of this year we had over a hundred sturdy dragons, each as large as those in the tower's thrall.

'By that time the king realised he'd made a mistake in not striking early, as his vizier had advised. But it was too late; we were a force to be reckoned with. Unfortunately, we were also a force to be dickered with. I and a large group of my brethren – some fifty in all, each riding a free dragon – were invited to the Tower to sign a treaty. But it was a trick.'

'Surely you could have seen through such a lame ploy?' exclaimed Daretor.

'There was a woman involved,' muttered Osric. 'A woman that I thought I could trust.'

'This sounds familiar,' mumbled Zimak.

'Whilst here, the massif was magicked back to this realm, to Ancient Q'zar, and in the confusion the king sprang an ambush. We were captured and imprisoned. And now my people – and the other free dragons – are marooned back on our adopted paraworld.'

Osric slumped as though weary. 'Yes, my people are finally free from the yoke of King Amida, but when the citadel departed, it took everything with it, our history is within its walls and its lands for many leagues around.'

Jelindel put a hand on his arm. 'Perhaps we will find a way to send you back,' she said. Osric looked puzzled.

'We don't wish to return. Q'zar is our ancient and rightful dwelling place. We *are* home. But I must find a way to bring the rest of my people here . . . with one exception.'

'Understandable,' said Zimak, glancing at Jelindel.

'Yet no one knows what will happen to us now . . . '

Jelindel told him about their interview with the Sacred One, and that they were charged with finding the dragonsight. Osric did not look happy.

'I fear you are being sent on a fool's errand,' he said. 'Nobody is more familiar with fools' errands than me. How can one find a bauble lost somewhere on a whole world?'

Zimak leaned closer and dropped his voice. 'Ordinarily, I would agree. But there's something you don't know.'

'If this is some scheme –' Daretor started, but Jelindel stopped him.

'Let's hear what he has to say,' she said.

'Glad someone's got some sense between the ears,' Zimak

said, flinching from Daretor. 'When I was brought here I wondered how they'd found me. After I had my audience with the old dragon downstairs, the king seemed to take a liking to me –'

'A story I find hard to believe,' Daretor grated.

Zimak ignored him. 'Anyway, one day I'm lounging around trying to get friendly with one of the court ladies when I see something that baffles even me. The vizier was wearing a moonstone ring on his little finger, and this wasn't just any moonstone; it was one of the fabulous gems from the collection of Skeel of Gratz.'

Daretor snorted. 'If your latest ploy is to bore us to death, then you are halfway there.'

'Shhh,' said Jelindel. 'Go on,' she said to Zimak.

'Well, a month before I was kidnapped, Skeel's gem house was raided, and his prized moonstones vanished. The rumour on the street had it that the gems were stolen by none other than our old friend, Fa'red, presumably to fund his war machine. Which is another reason why I was paying him a visit.'

'So you think Fa'red travelled to the paraworld of the dragons . . . ' Jelindel prompted.

'Or was invited there,' said Zimak.

'To perhaps dispose gems too valuable to be sold on this world?' Daretor guessed despite his doubt. 'So the vizier is behind this?'

'It's all supposition,' said Jelindel. 'There's no doubt that the vizier and Fa'red are alike in many qualities. But why bring the Tower Inviolate back to Q'zar?'

'It's some kind of ancestral rite,' said Zimak.

'It's our destiny,' said Osric. 'When the dragonsight went missing it was a great calamity, but in searching for the world of the supposed thieves, the dragonriders discovered Q'zar . . . the home of our ancestors, and the First Abode of the dragons. After that, there was no debate. They prepared the ancient dragon magic, a magic so powerful that normally it cannot be used by mortals, and hurled the massif on the return journey that was begun five thousand years ago.'

'A charming story,' said a dry voice behind them. They looked around to see Rakeem in the doorway. Clearly he had only heard the last fragment of their discussion. He beckoned for them to follow him. As they did so, guards fell into place around them.

'The Sacred One has spoken and the king has agreed that you shall be sent forth this day to find the dragonsight. Please note that your freedom – indeed, your very lives – depends upon your success.'

Two old men shuffled forward, holding vials. At a signal from Rakeem, guards immobilised the trio. Their mouths were forced open and the first old man forced the Q'zarans to take a sip of a vile-smelling greenish philtre. It made them gag and caused their eyes to water. The second man daubed their foreheads with a spot of what looked like red paint.

Coughing, the three shrugged off their captors and looked at each other.

'The mark is dragon blood from the Sacred One,' said the vizier. 'Even now it is depth-bonding with your flesh.'

'Binding magic?' asked Jelindel. The vizier nodded.

'Our dragons can now find you anywhere on this world. There is nowhere to hide,' Rakeem said. 'The philtre you drank is a slow-acting poison. You have less than six weeks to complete your task and return for the antidote. Mind that the antidote is peculiar to our world, and not to be found on yours.'

'Gah, six weeks are hardly long enough to scour the taverns of D'loom, let alone an entire planet,' spluttered Zimak.

The vizier smirked. 'Then you will need to spend your time wisely.'

'I gather Osric is coming with us,' said Jelindel, noting the red mark on his forehead.

'You will need transport and I see no reason to risk one of our own loyal servants. Yes, the traitor and his equally treacherous dragon will go with you,' said Rakeem, sneering at Osric. 'My assistants will provide you with supplies, and I suggest that you waste no time in commencing your journey. You have very little time. The poison is already at work within your bodies.'

'You have no honour,' said Daretor, scowling.

Rakeem paused near the door, then turned to face Daretor.

'I do my duty as I see fit,' he replied in a neutral voice. 'Why is that worse than running someone through with a sword?'

Daretor spat. The guards surged forward, but Rakeem stopped them with a cursory wave. He smiled.

'Let the barbarian be,' he said calmly. 'I want results, you want honour. Very well, then, you may have the chance to settle all accounts at the end of your little quest.'

'Be sure of it,' Daretor promised.

The dragon S'cressling had been fitted with a palanquin that easily accommodated a party of four. Two rows of saddles were mounted against a solid gunwale larboard and starboard. A double saddle occupied the bow, or what dragonriders called the mane.

S'cressling had grown considerably since Daretor and Zimak had last seen her, adding further credence to Osric's claim that time passed at a different speed between the two worlds.

They flew south at first, heading toward the Garrical Mountains before striking for Yuledan. While Osric guided the dragon,

Jelindel called Daretor and Zimak together to make plans.

'The first question is where do we begin?' she said. 'Gratz is the obvious choice, since that's where Fa'red was seen last.'

'He's in this up to his eyeballs,' said Daretor. 'I think we can all agree on that. Besides, finding Fa'red would give me the chance to squeeze his neck until his eyeballs pop out.'

Zimak cleared his throat. 'Er, Gratz might not be a good idea,' he suggested.

'And why not?' Daretor asked, his voice edgy.

'Fa'red has certainly *been* in Gratz, but I heard a rumour that he has shifted his headquarters.'

'Where to?' asked Daretor.

Zimak shrugged. 'Even the gossips are tight-lipped on some matters,' he said calmly.

Daretor scowled, as if Fa'red's absence might be Zimak's fault.

'Our lives depend on finding this bauble in time, yet you want us to base our search on gossip?'

'Well, let us hear your suggestion,' replied Zimak.

Jelindel spoke quietly to Osric. A moment later S'cressling wheeled slowly to the east, heading for the Dominer Pass. Daretor and Zimak looked mildly annoyed as she returned.

'So, do you have a revelation you might care to share with us?' asked Zimak.

'Once through the Pass we will turn north into Baltoria,' she explained, sounding impatient. 'There's no point in gallivanting about Q'zar, and I have a feeling I know where Fa'red is.'

'Our lives are at stake, yet Zimak wants to trust them to gossip, while you would rest them on a feeling,' said Daretor with a hand over his eyes. 'I'm not feeling very hopeful about the future.'

'My feelings aren't just vague fancies. Wants and desires cast shadows into the paraplane, and I still wander there as much in my sleep as I do in this world when awake. I have seen the ripples of people's intents and needs. From the ripples in a pond you may deduce that a stone has been thrown in, its size, and even its location.'

Zimak opened his mouth to say something but Jelindel held up a hand. 'No, I will not teach you how to tell which girls desire you. I'm afraid you will have to blunder about working that one out like every other male in the world. But because I am feeling malicious I will tell you that it can be done.'

Zimak nervously fingered the hem of his tunic, then rallied. 'So we're risking our lives on a dream of yours, are we?'

'Do you have better insights than I?'

'It's your life as well,' Zimak said moodily.

Jelindel looked at Daretor, who nodded reluctantly.

'Well, that's settled, then,' she said.

S'cressling negotiated the buffeting air currents of the Dominer Pass, staying clear of the snow-capped peaks that they passed on either side. The thin air was chilly, and far below they saw travellers on the high mountain road, stopped and staring up at them. Jelindel and Zimak waved. Some waved back, others scattered to take cover. A dragon carrying people was liable to be well behaved, but it was nevertheless still a dragon.

'They'll have a story to tell tonight when they reach the next inn,' Zimak laughed as they saw two men plunge into a snowdrift to hide.

The dragon turned north, crossing the Marisa River and heading across the heart of Baltoria, toward Dremari in the Passendof Mountains. Fa'red had chosen well. It was an ideal place to hide in and to defend. The inhabitants of the Passendof Mountains had resisted invasion for hundreds of years. They remained neutral while other low-lying kingdoms fought wars, and experienced rebellions and uprisings. The capital, Dremari, had a wondrous system of alpine canals that linked it to the lowland rivers and hence to the port city of Tol and the world's seaways. Most people found the idea of a mountain city being a port rather surprising, but this was Passendof's advantage. It enjoyed not only an enviable record of peace and neutrality, but was also rich from trade.

Despite the speed of their dragon transport, the journey was long and tiring. The ceaseless wind was chill, yet the sun burned their hands and faces because they were close to the equator. Flying was disturbing for all but Osric. While he slept, the others cried out in fear as they woke from yet another nightmare of falling. Thus they slept badly, huddled on the exposed deck, watching the stars, or peering at the inky darkness of the invisible landscape below.

They spotted the first outflung foothills of the Passendof Mountains early the next morning. Jelindel directed Osric toward the Valley of Clouds. Not only did the villagers there owe her a great debt of service for having rid them of daemons, but the cloud-enshrouded realm offered the best concealment for S'cressling.

They landed high on a mountainside in a forest clearing. While Osric remained behind to pack their gear, Jelindel, Daretor and Zimak made their way along narrow mist-enshrouded trails, past an ancient, weathered skull the size of a large boulder, to a wall-fort with a signpost that read: 'Fontimark Federation of Squires'. After bargaining with the two fort guards over the size of the bribe, they were allowed to pass into Fontimark itself.

Jelindel headed for the blacksmith's shop. As she made to enter, a massive, bearded man wearing gloves and a short cloak bumped into her as he stepped out.

'Excuse me, ma'am,' he said. He made to walk on, then he stopped and his eyes widened. 'Jaelin!' he exclaimed. 'But you're –'

'Yes, Drusan, I am a girl.'

'But, but –'

'When you knew me I had to go about in disguise. Forgive me, the deception was necessary at the time.'

'There is nothing to forgive. Come in, come in, you do me great honour by this visit. Your companions, too.'

He gestured them inside, calling for his wife to fetch ale and fresh bread, and what new baked honey cakes they had. While they ate and drank, Jelindel explained what she needed.

'You're not seriously telling me that you flew here on a *dragon*?' Drusan said in wonder.

Jelindel nodded, smiling at the incredulous look on Drusan's face.

'But they're figments of the imagination, stories told to frighten children into behaving.'

'Nevertheless, Drusan, the dragons have returned to Q'zar, their ancient home,' said Jelindel. 'Even now they roost at Dragon-frost and despoil the country thereabouts. Our dragon is better behaved than that, but I need your help to keep people away from her. She will also need feeding.'

Drusan's face fell. 'Not virgins, I hope. Not many of those around these parts.'

Jelindel closed her eyes and shook her head. 'A few sheep will do, and I don't think they have to be virgins. With luck, we'll call S'cressling before too long.'

She offered him money for the dragon fodder but he refused. Then her gaze fell on his gloved hands. Long ago, Drusan had been branded a coward; the backs of his hands had been marked with the sign. Even though he had proven his courage many times over, single-handedly battling terrifying daemons from which the town folk fled, the brands marked his skin forever. To keep his shame hidden he wore gloves. Even in the presence of his wife, he only removed them in the darkness of the bedchamber.

Jelindel took his hands in her own. Drusan almost jerked them away.

'It's all right,' Jelindel said. 'Drusan, when I was here last I was still an apprentice of my guild.'

'But you fought the daemons and won,' he exclaimed.

'I uncovered a plot, that was all,' she said. 'Remove the gloves, Drusan.' When he hesitated, she said gently: 'Trust me one more time?'

He took a deep breath and slowly pulled off the gloves, revealing the humiliating marks. Jelindel held his hands, massaging with her thumbs the fused and furrowed skin on the backs. She spoke magical words of plasticity under her breath, and a strange blue light flickered about her lips. Gradually, a blue glow appeared around Drusan's hands, outlining the brands so that they blazed more strongly than before.

Drusan whipped his hands away as if scalded, and muttered angry words to himself. The scars caused by the brands went deeper than the skin. The coruscating blue light shot back to Jelindel's lips, and faded.

'How are your hands?' she asked.

Drusan held out his hands before him and shrieked. The skin was without blemish, the scars sponged away as if they had been sooty grease. He raised his eyes and stared at Jelindel. She shrugged and spread her hands with a smile. Drusan's wife hurried in, saw her husband's hands, then burst into tears.

Drusan looked at her, perplexed. 'Why do you cry?' he asked.

'Your hands. The branding is gone.'

'You knew?' he exclaimed, tears running down his own cheeks.

'Of course I knew,' she said. 'I'm your wife, am I not?'

'But you . . . you stayed . . .' Drusan seemed lost for words. His wife sighed and gently wiped the tears from his face.

'Men are so foolish,' she said. 'You have been a wonderful husband and a loving father. Why would I leave you? Because you were once afraid in battle? Shame on you for thinking so badly of me. I'm not some silly hoyden with air between my ears.'

He threw his arms around her and they hugged. Over her shoulder he locked eyes with Jelindel.

'Thank you, thank you, more times than I can say,' he began.

Jelindel silenced him with a flick of the wrist, and then motioned for Daretor and Zimak to follow her outside.

'Hie, Jelindel,' Zimak said. 'I don't suppose you can make my scars vanish, too? Daretor's messed his body up a few times and –'

For several frantic moments Jelindel struggled to keep Daretor from getting his hands on Zimak.

'Enough,' Jelindel said. 'Zimak, not all the gold on Q'zar could persuade me to misuse the gift of healing on you.'

'I don't see how that would be misusing it,' Zimak said. 'No more so than removing Drusan's scars.'

'Daretor's scars were earned in honour. You may not be familiar with the word, but some people value it rather highly.'

Drusan joined them, and they walked most of the way back to the clearing in silence – apart from Daretor, who was muttering about how it was probably not 'murder' to kill one's own former body. Jelindel kept herself between her two companions.

Jelindel introduced Drusan to Osric, and the two men discussed the feeding of the dragon. In turn, Osric told S'cressling that Drusan would be bringing food, and that he was a friend.

'And you are sure he will not eat me or anything?' Drusan asked yet again.

Osric smiled. 'Only if you keep calling her a he.'

'He's a she?'

'Yes. The only female I trust. The dragons are a proud race, and they admire intelligence in whatever form it takes. They don't harm anybody, unless they're driven to it.'

'By being insulted while hungry,' Zimak joked, but no one laughed.

With the dragon's care and feeding arranged, the foursome set out along the narrow trails that led from the vales to the canal road that would take them to Dremari. The paths through the Valley of Clouds were narrow, windy, and somewhat precarious. The arches over the many ravines were usually constructed of cut stone cleverly laid together so that even a knife blade could not enter between them. There were no rails or handholds, and the paths had been cut into the sides of steep hills and even cliff faces. Invariably, one side of the trail dropped sharply away into the chasms between mountains. The vistas were such that often they found themselves whispering, as if in deference to the majesty of the landscape. Their normal voices echoed eerily between the peaks. Daretor remarked that the permanent cloud cover made it seem as if they were walking under water.

For two days they wound their way through the mountains as if they were ordinary travellers, concerned only with the cold, the damp, and not stumbling off the trail into half a mile of nothingness that ended in sharp rocks. As they approached Dremari, however, they became wary. All except Osric knew that Fa'red was probably the most formidable man on Q'zar.

To underestimate him, or to ignore his fox-like cunning, was generally the last thing that the more foolish of his enemies ever did.

They finally came down out of the clouds and encountered a real road, along which a fair number of pedestrians and horse-drawn wagons moved. They followed the road round a bend and there was the capital of Passendof.

Dremari was a city of wonder, festooned with tall, slender spires and towers, seemingly so fragile that they defied gravity and wind in remaining upright. The Q'zarans had been here before, but Osric's breath was taken away.

'It's . . . it's *beautiful*,' he cried out.

'That it is,' said Jelindel, 'but it has guards and gates like any other city, so we must gain entry.'

They queued at the customs checkpoint along with a dozen other travellers, paid their transit fee, and demonstrated that they could support themselves for a month or more. After finishing with the inevitable bribe, they were permitted entry.

On the way to a hostelry, they passed a long curving stone canal raised up on a series of red granite arches. In answer to Osric's question, Jelindel explained that this was the aqueduct that fed Dremari's artificial lake, and that it was linked to the main canals that flowed down from the mountains to the Marisa River in the lowlands.

They found a suitable hostelry beneath the battlements of the city's old castle, and immediately gathered in Jelindel's room to lay their plans.

'We must assume that Fa'red knows we are here, and why,' said Jelindel. 'He has many spies and perhaps still has some dead-moon warriors at his command.'

'What are they?' asked Osric, alarmed by the very name.

'They are highly trained assassins that do not know fear of death,' said Daretor. 'They are worthy adversaries.'

'Gah,' Zimak laughed. 'Daretor's prone to exaggeration, Osric. We've taken on many times our number of deadmoons. Why, even Jelindel bested a hundred of them once.'

Jelindel closed her eyes. 'I am going to count to three, Zimak. If you have not shut up by then, I shall disembowel you, and Daretor will hang you with your own intestines.'

Zimak took the hint. Osric nodded, as if he understood.

'Fa'red will be within the castle, if I know him,' Jelindel continued. 'Daretor and I will attempt to get inside tonight when only Specmoon is up. Zimak and Osric, you will keep watch. Till then, I want you to scout around, pick up any information you can. Try the taverns and markets.'

Zimak's eyes lit up at the mention of taverns.

'Daretor,' Jelindel said, turning to him, 'I want you to plan our escape route, should we need to leave in a hurry.'

'And what are you going to do till dark?' asked Zimak.

'I'm going to hire a palanquin and some lackeys for the afternoon. Then I will visit several gem merchants, pretending to be a rich young lady of leisure. If Fa'red has boasted about the dragonsight or shown it to anyone, then someone here will know.'

They each set out on their respective missions for the afternoon. Daylight was fading as they met again at the hostelry. They bought food and drink in the taproom, and retired to a private booth at the back where their conversation could not be overheard. Zimak took a deep draught of his drink and coughed most of it back up into the mug. 'Black Quell's butt! That must be the foulest muck I've ever tasted.'

Jelindel ignored him. 'Apart from the quality of ale leaving something to be desired, what did you find out today?'

'We visited many alehouses, as you suggested, and even spent some time in the marketplace,' began Osric. 'Your magician Fa'red is here all right. On the face of it, he is helping the new king secure his realm against the anarchy that is spreading across the lowlands.'

'Ironic really, given that Fa'red helped to overthrow the previous king,' Zimak pointed out, spoon halfway to his mouth. 'I was about to wed his daughter. Why, if not for my so-called friends here, I might well be the king by now.'

'Actually Zimak, I regret rescuing you from her. Had we not whisked you away from here, the princess would have fed you to her lepon in the morning, after your first night of amorous bliss. All her other suitors exited that way.'

Zimak waved the spoon. 'I only have your word on it,' he said. 'Besides, maybe the other suitors hadn't measured up in the pre-marital bed. I would have been different.'

'Well yes, she might have had you soaked in red wine first, to disguise the taste,' Jelindel sighed. 'Osric, please go on.'

'Many mutter that Fa'red has some leverage over the new king, so that the monarch has been forced to give him a wardship, a protected haven.'

'Sounds like Fa'red still has enemies,' Daretor mused.

'Sounds like the sun still rises in the morning,' said Jelindel.

'He's probably already doublecrossed Rakeem,' said Zimak around a mouthful of food. He was merely putting into words what everyone else thought.

'That may help us,' said Jelindel, 'but our task is unchanged. We must find the dragonsight.'

'Or die horribly,' Zimak reminded them. Suddenly not hungry, he dropped the bone that he had been gnawing and looked around gloomily. 'How come every time I get mixed up with you lot my life expectancy plummets?'

'Maybe Fate thinks you should be brought to book for your many misdeeds,' Daretor replied.

'You should talk,' Zimak said, sucking his greasy fingers.

'I have scouted three routes out of the city, should we need them,' said Daretor. 'I have also arranged horses to be stabled nearby.'

Jelindel nodded. She had her own escape route in mind, but followed the rule that the best kept secrets are those known only to one person.

'I had less luck than you three,' she said smoothly. 'None of the gem and trinket merchants know of any bauble matching the description of the dragonsight. If Fa'red has it, then he has not revealed it to anybody here.'

She cast her gaze about the tavern to make sure no one was near. Then she cleared a space in front of her and spread a parchment on the table, making quick deft sketches of the castle and its environs.

'Tonight,' she said, looking around for objections. She found none.

Zimak and Osric knelt among mountain ferns four hundred yards from the castle walls, while Jelindel and Daretor slunk through the moonlit plaza till they reached the granite arch of the aqueduct. Keeping to the shadows, they scaled the brickwork of the arch, and lowered themselves over the aqueduct wall into the chill mountain water.

'Ready?' Jelindel asked. Her teeth were chattering. Daretor nodded, releasing his grip on the wall. Instantly, the current pulled them into the middle of the stream where the water was deepest. In a few moments they saw the castle battlements speeding towards them. The dark gap loomed in the wall where the aqueduct plunged through part of the castle before exiting again on the other side.

Even in this light they could see that an iron portcullis had been lowered across the flow. 'I hope you know what you're doing,' Daretor muttered through cold-clenched teeth.

The aqueduct dipped and the water picked up speed, rushing towards the portcullis. Jelindel muttered a spell. Her teeth were chattering so much that it came out wrong, and nothing happened.

'I'm too cold,' Jelindel groaned. 'Besides, magic is weakened over water.'

Daretor held her tightly, sharing the heat of his body. She tried again and though blurry flickering light lit up her lips, nothing happened. The portcullis was growing larger; in moments they would be dashed against it with bone-breaking speed.

'*Arnash ir aramay*,' Jelindel enunciated slowly. Blue light formed at her lips and leapt across to the portcullis. With a muffled groan it slid up out of their path just as the current swept them into the dark mouth.

As soon as they were inside, the grille dropped down again. They hurtled along in near darkness.

'We'll only have one chance,' Daretor said. He pulled a metal hook from inside his tunic. It had a leather grip at one end. 'Hang on tight. Whatever you do don't let go.'

Jelindel's grip on his arms tightened. 'There it is.'

They saw light ahead, a rectangular shape set in the ceiling, a hatch cut into the floor of the castle's kitchen so that supplies could be collected and let down. As they rushed towards the hatchway Daretor surged out of the water and whipped the hook in a great arc over his head. He grunted in satisfaction as it slid over the lip of the hatchway.

'Quickly, scramble up!' he urged. 'I can't hold this for long.'

Jelindel climbed hand over hand up Daretor's body, grabbed the hatchway, and hauled herself up so that she was standing on his shoulders. Her head poked through the opening. She quickly checked the kitchen. It was empty. She scrabbled for a handhold, found one, and hauled herself up. She turned back for Daretor. Soon he too was slumped on the kitchen floor, shivering and panting. Then they moved away from the hatchway and found an alcove. Here they stripped off their wet clothing and dressed in the dry clothes that Jelindel had brought in a leather bag sealed with wax.

'Lead the way,' said Daretor. Jelindel nodded, still too cold to speak coherently.

The castle, like many ancient buildings, resembled a maze, partly from a sense of fun, and partly to confuse intruders. Fortunately, Jelindel had memorised a map of the castle's layout. Sold as a curio, the map was more than a century old. She doubted that there had been any significant alterations.

She guessed Fa'red would be in the east wing, which was normally reserved for visiting nobility. She could not imagine Fa'red tolerating anything less. The east wing was some two hundred yards from their current position, and the guest suites several floors up. There was no stairway to the upper floors from this service level, but Jelindel knew that there had to be a service stairwell or similar arrangement for the staff.

'Here,' she said, indicating a small rectilinear cavity in the wall.

'Are you seriously suggesting that I get in there?' Daretor asked.

'It's called a dumb waiter,' she said. 'The servants place food and drink in it, then pull on those ropes to the side. The whole thing goes up to whichever floor has ordered it.'

'Like Rakeem's elevator.'

'Exactly.'

'It's too small. I wouldn't fit in there,' he pointed out.

'Still forgetting you're in Zimak's body,' Jelindel replied. 'Squeeze in, because this is how we're getting up into the realms of royalty.'

Daretor scowled. She smiled sweetly back.

'You know I don't like small spaces,' he said. 'Poxy little body or not.'

'I'm sorry, Daretor, but there's no other way. I'll go first.'

'No,' he said, taking a deep breath. 'I will.' He paused. '*Why* must we go up? Surely we could use the stairs around the other side.'

'They will be charmed against intruders,' Jelindel said dismissively. 'Fa'red won't leave his suite of rooms, so we must meet him.'

Reluctantly, Daretor climbed into the tiny space, drawing his legs up to his chest. His face glistened with sweat and he was shivering. 'How will you know when I arrive at the right level?'

'Stop worrying. It's all marked here on the side. When you get to the proper level this marker will be next to the name of that floor. I told you, it's designed for illiterate servants.'

Daretor swallowed, then nodded. Jelindel closed the door and started hauling on the ropes; fortunately, the contraption was counter-weighted to rise smoothly and easily.

Inside, Daretor kept his eyes shut. He was a fearless warrior, known among the Preceptor's former legions and mercenaries as death on two legs, but this tiny cabin unnerved him profoundly. He sighed with relief when the dumb waiter jerked to a stop. He listened for a moment, then slid the door aside wide enough to peer out. The chamber was shrouded in shadows, and seemed empty.

Daretor pushed the panel wide open and climbed out, cautiously stretching his cramped limbs. Still nothing. He sent the contraption back down for Jelindel. In a short time she stood beside him, having endured the claustrophobic journey with less anxiety.

A tall, turbaned man entered the chamber, padding silently on soft slippers. He was holding an oil lamp. When he saw Daretor and Jelindel he froze, then opened his mouth and drew breath to cry out. Jelindel was faster. Her binding spell wrapped itself around him, shackling his legs and arms, silencing his cry. Daretor caught the lamp as the man toppled to the floor, mumbling for help.

'That won't hold him for long,' Jelindel said. 'We have to hurry. My plan will only work as long as we have surprise on our side.'

They peered out the door. No guards. They stepped out and hurried along the corridor.

Without warning, Fa'red attacked.

Zimak and Osric crouched in the shadows, conversing softly.

'They've been gone a while,' Zimak said.

Osric nodded. 'You say Jelindel is a great mage, and that she has bested this Fa'red and his deadmoon warriors before. Why then has she not displayed her magic? She was easily caught by Rakeem and his men.'

Zimak remained silent for a moment. 'There is more than meets the eye with that little vixen,' he said finally.

'You think she is a traitor?' asked Osric.

'I think she loves to be underestimated.'

Osric considered this. 'According to Daretor, she could have fled ere now, but stayed to free you both.'

'He's bound to say that,' Zimak scoffed. 'Daretor's in love with her. People in love say anything.'

'Why, then, are you so anxious?'

'I just don't like waiting. Besides, she's never really gone against Fa'red directly. He usually sends his lackeys to do his killing.'

'I suppose we just wait then.'

'As usual,' Zimak said sourly. 'But wait for what? If they fail, Fa'red's guards will be swarming over these grounds like ants.'

'Perhaps the only way to win is to lose,' Osric said.

'Osric, I hope that was meant to be a joke.'

Osric shrugged and settled deeper into the shadows. 'I am going to call S'cressling now. If all goes according to Jelindel's plan, there will be a sign shortly, and we must be ready.'

Zimak rolled his head, stretching his neck muscles.

There was some cause for Zimak's unease. Jelindel and Daretor had run along the corridor and burst into a large dimly lit hall. No sooner had Daretor closed the door, than seven deadmoon warriors rappelled from the ceiling, encircling them with startling speed.

Jelindel spat out binding spells reflexively, and three deadmoons collapsed instantly, their chests constricted so tightly that the air was almost squeezed from their lungs. The others launched a coordinated attack. Jelindel pivoted on her right foot, sending a spinning side kick into the jaw of one assassin. The other flicked out his arm and barely missed crushing her larynx. She feinted, dropped, and managed to knock him off his feet with a leg sweep, but he sprang up again as though on a trampoline.

Daretor was faring slightly worse. He managed to wound one attacker with an underhand knife throw, causing him to limp. But he fared worse with his next attacker, who sliced skin from Daretor's forearm. Daretor locked the deadmoon's arm beneath his own, and smashed his opponent's nose with a head butt, dropping him instantly. Cursing his carelessness, Daretor retrieved the deadmoon's blade from the ground. Blood was dripping from his arm.

The skirmish was all blurred arms, legs, and feet, each a lethal weapon. Jelindel could utter no more binding spells till the others released their victims and returned to her. Suddenly blue trails of energy warped the air and returned to her. The sorceric blast from her mouth sent the last deadmoon warrior hurtling against the wall, stunning him senseless.

Jelindel and Daretor leaned against each other, gasping for breath when, with an air-warping flash and a foul stench, something materialised in front of them. Even before half of its body could emerge from a paraworld, Jelindel was dragging Daretor away.

'Do something,' he shouted as he was dragged backwards.

'I am,' she wheezed. 'I'm fleeing. Why don't you join me?'

They sprinted across the hall, into an auditorium. The creature's pursuit was evident in the clattering echoes of its stampeding feet. Doors on the far side of the chamber opened onto a large courtyard.

Racing across the marble floor, Jelindel and Daretor reached a stone balustrade on the far side. Daretor turned as the creature burst into the courtyard, ripping the ornate doors off the hinges and flinging them aside as if they were sheets of parchment.

'Is this what you call doing something?' Daretor said, crouching with his dagger in hand. It seemed ludicrously inadequate.

'You won't need that,' Jelindel said. 'At least, I don't think so.'

Across the courtyard, something *was* happening to the creature. It was writhing and smoke was pouring from its segmented body. It gave a deep, painful bellow, which reached a crescendo. Then the abomination burst into flames.

Daretor flinched, shielding his eyes. 'What – ?'

'It's a Sivocan materialisation,' Jelindel explained. 'The tiniest amount of moonlight unzips the magic that binds it to reality.'

'You could have told me,' Daretor said. 'I would have run faster.'

'I doubt anyone could have run faster than that.'

They looked at each other. 'Except Zimak,' they said together, bursting into laughter. A voice interrupted them.

'I'm glad to see that you two are still entertaining each other.'

Daretor and Jelindel turned slowly, preparing for the inevitable attack. The man standing behind them was heavily built, but tending to excess weight. His face bore the scars of a narrow escape from death by burning some years in his past.

'Well met, Fa'red,' said Jelindel, recognising the voice of the archmage.

'*Always* a pleasure, Countess,' Fa'red replied.

The words were still emerging from his mouth when he flung a freezing spell at Jelindel; but the red light met her blue flame, and the two spells collapsed with a resounding pop. Jelindel felt the backwash sweep through her like pins and needles.

'I see your powers have grown,' said Fa'red.

'I see yours have declined,' Jelindel replied. 'Rest easy in Black Quell's pit, Fa'red.'

'I might say, "Ladies first",' Fa'red said guardedly. 'You were never one to be underestimated.'

Jelindel pulled a small metal cylinder from a pocket. She

put it to her lips and blew. Nothing happened. Daretor held his ground, clearly in the knowledge that his presence was superfluous.

As though reading his thoughts, Fa'red said, 'Put that blade away. You have no idea how silly you look.' All the while he remained staring at Jelindel.

Daretor sheathed the dagger, casting a quick glance to the palace gardens far below. They were two storeys down, which meant the flowerbeds would not break his fall, to any useful degree. He knew he was a liability to Jelindel. The instrument at Jelindel's mouth made no noise, yet Daretor would have sworn that a high ghostly sound on the edge of hearing had been on the air.

Fa'red watched Jelindel warily. 'A toy from a hard science paraworld?' he asked, then his lips broke into a cautious smile. 'You have risked too much this time, Countess. Your powers are no match for mine, despite the spirits you have claimed from your victims.'

'I'm still alive, Fa'red, so don't waste your breath with boasts. Where is the dragonsight?'

'The paraworld amulet? Is that what you seek? Rather charming of the old prophecies to turn out to be true, don't you think? Who would have guessed the dragons would return to the world from which they originated? Of course, I knew straight away that the dragonriders would need a guide once they arrived back in this world. They have been gone for centuries, after all.'

'So you offered your services,' Jelindel said. 'For a fee, of course. Now you have a paraworld army at your disposal and you don't even have to share it with the Preceptor.'

'How very perceptive,' Fa'red said, sounding amused.

'I'm sure you and Rakeem discovered you were kindred spirits. To the Preceptor you were just the hired help.'

'Once we dispose of King Amida, Rakeem and I will rule as equals, but what business of yours is that? I don't have the amulet.'

Jelindel's heart lurched. Their precious time was being leeched away without gain.

'Lies come so easily,' she said. 'They just roll off the tongue with no effort at all.'

'Why would I bother lying to one who is already dead? Mark you, Countess, Rakeem will never give you the antidote. You and the fools you call friends are merely pawns in a game more complex than you can imagine.'

'Do you care for the dragonsight?'

'Not at all.'

'Then no doubt you can tell a dying woman what the dragonsight is, and what it does.'

Fa'red's vanity was flattered. 'Ah, so your perception does know limits? Well, the dying should be granted one last wish. The dragonsight is a gem which gives the bearer the ability to glimpse the future and, to a limited extent, manipulate it. However, it is much more than that. It is in truth the eye of the dragon they call the Sacred One, removed from him a thousand years ago by a great mage called Keretch.'

'You're right, Daretor. Why do all great and momentous things happen exactly a thousand years ago?' sighed Jelindel.

'Don't mock. Whoever possesses the dragonsight holds dominion over all the dragons within their realm. You see, the dragons of the Tower Inviolate are little more than slaves, forced to do the bidding of King Amida and his elite band of dragonriders. If the dragonsight is not returned to its owners, the thousand year spell will be broken. It's falling apart already, as these things do. The Spell of Renewal ritual takes days to perform, hence your deadline to return the relic. Need I tell you that the dragons are annoyed about being enslaved for a thousand years, and will waste little time in rending King Amida and his minions into small, black, crispy things?'

'At which point, you will step in to restore the dominion and become king,' Jelindel suggested.

'You always were the clever one, Countess,' said Fa'red. 'Rakeem, as it so happens, doubts that the Spell of Renewal alone will work here on Q'zar.' Fa'red spread his hands expansively. 'My options are many. Return the dragonsight to my good partner Rakeem and be forever in favour; keep it and try to fathom its power, and wield it in time to save Q'zar *and* control the dragons; rid Q'zar of the dragons once they've toppled their current masters, and be the hero of all time.'

'You'll never be that, Fa'red,' Jelindel said.

'And you will never know. Now I tire of this. It's time for you to die, once and for all.'

'I think not,' said Jelindel. 'Perhaps you should take a look over your shoulder.'

Fa'red felt rather than saw the dark shape alighting on the roof behind him. He chanced a cautious glance and went rigid.

S'cressling was perched on the rooftop above the extended balcony. Osric and a rather dazed Zimak sat on her shoulders. S'cressling's long neck looped down and her snout, leaking smoke and fumes, was barely ten feet behind Fa'red.

Jelindel brought her guard down. 'Make the slightest move to leave, either by foot or by magic, and she will roast you. The flame that comes from her lungs is powered by dragon magic, and it will follow you into any paraplane in which you seek refuge.'

Fa'red's fire-scarred face remained expressionless. He stared vehemently at Jelindel. 'You too will die; the flames would reach you there.'

Jelindel's lips curled into a smile. 'I have spent many hours building the appropriate magical defence. You have not. I rather think that, even with your undeniable powers, it would take you somewhat longer to fashion one than the two seconds it will take S'cressling to roast you.'

Fa'red said nothing, but his shoulders slumped. 'Damn you for the witch you are,' he muttered.

'I should like the location of the dragonsight,' said Jelindel. 'And while you're at it, I should like to hear you recite The Oath That Binds in a statement that you will renounce all claim or use of the dragonsight from now unto the end of time. And just because I am paranoid, I shall invoke, with S'cressling's aid, the ancient dragon magic to tell truth from falsehood, and to bind you to your word.'

Fa'red's face darkened, but he rallied. 'You exceed your ability.'

Daretor tensed. If S'cressling released a fireball, he needed to get both himself and Jelindel off that balcony.

'Our time is short, Fa'red. Make your move now, or we shall reduce the number of villains in this world by one, then seek other help to find the dragonsight,' Jelindel bluffed.

There was more silence, punctuated by S'cressling's nasal breath. Finally Fa'red capitulated.

'Well, the day goes to you, Countess,' he declared.

His voice changed tone as he spoke the Oath That Binds beneath the watchful eye of S'cressling. He was unsuccessful, however, in keeping an edge from his voice as he swore under oath. As he spoke, he seemed to shrink like a pricked bladder.

'And the dragonsight?' Jelindel prodded.

Fa'red raised his bushy brow and scowled. 'It is with the Stone People. They guard it for me and will not give it up. Now that I have made the Oath you can ask no more of me,' he concluded with a triumphant smile.

'Which is why you gave in so easily,' Jelindel muttered to herself. 'I should have asked for the location before you uttered the Oath.' She paused to think. 'You will send Daretor and me to the land of the Stone People. My friends will follow on S'cressling. Do it now, and do it very carefully, Fa'red. The dragon's magic is ancient, yet she understands the nature and intent of our sorcery, though she regards it as the pastime of children.'

'Why should I?'

'Because I alone can allow you to reverse the Oath that you swore. In the unlikely event of you ever having both myself and the dragonsight in your power, you would really like that.'

'Very well. Until we meet again, Countess.' Fa'red muttered a spell and over the next few seconds Daretor and Jelindel faded from view.

Osric turned to S'cressling. 'Are they safe?'

The huge crimson dragon nodded in a slow gesture of assent.

'It is done,' Fa'red said. 'Now if you would be so kind as to leave, I have rather pressing matters to which I must attend.' He hurried out of the courtyard.

Osric and Zimak stared at the place where Jelindel and Daretor had stood.

'I wish to announce an uneasy feeling,' said Zimak.

Chapter 3
FORBIDDEN MAGIC

Daretor found himself in a great void, as if he had been sucked into the airless realm said to lie between paraworlds. Gasping for air, but finding none, he felt his lungs collapse, the last precious breath hissing from his mouth and nose. He tasted blood, and knew that in a few more seconds he would die. This must be how a fish feels, he thought, when it is ripped from its liquid world and cast upon the deck of a boat. Fa'red had tricked them.

But Daretor did not die. Sound and light and a world of sensation crashed suddenly back into existence. He gasped air, then lay panting. Somebody had thrown the fish back into the sea, thank White Quell!

The new world had its own discomforts. For a start, he was buried in something prickly, and the dust and grit nearly choked him. Daretor tried to move, to work out where he was. Raking a hand through the stuff that surrounded him opened a gap through which sunlight streamed. He blinked. At once he knew where he was: in the middle of a haystack, or something very much like it. Through the hole he could see a grimy cobbled street, and a line of ramshackle shops, their dirty windows reflecting back the scene before them. Looking closely at one of the shopfront windows he realised that the hay was piled on the back of a wagon. A pair of stout farm horses was hitched to the wagon, and several men were gathered nearby.

Before he could see much more the wagon lurched. One of the men, clad in a winter shirt woven of linen and horsehair, climbed into the driver's seat and stowed his purchases in the back. He flicked the reins and the horses lumbered into a slow clip-clopping walk down the street. It was only then that Daretor realised Jelindel was not with him. He felt around in the hay and whispered her name frantically, but there was no trace of her.

Daretor silently cursed Fa'red for his treachery. The fault was theirs, not Fa'red's. If one chose to trust a scorpion, whose fault was it when the inevitable sting came? He knew enough about magic to know that Fa'red could not have simultaneously sent them to two very different places; magic did not work like that, though it must be said that most of its workings were a mystery. He did not really *trust* magic, nor did he consider it honourable. Only a sword was honourable, although a good, honest punch in the face did have elements of honour. Magic was slippery. A little too much like life itself, Daretor thought, mocking himself ruefully.

Brushing aside idle thoughts, Daretor hoped that Jelindel was close by. Her situation might be better or worse than his; he did not know. Resolving to make no bold moves until he knew the lie of the land, he peered through the hole, learning what he could. He yearned for the quiet life that he and Jelindel had discussed not so long ago. *Maybe I should learn magic,* he concluded. *That way I could send* other *people on adventures.*

The wagon turned into a narrow, muddy lane. Daretor

squirmed towards the rear of the tray and made another opening for himself. He peered out. There were few people about and
those that passed looked downcast. He was about to jump off
the wagon when it rumbled to a stop in front of a small inn. The
driver climbed down and went inside.

Daretor waited till he was sure nobody was about. Jumping
from the tray, he brushed himself down. He wondered whether
to head back to the busy street, or enter the inn. Inns are wonderful places to acquire news, but strangers are always viewed with
curiosity or suspicion. Still, he needed information more than
anything else. He had several gold oriels on him, and some silver
argents. Precious metals are good currency in any paraworld, so
he would not starve. He entered the inn.

The interior was gloomy. Although it wasn't a cold day, a fire
was burning and by the looks of the smoke-filled room, the flue
was choked.

A bar ran along one wall, and a scattering of chairs and tables
stood in front of it. Odd looking devices protruded from the
walls: small black spheres that gleamed as if polished and composed of many small-faceted hexagons. Daretor tried not to stare
at them. He pulled up a chair at a table away from the bar. Half
a dozen idle drinkers had looked up when he entered, but most
had gone back to their drinks and conversations.

A serving maid approached, but she did not smile or greet
him. As he looked up, Daretor noticed a chalkboard on the wall.
The writing was in a language he understood. It was Delbrian.
He relaxed a little.

'What be your liking?' The girl's accent was thick and guttural.

Fortunately, Daretor could make sense of it. 'I'll have the
house ale, if you please,' he said. She looked at him oddly. His
own accent was as hard for her to follow as hers was to him.

'You be a foreigner, then?' she asked.

He nodded. 'From Skelt.' He grimaced inside. He had promised himself he would not volunteer information. He was here to learn.

'I've heard of the place. A far-off land, isn't it?'

'It is,' he said. The maid was obviously less travelled than most. He wondered how he might ask where exactly in Delbrias he was, but that was probably a bad idea. Perhaps there were other ways. The woman was not unattractive and she had eyed him twice now. 'You are a local lass?' he asked. 'I have no ear for accents.'

'Aye, I'm local.' She fetched his drink and returned. As she leaned down to place it on the table her mouth came close to his ear. 'I don't know how you got here, stranger, but you'd best get back the same way. They'll lock you up soon as look at you. I'll not be surprised if the priest-guards haven't already been called.'

Daretor handed her a silver coin and she gave him change. Though it seemed he drank at ease, inside he was in turmoil. What did she mean? In what way did he stand out and what law was he breaking that would warrant imprisonment? Obviously, coming into the inn had been a bad idea.

He drained the tankard and left. He hurried down the side of the building to a rear lane abutting the back of the inn. He had gone only a few steps into the lane when a hand shot out of a doorway and grabbed his coat. He was about to lash out when his assailant hissed: 'Follow me, if you want to stay free.'

It was the serving maid. Daretor hesitated, but the sound of many feet on the cobbles helped to make up his mind. He ducked into the dark doorway and followed the woman down a corridor and up a creaking flight of stairs. Finally, she led him into a cramped attic space. There was a sleeping pallet on the floor, a few personal effects, a wash basin, a makeshift table and chairs, and a pile of scrolls and pamphlets.

She motioned him to a chair.

'Are you the courier?' she asked, panting. Cautiously, she peered through a shuttered window. The laneway had become noisy.

He blinked at her, thinking swiftly. 'Are you the contact?' he said in response. She laughed then and moved away from the window. In that moment her face lit up and he saw that she was quite striking. Her eyes sparkled and some colour had come into her cheeks. She sat in a wicker chair and looked at him.

'You have no idea, do you?' she asked finally. Her accent seemed to have disappeared.

He decided to give up the pretence. 'I find myself in an unfortunate situation,' he said.

'Go on.'

'I mean, I didn't come here by normal means.'

'I know that, too. You would never have gotten across the border, let alone within the city gates unless you're a very clever spy. Are you a very clever spy?'

'Neither spy nor, it would seem, very clever. At least, I'm not clever enough to avoid detection by serving maids.'

'How then did you arrive?'

'I was magicked here,' Daretor said. She sat up straight, seeming uneasy for the first time.

'Are you a wizard?' she asked.

'No,' he replied. 'I am a simple fighting man, but a wizard sent me here. He is an enemy of ours . . . of mine. He tricked me, sending me here. I am on a quest and he seeks to thwart me.'

'Where were you?'

'Dremari in the Passendof Mountains.'

She stared. 'That far? Magic can do such a thing over so great a distance?'

'So it would seem and much more besides. But I am the wrong person to ask.' He paused, looking at her. 'Can you tell me why my appearance would cause trouble?'

'It is not so much your appearance as the fact that you are a foreigner. That is not a crime here, but it would justify any patrol demanding to see your papers. You would, of course, have none.'

'How did you know?'

'The way you talk. All newcomers are placed in detention for months at a time, during which they receive . . . rather forcible re-education. After that, you would not sound as you do.'

'Why are they re-educated?' Daretor asked.

'To cure them of magic, of course, though many do not survive the cure.'

It was his turn to stare at her.

She shrugged. 'Magic is forbidden here, unless you are a priest. To work magic is to risk imprisonment and heavy fines. Big magic, of the kind that brought you here, would earn you the death penalty.'

'Where am I? What is your name?'

'My name is Elorsa and this is the city of Ishluk.'

His heart thumped, causing his eyes to widen. 'Southern Gratz? I believed I was in Delbrias. The writing back at the tavern . . .'

'Delbrian and Gratzian is similar,' Elorsa said. 'No, you are a very long way from there. But I will aid you, if I am able.'

A vast dark shape circled beneath a ragged moon. S'cressling was questing the sky for a scent.

'I don't like it,' said Osric. 'If they were nearby she would have picked up their scent by now.'

'Can she actually smell the Sacred One's blood?' asked Zimak. He gingerly touched the daubed spot on his forehead.

'Ordinarily yes. But this is a magical scent. She is questing through layers of space and time, seeking them . . .'

The dragon banked hard and soared off to the southeast, climbing as she went.

Zimak clutched the sides of his seat. 'Well, she seems to have found something.'

'You had better prepare yourself for a long journey, my friend. I do not know where we are going but it will not be a short flight.'

'We should have roasted that fat pig Fa'red,' Zimak spat.

Osric frowned. 'I am sorry if we have misled you, but I don't think you understand, Zimak. Jelindel was only bluffing. There was little chance of S'cressling killing Fa'red. Not without having possession of the dragonsight beforehand. We need Fa'red to fall back on if we cannot find that which binds us to King Amida.'

Zimak's face paled. 'Don't tell me you need Fa'red alive.'

Osric leaned into the whistling wind. 'For the time being, until our quest is completed,' he said. 'Let us pray we find our companions.'

Prayers were the last thing on Zimak's mind. The dragon flew on, her great wings beating the night air like vast blankets being shaken out.

Jelindel did not know where she was. Worse, she did not know how she had arrived there. She had materialised inside a closet, accompanied by a great clatter of falling brooms and clanging buckets.

Then the door had been thrown open and several shocked faces stared at her.

'You young scallywag, get outta there!' cried an outraged woman in scullery garb. She grabbed Jelindel by the ear and hauled her out of the closet. Before Jelindel could gather her wits, the maid had rummaged through her garments and confiscated everything she found.

That had been five minutes ago. She was now sitting at a table. Opposite her was an anxious man in his mid fifties. He wore a neatly cropped white beard. His dark eyes regarded her furtively. He had quickly cleared the kitchen of its staff on his arrival. Had Jelindel been herself, she would have known that the man was actually fearful for her safety, although unable to show it.

'You will tell me how you came to be in my closet and you will tell me now,' he demanded, thumping the table. Jelindel flinched.

'I'm not sure,' she said, nervous.

'What is your name? Or are you too addled to tell that much?'

Jelindel frowned. Her frown deepened into puzzlement, then alarm. She looked up from the table. She found her inquisitor difficult to understand, but that didn't seem too unusual, for there were huge gaps in her memory. 'I don't think I know my name,' she said. 'What *is* my name?'

She was so obviously confused that the man's anger subsided. Judging by her clothes and accent, she was no urchin. 'Have you taken a bump on the head of late?' he asked, a little more gently.

Jelindel slowly felt her head. There was a tender spot at the back, and when she pressed on it she winced. Her fingers were smeared with blood.

The man nodded, satisfied. 'It is as I thought. I am a physician.

You are very lucky. I have encountered a case like this before, though not for some years. In my experience, your memory will return given time. However, the Provost will have to be informed. It is most likely you came here by magic, since it is impossible for you to have entered my house by any other means.'

Jelindel stared at him. 'Do I know magic?'

The man shrugged, then clapped his hands loudly. 'That is not for me to say. I will speak to the Provost about your amnesia. It is he who will be the final arbiter of this matter.'

A man in house livery dashed in. The doctor instructed him to escort Jelindel to the Office of the Provost.

As Jelindel left, the doctor called out, 'May White Quell be merciful.'

A moment later, Jelindel and her guard were in a cobbled street, walking past a dingy inn. High above an attic window glowed a friendly yellow light. It was in stark contrast to the din in the streets, where harried soldiers were obviously searching for someone.

Daretor awoke suddenly. He had been dreaming of Jelindel. She was being tortured to death. He woke sweating and shivering, calling out her name. Elorsa loomed above him. She motioned him to be still and closed the door, removing a cloak.

Daretor rubbed the sleep from his eyes. 'What news?' he asked. The dream had left him badly shaken.

'A woman appeared mysteriously in a house not a hundred yards from here. I know the owner. He is a physician, not unkindly. Still, he would have had little choice but to hand her over to the Provost.' She wrung her hands. 'His servants, and, well, anyone cannot always be trusted. It would not be worth his life to help her.'

The words alarmed Daretor and he started to his feet. Elorsa waved him back.

'What does that mean?' he demanded.

'She is not in danger, not yet at least. She is suspected of having used magic to get here, but she is very clever. She is pretending to have amnesia, it seems. Also, she is comely, which may sway the Provost when it comes time.'

'Time?'

'Time for her hearing. You still do not understand. Magic is a criminal offence here. To practise it, or benefit from it, is illegal. Only the priests may do so.'

'But how do they enforce such a law?'

'They have many ways. Wizards from other realms detect the use of magic. And there are also the Watchers.'

'Who are they?'

'*What* are they. Surely you noticed them. They're black crystals in brackets on the walls in every building and public thoroughfare. They not only detect magic of a certain power, but enhance the priests' sorcery by some means. While smaller spells may be practised in privacy, no potent magic can be worked here without instant detection.'

'Yet my friend and I both arrived by magic,' Daretor said.

'Yes, but the magic was worked elsewhere. The black crystals cannot detect such things, but you could not leave the same way without a horde of priests following.'

Daretor combed a hand through his hair. Apparently the local priests wanted all the action for themselves. 'Why are they so afraid of magic?'

'Why shouldn't they be? They fear the unpredictable. More than anything, the Provost fears that one day a powerful adept will come and subjugate *him*.'

'When I followed you up here you asked me if I was the courier. What did you mean?'

Elorsa gazed at him, biting her lower lip. She seemed to be struggling with a decision. 'There is a . . .' she started haltingly, '. . . a group of people who . . . who wish to see things as they were in the old days, before the Provost took over. They wish for . . .'

Her voice trailed off, but Daretor finished for her: 'The return of magic.'

She nodded.

'Is magic such a wonderful thing, then?' he asked.

'You do not understand. A bad king may be removed by magic. Tyranny is a difficult enterprise when many great mages and wizards inhabit your realm. It may not be an easy or quick cure, but it is a road back to freedom.'

Daretor sighed. 'I never thought of it like that,' he said. 'But then, tyrants like the Preceptor employ Adept 12s to ward off opposing magic. It usually boils down to who has the most powerful adept in their employ.'

'Better that than what we have now,' Elorsa said bitterly.

'One tyrant or the next, it's all much of a muchness,' Daretor said. 'But now, tell me of the woman who mysteriously appeared. Where is she being held?'

S'cressling streaked through the night, into the next day, then on into night again, moving across many lands. She flew over high mountains, deserts, and great, fertile flood plains. She soared above the homelands of men, and of creatures that were not men. Sometimes attack spells flashed as starbursts around them, but most were content to let the huge creature pass as long as it did not turn upon them. Not once did S'cressling stop for food. On her back, Zimak and Osric were near the end of their supplies.

'I never knew this much land existed,' Zimak moaned. His fingers seemed frozen to the saddle straps, and his entire body felt stiff as a sun-bleached carcass.

Osric was too miserable to move, even though he was used to riding dragons. 'Land is infinite,' was all he said.

Kagan, Head Priest of Ishluk and Provost Marshal of the Realm, gazed through lowered eyes at the captive standing before him. That she was very beautiful was indisputable. That she was beautiful *and* dangerous remained to be ascertained.

'The physician who found you,' said Kagan, 'believes the memory loss is genuine, rather than a clever ploy to cloak your true intentions.'

'Why would I lie?' Jelindel asked.

'Why indeed? Why does anybody lie? Perhaps you lie because you know your peril.'

'But I am innocent of any wrongdoing. What is it that I am supposed to have done?'

The Provost's eyes narrowed in momentary doubt. 'You have used magic.'

'I have? Perhaps I am a victim of magic.'

Kagan steepled his fingers and rested his chin on them. 'And perhaps you are a cunning witchling sent here by our enemies. How can one tell?'

'Don't you have some kind of test?' Jelindel asked.

'Possibly.' Kagan was beginning to think the physician was right. The girl did not act like the usual captives. Indeed, she did not seem to have any idea of the peril she was in. It was actually quite refreshing, he found. Whatever the matter, it put him in a good mood. Unfortunately, not good enough to spare her and miss the opportunity of impressing on the townspeople the need for constant vigilance against the practice of dark magic – dark magic being any type of sorcery not sanctioned by him. Furthermore, the pretty ones, as with virgins, made better sacrifices. For some reason, the commoners identified more with the winsome unfortunates, and even got quite emotional at times. Beauty was usually associated with nobility, after all. Finally, he sat back and glanced at the men stationed either side of Jelindel.

'I have made my decision,' he said. 'For the crime of illegal entry into our realm you are hereby condemned to a lifetime of slavery.'

'But I have done nothing,' Jelindel said, incredulous.

'And for the crime of Manifestation of Magic, that lifetime will be sadly short.' He flicked another look at his guards. 'Take her to the dungeons to await execution.'

Daretor walked the busy street, keeping out of the path of wagons and the main flow of foot traffic. He wore a brown nondescript cloak, rustic tunic, and leggings. His face was hooded. Thus dressed, he blended with the noonday crowd. Some twenty yards ahead, moving at a steady pace, was Elorsa. She had a basket over one arm. On her way to the markets, or so anyone would think to look at her.

And look they did. Not just at her but all who passed. 'They' were the Provost's priests. Robed in an austere regimental style with tasselled mitres, they hovered on most street corners and were subtly intimidating to religious people. They carried swords, and staffs of power. Handpicked, they all had thin cruel faces and the eyes of hawks.

Elorsa had schooled Daretor as best she could in the ways and manners of the Ishlukians. Submissiveness, never one of Daretor's strongest features, seemed the predominant trait, along with open-eyed guile. She had also worked on his accent and taught him some common phrases, which gave a clue to the grammar of the streets. In a stroke of irony, it seemed to Daretor that being in Zimak's body was a blessing in disguise. His bigger frame would have drawn attention, for these people were smaller in stature than most Q'zarans.

Nonetheless, it was a big risk. Daretor had never heard of the expression 'police state' but he was now deep in the middle of one.

'Stupidity is your best weapon,' Elorsa had told him. 'When in doubt, act dull-witted. Never try to argue or, White Quell forbid, try to prove you're right. If you can act the part of a simpleton, so much the better.'

'It's a shame my companion Zimak is not here,' he said.

With Elorsa's words firmly in mind, Daretor made his way along the street, always keeping the serving maid in sight and staying the same distance to the rear. The people they passed seemed gloomy and downcast. Few looked up or dared to meet his eyes. Elorsa had told him that betrayal had become a way of life in Ishluk, and many made their living from the sale of information.

Ahead Elorsa swung into a side street. Daretor followed, passing shops of a slightly higher standard. Even the clientele here appeared more prosperous. There were even outdoor eateries, and once he actually heard laughter.

'I shall be glad to leave this forsaken place,' he muttered.

A fox-faced passer-by shot him a look. Their eyes met for a second, then the man looked away. Daretor cursed himself for a fool. He should not have looked.

Elorsa changed her basket from one arm to the other. That was the signal. As Daretor reached the spot where she had done this, he casually glanced to his left and saw, built far back from the road and behind a high wall, a severe-looking building topped by turrets patrolled by armed priests. This was the Provost's citadel. If Elorsa's information was right, Jelindel was being held behind its walls.

Daretor glanced toward Elorsa and paused. She had stopped to look in a shop window. His breath quickened. It was the sign for danger. Trying not to betray his alarm, he casually looked around.

The fox-faced man was talking to a pair of priests and pointing in Daretor's direction. The priests looked up. They could not see Daretor's eyes beneath the cowl, but there was no doubt who they were talking about. They started in his direction – not running, but walking like hounds on the scent.

Daretor looked quickly about. The citadel was to his left. Ahead was a long line of shops and no cross street for nearly three hundred yards, not even an alleyway. He started to sweat. Elorsa was still peering in the shop window but there was nothing she could do to help.

He crossed the street to a recessed area marked by the signs and pennants of butchered animals. It was filled with stalls covered in garishly coloured awnings, each one with a carved and decorated pole that, no doubt, identified the stall's owner. Ducking between the nearest stalls he lost himself amongst the noisy vendors. The ground was covered in blood-stained sawdust and flies buzzed thickly in the air. Great slabs of raw meat hung from hooks attached to movable rigs, or lay on chopping slabs. Broad-shouldered bearded men in thick bloody aprons wielded heavy meat cleavers, while apprentices sawed doggedly at stubborn bone and sinew. Customers shouted demands for particular cuts. The place was a bedlam that suited Daretor's needs.

He grimaced as he squeezed between two stalls swimming in blood and entrails. Moving to the rear of one stall, he darted into a forest of hanging carcasses, shedding his cloak and hood in one quick movement. He came suddenly on a butcher who scowled at him.

'Sorry,' said Daretor, and snapped a short left hook that connected with the man's jaw. The butcher floundered, then went down. Daretor removed the man's apron, donned it quickly, then smeared blood on his arms and face. He rolled the unconscious man beneath the stall, picked up the slab of meat he had been carrying, and slung it over his own shoulder.

Then, brash as Zimak, he strolled back into the street. Daretor saw two or three other men dressed in aprons also carrying great chunks of meat. He followed them, deliberately bumping into Elorsa who was still hanging around the shop window.

'My pardon, lady,' he said. She started to respond then stared at him. She immediately looked away and hurried up the street. Daretor followed.

An hour later they were in a basement facing a fresh-faced youth with features similar to Elorsa. His name was Alin and he was a co-conspirator, it seemed.

'Why should you help me?' Daretor wanted to know. 'I have little to offer, except a few gold coins.'

Alin laughed. 'And a side of venison! Keep your coins, friend. Any enemy of the Provost is a friend of mine.'

'Why don't you simply leave the city?'

The youth shrugged. 'I am one of the few romantics left,' he said. 'And all good revolutions need a romantic or two, otherwise they become rather grim affairs, don't you think?'

Daretor was not particularly romantic, but he could not help liking the youth. If the Provost's priests had drained the spirit of the city, here at least was one they had missed. 'I don't have much experience with revolutions,' he said simply.

'I see,' Alin replied, glancing at his sister with the faintest smile. 'Your friend is to be executed tomorrow morning,' he continued, becoming suddenly serious. 'It has been posted about the city. There will be a big crowd. If we are to free her, it must be done this night.'

'How many men do you have at your disposal?' Daretor asked.

'You need not worry on that count,' Alin replied before his sister could say anything.

'You have a plan?'

'Perhaps,' said Alin. 'Tell me more about this Jelindel.'

At that moment Jelindel was hunched on a straw pallet in an ill-lit cell deep within the citadel. A tray of untouched food sat nearby. In a guard station opposite her cell, two priests sat playing some kind of card game that involved gambling with yellow pebbles. Their muttered exclamations were driving her to distraction.

Feeling thirsty, she started to fetch the water jug near the cell door. As she did so, the jug leapt into the air and flew across the room towards her. She cried out and ducked. The jug smashed into the wall, showering her with water and pottery fragments.

The priest-guards looked up. One of them, a surly fellow with a hare lip, lumbered to his feet and crossed to the iron bars.

'Throwin' things about ain't gonna do you no good,' he grated. He turned to his overweight companion. "Aving a tantrum, she is,' he said. They both laughed. The guard shambled back to the table. Over his shoulder he called out, 'Don't let's hear another peep out of you, or me and my friend here will come in there and pay you a nice long visit!' They guffawed again.

Jelindel wasn't paying them any attention. She was staring at the ceramic shards scattered across her bed and the wet patch on the single threadbare blanket.

The jug had flown across the room unaided. She could not have been mistaken. Was it possible the bump on the head had caused some kind of hallucination, like a waking dream? She actually wished she could speak to the physician in whose house she had materialised.

There was another possibility, however. A more intriguing one.

Magic.

Was it possible that she had worked magic, the very crime for which she was to be executed on the morn?

Did that make her a magician? Or a witch? She didn't *feel* like a witch, though admittedly she wasn't sure what a witch felt like.

She looked over at the guards. They had gone back to their card game and were paying her no heed. She glanced over the floor, then picked up a small chunk of pottery.

Taking a deep breath, she slowly stretched out her hand, and willed the pottery shard to come to her.

Nothing happened.

She tried again and kept trying until sweat stood out on her brow. Still nothing happened. She slumped back against the wall and exhaled, almost panting. Perhaps she wasn't a witch after all. She was oddly disappointed. But that still left a big question:

how did a bump on the head cause a sturdy jug to fly?

Upon *that* question she thought long and hard.

Daretor's head for heights was being sorely tested. His mouth filled with saliva and he experienced a lurching sensation in his stomach as he gazed at the ground some fifty feet below. He was on a ledge halfway up the side of a building, inching along with his face to the stone wall and his back to airy emptiness. He could feel the cool night air prickling his skin, which was already slick with sweat and, he had to admit, the stink of fear. He told himself that there was no shame in favouring the solid earth. If White Quell had meant for man or woman to fly, she would have given them wings.

He reached the end of the building. Now came the tricky bit. He had to round the corner. Unfortunately the ledge, up to now reasonably wide, smooth and unadorned, became somewhat ornate. It rose up like a wave out of which mermaids and fish protruded as if riding surf. This left little space for feet, and the sloping backside of the wave was slippery with night dew. Or perhaps, like him, the cold stone was sweating.

He was wondering what to do when an arm came around the edge and an impatient voice asked, 'What are you waiting for?'

'Wings,' he replied tartly.

'Wings we don't have. My strong arm we do. Grab it and hold on.' It was Alin. They were at one of three structures next to the detention building, which was barely a stone's throw away, looming some twenty feet higher against the night sky. Elorsa looked over impatiently.

Daretor gripped Alin's arm. Taking a deep breath, he placed his foot on the stone wave and twisted round the corner. He slipped.

Stifling a cry, he felt himself toppling, and slid off the ledge altogether. Then he was hanging in midair, still held by Alin. He looked up. Alin, visibly straining, managed a thin smile. His other arm was hooked through an open window, otherwise both of them would be bloody corpses on the flagstones below.

'Well caught,' Daretor gasped.

'I strongly suggest you get back up here, before my arm is wrenched out of its socket.'

Daretor managed to wedge the toe of his boot into the gap between two stone slabs. A moment later, now thankful to the craftsmanship of the design for its plentiful handholds, Daretor was back on the ledge.

From there they moved quickly to a spot adjacent to the roof of the detention building, but they were still two storeys below their destination.

Daretor checked the street and signalled Alin, who quickly threw a knotted rope up to the top of a balcony parapet. Its hooked, padded end caught. Moving rapidly, Alin scaled the rope and hauled himself over the parapet. Elorsa scrambled up next, moving with the agility of a cat. Daretor followed.

Once over the parapet, they forced the embrasured window, and hurried to the thick oak door on the far side of the room. Beyond the door was a locked grille that barred the top of a stairwell. Years spent travelling with Zimak came to Daretor's aid. Picking simple locks had been child's play for the little thief, and even Daretor had learned some of his skills. With the aid of two dirks he had the grille unlocked within seconds.

'A man of many talents,' Alin said in admiration.

They passed inside, moving softly in the leather slippers Alin had brought. The stairwell was unguarded, at least until they reached the ground floor.

Peering over the banister, they saw two priest-guards squatting by the main entrance. They were too far away to be caught by surprise. They were so close to the entrance that they could have easily escaped to warn others.

Alin considered their dilemma. 'What to do,' he thought aloud. 'Elorsa?'

Elorsa unbuttoned her tunic until her cleavage was displayed.

'No, wait,' Daretor said. He was contemplating the walls. 'I have seen no magic Watchers on these stairs,' he said.

'They do not watch their own,' said Elorsa with a soft snort of derision.

'Good,' said Daretor. 'I'm going to try something. Be ready. I don't know if it'll work or for how long.'

'What are you going to do?' Alin gazed at him, puzzled.

'Jelindel has taught me many things, even some I have little aptitude for. We shall see how much of a student I really am.' He concentrated on his conjuring. One false word, even an odd intonation, could have disastrous consequences. That much he *had* learned.

Muttering beneath his breath, as if chanting to himself, he started: '*Vec-akine! . . . Vac-kine! . . .*'

Alin and Elorsa exchanged a look that plainly said they had misjudged the foreigner. An error that could prove a dangerous liability.

'*Vec-takine!*' Daretor said triumphantly.

Just as Alin decided to do something about Daretor's apparent madness, a flickering blue light gathered about Daretor's lips. His brow beaded with sweat and he seemed to be under a great exertion.

Suddenly, the blue light leapt through the air and bound the two priest-guards in writhing cords. They fell to the floor, unable to move or call for help.

Daretor slumped heavily, spent. 'Quickly,' he gasped.

Alin and Elorsa did not hesitate. They hurled themselves down the remaining stairs at the guards, clubbing them unconscious. Seconds later the blue light unravelled and sped back to Daretor.

Alin bound and gagged the two men and dragged them to a cellar. Elorsa returned to the exhausted Daretor. She helped him to his feet and draped one of his arms across her shoulders. Together they stumbled down to the foyer. They found Alin by a small storeroom beneath the staircase.

Feeling somewhat safer here, Alin gave the group a moment's respite. Daretor was squatting on the floor, breathing heavily.

'A simple enough binding word . . .' he said. 'But it's how you say it that counts.'

Alin and Elorsa stared at him, partly in awe, partly out of fear. 'Was that . . . was that *magic*?' Elorsa asked, hardly daring to say the word.

Daretor nodded. 'Simple stuff. First year apprentice level. Had no idea . . . it was so . . . exhausting. . . . I'm not a natural . . .'

Alin clapped him on the shoulder, grinning. 'I thought it was amazing. The priests don't like to use magic in front of us. They're afraid we might learn how to use it.'

'Or might want to,' said Elorsa, her eyes gleaming.

'Are you ready to go on?' Alin asked Daretor.

Daretor climbed laboriously to his feet.

Jelindel was trying to sleep. She was scared. She was going to die at daybreak and she hardly understood why. It was like being accused of a crime that you thought you might have committed but couldn't actually remember doing.

It didn't seem *fair*. If only she could remember something about the past. It might explain how she came to be in this predicament.

At some point she must have slumbered, because she found herself in the middle of an uneasy dream. She was flying swiftly through a dark, unnatural plane in which globes trailing silken thread were harassing her. A noise woke her. She sat up, blinking.

Everything seemed normal at first, then she realised that the priest-guards were lying on the floor, unconscious. The table was upturned and the cards scattered.

Standing in the shadows, looking exceedingly wary, she spied three shadows. One of them stooped low, snatched up a set of keys, and crossed to her cell. A slim but muscular man stood there, smiling.

She stared back. 'Have you come to rescue me?' she asked.

'I have,' said Daretor. 'Make no noise, and do everything precisely as you're told.'

He unlocked the door and eased it open. Then he embraced her and pressed his lips to hers. Her eyes opened wide. Maybe this was the local reward for rescuing somebody, she thought. She shrugged mentally and returned the kiss, since she was clearly being rescued and owed the stranger a debt.

One of the others hissed at them. 'There's plenty of time for that later.'

It was a woman's voice. She sounded irritated. Jelindel pulled back from the embrace.

The man handed her a sword. She wasn't sure she liked weapons but it did feel familiar. She swung it experimentally.

'Are you well?' the man said, concerned.

'I am now,' Jelindel said.

Daretor took her hand and led her from the cell. They pattered up a short flight of steps, turned left, and raced to the end of a dark corridor. Here they paused, checking that the way ahead was clear.

Alin gave a signal. They darted across yet another corridor, into a courtyard.

They had almost reached the other side when, somewhere behind them, a bell began clanging.

'Time to move,' said Elorsa.

'We have to make the stairwell before we're seen,' said Daretor.

They raced down a corridor, spun into the next and came to a stop. Half a dozen priest-guards pounded into view. Someone was blowing a hitch-pitched whistle.

'At them,' yelled Daretor. He and Alin sprang towards the priests, and two went down almost at once. Elorsa engaged another while Jelindel watched. The sword in her hand seemed of little use. But she did manage to dispatch one of the priests who backed into her by whacking him hard on the head with the flat of the sword. He dropped like a stone, and she felt quite pleased with herself. At this point, a larger group of priest-guards appeared behind them.

'Stop them,' Daretor yelled at Jelindel.

She stared at him. 'Stop them how?'

'You know. *Magic.* A binding word. Anything!'

'I thought that was illegal here.'

Daretor turned frantically to their pursuers. 'Do you *want* to be executed?'

'Good point. There's only one small problem.'

During the exchange, the priests were advancing cautiously. Daretor and his companions were backing away slowly. With six of their brethren already on the ground, the priest-guards chose to exercise caution.

Elorsa's jaw set tightly. 'What exactly is the problem?'

Jelindel shrugged apologetically. 'I . . . ah . . . don't know any magic.'

'What?' asked Alin.

Elorsa looked suspicious and annoyed.

Daretor glanced at Jelindel. 'Then we're done for,' he said, noting the blank look on her face. 'You really did lose your memory. It wasn't a trick.'

Jelindel shook her head. Daretor started to say something when the priests attacked with a loud cry. The delay had been calculated. With further yells from behind, a band of more than twenty priest-guards charged from the far side of the courtyard.

Daretor pushed Jelindel behind him. '*Vec-vec-*,' He paused, trying to remember the intonation. *Vec-*'

He felt a hand on his shoulder. 'I remember a word that begins like that,' Jelindel said.

Before Daretor could engage with the foremost priest-guards, Jelindel said, '*Vec-takine!*'

Blue flickering light appeared on her lips. She waved her hand at the charging priests and blue light flashed across the space, binding every one of them. They fell to the floor, stunned and frightened.

The priests rushing from the opposite direction stopped, amazed and not a little alarmed.

Nobody was as amazed as Jelindel herself, however. 'By all the gods, did I do that?' she asked.

There was no time for Alin and Elorsa to marvel at Jelindel's power. They skirted the bound priests and made for the turret doors. Moments later they reached the stairwell and pounded up. Two floors from the rooftop, Alin paused to place a package on one of the landings. He caught up with the others as they reached the balcony. From there they scrambled across the scalloped roof to the adjacent building. From behind them came a loud explosion and a flash of light. Then great clouds of smoke billowed from the shattered upper floors of the citadel.

Alin grinned. 'We may not have the use of magic here, but we have developed other means of deterring our enemies.'

Using the rooftops, they crossed the city, putting distance between themselves and their pursuers.

Some time later, they returned to the basement where Daretor had first met Alin. They had barely spoken along the way. Now, with doors barred and windows shuttered, Daretor turned to Jelindel.

'How much do you remember?' he asked.

'Falling,' she said. 'Then I was in a closet amidst brooms and buckets.'

'Nothing else?'

'I had a strange dream that I was flying, that I was high up in the sky. But it was just a dream.'

'It wasn't a dream,' Daretor said. 'We are on a quest and we were sent here by an old enemy, a powerful sorcerer called Fa'red. He tricked us. Before that we were indeed flying in the sky.'

'Why doesn't she remember anything?' Elorsa asked. Her initial anger had evaporated the moment Jelindel had worked magic.

'I got a bump on the head,' said Jelindel. 'A physician said my memory should come back. Eventually.'

Daretor groaned. 'I was counting on your abilities to get

us out of here. Never mind. You're safe, and that's what really matters.'

'Sorry,' Jelindel said. She started to speak when she remembered something. 'When you opened my cell, you kissed me. Are we ? I mean, are you and I . . . friends?'

Daretor pulled her to him. 'We are life partners, you and I. Lovers and companions on many adventures, not least this one.'

Jelindel felt oddly secure, wrapped in this man's arms. 'So we . . . ah . . . do this a lot? Go off having adventures and getting into trouble?'

'Well, you are a young archmage, a very powerful sorceress, and many wish to hire your services. I have a good sword arm, and so I travel with you.' He paused, looking into her face. 'You don't remember anything?'

'You're sort of familiar, but everything is sort of familiar right now. It's a very unsettling feeling.' She turned to Elorsa and Alin. 'Are these people also our companions?'

'Sit down,' Elorsa said. 'There is much to tell, but I fear we have little time.'

Her words proved prophetic for there was a knock at the rear door. Everybody froze. The knock came again. Then it was repeated in a distinct pattern. Alin opened the door and two men entered.

'Pirin, Jod. Come in, quick.' Alin peered outside before closing the door.

The newcomers looked at Daretor and Jelindel in evident dislike.

'Well,' grumbled Pirin. 'You have roused the city, make no mistake of that.'

◈

Osric and Zimak peered at the city that lay some ten thousand feet below. S'cressling remained at the same altitude and held a circling pattern. The land was totally unfamiliar, nor did they know how they would be greeted by the locals.

'Why don't we just land in the town square and *ask?*' said Zimak, impatiently.

'And what if they're not the friendly sort?' Osric demanded.

'Why shouldn't they be? Why is everybody so suspicious?'

'There is treachery everywhere,' muttered Osric. 'Particularly in the hearts of women,' he finished off.

'They're not all like Jelindel,' Zimak said. I like a good wench.'

Osric nodded. After a while, he said, 'S'cressling knows that Fa'red did not send Jelindel and Daretor to the Stone People. Where this place is I do not know but one thing is certain: Fa'red did not send them here for their good health.'

Zimak gazed glumly at the dimly lit city. It seemed somewhat smaller than D'loom. Judging by the lights, it wasn't as densely populated either. He was sick of flying, sick of feeling queasy, sick of throwing up over the side of the deck platform. He wanted solid earth beneath his feet and he really didn't care where it was.

'Well, what are we going to do then?'

'We? We're not doing anything. I'll ask S'cressling to put down on one of those towers as soon as everybody is asleep and you're going to reconnoitre.'

'Me? What about you?'

'It was your idea to go down there and search for Daretor and Jelindel. Besides, somebody has to look after S'cressling.'

'Seems to me she looks after herself.'

'They're our friends down there,' Osric said flatly.

'Gah, I wouldn't exactly call them friends,' Zimak snorted. 'Especially that vixen Jelindel.'

'She has betrayed you,' stated Osric.

'She's cheated me out of powerful weapons, banished me to a paraworld, abducted me from a harem, robbed me of kinghood, seduced my best friend, and, and – do you want me to continue? I can.'

'Then why do you seek her company?' Osric asked. 'Men are more loyal.'

'Hie, Osric. Isn't that the truth? But why do we do a lot of things?' Zimak said. 'Why did Daretor and I save you from the Temple Inviolate?'

'Because without me you couldn't escape on the back of a dragon.'

Zimak turned in the saddle and glared. 'Of all the ungrateful wretches! Next time I won't bother saving you or anyone else.'

'Well next time is upon us, so make up your mind. In case it has slipped your attention, Rakeem's poison must surely be working on your body by now.'

'We're as good as dead anyway,' Zimak said. 'If the poison doesn't get us, Rakeem will.'

'Finding the dragonsight is only a portion of your future,' Osric predicted. 'Play that part, and another may present itself.'

'You're sounding more like a market charm vendor every day,' Zimak observed. 'All right, I'll do things your way.'

'Good. After we land, you find Daretor and Jelindel then signal me.'

'Signal you? How?'

'Improvise. Light a fire.'

'Hie, easy, as long as there's a tinder box lying around, along with a pile of hay and faggots stacked for me to light.'

'Ever the pessimist,' said Osric, shaking his head. 'Maybe Jelindel still has the whistle I gave her.'

At a command from Osric, S'cressling banked steeply and descended. Zimak held on tightly and cursed the day, several years ago, when he had left the D'loom markets in search of an enchanted mailshirt.

'What were you thinking?' demanded Pirin, pointing angrily at Alin and Elorsa. 'You have endangered the entire movement.'

Alin was unapologetic. 'It's time something happened around here, Pirin. We skulk and hide, and we plot, but we never do anything. It's only a matter of time before we're betrayed, and without doing anything.' At Pirin's silence, Alin added, 'Look how many of us are left. We're dwindling like coins to the Provost's coffers.'

'Alin's right,' Elorsa added.

'So you took matters into your own hands?'

'This woman is a powerful sorceress,' Alin said. 'She might even be more powerful than the Provost himself.'

Pirin laughed. 'If she's so powerful why did she sit so meekly inside her cell, waiting to be rescued? Why didn't she just blow the door open and walk out? Tell me that, Alin.'

Elorsa interrupted again. 'Because she's lost her memory.'

Pirin peered at Jelindel. 'Well, isn't that convenient. A sorceress who can't remember magic. She's as much use as a bow without an arrow.'

Daretor stepped between Pirin and Jelindel. 'You know nothing of what you speak,' he said. 'There are few mages in Q'zar who can rival Jelindel dek Mediesar.'

Pirin's companion, who had said nothing so far, cleared his throat. 'Perhaps we should discuss this more sensibly.'

Pirin withdrew, but shot his colleague a dark look. The smaller man gazed back, asserting his authority.

The man invited everybody to sit around the table. When they had done so, he introduced himself. 'I am Jod Ukin. By day I am a banker and merchant. By night I am as you see me now. A disreputable plotter and a traitor to my tyrant sovereign, the Provost Marshal of Ishluk.' He leaned his elbows on the table and looked closely at Jelindel. 'Are you truly a great mage, one of those we sometimes hear of when news reaches us from afar?'

Jelindel looked uneasy.

'She is,' Daretor said, taking her hand.

She looked into his eyes and silently mouthed, 'I am?'

Jod Ukin regarded them, then looked at Alin and Elorsa. 'She has demonstrated power?'

They both nodded vigorously. Jod Ukin thought for a long moment then stood up.

'Let us begin then,' he declared.

The others stood, not understanding. 'Begin what?' asked Pirin.

'The revolution, of course.'

The word went out. At the sixth hour the next morning cadres of revolutionaries were to strike across the city, taking over key locations. Old men and women who could remember the days before the current regime, and who had once practised magic, were to assemble at strategic places. Jod Ukin doubted they could muster any magic greater than a few weak curses, but every bit would help.

Daretor felt as if he had been caught up in a whirlwind. He was also none too sure that Jelindel would be of much help. He sat with her for some time, relating her own history. While she seemed to remember bits and pieces, it was fragmentary. Her responses to most of the stories was a gasp of amazement and something along the lines of 'I did that?'

For her part, Jelindel felt like she was listening to somebody else's life story, one that was fascinating, but in no way hers.

That night they got what sleep they could, but by the fourth hour everyone was gathered and ready. Daretor and Jelindel had agreed to accompany Alin, Elorsa and Jod Ukin to the Provost's palace. The Provost was, by all accounts, a powerful sorcerer in his own right, and would prove a formidable enemy.

Ten minutes before the sixth hour they were in position. Overhead, the sky was lit by the gibbous Blanchmoon, and piercingly bright stars. On street level, silent forces crept.

'Not exactly what we bargained for,' said Daretor, close to Jelindel's ear. She simply nodded. Daretor had written out as many spells and charms as he could remember, and Jelindel was memorising them. Binding spells and blinding spells would be useful, as well as shield spells that would repel projectiles. There was also a spell that made enemies move in slow motion, making them satisfyingly vulnerable.

Jelindel had grave doubts about her ability to work magic of *any* kind, let alone useful magic. Jod had placed her with his 'magic' contingent. Their job was solely to counter any spells emitting from the Provost's priest-guards. Jod would take on the Provost. Jelindel looked around. She saw only elderly, frightened men and women. Some even clutched reminder notes, in case they forgot their spells.

Jelindel's heart lurched. If these people had ever gained para-plane spirits, they had long since relinquished their hold over them. Without spirit-power, their magic would be weak. Jelindel's eyebrows knitted. How did she know that?

Jod appeared beside her. 'It's time,' he told the elderly bunch.

'Stay together if you can.' That said he raced across the deserted marketplace. The others followed. Cane ladders were hoisted up against the boundary wall. Within moments dark-clothed men and women were scaling the ladders. Two garrotted priest-guards lay on their backs, their dead eyes wide with surprise.

Jod waited for his people to clamber over the parapets. He then dropped his hand and everyone climbed down to the palace grounds. A wolfhound yowled in the distance, but it didn't slow the scurrying figures as they raced towards the imposing building fashioned from white marble.

Several wolfhounds, loping around the side of the palace, started barking, their hackles erect. Jod had given instructions that nobody was to use magic until the last possible moment. An elderly man took fright. Before he could complete a simple warding spell, several bolts struck the beasts. They tumbled in a whining heap, but they had roused the palace guard. Somewhere to the left swords clanged, then someone shrieked. Jod cursed beneath his breath. He had hoped to enter the palace before their presence was discovered.

He readied himself as priest-guards rushed them. Daretor vaulted an ornamental pond and engaged three of them. His sword flashed and whirled. A priest-guard dropped as the blade cut across his face, another clutched his abdomen and went down. The third dropped his sword and raised his hands, then babbled an incantation.

Daretor buckled over as something invisible thumped into him. The next moment he was flung through the air to land twenty yards away. The wind knocked from him, he saw several of the revolutionaries thrown in a similar fashion. Some crashed into stone walls and fell dead, others rolled on the ground.

Then Jod's sorcerers struck. The promenade became crisscrossed with purple, pink and blue flickering bolts of light. Tightening the grip on his sword, Daretor steadied himself. The fighting was thickest by the main entrance to the palace. Shaking his head to clear it, he made for the colonnaded steps.

Jelindel stood back and chanted spells, aiming them with sweeping gestures of her hands. The strange part of it was that they mostly worked. Blue light flickered out and wrapped itself around its victims, toppling and binding them. She felt giddy with this newfound power. But she became slightly dazed, as though drained. She saw Daretor being thrown across the court-yard, and immediately she cast a binding spell at the throat of his attacker. The priest-guard had not warded himself, no doubt unaware of the power in their attackers. His body twitched in sei-zure; he clutched at his throat as though he were being strangled, then collapsed. Jelindel walked towards the palace as though mesmerised, almost oblivious to the mayhem.

Daretor took the steps three at a time, once almost tripping over a body. He dispatched the only priest-guard left at the entrance, then entered the grand and richly appointed atrium. Here the fighting had reached fever-pitch. The Provost's elite guards threw themselves into the frantic, desperate fight, seem-ingly unafraid of death. They were disturbingly like Fa'red's deadmoon assassins.

Outside, dawn spread reddish sunlight that spilled through the atrium windows, revealing the carnage. It also revealed a squad of elite guards who had been rushed from the barracks.

Jelindel's mind cleared, and she tried a spell she had not yet used. The slow-motion spell ensnared the advancing guards, instantly slowing their movements. Against even the ill-trained rebels, they were easy prey. Demoralised, some of the defenders broke ranks and fled. Messengers arrived to report to Jod that the city had been taken, more or less. Jod nodded acknowledgement, but he was aware that their revolt was far from over. The Provost had not shown himself yet.

No sooner had he thought that, than a cry went up. All eyes turned towards a huge archway on the north side. Standing there, dwarfed by the arch, yet somehow filling it with his powerful aura, stood Kagan, the Provost Marshal.

The attackers ceased fighting. The Provost took a step forward and the front ranks crumpled silently to the ground. Those left standing seemed to be the immediate targets of crossbowmen who had appeared from the mansion's numerous balconies. Jod's people retaliated with a withering flight of arrows, but they seemed too few and too late to save those under attack.

The Provost waved his hand and half of the second rank went down as though felled by a giant invisible scythe.

Jod Ukin took a deep breath and shouted the spell, *'Velectum-bassius-sui!'*

The ground rumbled. Even Jod's people fled the lawn that was now undulating as though an earthquake was gathering momentum. Then something sprang from the ground like water from a fountain. It coalesced into a shimmering body of white light, and then solidified.

'Slissum-vec-takine!' Jod incanted, before sagging to the ground. His lifeforce was being drained to sustain the ethereal manifestation.

Jelindel shielded her eyes from the blinding apparition. She had to do something, but what? Jod had put everything into one spell. Somehow she knew this was foolhardy. If the paraplane creature failed him, he would be completely defenceless against the Provost.

The being hovered in indecision. Jelindel took a deep breath.

She then focused her mind on the creature, willing it to move. The thing pulsed on the lawn for a moment longer, then skimmed the surface of the grass and reached out for the Provost.

The body of light sought to devour the Provost, but as its outer aura closed in around him, it seemed to diminish. Within seconds it was flowing into the outline of the Provost as though he had inscribed a paraplane black hole around his body, and it was drinking in the light. Moments later, the ruptured lawn was all that remained of Jod's trump spell. Jelindel walked forward, leaving Jod's crumpled body behind.

Kagan gazed at her in genuine puzzlement. 'You? *You're* this rabble's secret weapon?' he said, mistaking her for the creator of the white apparition. 'You will rue the day you took up with this lot,' he concluded.

He waved his hand in a dismissive manner. A tongue of red light jagged across the lawn and struck Jelindel. She was lifted bodily and thrown against a column. She slammed against it and fell forward. A low moan swept the ranks of the attackers. Jod Ukin forced his eyes open and saw the triumphant Kagan. The Provost would kill them all.

'So we have all the rats in the one basket, do we?' said Kagan. His lips moved and a deadly red light gathered about him. It began to swirl, spinning faster and faster like a tiny tornado. Suddenly it bellied out towards the remnants of Jod's rebels. They scattered, but all fell under the might of the whirlwind. The wind increased, throwing them across the grounds.

'You want to see magic?' Kagan bellowed above the shrill whirlwind. 'Then I shall give you magic.' He raised his arm to cast the deadly vortex. It would cut them down like a storm in a field of corn.

Instead the red vortex imploded, quickly dissipating. The

Provost stared about him, stunned. 'What?' he gasped. 'Who dares defy me?'

'Me,' said a voice. All fighting ceased. Both sides turned and stared at Jelindel, whose outflung hand was still directed at Kagan. Leaning heavily against the palace wall, she was bleeding from a scalp wound. A moment later she let her right arm fall to her side.

Kagan muttered a word and raised both hands, creating a ball of writhing light between them. His face contorted in fury as he flung it at her. It singed the very air as it passed over the heads of the combatants. The power in it was felt hundreds of yards away. People ducked as the white light passed. None doubted that it would annihilate the wisp of a girl who was its intended victim, yet somehow that did not happen.

Jelindel raised her left hand, palm out, and chanted a ward spell. The ball of sizzling energy hovered in midair. She then clenched her hand and flicked her fingers out. The ball hurtled back at Kagan. His face had barely enough time to display absolute terror before the white light engulfed him.

The people on the lawn shrank back from the spectacle, mostly shielding their eyes against the blinding light. Those who dared look saw Kagan's body limned by the devouring light, before the flesh was shredded from its bones. Moments later, the Provost's skeleton fell apart and collapsed.

Jelindel could not comprehend her success. It had seemed to her that Kagan would easily dissolve his own creation and retaliate with such speed that she would be unable to block his counter spell. But at the precise moment she warded off the para-plane entity, the Provost had been distracted by something on the palace roofline.

People were moaning in fear, others dropped their weapons

as though they were redundant. Then Jelindel heard, rather than saw, someone running towards her. It was a hooded figure. A man with his hand gripping a long-bladed knife.

'Jelindel,' Daretor cried. Jelindel was already turning, but too slowly. She was groggy from the magical battle, and actually stumbled as she turned, starting to fall.

The knife fell from the man's fingers as he gripped Jelindel's arm, stopping her fall. At the same time the cowl fell back from his face. Daretor rushed beside him and looked on, dumbstruck.

Jelindel steadied herself. 'Nice to see you, Zimak. What kept you?'

'Gah, Jelindel. You know that adage, "As fast as a dragon"? Well, it's way overrated. Trust me.'

Daretor looked at Jelindel. She stood on her tiptoes and kissed him. 'You look rather silly when you get that expression on your face.'

'Your memory . . . ' he said.

'Is back,' said Jelindel. 'But I think the cure was worse than the disease.' She put one hand to her head and shut her eyes against the throbbing pain.

S'cressling was a majestic curiosity. She crouched in the town square, her immense, serrated tail flicking like the tail of a cat watching a mouse. Sensing this, the people kept a respectful distance. Despite the recent display of magic, nothing compared with seeing a giant crimson dragon land in the palace grounds. All of Ishluk knew of the existence of magic, but dragons were simply the stuff of folklore.

'She rather steals one's thunder,' Jelindel was heard to say.

It was two days since the triumph of the revolution. Jelindel had been partially healed by Jod, while Zimak and Osric had been brought up to date on events. The city was in the midst of joyous celebration. Within the first few hours of Provost Kagan's demise, all the Watchers were torn down and destroyed. The surviving priest-guards were rounded up for trial. They would have to answer accusations of crimes against the people; some would be banished from Ishluk, and others hanged; a few would stay in administrative posts which were needed in the running of the city.

Almost as soon as the city had fallen, Jelindel sent word asking if anyone had heard of the realm of the Stone People. Nobody had come forward at first, but while supplies were being loaded aboard S'cressling, a heavily lined woman hobbled up to them. In her youth, she said, she had heard a tale about people made of living rock. The tale claimed that their realm was deep beneath the Hazgar Mountains, hundreds of miles to the north-east.

The old woman was partially deaf. Jelindel asked several times how the woman wished to be rewarded, but she replied that the Provost's fall was reward enough.

An hour before noon they climbed aboard the dragon and bid their friends goodbye. Jod Ukin, the new Regent of Ishluk, conferred honorary citizenship on them and made them Stewards of the Realm.

'A Steward of the Realm has high rank and standing,' complained Zimak as they prepared to leave. 'Why are we leaving without enjoying the honour for at least a few weeks?'

'We're poisoned, and will die unless we find the dragonsight,' Daretor reminded him.

'Gah, Daretor. Do you have to spoil everything?' muttered Zimak.

Moments later, S'cressling stretched her enormous wings,

provoking a collective gasp from the crowd, and causing many to back away frantically. The wings rose then dropped with a noise like a thunderclap, and the dragon sprang into the air. Her wings beat laboriously as she worked to gain height, then she began to catch air currents and ascend in a graceful glide.

From below came a long cheer and much clapping. Jelindel and Daretor waved. When S'cressling reached a height of two thousand feet she veered off to the north-east.

'That was a costly detour,' said Jelindel. 'Best to avoid the like in future.'

Chapter 4
THADDEUS PIKE

They maintained the same course all that day and most of the next, only veering to avoid a massive storm system that Osric feared would toss them about like leaves. Jelindel and Daretor felt far from threatened after their recent ordeal. They regarded this part of the journey as a rest, time off from danger and desperation.

Jelindel blamed herself for being taken in by Fa'red's treachery, although she agreed with Daretor that they should have expected no less from one so cunning.

'Next time,' said Daretor, 'let us just ring his fat neck.'

'Maybe I could try that ball of power trick the Provost used. I can't think of anything more fitting for Fa'red than to be skinned alive,' Jelindel mused. 'Then again, he has survived fire before.'

'I don't know about that,' said Zimak. 'If it were up to me, I think I'd concoct a spell that removed his bones and left the rest.'

'Fillet him?' Jelindel said.

'Whatever,' Zimak said. 'Dissolve all the bones in his body instantly, leaving behind one big pile of useless human sludge.'

The next morning they sighted the Hazgar Mountains in the distance. The highest peaks rose nearly twenty thousand feet, too high even for S'cressling to fly over. The range stretched away into the distance. Many of the high ridges and peaks were blanketed in snow, while fir and birch carpeted the lower escarpments, even where great rocky gorges cut deep into the slopes.

In stark contrast, the lowlands were arid and empty. According to Jelindel it was not due to climate.

'Some terrible magic was wrought here long ago,' she said, studying the scorched land. 'A great battle between sorcerers maybe.'

The principal town in the territory was Ogven. It sat at the confluence of two rivers, one of which eventually ran into the Bay of Samile after nearly two hundred miles and many name changes.

S'cressling landed in a small valley some ten miles from the town. Leaving the dragon to forage for herself the group made their way to a nearby road, and hitched a ride on a slow, rumbling wagon.

'I hope this wagon ride is more auspicious than my last,' said Daretor.

'I wish we could avoid contact with towns altogether,' said Osric, glancing around uneasily.

'If you know how to find the Stone People, I am all ears,' Jelindel said. 'If not, then we must gather information as best we can.'

She spent the rest of the journey questioning the wagon driver about the town and its people. Ogven sounded pretty much like any normal town on the continent.

'Seems to me we end up in more danger in "normal" places than the other kind,' Zimak protested.

'You're such a pessimist, Zimak,' said Jelindel, laughing easily.

Zimak stared at her. 'You hang out with Mister Doom-and-Gloom here,' he said, indicating Daretor, 'and you call *me* a pessimist?'

The wagoner dropped them three miles from town at a fork in the road. Jelindel and the others waved goodbye and turned towards the distant huddle of buildings.

The land had a withered, blasted look, as if indeed a battle had taken place, one using vast quantities of magical power. Jelindel shuddered as they passed an earthen mound burnt blacker than the rest. 'Something is buried there,' she said, averting her eyes. 'Something that should never have walked the face of this world in the first place.'

'You mean it's akin to the fallen god that crashed into Sky-fall?' Daretor said.

'Don't remind me of that business,' Jelindel said. 'Just keep sentient mailshirts out of it.'

Zimak's ears pricked. If it had anything to do with powerful artefacts, then he wanted to know more. He was all for digging up the dead thing. 'Perhaps we could sell off parts of it as potent amulets,' he suggested casually.

'Zimak, shut up,' said Daretor.

Zimak kept his eyes on the ravaged ground. 'Ever since you two got together you've both lost your sense of adventure,' he said.

Neither Jelindel nor Daretor deigned to reply.

As they trudged towards the town, the air became noticeably chill. A shadow fell over them. Looking up they saw that the sky had become overcast. Thick grey clouds scudded across from the Hazgar Mountains, obscuring the sun, and cooling the land.

'Now that's odd,' Zimak observed, staring at the fast-moving clouds. Jelindel also stopped to watch the strange weather, frowning slightly.

'I have seen places where it is like winter on one side of a mountain and summer on the other,' said Osric. 'All other places roundabout are unaffected. Perhaps this is one of those.'

'Localised weather,' said Jelindel. 'I have visited one country that has four seasons all in one day. I didn't like it, either. I think we should get to town as soon as we can.'

She walked faster. The others matched her pace. 'What do you fear?' Daretor asked, striding by her side.

'I don't know,' she answered after a long pause. 'And I fear what I don't know.'

The temperature continued to drop. Overhead, clouds thickened and grew dark. The light was like that of early evening, though it had an odd bruised quality that made them look sickly. The wind began to strengthen, blowing in icy gusts that whipped up sand and pebbles, blasting the travellers.

'Is it my imagination or does this storm have something against us specifically?' Osric called above the howl of the squalling wind.

'Black Quell alone knows,' Jelindel answered, leaning into the gale. 'But if this is the worst of it, then we are safe.'

Zimak thought he heard Jelindel mock the inclement weather and hastily traced White Quell's sign on his chest to avert bad omens. As they continued towards the town, the wind swung around to blow directly in their faces, as if it wanted to force them back.

'This is no natural storm,' Daretor called. Everyone else had already reached that conclusion for themselves. Jelindel noted that snowflakes had joined the sand and pebbles on the wind.

'Snow in spring,' she said. 'Interesting.'

'Interesting?' scowled Zimak. 'If this gets any worse I'm going to have extremities freezing and breaking off.'

'I can think of one that won't be missed!' Jelindel called back.

'Those are my extremities, I'll have you remember,' Daretor shouted indignantly.

'Oh, very funny,' said Zimak. 'I'll be sure to collect them and hand them over.'

The temperature plummeted further, until the pain from its chill forced them to breathe through cloth masks. Jelindel's hands were numb from the cold and all feeling had gone from her legs and feet. The snow whipped past, but the wind prevented it from piling up on the ground. Visibility was down to a few yards.

'If we don't make the town soon we shall be completely lost!' yelled Osric, trying to be heard above the wind's howl.

They staggered on, clutching their lightweight garb tight about them, and peering into the relentless wind. Daretor walked ahead of Jelindel, trying to shield her from the worst of the wind's fury.

'We're going to die out here,' Zimak called. 'Do something, Jelindel.'

They needed little encouragement to stop. The four huddled together, making shelter with their bodies. Jelindel spoke some words of magic, but her teeth were chattering so much that they came out garbled. She tried again. It was still no good.

'I'm sorry,' she managed. 'Have to keep walking.'

'In what direction?' asked Osric.

'Into the wind, of course.'

'If this is an enchanted wind, whoever is behind it could be trying to fool us into thinking the wind is coming from the direction of the town. If he then changes its direction, we would still walk into it, and get lost.'

A garbled argument developed about the correct direction. Zimak pointed off one way, insisting the town lay there, but was unable to explain why. Osric suggested they follow the road, but they couldn't be certain they hadn't already strayed from it. It was merely a dirt track, little different from the rest of the wasteland. In this light, with so much snow on the wind, they could well be standing on the road, yet not know it.

While the others were arguing, Daretor peered intently into the murk. He raised a hand, pointing. 'I saw a light flare over there,' he shouted. 'Line up behind me. Everybody hold hands.'

They did as he instructed. Not daring to turn his head even by a fraction, Daretor walked carefully and doggedly in the direction of the light. Suddenly he stumbled and fell. He was so cold and cramped that he could barely move. His hands were so numb it took him a moment to realise that what he was clutching was not earth or sand but a stone signpost.

The others clumsily helped him to his feet. Daretor told them what he had found, but if they heard they gave no indication. Struggling on, they reached a wall made of ice-encrusted wooden planks. Groping his way along, Daretor found a door and pulled it open without the formality of knocking. One by one he pushed his companions inside.

The heat slowly registered on their freezing bodies. Blinking their eyes clear of grit and ice, they looked around to find themselves within the taproom of what seemed to be a well-appointed inn. The placard above the barrel bench said *The Dragon's Breath*.

'Damn dragon must eat ice instead of virgins,' wheezed Zimak.

A dozen surprised locals turned to face them. They were gathered around a great stone hearth in which a very inviting fire crackled and danced. They gestured for the frozen newcomers to join them. The innkeeper began to put drinks on a tray without even being asked.

'I'm Leot,' said the burly man as he handed the drinks around.

The liquid burned as if it were molten lead, warming them from within even as the fire soaked the numbness out of their limbs and fingers.

'I suppose I don't have to tell you that you were lucky to have lived through that?' Leot asked. 'Where did you come from?'

'Carter . . . dropped us,' gasped Daretor. 'Said town was . . . three miles.'

'How can we ever thank you?' said Jelindel.

'Now, now, enough of that,' said Leot. 'It's our custom to welcome strangers. The first drink is, by tradition, given free and with good will.'

'A wonderful custom,' said Zimak, basking in the heat. 'High time everybody took it up.'

The locals took this as a toast, raising their tankards and drinking deeply. The newcomers joined in.

Leot suggested they join the company for a meal as they sat steaming the damp out of their clothes. Rather than make people leave the fire, he dragged a table over and brought out a platter of roast lamb, fresh ryebread dripping with butter, and sauces. Vegetables were not a major feature of the meal, which was eaten with fingers off ryebread platters. Whatever else could be said of Ogven, its citizens ate well and heartily. Leot explained that the town was actually on the edge of the wasteland, and that the mountain valleys to the north were green and verdant, with good grazing and plenty of water.

'Why then build your town here?' asked Jelindel.

'For trade, of course,' Leot answered. 'Not everyone can be a farmer. We are on a confluence of byways for merchants from the north and west, and those from the far side of the continent.

Several roads and two rivers meet here. Indeed, if it weren't for the Great Rapids some fifty miles north-east of here, we would be even more prosperous. But we have joined with some other towns nearby to build a canal and a series of locks around the rapids. It will take many years but our children will be wealthy, and this town will grow into a city.'

Predictably, Osric complimented Leot on the fine name of his inn. Leot replied that it was also the locals' name for the wasteland hereabouts.

When the meal was eaten, they crowded closer to the fire, each with a tankard of mulled ale. Leot spread his hands flat on the table and looked at each of them in turn.

'First, let me say you are welcome here,' he said. 'As I am also mayor of Ogven it is my duty to ask your business. That storm descended with truly magical swiftness. I think it would only be fair if you told us whether you have magician enemies in pursuit.'

The others waited for Jelindel to answer.

After hesitating a long time, she said, 'We thank you for your welcome, and especially for your warmth and drink. As for our business, we come seeking old myths, stories, and lost magical things. On the matter of the blizzard, I cannot say for sure but I feel that someone does not want us to feel welcome. We have endured many storms, and that one did not come from nature.'

One of the locals, Uthven, snorted good-naturedly. 'Far from it, miss,' he said. 'I have not seen weather like this in all my years, and I am no youngling.'

The other locals nodded. Some shot nervous glances at the shutters, where the wind still hammered.

'We are on a quest on which our very lives depend,' Jelindel continued, 'and we have little time to complete it. Our bodies have been tainted with a slow poison. Each passing day makes our plight more urgent.'

'You could have left that bit out,' grated Zimak. 'I for one don't need reminding.'

'Nevertheless,' continued Jelindel, 'that is our circumstance. We were hurried on this quest by a treacherous archmage named Fa'red. Instead of sending us where we needed to go, he sent us to a place called Ishluk, in southern Gratz. We were lucky to escape alive. It is my belief that this storm is also his doing, and that he seeks to thwart us again. This does suggest that we are on the right track, however. Otherwise he would not be bothering with us. The trouble is that the storm is probably the least of our worries.'

'The least?' exclaimed Uthven.

Jelindel shrugged. 'Fa'red will use any means to destroy us. He will not stop at a storm.' She thought for a moment, her brow creasing. 'Have you defences for the town?'

Leot nodded. 'You think we will need them?'

Jelindel looked at him squarely. 'If we stay, yes. It would be better for you if we left as quickly as possible, but I fear it is already too late. If what we seek is here, then it is in Fa'red's interest to destroy your town.'

Leot's ruddy cheeks puffed. 'With whose help?' he laughed. 'The Preceptor is short on authority since his army was smashed.' He turned to his countrymen. 'Aye, we know of this Fa'red. He is a petty warlord with some skills in magic.'

The locals murmured assent. They did not seem especially fearful.

Jelindel smiled doubtfully. 'I think you misunderstand. Fa'red doesn't need armies to enforce his decrees. His alliance with the Preceptor was a mere convenience. No, he has a more nefarious agenda, one that requires no mortal forces. He can align himself with things not of this world.'

Uthven sat down heavily. 'One man has as much power?'

'Indeed he does,' Jelindel answered. 'But other powerful forces stand in the path of what he desires.'

Leot looked at her shrewdly. 'And would you be part of those forces?'

She nodded.

'Well, then, if what you say is true, we must certainly look to the defence of the town. Will this infernal blizzard last long? It makes everything more difficult.'

'Now that I have rested, I think I can be of some help,' Jelindel said. She walked over to the table, sliced one last chunk of meat from the leg of lamb, and stood chewing while she rubbed her hands together. The locals eyes her uneasily. Magic was something everyone had heard about, but rarely did the common folk come into direct contact with it. As such, anyone who said they had a flair for the arcane arts was usually treated with respect.

Jelindel went to the door, paused as if bracing herself, then quickly opened it and stepped into the storm.

'Jelli,' Daretor called.

Jelindel waved for him to stay back. A part of her lurched at the concern in his voice, before she closed the door against the pounding wind.

Steadying herself against the building, Jelindel spoke a long string of words in a language so old that it had never been heard in Ogven. Intense blue light flickered on her lips, then grew into a small vortex about her. After some moments it expanded several feet to form a perfect circle that swirled around her like a troupe of magical dancing girls. The pulsating ring expanded outwards, gathering energy from the very storm itself.

Roused by the sudden quiet, Daretor flung open the door. The locals gathered behind him. The air was again still.

Leot's eyes widened. 'The storm is gone?'

'No,' said Jelindel. 'See for yourself.' She looked very tired.

Leot pushed to the front of the crowd and peered out. He turned to Jelindel, awestruck. The others filed outside. It was still very cold but what caused mouths to drop in wonder was that the storm now raged some hundred yards away. Indeed, Ogven now existed in a bubble inside the storm. Beyond the bubble, the blizzard continued. If anything, it seemed to have grown even more ferocious now that it had been pushed back.

The townspeople could not believe their eyes. A snow storm stretched over their town like a giant eiderdown, yet not a snow flake touched the roofs. They were simple folk, and seeing this left them in awe of their guest.

Leot started issuing orders. Jelindel interrupted him to suggest he arm the townsfolk with fire and steel, and also call for any known mages.

'Do you think the storm is going to get worse?' said Daretor.

'I'm afraid so. Fa'red is behind this; I can smell his vile magic. He will stop at nothing to see us undone. On the positive side, the longer he strikes at us with the storm, the more his reserves will be drained.'

Zimak nodded, sneering. 'So much for oaths that you people swear by.'

'You're a fine one to speak, you little scad heap,' snapped Daretor. 'You should ally yourself with Fa'red. You two could spend your days betraying each other to your hearts' content.'

Jelindel stepped between them. 'Things would be so much better if you two would sort out your problems some other time. Zimak, Fa'red may have forsaken direct use of the dragonsight but he will find some other means to wield it, or to exploit the dragons. In the end it is dragon magic itself that he wishes to control, and no magic on Q'zar can oppose such power. It is fortunate that dragons are by nature noble creatures. If they wished, they could destroy Q'zar.'

'Destroy their birth world? Daretor said. 'They would no sooner do that now that they've found it than, well, than Zimak can walk past an unattended coin.'

'What will Fa'red do now?' asked Zimak, ignoring Daretor.

'I don't know. The storm may be part of a more subtle plan. I wish I knew if the storm was meant to kill us, or if it was meant to keep us imprisoned.'

'Either way,' said Osric, 'we are imprisoned. You can defeat him, can't you?'

'We will see. I have used a lot of energy holding back the storm. At least with the weather in check, we can see clearly, and organise defences. In the meantime, we can best help these people by getting what we came for and leaving quickly.'

'If leaving is a possibility,' added Daretor.

'I say we whistle up S'cressling and get out of here,' Zimak said.

Before Jelindel or Daretor could respond, Osric said, 'Were it that easy I would have called her when the storm first struck.' Worry lines creased his forehead. 'Something is blocking my empathy with her.'

'Some*one*, I would hazard to guess,' Jelindel said.

Leot returned. He had been busy. Behind him, it seemed as though the town's entire population had gathered to catch sight of the sorceress and her companions.

Leot placed several burly men at the door to keep the crowd back, then approached Jelindel. He outlined the town's defences and what he had so far accomplished. Jelindel then told him the nature of their quest, though there were parts she left out.

'I have never heard of the Stone People,' he said, scratching his head. 'Nor do I know who might.'

One of the locals spoke up. 'What about Thaddeus Pike? If anybody knows of these creatures, he might.'

'That old fool?' Uthven sneered. 'He's only good for selling potions to lovesick maidens, and prattling nonsense to those whose brains are addled.' Most of the others muttered agreement.

Leot raised his hands for silence. 'Still and all, after what we have seen here today, I for one might change my views where magic is concerned.' He pointed at the bluish light that held back the raging storm. 'Is there one among you who cannot see that this magic is strong?' Silence answered his question. 'I thought not. There is no one else who remembers the old stories as well as Thaddeus, so it is him that we must consult.

'Sarat,' he called. 'C'mere lad, and be smart about it.'

A freckled youth with a mop of red hair eased his way through the crowd. Leot told him to take the newcomers to Thaddeus's shack.

The boy looked alarmed. 'Thaddeus lives on the edge of town, close to where the storm now howls!'

'Nevertheless,' said Leot softly, 'I need you to take these folk to him. You'd not be thinking the witch can't look after you, perhaps?'

Jelindel winced at the word 'witch'.

Sarat misconstrued the wince and said, 'I'll go.' He looked nervous all the same.

Daretor said that he would stay at the inn and ready himself for any conventional battle that might threaten. In truth, he felt it was better to have a presence than to leave the townspeople to start blaming their woes on the foreigners. Sensing Daretor's purpose, Osric volunteered to remain as well.

Jelindel and Zimak followed Sarat. The crowd parted reluctantly, some of the people touching Jelindel as she passed, as though doubting her reality.

Sarat led them past the livestock palisades, towards the edge of town on the east side. The streets were for the most part cobbled and lit by oil lamps, but the storm affected the lighting so that it was gloomier than it ought to have been. Meltwater had turned the ground to slush. There was no escaping the cold. Nor did they try – their clothing and footwear were sodden, anyway.

'What can you tell me about Thaddeus Pike?' Jelindel asked Sarat.

The youth shrugged. 'He's old,' he said, as if that was all one needed to know. When he saw that Jelindel expected more he thought carefully. 'I don't know,' he said. 'My mother reckons he was once a powerful warlock or something. That was back in my grandfather's time. Anyway, it's just stories Thaddeus tells the idle children who listen to such tales. He's just a crazy old man. And we're not allowed to speak of him in case he turns us into toads or something worse.'

Jelindel groaned inwardly. Such ignorance gave her occupation a bad name.

They came out of a narrow lane and headed towards a small hut standing some distance from its nearest neighbours. The storm raged only a few yards away. Zimak gazed at it nervously. He reached out to touch it, for the coruscating bubble looked like water defying gravity. When his finger touched the bluish light, it sent out ripples as would a stone thrown into a still pond.

'I wouldn't if I were you,' was all Jelindel said.

'It looks as though it might cave in at any moment,' Zimak said.

The winds were more powerful now and the snow was piling up at the boundary line, as if whatever guided the storm sought to bury the town beneath a great weight of snow and ice. Sarat might have bolted had Jelindel not foreseen his reaction to Zimak's comment and held on to him.

Sarat knocked on the door. 'Go away, Sarat,' an ancient voice croaked.

The youth looked startled but did not leave, though he clearly wanted to. He pushed open the door and yelled, 'Visitors here to see you.'

Jelindel relaxed her grip on his arm. The moment she did so, Sarat took to his heels without a backward glance.

Jelindel and Zimak stepped inside and shut the door behind them. 'I'm not reading the cards today,' said the voice. A small fire flickered in a grate. By its light they could make out a bent and huddled figure sitting in a chair by a rickety table. The wrinkles on Thaddeus's face were like fissures of an ancient mountain. His fingers resembled claws, and his sea-green eyes shone bright and inquisitive.

'You're not here for the cards, are you?' he said as they came closer.

'My name is Jelindel dek Mediesar and this is Zimak. We are from D'loom in Skelt, in the far lands that border the Tanglesea Ocean.'

'A long way from home, you are,' said Thaddeus, peering. 'What would you ask of Thaddeus?'

'May I?' Jelindel asked, gesturing to a chair. The old man nodded. Jelindel sat down while Zimak stayed by the fire. 'I am a mage. I trained in the Great Temple of Verity in Arcadia.'

Thaddeus's eyes flickered. 'Under Lindkeer?'

Jelindel sat back, surprised. 'Why yes, she was Head Priestess at that time, though she passed away before I ended my training. Kelricka succeeded her.'

Thaddeus sighed. 'So my empathies have not dulled after all. It is as I thought. I felt her passing some time ago, but doubted myself. She was a Great One, you know. I trained with her in the Passendof Mountains long before she joined the Great Temple of Verity. I was young then, younger than you are now.'

Jelindel felt humbled. She was sitting opposite one of Lindkeer's peers. Surely he must be the last of that great line.

Zimak said, 'We're seeking information about –'

Thaddeus silenced him with a wave of his hand, his eyes not leaving Jelindel. Somehow he managed to quell the anger that rose in Jelindel at Zimak's crass interruption.

'Make a pot of tea,' Thaddeus said. Jelindel suppressed a smile. It was the Temple's old pecking order. The younger women were always put in their place by being asked to make pots of tea. Jelindel did not mind; indeed, she felt it was the old man's due.

She poured water into a blackened pot and hung it from a bracket so that it dangled low in the fire, close to the glowing coals. She then fetched herbal tea, honey and cups from a shelf above the table and started to carefully measure out the correct amount of tea.

'No, no, you're doing it all wrong,' said Thaddeus. 'Warm the cups first. Careful you don't bruise the tea. And you must turn the pot clockwise.'

'Didn't they teach you anything at the Temple?' Zimak joked. The laugh died in his throat when Thaddeus glanced at him.

Jelindel hardly noticed Zimak, and she did as instructed. Memories, unbidden, flashed upon her. She remembered making tea for Kelricka, her friend; she remembered long night-time vigils with the other acolytes, during which they talked about the world outside the wall of the Temple, of men and magic, and their futures.

Having warmed the cups and placed tea in the pot, she ladled several spoons of honey into each small cup. Herbal tea in the Temple of Verity was taken without milk. It was more like a hot liqueur, so sweet was it made.

When the water boiled, Jelindel poured the tea, handing the first cup to Thaddeus, and the second to Zimak. Thaddeus did not scold her again. He seemed satisfied with the brew.

They drank in silence, savouring the tea. Then Thaddeus spoke. 'Tea made by another's hand is always nicer than one's own. Why is that?' he wondered. 'What is it that you think you seek, Jelindel dek Mediesar?'

Jelindel put down her cup. The old man's question suggested that he knew what she was seeking, and that she did not. 'The Stone People,' she said uncertainly.

Thaddeus gazed at her. 'They are a solitary race that relish isolation. Why do you seek them?'

Jelindel wondered how much to tell the mage. She decided that any attempt to hold back the truth would be foolish. Besides, in all probability Thaddeus already knew the answer.

Jelindel explained their quest in more detail than she had given Leot and the other townsfolk.

When she finished, Thaddeus sat back and regarded her appraisingly. 'So the Dragons of Q'zar have returned, and you have come to the heart of Dragon's Breath to seek the heart of the dragon.'

Jelindel drew a lengthy breath. She had not thought of it like that, but now that it was laid out before her, she saw the true significance of their quest. Was it possible that she and the others were fulfilling an ancient prophecy? Had they been brought together to restore the dragonsight to the Sacred One, thereby bringing the dragons back to Q'zar?

She started to ask a question, but Thaddeus held up a hand. 'There are no coincidences,' he said, 'and the naming of things and places, and people too, is no accident.'

'Then this was foretold?'

'To those who can read the ancient riddles, which they called "foretelling", yes.'

'Well, what's supposed to happen?' asked Zimak.

Thaddeus lifted his eyes and gazed at him as he might a recalcitrant child. 'Impatient, aren't we?' he said. 'If you were supposed to know what happens before it happens, then you would know already, would you not?'

Zimak was about to reply but a sharp glance from Jelindel cautioned him.

Thaddeus tilted his head as though listening for something. 'You must go shortly,' he said.

'Why?'

'Things come.'

Jelindel finished her tea. There was much of Lady Forturian in Thaddeus. If the old man said leave, then he had good reason. Still, she needed to ask questions. 'What things? Where?'

The old man clucked his tongue as though Jelindel were dim-witted. 'Out of the storm, girl. Dreadful things. The others will need you.'

Jelindel placed the china cup on its saucer and sat back. 'Can you help us?'

Thaddeus pursed his thin lips in thought. 'My time is nigh,' he said simply.

'And the Stone People?'

'The legend of a story of a myth, so old it makes mountains seem young.'

'They do exist,' Jelindel hedged. 'We were told they are in the Hazgar Mountains.'

'You are mistaken,' Thaddeus said. 'But if you had not come here then you would never have found them.'

'That does not follow the rules of logic,' said Jelindel.

Zimak grew impatient with the old man's riddles. He must have made a derisory sound because Thaddeus remarked over his shoulder, 'Curb your fretting, tadpole, or the frog of your future will fail to croak.'

Zimak stared at him, confused.

Thaddeus gave Jelindel a toothless smile. 'The Stone People dwell far underground in some hold nigh inaccessible to mortal man. Beneath mountains they live, that is known. That they live beneath a city built by men is not.'

Where better to hide from inquisitive men than right beneath their very noses. 'Which city, Thaddeus?' Jelindel asked.

'I do not know. In the language spoken by men before they came to Q'zar, the city was called Hadirr.'

'I don't understand,' Jelindel said. 'Before men came to Q'zar? Weren't men always here?'

'No, only the dragons and the Stone People. Some say a rift occurred between paraworlds and men poured through into Q'zar. Others say a great battle took place between wizards and a portal opened. Indeed, some believe the Dragon's Breath is where the portal first touched down and anchored itself.'

'Then Hadirr is a word in the language of another paraworld?'

'So I would fathom. Now you must go. You are needed. I shall be along when I am prepared.'

Outside, Zimak hugged himself against the cold and scowled. 'A complete charlatan,' he said. 'He wouldn't last five seconds in the Charm Vendors' Guild.'

'Zimak, if you can't make considered judgements, don't make them at all.'

'I've met considerable charm vendors,' Zimak said. 'Got to know some of them quite well, in fact. There was one in the D'loom marketplace that –'

Jelindel stopped. Zimak ran into her outstretched hand. 'I am not remotely interested in your conquests,' she said coldly. 'If you directed as much focus to the problem at hand as you do on your sordid past, then we would fare much better.'

Zimak brushed her hand from his chest. 'All right. Since you believe everything you hear, Hadirr seems to be in another paraworld. How many paraworlds are there?'

'How many grains of sand are there?'

Zimak slapped his forehead. 'Gah. The only thing between us and slow death by poison is the little matter of a billion billion paraworlds.'

They continued walking. 'You're so negative,' said Jelindel.

Zimak came to a complete stop. Jelindel kept going. He stared after her. Him? Negative? That was *so* unfair. He hurried to catch up. 'Someone around here has to make sense of all the scud that goes on . . . '

Leot and his militia were at the inn as Jelindel arrived. She was followed by Zimak, who was still arguing his case. She pushed her way to the front.

'Creatures will be coming out of the snow,' she said.

'Surprise, surprise,' Zimak said dolefully.

'What manner of creatures?' Uthven asked, ignoring Zimak. His mood had changed, Jelindel noted. No longer affable, his face was ruddy and shone with perspiration. A quick sign from Daretor indicated there had been some argument.

'Who can say? Bring axe and steel and pike. Light fires at all points about the town's edge. Gather the archers, and find pitch for the arrows. Have you stocks of the dark oil that burns?'

'We do. We distil it into spirits for the lamps.'

'Dig a trench on the north-west side of town and fill it with the oil. The brunt of the attack will come from that direction,' Jelindel said. When no one made a move she snapped, 'To attack us from any other front would be madness – they'd have no cover. Get moving if you still want your town to be standing in the morning.'

Leot and Uthven shouted orders. Men and women scurried to carry out Jelindel's commands.

Left alone in the inn, Daretor and Osric related how several of the locals blamed their current plight on Jelindel's arrival. Some had even suggested running her out of town, or handing her over to whoever had released the storm.

Daretor said that the situation hung on Leot's word. Uthven sided with Leot, so long as Daretor could prove that Jelindel could best Fa'red. At that point, Osric had stepped forward to confirm that the archmage was a traveller between paraworlds, and that he himself came from one such paraworld.

That had set everyone arguing and exclaiming. Uthven had challenged Osric to prove his story. Without hesitating, Osric unsheathed his keen blade and slit his palm. From it oozed a yellow substance the consistency of blood. He had then held up his hand for everyone to see.

'A charm vendor's trick,' someone scoffed, but he was hushed quickly enough.

'You could say all this is getting out of hand,' Zimak quipped, and everyone groaned.

Some time later, a commotion started outside. Sarat burst in, breathless. His face was deathly white. 'Things . . . ' he said, his voice a croak. '*Things . . .* '

Jelindel and Daretor rushed outside, followed by a reluctant Zimak. They followed Sarat to the outskirts of town where the youth pointed into the storm.

Huge shapes were standing still as stone, shadows inside the swirling chaos of the storm. 'Snow trolls,' Jelindel said tonelessly.

As if the naming of them brought them to life the monsters surged forward. Smaller, swifter shapes moved at their sides.

'Wolves,' said Daretor. 'Will your barrier stay them?'

Jelindel chewed a nail, uncharacteristically indecisive. 'I fear not, else Fa'red wouldn't have bothered sending them.'

True enough, the first wolf leapt through Jelindel's shield. Daretor met the beast on its second bound. His sword flashed and the predator tumbled to the ground. It was a wolf as might be painted by an artist who had never seen a wolf, and had only read about them. It was long and lean in the body, but misshapen, with hind legs like those of a hare, and claws resembling five-inch scimitars.

More deformed wolves sprang out of the storm. Daretor and Zimak's swords cut and slashed, never stopping. Many other fighters also gave a good account of themselves. Jelindel bound several wolves with magic, making them easy targets for the younger and less experienced fighters, but she found that her magic was to some degree repelled, as if the creatures were protected by powerful charms.

She did not have long to ponder this as the snow trolls lurched against the shield. It warped as they struggled through it. Pockets of the shield fractured, and sheets of snow spat through the fissures. Seemingly by brute strength, the trolls pushed their way through the bubble.

They were fully sixteen feet tall and seemed to be made of ice, as if someone had hewn slabs of it from some glacier and stacked them atop one another until a troll was fashioned.

Daretor met the first. His blade bit deep and silvery blood spurted from severed arteries. The troll howled and stumbled to its knees. Daretor pulled his sword from the creature's chest, and slashed its throat, opening a gap. More silvery blood splattered across the troll's chest. It pitched forward like a felled tree.

Daretor had no respite. More snow trolls appeared, and still more wolves. For all their provincialism, the Ogven militia were acquitting themselves well. The archers wrought havoc among the wolves; their flaming shafts hissing through the air and into the flanks of the beasts, burning those they failed to kill outright.

Jelindel, realising she had extended herself to her magical limits, waded in with her sword, slashing at wolves and trolls. All around her the townspeople were dropping. There seemed no end to the attackers.

A wounded wolf struggled to its feet and lunged at her. She dodged, stumbled. Then Zimak charged the wolf. It changed direction to meet the new adversary, but it was too late. Zimak's speed took him into the wolf. Beast and human tumbled to the ground, and Zimak's knife left the wolf twitching in the slush. Zimak rolled from the animal's back, noting the approach of still more through the bubble.

'The trench,' Zimak panted. 'Light the trench.'

In the mayhem Jelindel had forgotten about the trench. The command passed from mouth to mouth. Then, in opposite directions, torches flared, rose high for a moment as if in salute, then dipped low to the ground. Instantly, two great blazes bloomed and raced towards each other. When they met, a snow troll happened to be stepping across the trench. The conjoined flames erupted into a fireball, engulfing it. The burning creature stumbled against other trolls, embracing one in a desperate grip, and igniting it.

More flaming arrows arced high in the air, raining down on wolf and troll alike, scattering them. Daretor led by example. With Osric at his side, he rallied the townspeople to harass the retreating trolls. They pushed the trolls back to the shimmering wall. At that point the townspeople fell back, as though to touch something magical might be their ruin. No wolves had survived.

Daretor sheathed his sword and returned with Osric. 'They'll be back,' he said. 'Make no mistake on that count.'

'You have bizarre creatures indeed on Q'zar,' Osric said.

'Says he who rides dragons,' said Zimak. He was busy kicking sand into the trenches in an effort to quench the fire before refilling them with oil.

While Daretor and Osric joined Zimak, Jelindel consulted Leot and Uthven. 'How many did we lose?' she asked.

'Fifteen good people, killed or wounded,' Leot said.

'I'm sorry,' Jelindel said.

'And well might you be,' said Uthven. 'If you are a powerful sorceress, how is it that those creatures breached your defences?'

Jelindel knew their frustration for her own. There were just too many things she didn't understand.

'Well?' demanded Uthven, watching the bodies of his friends being carted away.

'Picture a full well,' Jelindel said. 'Take a hundred barrels of water from it and the water level goes down. It doesn't go back up until it is replenished. And so it is with magic.' She looked at the bubble. 'To maintain the shield is draining for me. Were I to let it dissolve I would have my full powers restored.'

'But the creatures broke through your barrier,' Uthven snapped. 'What good is it?'

Uthven was towering over Jelindel. Daretor and Zimak were heading their way, and several of the townspeople had stopped to listen.

'Perhaps you should let the girl speak,' Leot suggested.

Jelindel took a deep breath. 'Uthven, I am truly sorry that you have lost friends today, but understand this: were it not for the shield, your entire town would have fallen by now. Your militia would have been fragmented, disorganised and separated by the storm. The trolls and their wolves would have simply gone from building to building, killing everyone.'

'It makes sense,' Leot said.

Uthven spat on the ground. 'None of this makes any sense,' he said, leaving.

Leot sat while someone dabbed at a cut on his forehead. 'I apologise for Uthven,' he said to Jelindel. 'Ogven's never lost so many militiamen in one day. Why, even when the Preceptor swept the continent he left our town in peace.'

Jelindel watched the wolves being hitched to horses and dragged across the ground. 'Your people gave a good account of themselves,' she said.

Leot nodded gravely. 'Eight trolls, and I doubt that any of the wolves escaped. They'll not forget that, to be sure.'

'But they'll be back,' Daretor said. 'Jelindel, what do you say?'

She nodded. 'If Fa'red is controlling them, they will have little option. Distance alone favours us, for his magic will be stretched. Only if he travels here will his control strengthen. The trolls' sense of self preservation sent them running, but we can't count on that when they return.'

'We'll at least be better prepared for them,' Leot said.

He had already ordered his men to mount a palisade around the perimeter. Jelindel had not the heart to tell him that the pointed staves would be useless against the forces that Fa'red could rally. Next time it could be something worse than wolves or trolls.

During the respite they quickly ate and warmed themselves with mead. Hardly had they finished when frantic shouting warned of the next attack. This time it was only the trolls, and the town militia triumphed for the loss of only two men.

The townsfolk rejoiced as the last troll limped away through the barrier, but Jelindel motioned for quiet. She sensed that the most dangerous attack of all was imminent.

'Everybody get back!' she shouted. 'What comes now comes for me.'

The others fell back a little way. They all had a profound respect for the girl who could fight with steel as well as magic, and were reluctant to let her stand alone.

Daretor, Zimak and Osric joined her. 'What do you see out there?' Daretor asked.

Jelindel bit her lip. 'I'm not sure.'

From behind came a noise, the sound of jeering, even laughter. Jelindel turned to see Thaddeus Pike hobbling with the help of a walking stick, his back bent, his feet shuffling.

'Get back to your hut, Thaddeus,' called one of the men, while others continued to jeer.

Thaddeus made his way to Jelindel's side. To the three men he said, 'Join the others.' They did not move until Jelindel waved them away. Reluctantly, they went to stand with Leot and Uthven.

Leot was puzzled. 'What does the old fool want?'

Daretor shook his head. 'I've learnt not to question the ways of magic. But know this, if the old one and Jelindel fail, take your people and flee, have them scatter in all directions. What comes through that storm will not take kindly to being called here.'

'There are few trolls left,' Uthven said, clenching his sword handle so tightly that his knuckles whitened.

Daretor and Zimak exchanged looks, but they had no time for further talk. A dark shadow oozed out of the snow-covered earth and shaped itself into a slab of darkness that covered the ground as far as the eye could see. At the same time the storm abated somewhat, and visibility improved.

'He wants us to see our doom all the more clearly,' said Jelindel.

'No, it's that he cannot sustain both the storm and this adversary,' said Thaddeus.

Rank upon rank of otherworldly creatures stretched away endlessly. Each one had two pairs of arms, wielding a sword or axe or pike. The bodies were covered in thick scales – a natural body armour – and the heads were snapping, slathering jaws that could swivel and attack in any direction: front, side, behind. They were mesmerisingly menacing.

The thing that chilled Jelindel's heart was not so much their bestial appearance, but their discipline and precision. These were no dumb beasts sent to the slaughter. They were highly trained soldiers.

Her heart faltered. 'By all the gods,' she breathed, 'what on Q'zar could have created such things?'

Beside her, Thaddeus snorted. 'A riddle too easy to solve,' he said. 'Nothing on Q'zar created them. These were hatched on another paraworld.'

Jelindel stared at the uniform ranks. They started chanting a guttural mantra that filled the air. 'There are too many,' she said. 'And I'm nearly spent.'

'Then don't spend so much next time,' said Thaddeus.

Jelindel shook her head. 'More would have died if I had not,' she said, then promptly dissolved the bubble covering the town. It seemed the sky fell in on them, for a sheet of ice collapsed with the bubble. It was followed by a light drizzle – all that remained of the storm's fury.

Jelindel straightened as power surged back to her.

'What of their deaths?' Thaddeus asked. 'You think dying is some kind of an end? Would you stop a caterpillar from becoming a butterfly just because the caterpillar thinks it is about to die?'

Jelindel said nothing.

'We all die and we all become butterflies. There. Are you happy now?' The mage's eyes sparkled with mirth.

Jelindel looked at him with wonder in her eyes. 'You speak of this like it is fact.'

'Of course it is fact. Mind you, not all creatures become butterflies. Some become maggots, like those abominations out there. They are, if I am not very much mistaken, about to charge.' He then wove a spell about Jelindel with his hands.

Jelindel shivered as something coursed her veins. 'What did you do just then?'

Thaddeus sagged a little, as though the spell had drained him. 'A simple thing,' he said. 'For later, perhaps. A charm against pimples.'

Jelindel did not bother to unravel his jest. She looked back at the ranks of their enemy. 'There are too many,' she said again.

'Quality is far more important than quantity, child.'

Jelindel's heart thumped out of rhythm. She remembered Lindkeer at the Temple in Arcadia saying precisely the same thing in precisely the same reproving tone.

The abominations charged. The creatures' chanting rose to a

crescendo, filling the heads of everyone; it grew into a kind of subsonic screech that made strong men clench their eyes in pain and forced others to their knees.

Jelindel felt the assault on her mind, but her training provided some protection from it. Thaddeus did not appear to be affected at all. He seemed tranquil, as if seated in his kitchen.

Jelindel started mustering a magical counter-assault. She built her spells and charms quickly, layering them one upon the other, connecting them in intuitively brilliant ways, fashioning a deadly instrument with which to repel the attack, knowing all along that it was pitifully inadequate.

Thaddeus laid a hand on her arm. 'Hush,' he said. The spell that was in Jelindel's mind fell away. Instead, she heard a soft lilting voice she knew to be Thaddeus's when he had been a young man. 'Open yourself to me, child,' he said. 'Flow through me . . . let it grow.'

Jelindel opened herself to Thaddeus, her heart, her mind, her soul, her memories. She felt a raw power flow down her arm and into Thaddeus where his old withered hand gripped her. Then she was falling, not painfully, but slipping to the ground, as though there was no energy left to hold her up.

Thaddeus released Jelindel and she felt a heady feeling, as if waking from a dream. Behind her she heard an odd groan from the ranks of the defenders. She looked around. The enemy was sweeping in with awesome speed, a tidal wave of death and horror. Jelindel heard, rather than saw, the townspeople break ranks and flee. Someone, Leot perhaps, was ordering them to hold firm. Daretor had just screamed her name.

In the melee, Thaddeus flung aside his staff and walked out to meet the charge. He held out his arms in a welcoming gesture, as if inviting the monsters to come to him.

Jelindel noted that Thaddeus's flesh was glowing, or else it was becoming translucent and a light from inside – or from some other place – was shining out.

The first of the creatures slammed into him but there was no impact. Snow storm, clouds, creatures . . . it seemed as though Thaddeus had become a portal and sucked in all evidence of Fa'red's invasion.

And, as with many portals, it snapped shut, taking its creator with it.

Chapter 5
THE DRAGONS COME

Of the Ogvenians, Leot alone stood his ground. He walked unsteadily to Jelindel. Daretor and Zimak had just helped her to her feet.

'What in White Quell's name just happened?' Leot asked, shaken.

Jelindel took a deep breath as her body reacted to a surge of power. When she had the strength to answer, she said, 'I believe Thaddeus has rid your people of some ancient curse. You will have sudden prosperity . . . I sense a cleansing of the air.'

Leot's eyes hadn't left the spot where Thaddeus had embraced the charging creatures. All that remained was a charred circle the circumference of the old man's outstretched hands.

Jelindel went to the fused, glassy sand and broke off a fragment. She nodded. 'If I were you, I would collect this glassy material before the wind buries it. Secure it in an urn and place it in a cairn at this spot. Dedicate it to Thaddeus Pike, Archmage,' she said to Leot. She looked towards the basin that was once the

Dragon's Breath. To her enhanced senses the once blighted land seemed to be changing before her very eyes. 'It is as he foretold,' she added, almost to herself.

'I'll see to it immediately,' Leot said, sensing the urgency in Jelindel's words.

When Leot had left to find a stonemason, Daretor said, 'What exactly *did* happen, Jelindel? *What* did Thaddeus foretell?'

Jelindel gestured helplessly. 'It will take too long to explain.'

'Try,' Zimak said. 'There's something not quite right about this place. And if I know Fa'red, he's going to jump on it from a great height.'

'Not if we leave he won't,' Jelindel said wearily. 'Take away the fuel and there is no fire. As for what happened here today, Thaddeus foretold of a "cleansing", which involved our arrival. He's been holding on to life, waiting patiently for us. To save this place, he needed to sustain his life force, and in doing so, he drained vital energy from the earth. Hence its barrenness of recent years. Had he not been alive to assist me, this town would have been destroyed. And us along with it.'

'What a lot of codswallop,' Zimak said. He almost said 'prove it', which might have been fatal, for those words were like flinging down a gauntlet to Jelindel.

'*Exactly* why I didn't want to explain everything,' Jelindel said. Before Daretor could say anything, she said, 'We need to find the Stone People. Luckily, Thaddeus has shown the way.'

'So now you're saying we have to travel to some other paraworld?' Zimak glared at Jelindel, obviously displeased. 'Because I have to tell you that my experiences with paraworlds have not been positive. I just want you to know that.'

'Then don't come,' Jelindel snapped.

Daretor put a placating hand on Jelindel's arm. 'Normally I

would be the last person to agree with Zimak, but this time I am inclined to take his side.' Noticing Zimak's wide grin, he added, 'Just this once.'

'There you are,' Zimak said, as though Daretor's backing settled the argument.

Daretor ignored him. 'On the other hand, should you explain your motives much better than you have, I might change my mind.'

Jelindel took a deep breath. 'Going to other paraworlds is a last resort. The process of discovering which one we need to visit would probably give us the information we need anyway.'

'And what information might that be?' said Zimak.

'The name of the city that was Hadirr,' responded Jelindel.

'Could there be a correspondence between the old name and the new?' Daretor asked.

'Of course there could,' Jelindel said. 'But the name could also have been changed by later conquerors, or it may just have evolved, or it may be the same name in a different language. For instance, D'loom means "Gem of the Sea". Two thousand years ago it was called *Liallon*, which means the same thing in the language of the Musea'a.'

'This is all fascinating but let's just *do* something,' Zimak said. 'We're being poisoned, remember?'

Jelindel narrowed her eyes. 'Very well, pack up.'

Zimak smiled. 'Great.'

Jelindel looked at Osric. 'I hope S'cressling hasn't forgotten us.'

'Now that the weather has cleared, she will come,' he said confidently. 'S'cressling will always seek me out.'

'Reminds me of a certain witch,' Zimak mumbled.

They bid goodbye to Leot and the other townsfolk who came

out to see them off. Jelindel found it hard to look Leot in the eyes. She blamed herself for what had happened.

Leot understood. 'Do not feel badly,' he said. 'It may be true that these things would not have occurred had you not come but we have learned much. There is a sense of unity and achievement in Ogven not felt in my lifetime.

'More, such fantastic events may well draw the curious who no doubt will stop here a time and spend their money. We also discovered that one of our own, who we had long slighted, was a great mage. I wish I had known that before. Many times I sat at Thaddeus's feet as a child and listened to his wondrous tales.' He sighed, and for a moment seemed lost in memory.

'But there is something else we got out of this,' he went on, lifting his head proudly. He turned and pointed to the north-west from where the attacks had come. 'Whatever has happened, whether because of Thaddeus's magic, or the great quantity of snow, I do not know, all the wasteland to the south of here is now alive. Green buds and grass are sprouting, growing at an incredible rate. Underground springs have bubbled to the surface and streams are finding their way through the Dragon's Breath. It is truly a miracle and will bring growth and prosperity, perhaps forever.'

'We thank you for your understanding, and your kind words,' Jelindel said, shaking the man's hand. Then she and the others hoisted their packs to their shoulders. Osric put his fingers to his lips and blew a whistle that none could hear.

Moments later a dark speck appeared in the sky, rising up from the foothills of the Hazgar Mountains. As they watched, it grew larger. Leot shaded his eyes and squinted against the sun.

'What manner of thing is this?' he asked, puzzled. Many other townsfolk also shaded their eyes and watched the speck grow.

When it could be seen clearly the Ogvenians moaned in trepidation and in wonderment. A dragon in the Dragon's Breath.

Leot stared at Jelindel. 'Is this possible?' he asked. 'A creature out of the fairy tales told to children now comes?'

'The dragons have come back to Q'zar,' Jelindel said, smiling apologetically. 'I kind of left that part out before. It would have taken too much explaining.'

S'cressling swooped overhead, huge and majestic. Leot swallowed. 'You left out rather a large part, I am thinking,' he said, awed.

S'cressling landed with a great whoosh. Jelindel and the others climbed aboard.

'Tend Thaddeus's cairn as you would your mother's,' Jelindel called to Leot.

Leot waved acknowledgement. Flowers had already been placed where the archmage had vanished. Even the disbelievers felt some kind of power emanating from the spot. Jelindel hoped that the marking spell at the cairn site made its presence felt long enough to instil some respect in the locals.

Soon they were heading south-west at a swift pace. Jelindel had decided they should head back to D'loom. She needed to scour the oldest libraries in Q'zar and to talk to other archmages. Along the way they would call in at Yuledan and look up Theroc, whose money they had taken in good faith.

Zimak laughed. 'Wait till he sees us flapping in on the back of one of his aerial predators.'

Osric bristled. 'S'cressling is not a predator.'

'Try telling that to the people taken by Rakeem's dragons.'

Osric stroked S'cressling's red mane. 'Then it is Rakeem who is the predator. For the Tower Inviolate dragons are under his control.'

Daretor squeezed Osric's shoulder. 'We shall see about that when we have found the dragonsight.'

Osric slumped back into his seat. How could these Q'zarans not realise that their lives were forfeit when they completed their task? he wondered. Or did they not care?

They flew west for the next two days, veering south when they crossed the Serpentire River. Stopping occasionally to rest S'cressling and replenish their water bladders, they otherwise flew on relentlessly. Leot had given them ample supplies of food. Their only enemy was the cold that never ceases to claw at those who fly.

On the morning of the fourth day they sighted the Garrical Mountains far to the south-west. Osric asked S'cressling to stay low and get as close to Yuledan as possible without being seen. They did not want to alarm the already terrified townspeople, yet they did not want to land some distance away and face yet another long and probably dangerous walk.

'How do you know Fa'red won't try something here?' Osric asked Jelindel.

'Why should he?' she asked. 'I doubt very much that he thinks we can learn anything in Yuledan. We already know the nature of the aerial attackers that have been preying on the town.'

Osric was either inexperienced at low-flying manoeuvres or he had been distracted by thoughts of Fa'red. In any event, he overshot the landing spot and they were, all of a sudden, directly above the town. Frightened men and women looked up and ran for cover, gathering children as they went. Alarm bells began to toll.

'Land over there,' Jelindel told Osric. 'If we delay they'll start firing arrows at us or worse. Let's get down quickly so they can see that we're friendly.'

'Somehow I think they won't ever see a dragon as friendly,' Zimak said.

Osric guided S'cressling to the large open area Jelindel had indicated. It was the town green, a place where children played, lovers strolled, and where fairs were held in summer. It ought have been a picturesque spot but it had a blighted look. Some of the trees were burnt and there were scorch marks on the ground.

'The marks of dragons,' said Osric, looking about in alarm.

S'cressling settled onto a low mound near the centre of the green but did not relax. Her nostrils flared when she sensed the fear in the town. She could smell the presence – faint now and several days old – of other dragons. Dark mucus dribbled from her snout and she moved her head restlessly from side to side, watching.

She did not have long to wait.

A group of archers appeared at the north end of the green and ran quickly to pre-arranged positions. Jelindel stood on the prow and waved a white cloth for all to see. Holding this aloft, she and Daretor climbed down and advanced towards the archers who fingered their arrows nervously and never took their eyes off the pair, as though they were daemons.

'Come no closer,' shouted a mountain of a man, with a yellow beard and no hair on his crown. 'Go back where you came from. You are not welcome.'

'Not welcome?' Jelindel called back with deceptive composure. 'We were invited.'

The man's eyes were stony. 'None here did so.'

'You are mistaken. I am Archmage Jelindel dek Mediesar. Theroc engaged our services.'

A grizzled scarecrow of a man pushed forward. He shaded his eyes and peered at them. He exclaimed, coming forward with a smile on his face.

'Archmage,' he said, eyeing the dragon nervously. 'You came.'

'These are taxing times, Theroc. I apologise for our tardiness. It is often said: better late than never. I hope this is one of those times.'

'I beg forgiveness for our reception but the manner of your coming . . .' He looked again at S'cressling who stared back at him. 'The manner of your coming is . . . er . . . somewhat unexpected.'

'You have seen then the nature of the beasts that assail you?' asked Daretor.

Theroc nodded. 'We have.'

'They are dragons?'

Theroc nodded again, still eyeing S'cressling. 'They are dragons indeed. Like this one here.'

'Do not fear our friend,' Jelindel said. 'Call your people. Let us talk. There is much to explain.'

Two hours later they met in the Town Hall. The meeting got off to a bad start when a thin man with one eye and a flash burn across his left cheek accused them of being in league with the dragonriders.

'I lost my wife in the last raid,' he growled. 'Why should we deal with you? How do we know you're not here to study our defences and spy out our weaknesses?' There were angry agreements, and much muttering and argument followed. Theroc did his best to calm everyone down, but they were in no mood to listen. After an hour Jelindel lost her patience.

She uttered a binding spell that shot out in all directions and bound the mouths of every man and woman there. Speechless, they clutched and clawed at their mouths, staring at her in fear.

Jelindel stood at the front of the hall and addressed them. 'As you can see,' she said, 'if I wished to harm you I could do so without the help of dragons. Since you prefer shouting to listening, you must stay mute until I have had my say. After that, you can decide as you wish.' She gave an account of the return of the dragons to Q'zar, the evil King Amida and his vizier, Rakeem, and the fact that the dragons were enslaved by the very object she and her companions sought.

Finally, Jelindel asked Daretor for the purse of gold oriels that Theroc had given them. 'I hereby return the better part of your fee,' she announced. 'That which I have taken, was spent in a good cause. I need no gold to persuade me to stop Amida and Rakeem and so free all lands from the predations of the dragon-riders. I offer to teach your mages such spells as may be useful here. The weakness of the dragons is their riders, and it is they who must be bound or blinded.'

She withdrew the binding spell and a soft gasp swept through the room. Oddly enough, now that they could talk again, the people seemed loath to do so. Daretor leaned close to Jelindel's ear and whispered, 'I shall remember that one for when we have a clutch of noisy children.'

Jelindel gave him a sidelong glance. 'No child of mine will ever behave like this lot.'

'So say all women before bearing children,' Daretor replied, shaking his head.

Theroc stood, averting his eyes apprehensively, as if he expected to be struck down at any moment. 'Archmage, let me apologise again for the reception you were given. Our excuse is that we have lived under great fear for so long that we can no longer tell friend from foe.'

Jelindel told him it was she who must apologise, and related how they had been waylaid. 'Not only have we arrived late, but on, of all things, a dragon.' Her tone suggested that it was a joke, and nervous laughter rippled around the hall.

All that day and the next, Jelindel worked with Yuledan's mages, teaching them intricate, powerful spells to use against the dragonriders. Daretor and Zimak helped reorganise the conventional defences of the town. In all these things Osric was the chief consultant. Only he truly knew the ways of the dragons and their riders; only he fully understood the dragons' aerial manoeuvring capabilities, the reach and power of their fire, and even some ways to turn aside the fire without harming the dragons. It soon became apparent, however, that Yuledan's citizens really did not care if the enslaved dragons were hurt or not. Too many of their number had been eaten for any sort of sympathy to be possible.

During this time the swaggering Zimak wooed many young maidens, who were delighted to meet a man who flew on the back of a dragon. The way he told it, dragonriding was much more dangerous and exciting than it actually was; and that only entranced the girls all the more.

As Jelindel worked with the local mages, she questioned them about the origins of human language on Q'zar, asking if they knew of a city that was once called Hadirr. As she feared, they knew less than she did. She told the others that they must reach D'loom as soon as possible for her to research the libraries. If that proved fruitless, then she would seek other sources, such as Lady Forturian, and the Library of Hazaria. The problem was that time was a commodity they could ill afford.

Their last night in Yuledan was as bitterly cold as any desert night can be. A sharp chill wind swept the sand like a giant broom. There were no clouds, just the stars, highlights on a sky of black crystal. Jelindel and Daretor were on the roof of Theroc's house. They had eaten and had brought a bottle of honeymead wine with them. They were still flushed from food and fire, and did not feel the cold at first.

Jelindel stood for a long time looking up at the stars. Spec-moon was in the sky, yellow and pockmarked with grey craters. Daretor came up behind and put his arms around her, kissing her neck.

'Hmn,' she said. 'You have an hour to stop doing that.'

'I'll take as long as I need,' Daretor whispered, nibbling her neck. 'Or have you forgotten how to enjoy yourself?'

She giggled. 'We haven't had much time to ourselves, have we? We seem to stumble from one calamity to the next.'

'Or are pushed.'

'Yes. I have been thinking that,' Jelindel mused, almost to herself. 'So far, Fa'red has called the tunes.'

'And we dance to them.'

'Well, then, we must make our own music.'

'I know what you told Zimak,' Daretor said, 'but I feel that you intend to search out other paraworlds if necessary.'

Jelindel sighed, resting her head on his shoulder. 'If it comes to that,' she said, 'then we have little choice. It will not be other paraworlds, Daretor, just one, if we can find it. And even then there's no guarantee that the first language of Q'zar is still spoken there, or remembered.'

Overhead, something blotted out the stars. Instantly, from the other side of town, a bell rang out. Another joined in, then another.

❖

141

A shepherd shivered in his sleep. Only half waking, he dragged more furs across his body. Nearby, in a hollow, dozens of sheep stood or sat in a tight clump, eternally wary of the night, as if ancient memories plagued their waking sleep.

Tonight the memories were justified.

A terrified bleating woke the shepherd. He jumped to his feet, wiping sleep from his eyes. Stumbling to the hollow, he held his staff before him like a weapon. Then he instinctively ducked as a dozen dark shapes flew low overhead.

He looked up and froze. The shapes were enormous bat-shaped creatures whose vast wings clutched the air and hurled it at the ground, where it shook the trees and raised the dust of the arid earth. In moments the shepherd was engulfed in swirling dust. He could see nothing, which was bad, but he could still hear, and that was worse.

Above the rush and tumble of the wind, the creaking acacia trees, and the bleating of the sheep, he heard the roar of night creatures and their daemonic riders, dwindling in the distance. He rose to his knees and gave thanks to all the gods he had ever worshipped for his deliverance.

Seen from high above, the desert glowed softly in the light of Specmoon. The swirling dust resembled a boiling river that appeared in the wake of the dragon squadron, stretching out far behind them, pointing like an arrow back to the heart of Dragonfrost.

On the lead dragon, the pilot sat in his saddle and surveyed the moonlit landscape ahead. He had made this trip several times already and despite the horrors that lay ahead for Yuledan, and the part he would unwillingly play in them, he was not unmoved by the awesome beauty of the desert at night or of the grandeur of sailing above it on a creature as ancient as the hills themselves. The dragonrider was not a poet. He was a fighting man who was resigned to the necessity of what he did. He had the sense to keep such thoughts to himself, however. Behind him flew his command, marked by the heavy throb of their beating wings. Woe betide the citizens of Yuledan, he thought, trying to feel detached from what he was about to do.

Below, armed men and women poured onto the streets; a clamour swept through the town. As Jelindel had instructed, no lights burned. She noted that her orders were being followed. Good discipline had developed in the village under the scourge of the attacks. From high above, one of the watch cried out:

'They come!' he shouted. 'The dragons come!'

'Quickly,' Jelindel said to Daretor. 'Tell Osric that S'cressling must defend the town. Go with them.'

Daretor hurried away. In the dim moonlight, Jelindel could see other rooftops. On many of them small figures stood perfectly still, faces upturned. These were the mages of Yuledan. She had taught them how to enmesh and interlink their powers and so act as one. She did not know if it would work. Many risks would be taken this night, and this was but one of them.

More stars were being blotted out as a gout of greenish fire spurted down, raking a street as the dragon tried to provoke panic. Fortunately, as far as Jelindel could see, no one was hurt. The citizens of Yuledan had learnt wariness, and knew that to give in to panic was to invite death.

She sensed the mages had begun weaving a complicated defensive spell. A faint blue lens appeared above the town. The next dragon that dropped down was unaffected by the light but when it belched fire, the flames deflected against the lens. The spell could not stop dragons; it turned aside their fire.

From the town's main square, a large body leaped into the air, soaring quickly up. S'cressling dove and spun amongst the attacking dragons. Osric would not use fire against them, and nor would S'cressling. Instead, he used the dragon's greater weight and momentum to ram the other dragons and throw them off course. Several dragonriders were unseated, plunging to their deaths, and the riderless dragons flapped away quickly, no longer compelled to stay.

The sudden attack from S'cressling and the sorcerous defence of the town was so unexpected that the dragonriders broke off the attack after only a few frantic, confused minutes, scattering into the night.

A great cheer rose up from the town. It was the first time they had hit back decisively at their tormentors. It felt good.

'With any luck,' said Theroc, later that night, 'it will be some time before they come again looking for dinner.'

The next day dawned bright and hot. Jelindel and the others had a last meeting with Theroc and the town council, promising to return to see how they were faring. Then they made ready to leave, at which point they realised that no one had seen Zimak since the night before.

'I thought it was unusually quiet,' said Daretor, before he could help himself.

They scoured the town. Theroc ordered a house-to-house search. No trace of Zimak was found. Daretor's theory was that Zimak was lying asleep with a local girl, and would show up when she got bored with him.

'It's in the clown's nature to bore, so we should not have long to wait,' said Daretor as they waited.

'Zimak's not so stupid as to seek dalliance when there's fighting to be done,' Jelindel said. 'If Yuledan had fallen, so would he.'

Theroc advanced the theory that Zimak had been seized by one of the dragons and carried away.

'That's possible,' said Jelindel, 'yet no dragons landed, nor any of their riders. Not alive, at any rate.'

'Well, what can we do about it?' Daretor asked. 'The days are passing, and we have few of them left.'

Jelindel squeezed his hand. 'There's only one thing to do. We must find the dragonsight.'

D'loom basked in spring sunshine. The streets were crowded with hawkers selling their wares, haggling customers, beggars and thieves, and even impoverished nobles selling letters of recommendation. The air was festive, which was a pleasant change from the grimness of the last few days. Even the presence of the brigands and other disreputable types, swaggering along the streets, or holding forth in taverns, could not mar the pleasure Jelindel and Daretor felt at returning to what they called home.

They had arrived the night before, landing on a dark rooftop beneath an overcast sky. Osric sent S'cressling to roost on a nearby rocky islet that stood a mile offshore, and had the kind of craggy terrain that would conceal a large dragon. Nor could boats draw close, as there was no beach; just treacherous reefs.

They found a tavern that was not quite so rowdy as the others, and discussed their plans. Zimak's disappearance was not mentioned.

'I will visit the Temple of Verity and consult the High Priestess,' Jelindel said.

'I thought the Order had fled across the continent,' Daretor said.

'The moment word spread that the Preceptor had been defeated, Kelricka promoted her seniors to High Priestesses and re-established the Temple of Verity in key cities.' To Osric, she said, 'I want you to go to the university and seek out the professors of history and languages. Daretor, I think we need to know what our friend Fa'red is up to. I doubt very much that he has forgotten about us.'

'Nor us, him,' Daretor grunted. 'The man has an uncanny knack of knowing exactly where we are at any given time. How is that?'

'I can only guess at the powers of an Adept 12, Daretor,' Jelindel said. 'There's also the Sacred One's blood on our foreheads, remember. Perhaps there's a connection between Fa'red and Rakeem . . .' She reached out and squeezed his hand. 'Fear not. I have it on good authority that we too are being looked after by a powerful friend.'

Daretor looked suspiciously around the tavern.

'Not a mortal guardian, silly,' Jelindel laughed. 'Something higher up. And don't go looking at the ceiling.'

Daretor took a gulp from his tankard and swallowed. 'Very funny. I'll leave the mage mongering in your capable hands,' he said. 'In the meantime, I notice that we have company.'

Jelindel and Osric glanced across the room. There was indeed someone seated at a table in the corner. Noticing their eyes on him, he slumped further into his seat and looked away.

'He came in after us and I am almost certain I saw him earlier near the marketplace,' Daretor said. 'He must be the sorriest looking deadmoon that I've ever seen, though.'

'To underestimate your adversary is to court death,' Jelindel mused. 'But I sense no malice in that one.'

They finished their drinks. Jelindel and Osric rose to go. Daretor lounged back, and looked as if he were settling in for the rest of the day. 'I think I will stay awhile,' he told them.

As they left, Daretor watched the man in the corner. He seemed suddenly flustered, as if he did not know whether to follow Jelindel and Osric or stay. At the last minute, he made up his mind, and nonchalantly left. Daretor went after him, maintaining a safe distance. He lost him once or twice, but picked him up on each occasion. It seemed the man was in no immediate hurry, for he stopped at stalls, halted twice to curse at holy shrines, and once he kicked a beggar who would not leave him alone. Stopping at a market stall, he haggled with the vendor over the price of a melon. The bartering ended when the man swept half the produce from the stall.

To Daretor's surprise, the man had tracked neither Jelindel or Osric. Instead, he headed for the docks, and after speaking briefly with a one-armed man, boarded a caravel.

Daretor leaned against an empty water barrel, pondering what he had seen. He was sure that the man had been watching them at the tavern. But it would seem Jelindel had been right. Perhaps the man meant them no harm. Putting him out of mind, Daretor turned back to the city and went looking for those who earned a living by knowing more than was good for them.

Chapter 6

SEA GATE

Onala, the High Priestess of the Temple of Verity in D'loom, was new to the post and keen to prove herself. She knew the so-called 'Archmage' Jelindel dek Mediesar, and was not impressed that she had sought an audience. Onala hadn't forgotten her first meeting with Jelindel when she was a mere neophyte. Jelindel had ensnared her with a binding word and humiliated her in front of her fellow seniors. Onala did not forget that sort of thing, and she looked forward to putting Jelindel in her place.

The High Priestess donned her most impressive vestments in a leisurely manner: a burgundy-trimmed robe with flared cuffs, a black velvet mitre with stiffened wings bordered with exquisite silver and gold embroidery. She placed her ceremonial crosier with its staff-long tassels by the table.

Onala kept Jelindel waiting two hours. Finally she sat behind her desk in a high-backed chair that looked more like a throne. Satisfied, she had Jelindel ushered in by a fawning neophyte. Her brown tabard with the Temple's rising sun emblazoned in golden yellow across the front were the only colours allowed such lowly clerics.

'Leave us,' the High Priestess said imperiously to the neophyte, who seemed to almost worship the famous archmage. Only at Onala's command had the infatuated girl scuttled out, leaving the door slightly ajar.

'Close it,' Onala added.

Jelindel smiled faintly at the click behind her. The bullying of the recently appointed High Priestess brought back memories, even fond ones. Onala thought the smile somewhat mocking and her face tightened.

'I am quite busy today,' Onala said. A look of disdain swept her face at Jelindel's weather-beaten appearance. 'You are lucky I am able to see you at all.'

'I am grateful for the audience,' said Jelindel. Her obvious sincerity caught Onala by surprise.

'How may the Temple be of assistance?' she asked, affecting weariness.

'I am seeking information about the earliest human language on Q'zar.'

'Quech. Any third-year servitor would know that.'

Jelindel ignored the jibe. 'What do *you* know of it?'

'I know what everybody knows, which is little enough. It was called Quech, as I have just said. No living being knows how old it is or where it originated. Why do you ask?'

'Is it possible to study the records?'

'With the proper permission,' said Onala.

'I don't have much time.'

'I cannot help that. You must obtain permission from the Temple in Arcadia. You of all people should know that,' Onala pointed out.

'I had hoped –'

'You hoped in vain.'

'So I see.' Jelindel rose to her feet, bade the High Priestess good day, and made to leave. Onala allowed herself a brief smile of satisfaction.

At the door Jelindel turned and for a second Onala's innate timidity surfaced. She stifled a squeak.

'It was wrong of me to try to bypass our ancient ways,' Jelindel said in a tone that was nevertheless ambiguous. 'I'll pray to White Quell for forgiveness. Fare you well, Onala.'

Onala did not trust herself to reply.

When Daretor and Osric returned that evening they found Jelindel pacing the floor of the tavern room they had lodged in. Before they could even open their mouths Jelindel came to a sudden stop, eyeing them belligerently.

'We're going about this the wrong way, I am sure of it,' she said.

'I take it,' said Daretor, 'that you fared poorly at the Temple?'

'On the contrary,' Jelindel said, her voice rising, 'I learnt a great deal. I learnt that the High Priestess is an insufferable fool who should be stuffed into a barrel of rancid whale blubber and dropped in the middle of the Tanglesea Ocean. No, I take that back, she should be kept alive to suffer the stink.'

'There's no need to lose your temper,' Daretor said.

'Who's losing their temper?' Jelindel said, stamping her foot and waving her hands. Daretor and Osric tried to give her their attention while not looking directly at her. 'Oh, you think this is funny, do you? Well, what did you two find out?'

Osric sat down and with relief pulled off his fur-lined boots.

'I found out that I prefer riding dragons to walking cobblestone streets.'

'Enlightening. What else?'

'No one at the university knows anything, nor are there any records going back that far. None of them could understand why I was interested in what they called a "dead language" anyway.' He massaged his feet as he spoke. 'One professor insisted that there was no original human language on Q'zar, which seemed to hint that it had to come from somewhere else. That is all he seemed to know.'

Daretor had found some bread and cheese left over from breakfast and was busy finishing it off when Jelindel turned to him. 'Well?'

'Fa'red was here.'

'What?'

'He came three days ago and, according to my source, left this morning. Apparently he was heading back to Dremari.'

'Did your source say why he came here?'

'He did not. But he had a guess.'

Jelindel and Osric both looked at him. 'And?' Jelindel asked.

'He met with one of the pirate captains, and they conferred for several hours. It seems Fa'red seeks to replace the Preceptor, starting with the prince here in D'loom. Why not? The entire coast is overrun by pirates, and there are rich pickings to be had. And where there are pirate lords there are pirate lordlings, smaller fry that seek some sort of security, otherwise they will be rammed and burned as the more powerful pirates consolidate against them. Quite possibly Fa'red is playing both sides of this game.'

'Out goes the prince, and in strides Fa'red as overlord or regent. Mind you, the pirate lords will find themselves in even deeper water with Fa'red at the helm,' Jelindel mused. 'One step out of line and it's the last mistake they'll make.'

'By the way, remember the man I thought was following us this morning? He went from the tavern to the docks and there boarded what turned out to be a privateer.'

Jelindel considered this. 'The one belonging to the same pirate captain Fa'red was speaking with?'

'The same.'

'So what is going on?' Osric asked.

'Apart from the obvious fact that there is a conspiracy, I wish I knew,' said Jelindel. 'Whatever it is, I am sure Fa'red means to delay us or stop us if he can. He's effectively cut us off from leaving by sea, but then he must surely know we arrived by other means.'

That night they had a stodgy meal of fried potatoes mashed with over-cooked greens. They had already been two weeks on their quest, and time was in depressingly short supply.

Jelindel finally pushed her plate away, having barely touched her food. 'We need to attack from a different angle,' she declared.

'And that would be?' Daretor asked, raising an eyebrow.

'We race here and there to find the Stone People, and get no closer to solving the problem. There is one who knows exactly where they are.'

Osric frowned for a moment, then exclaimed, 'Fa'red.'

Jelindel stood up. 'I am going to pay him a visit –' She stopped as though sensing something.

'No need,' said a voice. She knew before turning that Fa'red had silently entered the room behind them. She turned as an intense red light blasted towards her. She put up her hands to ward it off, but she was unprepared for the sheer ferocity of the magical attack. The impact threw her halfway across the room. Her head slammed into the edge of a table and she lost consciousness.

In the blackness that followed, she thought she heard a jumble of noises, followed by distant mocking laughter. The sounds followed her into sleep.

Everything was blurry. Jelindel managed to open one eye but quickly shut it again. Blinding pain throbbed behind her temples and the room swayed. Her stomach lurched and she clamped her mouth shut to hold down the little food in her stomach.

Slowly forcing herself into a sitting position, she peered around. It was a small cabin, well appointed, and dimly-lit. A large metal cage swung from the ceiling, moving in the opposite direction to the swaying of the room. The effect was sickening and she felt bile fill her mouth. As she moved, her foot kicked something. A bucket. She grabbed it and vomited.

She sat up, half afraid she might be sick again, and looked at the cage. This time she realised there was a body crumpled inside.

She tried to rise but couldn't co-ordinate her legs properly. She slid off the bunk and crawled on hands and knees across the heaving floor. She collapsed twice before regaining her balance. Reaching the cage, she grabbed hold of it to dampen its swings, and looked inside. A pale face looked back. Daretor. He managed to smile at her.

'I think we really are on a boat this time,' she said.

He nodded. 'Salt.'

'Salt,' she agreed, sniffing the air.

'I think I'd rather be back on the dragon,' she said, cupping her mouth as another spasm took hold.

Daretor sat up and gripped the bars. 'Funny they should lock me up and leave you free,' he said. 'You're the dangerous one.'

She rested her forehead on the bars. 'I'm only a danger to myself right now,' she groaned.

'Can you get me out of here?'

Fighting the throbbing in her head, Jelindel concentrated. She flicked her hand at the lock and muttered a minor incantation. Nothing happened.

Perplexed, she tried again. 'Nothing.'

'The blue weirdling light,' Daretor said, 'that gathers on your lips . . .'

'What of it?'

'I didn't see it.'

Jelindel looked at him, trying to assimilate this information. She crawled back to the bunk and climbed up. Here a small mirror had been fixed to the wall. Gazing closely at her own image, she muttered another spell, one she used almost every day of her life. Then she sat back, stunned.

Slowly she turned to Daretor. 'He has taken my powers,' she said, so quietly he could hardly make out the words.

The door burst open and a large man with a scar on his left cheek entered. He was completely bald. With him was the one-armed man Daretor had seen the day before, talking to the one who had followed them through D'loom.

'Welcome to the *Sargasso*,' the scarred man said. 'I am Captain Helnick. Bring her.' The one-armed man grabbed Jelindel by the hair and dragged her from the room. He was immensely strong. Daretor roared abuse and strained in vain at the bars of the cage. Helnick smiled at him. 'Wait your turn.' He slammed the door behind him.

The one-armed man, whose name was Tarlig, dumped Jelindel on the middle deck. Helnick stood over her. 'You have two choices,' he said. 'Work, or go over the side. It makes no difference to me.'

She uttered a quick spell and flung it at him. Nothing happened. He laughed. 'Perhaps you need a spur,' he said. 'Shall I have the man downstairs flung overboard, still locked inside his cage? His life is in your hands.'

Jelindel stared at him a moment then let her head droop in defeat.

'As I thought,' Helnick laughed.

Tarlig shoved her aft to a storage compartment that contained mops and buckets. He set her to scrubbing the deck and later sent her to the galley, where she worked under the guidance of the cook.

Later still, Jelindel and Daretor were moved from the cabin to a chamber low in the ship. That first day, the ship encountered high seas, and the floor ran with stinking bilge, all of it slopping across the deck. That night, coming back covered in bruises and cuts from the attention of her guards, Jelindel could not find a dry place to lie down. She slumped in a corner. For the first time since the death of her family, she felt utter despair.

Daretor buried his face in his hands when he saw her. 'If I get out of here, I will kill them,' he vowed. 'It is as simple as that.'

'Me first,' Jelindel muttered.

The unsavoury looking man from the tavern served them one meal a day in the early evening. He said his name was Hakat. Despite his unpleasant appearance he did not treat them badly, but he refused to enter into any kind of conversation.

One evening, after Hakat had brought their meal, Jelindel sat close to Daretor's cage. They had fallen into the habit of talking in whispers, in case anyone was listening.

'Helnick makes out that the crew doesn't know where we are bound,' Jelindel told Daretor. 'But they're extremely calm about what's happening. It's my guess they've done this trip many times.'

'White Quell forbid something should be straight forward for a change. How do you come by your theory?'

Jelindel pursed her lips. 'Just things they let slip every now and then. Besides, the ship has set out for the deep ocean, but it isn't provisioned for a long journey.'

'Perhaps we are to meet another ship,' Daretor said. 'Or stop at some island.'

'Somehow I don't think so.'

Jelindel thought back to several conversations she had overheard. None supported Daretor's theories.

'Any sign of Osric?'

'I think they killed him,' she said. Daretor winced. 'He's not on board. But then S'cressling wouldn't have let anything happen to him if she were alive. Pray to White Quell he escaped.'

Daretor made a spitting sound. 'Why would Fa'red bring us out here?'

'Perhaps for the same reason he hasn't killed us, whatever that is.'

That night they did not sleep well. The ship entered a region of choppy water and around midnight a squall engulfed them. The *Sargasso* tossed and heaved throughout the night, crashing through troughs before rising high to crash again. Mountainous waves broke across the deck, pounding the sodden timbers. The noise washed through the ship like the footfalls of an army on the march.

The next day dawned bright upon a calm sea. An inconveniently calm sea. There was no wind, not even a breeze. The ship sat becalmed on the great ocean. Jelindel was scrubbing the decks once again. She noted that although Captain Helnick paced the upper deck and peered at the horizon through his farsight, he did not seem concerned. Indeed, he was more relaxed than the crew, which had become irritable.

The reason for Helnick's calm soon became apparent. Exactly at noon a wind sprang up from the south-east. The canvas billowed, the rigging creaked, and the *Sargasso* knifed through the water. The crew cheered, but Jelindel sensed that it was no natural wind. It was magecraft, and only Fa'red was powerful enough to be behind it.

Jelindel overheard the first mate and the bosun talking. The latter spat, calling the waters they were in the 'Accursed Eye', a place where the elements fought one another to a standstill.

Jelindel had heard of the Eye. One did not live long in a port city without hearing all manner of sailors' tales. That afternoon, when she managed to slip away for a few minutes, she reported to Daretor.

'The captain was not surprised?' Daretor asked.

'Not at all,' Jelindel said. 'On the contrary, he seemed to be expecting it. The crew, too, I'd say. They're definitely unhappy. Though, of course, they'd be edgy where magic's concerned.'

'So Captain Helnick steers deliberately into an area of dead calm, in the middle of the ocean, then sits patiently waiting for a mage-wind.'

'I heard Tarlig muttering. He fears this place. No breath of natural wind ever comes here,' said Jelindel. 'Apparently we're heading even deeper into it.'

Daretor gripped the bars. 'It's madness to go farther. What if we're stranded? Who could rescue us from such a place? It makes no sense.'

'All I know is that if I don't get back to the galley, I shall have a dozen extra bruises tonight.'

Jelindel kissed Daretor through the bars, then darted out. Left to himself, Daretor stared morosely at a rat hole in a corner. Two tiny red eyes peered back at him.

'Well, what do you want, Zimak?' he said, addressing the rat.

He slumped down. For the first time since leaving Yuledan, he thought at length about what might have happened to the thief. A low life he might have led, but at that moment Daretor would have welcomed him with open arms. Zimak's stealth, and his ability to get into and out of secure places, was almost legendary. Money and women's admiration were a particularly powerful incentive.

The *Sargasso* sailed for another three days, propelled by the mage-wind. Though happy to be moving, the crew was nevertheless uneasy; visit potential death a thousand times and it doesn't get easier. Their disquiet broke the surface frequently as squabbles and fights erupted. Jelindel noted that a lot more firewine was being stolen from the stores.

Spirits had always been rationed out to seamen on long voyages as a reward, or to raise morale. The Merchantmen's Guild tried to regulate, and indeed ban the provisioning of ships with powerful distilled spirits. In the end they had given up. Mutinies, ship wrecks, sabotaged gear, and murdered officers caused by even temporary prohibitions cost the ship owners dearly. Their puritanical regulations were not enforced, and officers went back to rewarding crew with firewine, the currency of the seaways.

Despite having worked as an officer and navigator on previous voyages, Jelindel had developed a great deal of sympathy for the common sailor's point of view. Life on board the great sailing ships was hard enough without some way to relax and forget one's troubles. Like the others on board, she was given a ration of firewine, which she always gave to Daretor. He swallowed the liquor in one gulp.

'I tell you Jelli, I'm going mad in here. It's all right for you. You get to see the sun, and breathe fresh air. I can't understand why they don't have me working above decks.'

Reaching through the bars, she stroked his face. He bowed his head, ashamed of being so helpless. How could she explain to him that she too felt completely trapped without her magic? Hers was as devastating a prison as Daretor's cage, but one she knew he could not understand.

'I don't know if I can endure this,' he said softly, then looked into her eyes. His eyes were red-rimmed and bleary, and his cheeks puffy. Lack of exercise and sunlight were taking their toll.

'I've noticed,' Jelindel said, her stomach cramping. 'I suspect they keep you down here as a hold on me. What they think I could do out here is beyond me. Even if I miraculously got my powers back, the mage-wind would stop and we'd all be at Fa'red's pleasure.'

'If something doesn't happen soon,' said Daretor, with feeling, 'I *will* go mad.'

'Our futures don't look bright,' Jelindel said, staring into his desperate eyes. 'One could almost hope that Rakeem's poison takes us before Fa'red.' She brightened for a moment, and at Daretor's querying look she went on. 'Fa'red mistakenly believes that I have trapped all the paraplane spirits from the adepts I have slain. He'll be present when our time comes. Only there won't be one solitary spirit for him to take.'

'Which doesn't help us,' Daretor said sombrely.

'No, but it gives us the last laugh. Besides, it also means that he expects to see us before the poison runs its course. If I die alone, he can't harvest the spirits he thinks I've enslaved.'

Daretor pulled her closer to him and through the bars they rubbed noses. 'I love you despite your nonsense . . .'

The next day Jelindel was on the poop deck, polishing brass work, when a cry went up behind her. She turned to see a colossal shape taking form across the ocean, some two or three miles to starboard. It was easily two hundred feet high and sixty wide. It looked like a huge serpent's iris. Whatever it was had the consistency of smoke and the colour of rust, and it was clearly sucking in the surrounding air.

All the crewmen stared, pointed, and talked excitedly. Jelindel climbed onto a spar to get a better look. She gasped as she caught a clear view. Wind and water were pouring into the iris, speeding up and foaming as if there were rapids on the other side.

'It's a portal,' she said to herself.

A voice next to her replied, 'That it is, Archmage.' She turned to see Captain Helnick watching her.

'You're taking your ship to a paraworld.'

'Aye, that I am.'

'This is Fa'red's doing.'

Helnick bowed slightly. 'We are his servants, are we not?'

'I hope he's paying you in gold and silver,' Jelindel said.

Helnick frowned slightly. 'And why is that, my lady?'

'Because it's unlikely, having expended so much power to get you there, that he will ever bring you back. And gold and silver are more universally used on paraworlds than other coinage.'

The captain stared at her for a long moment then snorted. 'That's mutinous talk that is. But you'll not be walking the plank, young lass. There's a much better fate in store for you.' He strode away, shouting orders to the bosun and the first mate. The bosun swung the wheel, adjusting course, and heading for the iris. When the captain wasn't looking, the bosun swallowed nervously and muttered a quick prayer to the sea god, Na'del. A young crewman nearby did the same.

The canvas was shortened and everything on deck battened down. 'We may be in for a rough ride,' the captain told his officers. 'Have the men roped to their stations. All others are to go below.'

'What about her?' asked Tarlig, hooking a thumb at Jelindel.

With great relish, Helnick said, 'Have her roped to the forward spar. We'll give her the best view of the ride.'

Jelindel was taken forward and tied to the mast. All the while the ship picked up speed as it entered the current pouring into the iris. With each passing second, the water washed higher and higher, now at Jelindel's legs, now at her waist. Soon she was holding her breath between waves that washed over her head with each pitch and plunge of the *Sargasso*.

The vermilion portal filled the sky and hid the horizon from view. Jelindel thought she saw stars within the vertical slit that loomed like a rent in the fabric of space itself. At this distance, she could see that the water at the base of the iris was ragged foam, boiling and churning, as though a sea serpent was thrashing beneath the surface.

Jelindel glanced down at the rope binding her to the mast. No matter that I'm bound, she thought fatalistically. If the ship founders, we all go down.

'All hands secure yourselves!' called Tarlig.

Everybody, though roped securely to the ship, grabbed stanchions and gunwales or anything else nearby. The ship began to shudder as it hit the roughest section of the churning water. Waves burst over the deck, and spray lashed over Jelindel like horizontal rain.

The bow nosed down. Jelindel was completely submerged, her hair swirling in her face, foam and bubbles surging about her. She had had no time to take a final breath, and soon her lungs were bursting. Just when she thought she could hold her breath no longer, the bow tipped upward. Seconds later it broke the surface, shedding tons of roiling water back into the sea.

The ship plunged into the iris. Instantly the prow pitched down, dropping abruptly. For a moment, the deck tilted at an acute angle, as if the whole structure was going to sink. There was a massive impact, like somebody belly-flopping into a pool, then the prow was rising again. On all sides, the water churned and chopped. The ship's timbers groaned and creaked, and spume flicked through the air, stinging Jelindel's face.

A vortex grew slowly beneath them and the ship began to rotate, caught within its grip. A tube formed within the swirling water, and quickly bloated as the swirling accelerated. Jelindel knew enough about ships to realise that the vessel was about to shatter; ships were not built to endure conditions like this. Then she saw Helnick on the upper deck, one hand raised aloft. In the palm of his hand was a black crystal shaped like a runestone. She saw his lips moving, but she could hear nothing above the thundering of the vortex and the wind that howled through the iris. Even as she watched a livid light gathered about the crystal, which seemed to be throbbing as if it were alive. Helnick suddenly shouted, '*Vishnak atu!*' What seemed to be a solid bar of light speared the iris like a lance.

The anomaly was some thirty yards behind them as it began to close. The wind passing through it shrieked at an ever increasing pitch, rising to a crescendo that had everyone on the *Sargasso* shutting their eyes tightly and cupping their hands over their ears.

Silence descended like a falling axe.

Jelindel opened her eyes. The iris had closed. The vortex, which had been fed by the water roaring through the portal, quickly dissipated, and the *Sargasso* was bobbing on a slight swell.

Two days later they pulled into a port and docked. The town rose tier upon tier above the harbour, built into the side of a granite massif that rose steeply to a summit lost in cloud. The town's buildings were built upon broad terraces carved into the rock. Roads and footpaths criss-crossed the surface. Enormous caverns also pockmarked the cliff, with roads leading into them. Long looping bridges, fashioned of stone bound by metalwork, spanned natural clefts and chasms. Everywhere Jelindel looked she saw great crowds going about their business. Altogether, it was the most awesome city she had ever seen.

Cargo was off-loaded with no particular haste, and the captain was away from the ship for most of the first few days. Jelindel was confined to the hold with Daretor. They had no idea what was going on. One evening she was pacing the cramped space lit by a hanging oil lamp given to her by Hakat. Distracted, she walked into the oil lamp, banging her head and knocking it from its hook. She cursed. Without thinking she muttered a spell to raise the lamp. Nothing happened, of course, except –

'Do that again,' said Daretor.

'Very funny,' Jelindel said, rubbing her forehead.

'Jelli, I meant no joke. When you tried to work magic just then, I think I saw a tiny blue flicker.'

'But nothing happened,' said Jelindel.

Daretor rattled the bars in frustration. 'So try again.'

Jelindel swallowed, but could not find the courage to try again. She had not been able to express to Daretor how devastating the loss of her magical powers had been. The equivalent for Daretor would have been to have had his sword arm cut off. Jelindel's loss had left a great void. Indeed, the endless wearying work on deck and in the galley had been a kind of godsend, tiring her mind beyond the point where she might brood on such things. Now she was far from sure that she wanted to reconfirm her worst fears.

'You probably just imagined you saw something,' she said, suddenly licking her dry lips.

'Try.'

'No Daretor, I'll not. They're gone. My powers are gone. Please, be silent.'

She turned away from him, so that he could not see her face. Daretor continued speaking, but his voice was softer now.

'You're my beloved,' he said, 'and I will love you with your magic or otherwise. But I swear on my right arm and all that I hold dear that I will throttle you if you don't turn around right now and try again!'

The threat, delivered so gently, took Jelindel by surprise. Despite feeling so woebegone, she burst out laughing and turned around, her eyes sparkling.

'Well?' he said. 'Don't just stand there like an incompetent jester waiting for applause. Do something.'

Jelindel cocked her head. 'A touch of romance at last. And you look so cute locked up in a cage.'

'Jelli . . .'

'You're serious, aren't you?'

Daretor gripped the bars. 'Maybe something in this paraworld weakens Fa'red's spell on you,' he suggested. 'You have to try, Jelindel.'

'Don't call me Jelindel,' she said, distracted. She realised she was frightened, and could not bring herself to do it. 'What if my powers are really gone forever? I don't know if I can live with that. I think I would want to die.'

'If you don't get them back there is nothing surer,' he said. 'For both of us. We know the *Sargasso* will never take us back to Q'zar. We are to die in this paraworld, if Fa'red has his way.'

She gazed at him a moment. 'A plague on your pessimism,' she said.

'As you like, but I am right nonetheless.'

'No doubt,' she said, weary. She steadied herself and focused on the cage. This time she felt the telltale tingling on her lips. Hope surged. She felt so excited that the spell came out askew. Nothing happened. She took three deep breaths and tried again, aware that she was trembling, that she had never been so desperate for success. Tiny blue lights flickered on her lips. She let the subtle forces build, nurturing them, trying to stay calm, despite the fact that her heart hammered within her chest.

She closed her eyes for a second and uttered the word that sent the flickering light spitting from her lips to the lock on the cage. For a second nothing happened, then she heard a faint noise, as if some part of the inner mechanism was creaking against another part. She stared at the lock for a long moment, then at Daretor. She rushed forward and thrust her arms between the bars, and embraced him. Daretor kissed her as well as the bars permitted. Jelindel realised that she was trembling.

Between sobs and kisses, she managed to say, 'It's coming back. My powers are returning.'

He pushed her back a step. 'Then get me out of here.'

'What? Oh, of course. Sorry.' She tried the lock but it still held fast. She tried the spell again but it had no further effect. She eyed the mechanism, puzzled.

'I think I know what's happening,' she said, thoughtfully.

'Fa'red's power was not able to span the portal, and whatever magic he worked on me only dampened my power. It didn't remove it entirely, as I'd thought. Now the dampening effect is wearing off and it comes back, bit by bit.'

'How long till it's fully back?' Daretor asked.

Jelindel closed her eyes. 'Who can say? It might be hours. Days. Weeks.'

Daretor rattled the bars, frustrated. 'I doubt that we have days, Jelli, much less weeks.'

'I'll keep trying.'

'Wait,' he said. 'It's possible that repeated attempts at this stage might delay the full return of your powers.'

'This has never happened before, Daretor.'

'Perhaps there's a gentler magic you can work that might free me.'

She looked at him. 'I'm listening.'

He glanced down at the rat hole. Jelindel's gaze followed his.

Chapter 7
THE UNSPEAKABLE CITY

The rat's nest was in a narrow, dark space. It was the way the creature liked it. Normally it would never have emerged while humans were out and about, but some subtle feeling was giving it purpose. It was more single-minded than it had ever been in its entire brief life as it set off, knowing exactly where it had to go.

The walls on either side rose steeply upwards, but the rat's claws found plenty of purchase, and it ran straight up. The entire ship was a town full of roads for the rat. It could reach any part of the vessel with ease. It pattered on, moving with a strange new purpose that was both exhilarating and frightening. It had never known a sensation like it.

At each fork in the path it took the turns without hesitation, until it stopped beneath a tarry beam that became a kind of ceiling. To one side was a narrow gap that appeared far too small for even a rat to pass, yet it wriggled through in moments. Next was a knothole on the inward side of the narrow corridor. The rat crawled through without even pausing to check for danger. It was by now inside the first mate's cabin. There, hanging on the wall, was a bunch of keys.

Jelindel and Daretor waited in silence. Jelindel seemed preoccupied, as if her mind was melded to that of the rat. The truth was that she was apprehensive. She feared that something would go wrong. The loss of her powers, even though temporary, had shaken her confidence. It would be a long time before she would dare take her powers for granted again. However, there was an odd reassurance in all of this. She knew that if Fa'red could have rid her forever of her abilities, he would have done so without hesitation. The fact that he had not strongly suggested that the power of magic was innate, something so fundamental that it could no more be removed from a person without killing them than could their heart.

There was a soft clinking noise at her feet. She looked down to see the rat, sitting on its hind legs, with a bunch of keys in its mouth. Daretor sighed loudly. He had had doubts as well, although he kept them to himself. Moments later he was out of the cage and hugging Jelindel, but this had been only the first small step of many yet to be taken. They had to escape the cabin, the ship, and even the paraworld. Jelindel also needed time for her full powers to return. She had a feeling that she would need them in order to get back to Q'zar.

Daretor had problems too. After having been imprisoned for so long, his legs were stiff and wasted. He could barely stand, let alone walk or run. Jelindel spent the first hour of freedom massaging Daretor's legs, and he just groaned.

'White Quell,' he muttered between clenched teeth. 'It's like having red hot needles jabbed into my flesh.'

Nevertheless, he bore it, though before long he was bathed

in perspiration and panting heavily, as if he had run a gruelling race. Finally he was steady enough to stand. He tottered from one end of the chamber to the other, and back again.

'That much movement will have to do,' said Jelindel. 'I'll support you.'

Jelindel unlocked the chamber door and eased it open. She peered cautiously through the gap. No one was in sight and there was no sound of anyone walking nearby. They had long ago become used to the noises of the ship, and sensed that most of the crew had gone ashore. A skeleton crew was sure to have been left behind to deter thieves, but they would not be expecting the prisoners to escape.

They made it to the stairs leading to the middle deck without encountering anyone, then their luck ran out. A pair of legs appeared, shod with rough hobnailed boots. The same boots worn by the first mate. Daretor immediately lunged forward and wrapped his arms around the man's legs. With an oath, the first mate toppled down the gangway and into the corridor. When he saw his assailants, he tried to raise the alarm. Jelindel was faster. She intoned a binding spell that wrapped his body in blue flickering light. He fought against the bindings, trying to call out, then stopped, staring with frightened eyes.

'Don't fight,' Jelindel advised him, 'or the bindings will grow tighter. You're lucky I've allowed you to keep breathing.'

They dumped him on the floor of a nearby cabin and locked the door. By now Daretor's legs were functioning. They climbed the gangway to the middle deck and scouted the ship. As far as they could see, there were only two crewmen on guard.

The easiest and quickest way to get off the ship was the gangplank that had been lowered to the dock, but they were not dressed like the crew, and were sure to be noticed.

'Make us invisible,' Daretor said. 'You have done it before.'

Long ago, they had been on another boat, a river barge, and Jelindel had led them safely past prying eyes. She nodded. 'There's no time to lose doing it the hard way. I just hope my full power has returned. Invisibility's taxing enough as it is.'

She chanted a spell and wove a complex sign in the air. Unfortunately, there was no way for them to tell if it was working. They hesitantly stepped out onto the deck and headed for the gangplank. They had nearly made it when a voice called out. They froze.

'What do you think you're doing?' the voice called a second time. They turned to find one of the crewmen looking in their direction. Jelindel opened her mouth to reply when a voice behind them answered.

'Minding me own dummart business,' it grumbled, 'as you should be doin'.'

'You go fallin' asleep again and the captain'll have your guts for garters, and no mistake,' said the first crewman. 'Now look lively.'

'Oh, aye aye an' all that,' said the man, climbing grudgingly to his feet and trying to look like he was guarding something.

Jelindel and Daretor breathed a sigh of relief and stumbled across the gangplank to the dock. They made for the first shadow they could find. From there they peered back the way they had come, looking for any sign that they had been spotted. All remained quiet.

Jelindel relinquished the spell. In doing so she sucked in a huge breath.

Daretor clutched her shoulder in alarm.

She breathed out and then drew heavily on the air. 'I'm all right. It's just left me a little giddy. No worse than you exercising after a long spell of doing nothing.'

Daretor ruffled her hair. 'What a pair we make.'

They headed for the city. It loomed above them, adorning the massive cliff face like barnacles on a ship's hull.

They found themselves in a dark, narrow alleyway that wound between two warehouses then curved up and away to the left as it started to climb the cliff face. Since most of the city was above them they had little choice but to follow it, and hope that the hour was late enough to prevent them from meeting any locals.

They climbed what must have been five or six hundred feet in elevation before reaching the city's edge. Here they came upon several dwellings lining the sloping path. Next to them was a row of inns. Given their proximity to the docks, they were probably designed for the patronage of sailors. Despite the more gothic and forbidding structures higher up, the inns seemed relatively normal, even homely. Jelindel and Daretor stopped outside to consider their situation. They were still in shadows, and fairly safe from casual glances. So far they had seen no one.

'My legs feel as if they've walked across Q'zar as well as climbed its highest mountains,' declared Daretor.

'How steady do you feel?' asked Jelindel.

'I've not fallen over. Yet.'

'How would you be in a fight?'

'Hopeless, without another day or so of stretching and walking.'

'Well then, here we have an inn,' Jelindel said. 'Inns are where drink is sold, and information is on the house, if you can talk smoothly.'

Daretor shook his head slowly. 'I don't think we should chance it,' he said. 'Look what happened the last time I used an inn to get information.'

Jelindel smiled. 'It worked out all right in the end. And we need to know where we are and what kind of people live here.'

'Some of the sailors from the ship could be in there,' Daretor pointed out.

This was correct. It was too big a risk, yet Jelindel was hungry. She had lived for weeks on gruel and scraps, labouring harder than she had for years. She was weary and in need of real food and a bath. There was even the temptation to do a few vaguely unpleasant things to some of the crew. On the other hand, Daretor had suffered even more, and he could not face returning to the cage.

They kept going, using the darkness as cover, and trying to make as little noise as possible. They had gone only a few hundred yards, and were nearing some odd-shaped buildings, when a sibilant voice called out from the darkness. They stood waiting, expecting the worst.

The voice came again. 'Over here. Come on, move it, you dullards.' This time it sounded vaguely nervous.

Jelindel sighed and headed towards the voice, still half supporting Daretor. There seemed little point in trying to run. At the very least she knew that her binding spells worked well enough in case of danger. They approached a line of scraggly ornamental bushes. A man, still masked by the shadows, stood up and beckoned them to follow. They did so, though Jelindel felt Daretor's sword hand grope for the missing grip of his weapon. Daretor without a sword was more naked than Jelindel without her powers.

The stranger led them through a stand of trees and into an alleyway that led to a ribbed plank, similar to a gangplank. It was very steep and had handrails. Jelindel eased Daretor up the plank. Ever vigilant, she wondered if they were being led into a trap. What was the reward for spies on this paraworld?

At the top of the ladder a small landing gave access to a round porthole-shaped doorway in the side of the cliff. A door whispered open on silent hinges and they were ushered inside. A faint smell of incense and cooking touched Jelindel's nostrils. Other than that she felt no sense of alarm.

A bright light came on overhead. Jelindel squinted at its intensity, but was unable to tear away her gaze. She had never seen anything like it: a glowing line of brightness encased inside a globe of glass. The man that had led them to this place was standing near the wall, his hand resting on a small lever. He laughed when he saw their expressions. Jelindel realised that she knew him.

It was Hakat, from the *Sargasso*.

The girl was gone. Zimak brushed straw from his clothes and picked a strand or two from his hair. He opened the hayloft doors, staring out across the darkened town of Yuledan. The barn was on a slight rise, giving him an excellent view. Zimak could see the town mages dotted here and there on rooftops – unmoving sentinels, faces scanning the dark skies.

He knew he should be out there, playing his part in the defence of the town, but he felt lethargic after his tryst with the dark-haired girl who had found the flattery of one who flew on dragons more than she could resist.

In any case, it was not yet time. The dragons did not come till the darkest hour of the night and that was still some thirty minutes away. Zimak decided to rest for a while longer, then make his way to the nearest rooftop and be ready with his sword. Much good that would do me or anybody against fire-breathing dragons, he thought. But one had to put on a good show for the locals. A bit of flashing steel always reassured people. Indeed, if he played his cards right and impressed enough locals sufficiently, by this time tomorrow night he might well be even more exhausted after bidding yet more admirers goodnight.

His sword hilt was poking him in the kidneys, yet he almost couldn't be bothered changing position. Finally he decided that comfort outweighed sloth. The movement probably saved his life.

To shift the sword, he first took hold of the hilt, then tugged it into a new and more comfortable position. While his hand was still grasping the hilt, several shadows swooped out of the night sky and into view scant yards from the hayloft doors. With a soft and sinister *whoosh* of air they hurtled towards him, gleaming swords at the ready.

Zimak barely had time to draw his sword from its scabbard to deflect the first assailant's blade. Then he rolled aside and managed to get to his knees as two more blades slashed at him. He parried and jabbed, sinking the point of his sword into one of his attackers. The man barely reacted, which told Zimak that he was up against deadmoon warriors. They were trained to ignore pain and fear nothing, not even a painful death. But Zimak had no time to think on all this. The fight was on, and it was one that he had not been expecting.

At first he could not make out how many attackers there were. They said nothing and made little noise, except for the soft padding of their feet in the straw and the ringing clash of their blades. Fortunately, the hayloft was long and narrow and no more than two of the would-be assassins could engage him at once.

Desperate to stay alive, Zimak was barely aware that gouts of fire were now flashing out in the night sky. He dimly heard screams of terror and pain as he struggled to defend himself. His blade bit flesh, a deadmoon fell, but another replaced him. Parry, chop, lunge, back away – despite the advantages of occupying Daretor's larger frame, Zimak wished for his old body, along with its agility and speed.

Although he was holding his own, the onslaught was merciless and the numbers were still in favour of the attackers. He gave ground slowly but gave it he did. Behind him, looming closer, was the edge of the loft, promising a sudden drop to the straw-strewn floor some fifteen feet below.

Zimak's heel touched the ledge. He knew there was a ladder somewhere behind him. He and his companion of earlier in the night had used it to get up, but climbing down now was not an option. A sturdy rope was tied three feet to his right. He knew, without looking, that the rope went up and over a hoist that was attached to a metal track. The other end of the rope was securely tied around two large bales of hay.

Zimak had no time for finesse or stylish manoeuvres. He parried a thrust that nearly spitted him, feinted twice in quick succession, then spun about, slashing the rope as he did so and forcing his opponents to step back out of the deadly arc of the whizzing blade. The rope parted, and a dark mass of hard-packed hay dropped from the rafters, side-swiping two deadmoons. Both fell instantly, clutching broken shoulders and arms.

Zimak took the opportunity to scan the edge of the loft. The ladder was poking several feet up over the edge. He grabbed it and pushed off. The ladder arced over into empty space and then plummeted downwards. Zimak was on a middle rung of the ladder when it slammed into the adjacent wall. Jarred from his unstable perch, he fell the remaining six feet, rolled onto his feet, then ran into the street.

Ignoring the spot fires that were spreading through several tenements, Zimak skirted lines of townsfolk carrying water. He ran recklessly in the gloom, in no doubt that the deadmoons would pursue him. He had to alert Jelindel and Daretor to the new danger. While the presence of the assassins did not prove that Fa'red was in league with the dragonriders, the coincidence was too great to ignore. Even if Fa'red was just taking advantage of the mayhem, he couldn't be too far away.

Zimak kept running, guided mostly by his ears: the menacing hiss of dragon breath sounded all about, but seemed concentrated ahead, near the town centre. From there also came the sound of voices, confused and loud.

Zimak made it to the corner of a small square, in the middle of which a fountain bubbled. The tinkling sound of water seemed incongruous in this night of death. The square was busy with townspeople dipping their buckets in the fountain. The sky here seemed clear of dragons and flying assassins. He pushed through the crowd, sighting Jelindel in the clock tower. Daretor stood beside her. Zimak took a deep breath and broke into a run across the square.

He almost made it.

A brick, torn from the parapet of the courthouse, flew out of the darkness and, with unerring accuracy, crashed into the back of Zimak's head. Bricks might not fly, he would later allow, but they did pretty well as missiles.

Zimak gave one sharp cry and fell flat on his face, unmoving. A bright flash lit the courtyard, temporarily blinding the people. Three black-clad figures swooped down and landed beside Zimak. They tied a special harness about him, each taking a leather strap, then sprang aloft again, lifting Zimak's limp body from the ground.

Jelindel stared at Hakat, mentally preparing a spell to disarm him if necessary. But he smiled and gestured around the room.

'Welcome,' he said. 'Welcome to my home.'

Daretor looked around. The room was like nothing he had ever seen. Certainly he did not recognise the function of much of the furniture and hangings. He also noted the light source. 'You live here?' he asked.

Hakat nodded. 'Amuse yourselves for a moment,' he said.

He fetched plates, cutlery and cups from a wall unit. He then placed a fresh loaf on the table, several aromatic cheeses, a side of jellied ham, a bowl of what looked like tomatoes, along with a jug of wine.

All the while Jelindel and Daretor watched, wondering what was going on. When Hakat had fully laid the table, he sat down and beckoned for them to join him. They did so, slowly, still suspicious. Hakat handed them a bowl of scented water and they washed their hands. Then their host set upon the food with gusto. Jelindel and Daretor watched for a moment then joined in, ravenous. They managed to keep enough wits about them, however, not to touch anything that Hakat did not sample first. There was no point in taking chances.

When he saw that they were eating heartily, Hakat poured wine, drained his in one gulp, then laughed, raising another in salutation. 'To the captain,' he said, ignoring Jelindel and Daretor's surprise. 'May he rot in a hell of our choice!'

He drank deeply, savouring the toast, then wiped a sleeve across his lips. 'I see from the look in your eyes that you have questions,' he said amiably.

'Why?' Jelindel asked.

Hakat laughed as if she had said something very funny. 'Why?' he repeated. 'Well, I could give you many answers, Archmage. I could say that Captain Helnick is a brutal tyrant who deserves death far more than he deserves loyalty, and I think that would be enough. I could say that none who serve the interests of one so foul as Fa'red should be trusted, let alone obeyed. And I could even add that on a night long ago, when Fa'red's forces killed your family and destroyed your home, there was one lowly stableboy who was taken away and made a slave, but who has never forgot the loyalty he swore to the Count Juram dek Mediesar.'

Jelindel stared at him, memories spilling out from the dark part of her mind that she had slammed the door on several years before, and even now had little wish to reopen. But suddenly the man before her seemed familiar. It was as if his face metamorphosed before her eyes. Slowly her mouth dropped open.

'Hak*at*! It is you? It is truly you?'

He nodded, smiling, and Jelindel found herself hugging the former stableboy. Daretor relaxed, breathing out. He felt safer than he had in a long while.

Hakat and Jelindel sat back. Jelindel continued to stare at him. It seemed as if she had lost the power of speech. Hakat seemed embarrassed and looked at his feet several times.

Finally Jelindel said to him, 'So many times we played together, racing through the stables or over the rooftops.'

'Aye,' said Hakat, 'and many's the time you got me into trouble, too.'

She placed her hands on his and said with an intensity that embarrassed Hakat further, 'Please, I do apologise, Hakat –'

'Enough, enough, that was only a joke, Countess. We was just children.'

Jelindel breathed out and a tiny shudder shook her. 'Yes. Till that night. But tell me, how did you come here? And you've changed so much.' She stopped short of mentioning the scars that crisscrossed his face, and the fact that he seemed to have aged ten years.

Hakat shrugged. 'They grabbed me that night, along with one or two others. We was taken onto a ship in the harbour and locked up for a time. Then the others were taken away. I never saw 'em again. Me, I was kept on board as cabin boy and treated worse then a cockroach. Then, some time later, we was sank by pirates and I became the cabin boy for Captain Helnick. Eventually, I was made part of the crew.'

Daretor looked at Hakat's well-established house. It looked as though the man spent more time here than on Q'zar. 'Why didn't you escape?' he asked.

'I did once.' His eyes seemed to dim at some dark memory. 'And swore I'd never try that again. They had some way of finding me, some sorcerer's way, I think. Helnick's been in league with Fa'red for years. Two of 'em are thicker than thieves. Only crueller.'

Daretor thought on that for a moment. 'You must have been valuable to Helnick for him to enlist Fa'red's help in finding you.' Daretor felt Jelindel squeeze his hand for silence.

''Tis okay,' Hakat said, noticing the admonishment. 'I've never been wise to the ways and wiles of mages, but I daresay Fa'red knew where I was from. How he meant to use me, I suspect I'll never know, and hope not to.'

Jelindel inscribed a sign in the air about Hakat. 'If your recapture was due to Fa'red's interference, he'll not intervene again. Now, what of this paraworld we've come to?'

'Thank you . . . Jelli.'

Ignoring Jelindel's grip on his arm, Daretor said, 'You're a different man from the one I followed to the *Sargasso* in D'loom.'

Hakat laughed. 'All the cussing an' mess I made of the stalls, you're meaning? You almost lost me twice, an' I needed you to follow me to the ship. I couldn't approach you in the tavern 'cause Helnick's eyes an' ears are ev'where, if you're understandin' me.'

'Enough, Daretor,' Jelindel admonished. 'I'd trust this man with my life. Where are we, Hakat?'

'Farvane, an' it's a hellhole, make no mistake. Helnick's been trading here for the last year and a half with Fa'red's help. Seems the archmage covets some of the devices that the Farvenu . . . acquire.'

'Like the light?'

'Nah. That's what they call science. It looks like magic but it ain't. I don't rightly understand it meself, but it makes a change from smelly old oil lamps an' dripping candles. Better on the old eyes, too.'

Jelindel reached up to touch it, but drew back quickly. 'It's hot, yet there's no flame. How does it work?'

Hakat sucked at his teeth. 'Something called electricity. Don't ask me what that is or how it works or where it comes from, 'cause I ain't got a clue. But the Farvenu are pirates, of a sort. Only they don't raid ships. They raid paraworlds, and they're packrats, ten times over. They steal anything they can, not knowing what most of it is, then sell it in a huge market that draws folks from fifty paraworlds.'

'They're dangerous?' asked Daretor.

'You wait till you see 'em,' said Hakat, his voice catching. 'You'll know 'em right off. Burned into your senses they are, already, only you don't know it.'

'Can we move about the city?' Jelindel wanted to know.

Hakat nodded. 'You can, but you gotta be careful. They have a dozen different races livin' here at any one time. Some of 'em look like us, and others don't, including the Farvenu themselves. But they'll be lookin' for you two by morning so we gotta do something to change your looks.'

Jelindel frowned. 'There's something you're not telling us,' she said gently.

Hakat ducked his head then brought it back up. 'This is an awful place, Countess. When I say it's worse than hell I ain't kidding. If they catch you, you'll be for the kitchens. They won't even put you up on the slave blocks. That's Fa'red's orders, where you two was destined to go. I heard Helnick say so himself.'

Jelindel shrugged. 'I've just worked in the ship's kitchen for the last week, Hakat, how much worse can it be here?'

Hakat swallowed. 'You got me wrong, Countess. They don't intend to work you in the kitchens. They intend to serve you up.'

Jelindel and Daretor stared mutely at Hakat.

'They're cannibals?' Jelindel said at length.

'They ain't cannibals,' said Hakat. 'They don't eat their own kind, just ours, if they can get us. That's why you was sent here. I was planning to rescue you both from the ship tonight, along with the other fella. Then I seen you break out of the lockup, and then I *didn't* see you, if you get my drift. I figured you'd have to come this way so I circled round an' waited in them bushes where you found me. An' here we are.'

Jelindel said, 'Thank you, Hakat. I wish my father and mother were still alive to know of your loyalty.'

Hakat looked both pleased and embarrassed. He started to say something when Daretor interrupted. 'You said "that other fella". Who do you mean?'

'They had another prisoner on board. Fa'red's men was guarding him. He's for the kitchens, too, I'd say.'

'Did you see him?' Jelindel asked.

'Aye, I did. Took him his food, same as you.'

'What was his name?'

'Zimat, I think. Something like that.' Hakat scratched his chin. 'Dark-haired fella, tall, strong, but gone to fat, like. Complained a lot, especially about the food.'

Daretor sighed. 'That's Zimak all right.'

'He's our friend, Hakat,' said Jelindel.

'That's stretching the truth a bit,' muttered Daretor.

'We will have to rescue him,' said Jelindel.

Hakat nodded. 'I already tried, before I saw you two breakin' out. But he was gone by then. They'll have him up at the palace, gettin' him ready.'

'Ready?'

'Yeah, for eatin'.'

Jelindel paled and stood up. 'Then we must hurry.'

'No, no, sit down, Countess,' said Hakat. 'There's no rush. They'll fatten him up first. Force-feedin' they call it. Be a week before they send him to the cook. Maybe more.'

Jelindel relaxed and took her seat again. She thought of something else. 'How long before the *Sargasso* returns through the portal?'

'She usually lays over five days, no more. But you can't go back on her.'

'Why?' Daretor asked.

'Because if they don't find you here then they'll be expectin' that. They'll wait till they're out to sea then they'll scour the ship stem to stern. Won't be a single rathole they won't poke their noses into, and make no mistake.'

Jelindel thought for a moment. 'My magic powers are back,' she said. 'I could make us invisible again . . .'

'Might do it,' said Hakat, 'an' might not. If I was them and

I figured you was aboard, why, I'd fetch along a nice nosy little mage with me *before* we set sail, and have him cast all manner of spells.'

Jelindel felt a profound weariness seep through her limbs. 'Is there another way?'

'There is,' said Hakat, 'but it ain't easy.'

Daretor leaned forward, pouring himself another cup of wine. 'It rarely is in our line of work,' he said. 'So you might as well just tell us.'

'Like I said, the Farvenu are pirates. Paraworld pirates . . .'

Jelindel blinked. 'Of course. They have some means of opening gates between the paraworlds.'

Hakat nodded. 'That they do, Countess, only it ain't magic. It's more of that science stuff of theirs. A machine they snatched long ago from some other paraworld, when they was still using magic to get them through the paraplane.'

'A machine?' Jelindel asked doubtfully.

'Aye. You won't like it, is my guess,' said Hakat. 'And your magic may not work on it, one way or another. But it does work. And there ain't nothin' Fa'red can do to stop it, either.'

'Where is this machine?'

'There's more than one. Each clan, and there's dozens of 'em, has its own. They're always fighting with each other, trying to outdo their rivals. They're a bloodthirsty lot.'

'So we pick a clan headquarters, break in, find the machine, then get back to Q'zar.' Daretor looked around, waiting for objections.

'Nah,' said Hakat. 'Lessin' you don't mind dyin'. But there is a way. Problem is, we can't do nothing for a week, and your friend might be in hot water by then, along with some onions an' 'erbs.'

'So we break him out first.'

'We might. Then again, we might not,' said Hakat. 'Break 'im out and the hue and cry'll be ten times as bad. Let's just wait and see. I know a girl in the kitchens there. I'll get word to her and we can find out when your friend gets 'imself on the menu, so to speak. After that, we'll have about eight hours before they start cookin' 'im.'

Zimak refused to eat. They had been stuffing him with food ever since he arrived. At first it was a welcome change from the meagre rations on board the *Sargasso*. But it was possible to have too much of a good thing.

He had reached his limit. He spat a mouthful of food back into his plate and pushed it away. The servitor frowned. He was a small dark man with odd-shaped pupils and eyebrows that met in the middle of his forehead. Zimak had gleaned from him that he was not native to this paraworld. The man spoke a form of Q'zaran, and only knew it well enough to get by in the market place. With a combination of words, signs and gestures, he had made Zimak understand that he was to eat. And eat a great deal.

In principle, Zimak had no problem with the concept of overeating, and he would never have believed he could fail to do so in practice. But now the old adage that one's eyes were bigger than one's stomach was beginning to ring true.

The jailer scowled and muttered as Zimak sat back. The man gestured at Zimak, then at the food. He then abused him roundly in several languages, none of which Zimak understood. Finally, he pressed a stud on a small metal box fastened to the wall and spoke into it. Zimak thought this was odd behaviour, but assumed that there was a spirit or djinn inside the box. Another adage on Q'zar was, when in the henhouse, act like a chicken.

Zimak had no idea how prophetic that saying would prove to be.

A few moments later, clearly summoned by whatever messenger was in the box, the door swung open and three barrel-chested guards of an unknown race strode in. They were carrying things that looked like kitchen utensils designed for torture. The men were heavily muscled, and had no neck. Their shaved heads gleamed like helmets, and they had to stoop to get through the door.

Zimak got ready for a struggle, but the guards were expert at handling desperate, aggressive prisoners. Flinging his plate at the head of one guard, Zimak doubled him over with a kick to the stomach, then pushed him into his companion. As Zimak bolted for the door, the third guard dropped his load and slammed it shut. With the advantage of surprise gone, Zimak did not last long.

They trussed Zimak and strapped him to a wooden trolley. At the creak of a lever the trolley hinged upwards like a chair. A metal helmet was rammed over Zimak's head. It was completely enclosed, except for an opening at the front. The helmet was then fixed to the headboard of the trolley. By squinting down, Zimak could just see part of his lower body. His struggles tightened the bindings all the more.

A flexible hose was inserted through the mouth hole and forced between his lips; it did not stop there. The little man kept feeding the hose in until it hit the back of Zimak's throat and he started to choke. Zimak clenched his teeth down on the tube, but a stabbing pain across his scalp made him scream. Again and again he tried biting the tube, and each time they made him scream before pushing it in further.

The hose pushed through the back of his throat and into his

oesophagus. He kept gagging but, after a few moments, the sickening feeling of being strangled from the inside out dimmed and he found he could breathe. Zimak's eyes watered. He tried to spit out the metallic taste in his mouth, but the bile kept sliding down his throat. He could hardly see anything now and his panic grew. It can't get any worse, he assured himself. All the same, he had a feeling that he did not know the half of it.

There were sounds of lids being removed from containers, then stirring. Somebody grunted as though lifting something heavy, and suddenly warm liquid was pouring into Zimak's stomach. He made a determined effort to resist, but he did not succeed.

'Zimak's probably fine,' said Daretor, taking another bite of jellied ham and washing it down with mulled wine. 'If they're feeding him, he'll be as happy as a pig in a turnip field.'

Hakat looked grim. Jelindel saw the brief unhappy look he gave Daretor. She guessed that Hakat knew more about the feeding methods than he was telling. Jelindel yawned, then rubbed her eyes.

'I know we should start making plans,' she said, 'but I have to get some sleep.'

Hakat immediately jumped up, apologising profusely, and opened a panel in the wall. Behind it was a bed that slid out on rollers.

'So clever!' Jelindel exclaimed. 'In a way that is more marvellous than a magical spell.'

'They don't put much store in magic here, Countess,' said Hakat. 'Except as something to trade to the paraworlds as value it. The Farvenu are too practical for magic, if you ask me. They like hard, solid, bright things made of metal and wire.' He gestured idly at the ceiling light. 'And fancy stuff. Speakin' of which . . .' He pulled out a square black box and held it to his eye. 'Say somethin' nice. Oh, an' this doesn't hurt one bit.'

'Is it more Farvenu science?' Jelindel said. A bright light flashed and she smarted.

'Daretor? Would you be so kind as to smile for me camera?' Hakat asked.

Jelindel finished rubbing her eyes. 'I hope that thing doesn't steal anything . . .'

Daretor looked at Hakat suspiciously. The camera flashed and Daretor grunted.

Hakat put the camera down. 'Steal something?' he laughed. 'Like your soul? No, Jelli. The thing makes an artistic likeness of whoever it's aimed at. I'll show you the paintings when they're . . . what's the word? Developed! Once they're developed. I need 'em for your papers.'

'You have strange machines here, Hakat,' Daretor said, finally looking away from the camera.

Jelindel climbed into bed, luxuriating in the softness of the quilt and the pillows. 'They can keep their machines,' she said sleepily, 'as long as they let me do it my way with magic.' Moments later, she was asleep.

Hakat lit a fire in the grate with a 'match' and placed a wire grille across the front. Daretor showed no sign of wanting to go to bed. He poured himself more wine and beckoned Hakat to do the same. The two men sat before the fire, talking into the night.

Jelindel woke with sunlight on her face. She had a feeling of wellbeing that was quite unfamiliar, given what had been happening over the past weeks. It was as if she had awakened from a long dark nightmare and had finally come into the light of a new day. She stretched, yawned and rubbed her eyes, then sat up and looked around.

Daretor snored softly beside her. They were in a strange bed in a strange room. A few feet away stood a table littered with the scraps of a late-night meal. She gazed up through a transparent skylight, and stared at the astounding cliff city of the Farvenu.

Memories flooded back, and the peace she had felt receded into mere relief at being free again. She got up carefully and went to the washbasin, where she washed her face and hands. For a time she played with the wonderful taps, which poured a seemingly endless stream of clean water, then she cleared the table. A search of the cupboards revealed that one was a pantry, with dried fruit, cheese, bread, small salted fish, and nuts. She had laid out breakfast by the time Daretor opened one eye and grunted something unintelligible.

'If that's good morning, then the same to you,' said Jelindel, smiling impishly.

'Could I have some bread and cheese in bed?' he asked.

'No. This is on the table as incentive for you to get up.'

Daretor sat up, clutching his head, then lay back again.

'Five bottles of wine. No wonder you are feeling like that,' Jelindel pointed out.

'I was establishing a bond of male comradeship with Hakat,' mumbled Daretor.

'I knew there were advantages in being female,' replied Jelindel. 'Get up, drink some water from the spigot at the washbasin in the corner, then get yourself into the privy. It's behind that door that looks like a cupboard.'

'Everything in here is so small and compact.'

'But a lot less so than your cell. Come now, move.'

Daretor got up and meandered to the corner to wash his face. He entered the little room beside it, and Jelindel heard clattering and curses for a short time. Daretor returned to the washbasin next, turned a spigot and cursed as he unexpectedly got hot water instead of cold.

Hakat was nowhere to be seen but Jelindel was not worried by his absence. He turned up halfway through the meal with several packages, one of which contained fresh-baked bread and a thick chunky fish soup.

'I've been higher up in the city,' Hakat said in answer to their queries. 'Getting supplies and finding out stuff.'

'And what have you found out about us?' Jelindel asked.

Hakat frowned. 'I don't understand it meself,' he said. 'No alarm's been sounded. They gotta know by now you escaped. I wonder what their game is.'

'If we were caught, would we be turned over straight away?'

'No. Not unless there's a reward, and maybe that's all there is to it. The bigger the hue and cry the larger the reward would have to be. Maybe they'll just stick you on the list of escaped slaves and leave it at that. It's not like you can go anywhere.'

'Why do you have a house here, Hakat?' Daretor asked. 'You said the *Sargasso* usually lays over only five days.'

'Aye, that it does,' said Hakat. 'I'm a kind of quartermaster, you see, and they often leave me here between trips to get the best price for the cargo and set up deals for when they come back. They can't stay more than five days; I dunno why, something to do with the magic that opens the sea portal.'

'Don't you mind staying here?'

'I do and I don't. Mostly I hate it, but more than that, I hate being on board the *Sargasso* and under Helnick. I know what's likely to happen to me. One day the *Sargasso* won't come back and I'll be left here. It could be worse. There's some things here . . . there's a girl, you know . . . ' He shrugged.

Jelindel leaned forward. 'If we find a way back, do you wish to come with us?'

Hakat gazed at her, as if she was offering him something he could not comprehend. 'Go back? To Q'zar?'

'And be free,' said Daretor, glancing perplexedly at Jelindel.

Still puzzling over the idea, Hakat said, 'I'm sort of free here, mostly. Where would I go? What could I do?'

'We need all the help we can get,' said Jelindel.

Hakat looked out the window. 'Could I bring someone?'

'Someone, as in a female someone?'

'Aye.'

'Someone who can cope with hardship, and who only screams when it is absolutely necessary?'

'Er, I s'pose so.'

'Then why not?'

Hakat sat back, laughing to himself. 'Well, imagine that,' he said. 'Imagine that. Me, free as a bird, away from all these devils.' Then doubt passed across his features. 'Dreams are good an' I'll keep that one to meself for now, if you don't mind. Makin' it come real is the trick.'

'Good,' said Jelindel. 'What do we do now?'

'First, you gotta know what this place is like.' He told them as much about Farvane as he could. Although he spoke for more than two hours, there was something he left out. He never described the Farvenu themselves. Eventually Daretor raised the point.

'I was comin' to that,' Hakat said with strange reluctance. 'You gotta see 'em for yerselves. The truth is, you already seen 'em, in your nightmares.'

He would not elaborate. Instead he unpacked the bags he had brought from his visit to the city. He gave them local clothes and the necessary papers they might require. These were fairly crude identification documents, each one bearing a strangely sharp and accurate sketch of Jelindel and Daretor, which Hakat called a 'photograph'.

'The likeness on these papers is uncanny,' Jelindel said.

'They're good all right,' Hakat agreed. 'But to the Farvenu we all look alike anyway. They can't tell us apart, except by hair colour, size, and whether we be a man or a woman or other.'

Daretor's eyebrows went up. 'Or other? What else is there except man and woman?'

Hakat looked at him as if he were asking a silly question. 'You'd be surprised,' he said. 'Now get dressed. We need to scout the headquarters of some clans.'

'It's still odd,' said Daretor, 'seeing Zimak's face with my name under it.' Jelindel quickly squeezed his arm.

An hour later they were in the city proper. Up close, the architecture had a gothic look, ornamented by carved grotesque figures that were fantastic in appearance and cruel in mien. Jelindel shuddered, wondering about the nightmarish paraworlds the creatures must come from.

The streets were narrow and paved with a white stone that was smooth and very hard. It had a milky opalescence that contained intriguing depths. When Daretor gazed down into the depths, he gasped and stepped back.

'What is it?' Jelindel asked.

'Faces,' he said. 'Faces inside the stone.'

'Don't stare,' Hakat hissed at them. 'Of course there's faces. They make this stone in a factory down by the ocean an' in it they place the severed heads of their enemies. Some say the heads are still alive, frozen in the stone like the sea shells that turn to rock. They're said to be alive, aware, but insane.'

Daretor swallowed. 'What manner of beings would . . . ' he began, but trailed off. He attacked problems with a sword and sought, at worst, an honourable death. There was nothing honourable in having a head encased in rock for the city traffic to roll over endlessly.

So far they had not seen a Farvenu. Hakat had explained to Daretor the previous night that they were largely nocturnal, moving about by day only when necessary, and then usually in a drowsy state, as if sleepwalking.

They reached the first clan building. The palatial façade was built five hundred feet up into the cliff. It had numerous apertures dotting its face, each with a small ledge instead of a sill. Like most Farvenu buildings, it was built half into the cliff face, while the rest jutted out from the granite. Hakat pointed out that most such structures went back into the cliff for hundreds of yards, taking advantage of a network of tunnels and caverns that had been dug out of the rocky massif over generations.

On an outcrop near the clan building stood an inn. It was part of a larger structure that fell away down the cliff face on the ocean side of the street – only the façade could be seen from the street; the rest was in the rock. At the foot of the structure was a street built into a ledge. Thus the Farvenu city was built, tier upon tier, climbing the vast massif to the very top, thousands of feet high.

They entered the inn and settled at a table with a view of the clan building. It was then that Daretor noticed something odd. Several of the windows had staircases sloping up and away. It was as if the staircases were designed to lead to the windows and nowhere else.

He was about to remark on this oddity when a creature came into view. It descended a stairway, before standing on the ledge at the base of a large window. Jelindel saw it too, and covered her mouth with her hand.

'Don't react,' Hakat whispered, glancing around. It seemed everybody was preoccupied with their own affairs, though a woman at the bar looked away too quickly.

Jelindel and Daretor eased back into their chairs, forcing themselves to relax. The creature at the window had wings and was easily eight feet tall, with leathery skin the colour of red wine. It sported two small horns on its head, and a tail that ended in a vicious barb. Its eyes were bloodshot, the irises yellow, like parchment. There was no expression on its face, which made it more unsettling. Stepping out onto the ledge, it stretched its wings, flexed once or twice, and took to the air, flapping away and dropping in a lazy spiral that quickly took it from view.

Jelindel and Daretor breathed out and looked at Hakat. 'I've met creatures from forty different paraworlds,' he said, shrugging, 'and every one of them has a tale, a fable, a nightmare, about a creature like the Farvenu. They call them devils, daemons, ghouls, vampires . . . it's all the same. Something that comes in the night and terrifies all who see it. Something that eats the living and damns the dead to eternal torment.'

'They have been to Q'zar then,' Jelindel said. 'Maybe thousands of years ago. And now they are part of our myths . . .' She gulped the juice that Hakat had bought her. 'Strange how you never quite escape your childhood nightmares,' she concluded.

'The faster we leave this paraworld the better,' Daretor said, and the others agreed.

Jelindel's brow furrowed, making Daretor wary. When she got that expression it usually meant trouble.

'What worries you now?' he asked.

'Nothing worries me, but if these creatures came to Q'zar long ago they may have records, or even memories, of that time.'

'So?'

'They may know the first language of Q'zar. Perhaps we have come here for a reason. Perhaps here we will find the meaning of Hadirr.'

Daretor sighed. 'There's just one small problem.'

Jelindel looked at him, her eyes twinkling. 'And that would be?'

'Someone would have to question one of those things,' he said. 'And I just remembered that I'm a simple swordsman, not an interrogator. I do not torture.'

'Neither am I, so where is Zimak when we need him,' she said, laughing.

Jelindel turned to Hakat. 'Tell me about the clan building; its entrances, layout, defences.'

They spoke quietly and kept ordering drinks. No one seemed to be paying them special attention. Hakat noted the serving woman's departure, and relaxed.

Over the next few days they made several reconnoitring trips past the clan building. They also checked out several others, but the first had the advantage of being close to the edge of the city and the port below, which was familiar territory for Jelindel and Daretor.

During this same time they noted the loading and unloading going on at the *Sargasso*. Hakat was unavoidably involved, and was away for long hours. In his absence, Jelindel and Daretor went over their plans again and again, partly with the help of the strange 'photograph' sketches of the clan building that Hakat had taken. Though Jelindel and Daretor viewed the enchanted box he used with unease, they admitted its usefulness.

At Hakat's suggestion they did not venture out when he was not present. There was no point in taking unnecessary risks. But as the days passed risk could not be avoided. Their plans received a jolt three days later.

Captain Helnick wanted Hakat to return to Q'zar with the *Sargasso*, which was due to leave a day before the attempt on the Farvenu's paraworld machine. Jelindel and Daretor would need Hakat to work the contraption, and to translate should they get any information out of the devil creatures.

'Oh, they speak Q'zaran all right,' Hakat said. 'There's other stuff –'

'Have you ever missed a sailing before?' Jelindel interrupted.

'Once,' he said. 'I got rotten drunk in a tavern and they couldn't wake me, so they left me here.'

'Would that work again?'

'Who knows? Maybe Helnick's not planning on coming back. I dunno.'

Daretor put a hand on Hakat's arm. 'You must decide then,' he said gently. 'Do you throw your lot in with Jelindel dek Mediesar, and take a chance, or go back on the ship?'

Hakat looked at them both. 'What if you fail? My girl and I'll be stuck here, maybe forever.'

'Maybe,' said Jelindel.

She made no effort to persuade him. She believed that human beings tread the path to their own destiny; their decisions must be their own. Her calmness affected Hakat. He swallowed once and his rapid breathing subsided. He nodded quickly, as if he didn't trust himself to speak.

'Good man,' said Daretor. 'Now, we must anticipate their moves. What happens next?'

'As soon as they miss me, they'll come here and search the

place. They mustn't find any trace of you two, or they won't go at all. I still don't know why no alarm's been raised. It ain't right.'

It took two hours to collect their things and scour the small dwelling of all traces of their presence. Jelindel found several long hairs that clearly did not belong to Hakat and which were a different colour to that of his sweetheart.

When all was done they hurried through the evening streets. Hakat led the way, Jelindel followed several paces behind him, and Daretor was farther back. It was the hour after sunset, just before the Farvenu emerged for the night. They were heading for Hakat's sweetheart's boarding house. She had recently moved there, which would confuse their trail further. Hakat doubted his shipmates would make more than the most perfunctory effort to find him. Now that he was protected by Jelindel, he seemed to have a light step to his walk.

They were two hundred yards from the boarding house when three Farvenu dropped out of the sky with a suddenness that was almost heart-stopping. Jelindel gasped and involuntarily took a step backward. Daretor had the presence of mind to hurry forward and grip her elbows to steady her.

One of the Farvenu barked a command and held out his hand. His voice was deep, almost *basso profundo*. Hakat answered in the same staccato speech. It sounded like a language creatures in the bowels of the earth might speak.

Jelindel and Daretor saw Hakat reach for his identification papers. He did this slowly, giving them time to pick up on the cue. Then all three held out their papers. Each Farvenu took a document and peered at it. Eons of time seemed to grind slowly by. Daretor tensed. In a moment those huge taloned hands would flash out and seize them.

The hands did flash out but only to hand back the documents.

One creature's nostrils flared, as though scenting fear, but its colleagues seemed oblivious to its concern.

Jelindel and Daretor breathed a soft sigh of relief. Then came a woman's shout, and a figure hurried towards them. It was the woman from the tavern. Neither Jelindel nor Daretor had paid her any attention, but Hakat recognised her immediately.

To Jelindel he whispered, 'Stop her. Quickly!'

The Farvenu were looking in the woman's direction. Jelindel whispered a spell, cloaking the blue light, and flicked her hand. The woman hurried past without so much as a glance in their direction, staring ahead as if she had seen someone she knew.

Jelindel, Daretor and Hakat took back their papers. The Farvenu sprang into the sky and soared away, as swift and graceful as eagles.

Hakat took a trembling breath. 'My ticker's not up to this,' he said. He explained how he had seen the woman in the bar. 'What'd you do to her?' he asked Jelindel.

'I clouded her mind,' Jelindel said. 'Made her think she'd seen a friend and that it was urgent she catch up with him.'

'Thank White Quell you was with us, Jelli.'

They continued on their way. Within a few minutes they stood in QeSu's cramped bedchamber. She was small and dark-haired, with a friendly face and eyes that were bright and curious. She already knew their story and quickly admitted, in stilted Q'zaran, to a fascination with magic. Little of it was practised in the city of the ever-practical and machine-loving Farvenu.

Jelindel promised to show her more magic, but right now they needed to know how Zimak fared and his exact location. QeSu became excited. She had news of her own.

'He's on the breakfast menu,' she said.

Daretor said, 'Could I get a copy of that menu?' When Jelindel sneered, he shrugged. 'I'm as anxious about him as you, don't worry.'

'Ignore him, QeSu. Now. How do we get to Zimak?'

The young woman looked at each of them in turn. 'Then it's tonight?' she asked, a tremor in her voice. 'We will journey to a new world tonight?'

Jelindel took the girl's hands in her own. She could feel them trembling. 'Everything will be all right,' Jelindel told her. 'You will like Q'zar.'

'There are none of *them* there?'

'None.'

That seemed to reassure her, and she went on to tell them all she knew about Zimak and where he was being kept. It became clear they would have to split up, with Jelindel and Hakat going after the machine. Jelindel explained to Daretor that, should the opportunity arise, she would force a Farvenu to tell her what Hadirr meant.

'Promise me you won't attempt such a thing,' Daretor said, gripping her shoulders. 'With the machine we can visit any paraworld we want. Someone else will know the answer.'

'The machine is my first priority,' Jelindel said, and rubbed noses with him. 'Good luck finding Zimak, and don't take any unnecessary risks. Worse comes to worst, we'll try something else.'

Daretor clutched her tightly then released her. 'Leave the Farvenu alone,' he insisted.

'Willingly,' Jelindel said. 'Now to the finer detail.'

They arranged to meet either at a small fountain that had been shown to the Q'zarans earlier, or at QeSu's bedchamber, if things went wrong. The *Sargasso* would sail with the morning tide, some two hours before dawn. If they failed to obtain the paraworld machine, they would try, with the help of Jelindel's magic, to hide on the ship. Hakat could legitimately show up at the last minute, claiming he had drunk too much and dallied too long.

It was fortunate their plans had been well laid before this night. There was little time now to change or to improvise. Except for QeSu, they each knew what had to be done.

Daretor held Jelindel and kissed her lingeringly. Hakat and QeSu held hands shyly, and stared into one another's eyes.

Jelindel brushed her fingers across Daretor's lips. 'Be careful,' she whispered.

'As always,' he said.

Jelindel pulled away and nodded to Hakat. They would leave first.

Daretor gave them twenty minutes then – after he and QeSu had donned the clothes of kitchen workers – they exited. Outside, they immediately turned right, heading higher into the city. Zimak was being held by the Clan Kazor, a middle-ranking clan whose headquarters were roughly a mile from QeSu's room.

They covered the distance quickly, passing few pedestrians, though a great number of Farvenu swooped overhead. Some dropped low and seemed to study them before flying off again. QeSu said their uniforms were responsible for the slight attention they were receiving. To the Farvenu, the lower species were little more than bright animals, like dogs or horses, with little reasoning capacity. The more docile and obedient, the less visible they became. Only opponents acquired status in their eyes. Enemies who fought back were considered honourable, even though they were quickly killed.

They came to the headquarters of Clan Kazor, and QeSu led Daretor around the side to the entrance intended for barbarian species. Daretor's sense of honour would have demanded he enter the front gate as an equal, but he had grown wiser in Jelindel's presence.

QeSu was puzzled by the fact that Daretor seemed to detest Zimak yet was risking his life to save him. She pointed out that if they failed they would soon be on the same menu, as entrees due to their diminutive size. Daretor thought about what QeSu had said.

'Have you ever had a thorn in your foot for so long that it hurts more to remove it than leave it alone?'

QeSu laughed. 'That's what my ma used to say about my pa.'

There was a guard inside the entrance. He knew QeSu by sight and waved her in. She explained that Daretor was seeking work as a casual kitchen hand. Cleaners were of such lowly status that the guard barely glanced at Daretor, and certainly did not deign to speak to him.

'Tell him to mind his manners and work hard,' the guard said to QeSu. She promised she would do just that. Daretor bit his tongue.

Being almost invisible due to one's lowly status had clear advantages. For one thing, if found in the wrong place, Daretor's error would be put down to stupidity, rather than calculation. Free slaves did not scheme, and while they told lies, they were of little interest to those above them. Everyone, with the exception of those on the menu, was above Daretor.

They were soon in the kitchen. There Daretor was assigned tasks that anyone could perform, and was left to his own devices. Nobody checked up on him. Nobody kept an eye on him. It was just as Hakat and QeSu had predicted.

Daretor wanted to look for Zimak's cell immediately, but QeSu would not let him. 'You must be designated first,' she said. When he looked puzzled, she added, 'You must have a place where you belong. Then, if they find you elsewhere, you simply say you are lost. Everybody gets lost here. The building is designed for those who fly, and walk only on the perches up there.'

She pointed overhead. The rooms were oddly shaped in that the floors were smaller than the cathedral ceilings. Many rooms were huge caverns with the floors partitioned into rooms, offices, corridors, and such like, for the benefit of the pedestrian species. Up near the ceiling, jutting several feet from the walls, was a series of round beams, like those in a bird cage. Often Farvenu perched on these to chat or even strut from one to the other. Daretor saw a sleeping Farvenu and was amazed to discover that they slept upside down, clinging to perches like bats. It made them even more sinister.

Daretor was assigned to cleaning out huge pots, each one easily large enough to hold three men the size of Zimak. The fatty residue that clung to the insides filled Daretor with such seething anger that he was unable to go near them, let alone touch them.

Following QeSu's advice, Daretor waited half an hour then left the scullery. Pilfering two meat cleavers from a chopping block, he made his way to a prearranged rendezvous and waited for QeSu. He was nervous and jumpy. As the minutes dragged he became more agitated. Could something have happened to her? Surely no one could have discovered their duplicity? Then he wondered whether he had been led into a trap by the girl. Certainly it was odd, as Hakat had often said, that no one seemed to be looking for them.

He had just decided that he must either go looking for QeSu, or escape this place, when he sensed a presence behind him. He spun and flung back his hand, ready to throw a cleaver. Only QeSu's stifled gasp saved her. He promptly stuck the cleaver into his waistband. 'Where have you been?' he said tersely.

'I needed to steal a tool from the soup chef. He keeps it on him at all times,' she explained. 'Are you all right?'

'I'm fine,' he lied.

QeSu led him to a stairway that spiralled down for several levels. A corridor led into the cliff and was straight as an arrow for at least five hundred yards. The sheer engineering skill involved impressed Daretor, despite the fact that he loathed the engineers.

Two hundred yards in they turned left into another corridor, then right. Daretor tried to memorise the turns, in case he had to come back alone. QeSu nudged him, pointing silently at a bend in the corridor.

Around the bend was a guard station. Three human guards were normally positioned there, QeSu explained. They were armed with swords and pikes. Such guard duties were considered little more than precautionary: no one had ever broken out of the food pens, and certainly no one had ever tried to break in.

Daretor indicated to QeSu that he was ready. Together they marched around the bend and presented themselves to the guards. There were, in fact, four guards. One was visiting from another station, as bad luck would have it.

They straightened up when they saw Daretor and QeSu, but seemed in no way suspicious. QeSu immediately stepped forward. 'I need to see consignment 787,' she explained.

'What for? He's on the menu,' said one of the guards, obviously bored.

'Cook thinks he may have been regurgitating. Need to check his fat content.' She held up a pair of pincers used to grip rolls of fat and measure their thickness.

The guard tossed QeSu a key, too lazy to go himself. 'That way. A dozen pens along. Make it quick. The food wagon's due any moment,' he said.

The guards went back to their conversation. Daretor breathed a sigh of relief. This was too easy. That made him worry. It *was* too easy. But who was to say that this time luck wouldn't go their way? Without a doubt, the mission to recover the dragonsight had, so far, been anything but uneventful. It was time White Quell allowed them easy passage.

Jelindel and Hakat gained entry to the headquarters of Clan Morla – the clan they had reconnoitred – with equal ease.

For them, things would be very different. For one, they would not be dealing with human underlings and their domestic domains, but with the quarters of the Farvenu themselves. This would be trickier. Worse, the paraworld machine was kept in the clan chieftain's quarters.

Jelindel had magic on her side. Getting to the machine would be relatively easy. The Farvenu would not be expecting her or her abilities, but she suspected that getting out might be a lot more difficult.

Hakat, as chief negotiator in the absence of Captain Helnick, had met many Farvenu chieftains. This was partly because the clan leaders did not trust their brethren. Hence anything to do with the transfer of money and the acquisition of profit tended to fall within the exclusive domain of the chieftain himself. Hakat had met the Clan Morla chieftain. His name was Faruk and they had sat in his private quarters, haggling over everything from a barrel of jellied pigs' trotters to rare black Q'zaran pearls.

Hakat knew the way, Jelindel knew the spell, and surprise was on their side. As soon as they were inside, she used a semi-cloaking spell to render them inconspicuous – anything more potent would drain Jelindel too much. They quickly made their way to a long, sloping corridor that zigzagged upwards for at least half a mile. The angle was so steep that they were soon sweating heavily. Fortunately, it was a broad corridor and although they passed several pedestrians, nobody paid them any heed. The Farvenu flapping lazily overhead gave them even less attention.

At the top of the ramp was an empty office. They rested for a few minutes, then set out again. Hakat led the way up more ramps, along dark corridors, and sometimes through huge caverns unused for centuries. The path always led upwards. The chieftains habitually lived on the topmost level, the underlings in descending order beneath him. It was a very hierarchical society, in every sense of the word.

They came upon Faruk's quarters sooner than expected. Hakat thought they still had one more level to go, but abruptly they were face to face with a ceremonial guard. She was a Farvenu, and instantly saw through Jelindel's cloaking spell. The creature knew that the two humans were not meant to be here. With a speed that was frightening, her wings shot out to either side and backwards, propelling her forward so fast it almost proved their downfall.

Jelindel had been preparing a binding spell and, by sheer luck, she had just run through it. Even as the creature lunged, screaming shrilly, talons flashing, Jelindel struck. Before Hakat could cry out, the huge warrior tumbled to the floor, bound.

Hakat jumped clear as the Farvenu rolled beneath him. She writhed frantically for several moments, then lay still, glaring at Jelindel with a hatred and fury that seemed worse than the attack. Hakat leaned breathlessly against the wall, feeling weakened by the Farvenu's hateful glare. 'Evil spawn,' he said, giving the creature a wide berth to get to the door. His lock-picking skills came to the fore. The locks in this area were simple, more for show than security. A moment later they were inside Faruk's inner sanctum.

'It smells of carrion,' Jelindel observed.

Hakat went straight to a curtained alcove and pulled back a leathery hanging to reveal a series of barred recesses, no bigger than dog kennels. Hanging from the red-hued stone walls were long, thick chains with shackles.

'Midnight snacks,' Hakat said, making the sign of White Quell. 'Can you get us past these bars here?'

'We'll see,' said Jelindel. A moment later, two bands of blue light wrapped around two bars and slowly pulled them apart.

'Such fantastic strength!' exclaimed Hakat.

'Not so, the iron is rendered soft by the spell.'

On a small table within the alcove sat a gleaming metal box the size of a small artisan's pack. Hakat turned side on and squeezed in as far as he could. With effort, he hooked the box's handle. Standing back from the alcove, he flipped open the lid and checked the controls. He turned a switch marked with a Farvenu symbol. A light came on and the contraption hummed softly. 'Good,' he said. 'It's fully powered.'

'Powered?' asked Jelindel.

'Er, it's sort of fed, with sort of machine food.'

'Can we go now?'

'That we can.'

'Stay,' said a deep voice. They turned slowly to find two Farvenu studying them.

'Faruk,' Hakat managed to breathe.

The larger Farvenu grimaced, and then the creatures attacked simultaneously, wings thrown back, lunging forward and slashing with lightning speed. Jelindel spat out a holding spell, but not before a talon raked Hakat's forearm, gouging a deep gash that oozed blood. Hakat screeched, clutching his bloodied arm. The two creatures were now frozen in midair, straining at the mage light that held them.

Jelindel was sweating as she maintained the spell. She had never encountered such brute strength before. By sheer muscular power the two Farvenu were slowly draining her magic. Then she realised that Hakat had already fled to the door. He had only stopped because the fallen guard had somehow manoeuvred herself to block the entrance.

'Bind these two,' Jelindel managed to mutter between clenched teeth. 'The chains from the alcove . . .'

Hakat looked pleadingly at her. Sweat ran down his face in rivulets. 'I can't,' he said hoarsely. 'I can't!'

'They're escaping,' she hissed.

Hakat shook with indecision. Without the mage he would never reach the bottom level. To stay was to court death. Even now the Farvenu were drawing closer to Jelindel, daemonic creatures defying gravity, floating inches above the flags, drawing inexorably closer to the countess. Countess. Duty to the title swayed him. Count Juram's daughter needed him. He walked to the alcove, eyes not leaving the Farvenu. Clasping the chains, he trailed them towards the floating creatures. Even as he clasped the shackles around the smaller Farvenu, Jelindel released the creature and it dropped to the floor. Jelindel concentrated on Faruk himself.

The released Farvenu spat and hissed and writhed like a demented thing. When it found it could not free itself, it sank into a kind of patient stupor, red eyes blazing. Jelindel could not tell if it was merely waiting for a chance at freedom, or if imprisonment rendered it torpid.

'Now the others,' Jelindel panted.

Hakat wound the chain around Faruk's legs and hands, then

he looped it around the creature's wings for good measure. With scarcely enough chain, he manacled the female by the door. Not happy with his handiwork, Hakat stepped back quickly. There is not enough chain in the paraworld to hold these creatures, his brain screamed.

'They won't hold for long,' he said miserably.

Jelindel muttered a binding spell and allowed the other, more difficult and tiring spells, to dissipate. She breathed out, then drew in the heady power of the first spell as it returned to her. Incarcerating three creatures even with simple binding spells was more debilitating than she had thought possible.

Faruk grunted when he dropped to the ground. After an initial struggle, he lay still. Jelindel approached him with great caution. She did not trust either the earthly bonds or the magical ones to restrain him fully.

'Better bandage that arm,' Jelindel said to Hakat. 'Predators like these can probably smell blood a long way off.'

Hakat found a cloth hanging and tore it into strips. Meanwhile, Jelindel crouched so that she was at eye level with Faruk. His mesmerising eyes transfixed her. In them she read the promise of dreadful retribution.

'Magic user, you are,' he slurred. Saliva dripped from his incisors.

'True,' said Jelindel. 'I can kill you with a word. And I will, if you don't answer my questions.'

Faruk gave no indication that her ultimatum worried him.

'You speak some of my language,' Jelindel went on, ignoring the creature's fetid breath.

'Speak many tongues.'

'You have been to Q'zar?'

Faruk grunted.

'Your ancestors went there long ago?'

His eyes never left hers. Jelindel stared impassively back, confident that her binding spell would hold till she released it.

'Long ago,' said Faruk.

'When men were young?'

'Before.'

'Before men came?'

'Dragons then.'

'You fought dragons?'

Faruk smiled, grim but also admiring. 'Dragons great enemies. Destroy many Farvenu. We go.'

'When men came, Farvenu were there?'

Faruk blinked, bored with her questions.

'Did your people know the language of the first men?' Jelindel leaned forward, almost holding her breath.

'We learned.'

'Do you remember it? Was it passed down? Are there records of it?'

'Who cares?'

'I care.'

'I don't.'

She muttered beneath her breath and the binding around Faruk tightened. He grunted in pain but showed no other sign of discomfort. 'There is a word in the language of the first men. I must know its meaning.'

Faruk opened his mouth in a parody of a grin. He laughed scornfully, as if she had said something stupid.

'Children forget.'

Jelindel sighed. 'Yes, we have forgotten. I think your people live a long time. It is easier for you to remember.'

'What word?'

'Hadirr. Do you know it?'

'No.' That scornful grinning laughter again.

Jelindel felt defeated. She doubted she could extract the information from this creature even if she had the will to torture it. She stood up.

'Let's go, Hakat. We have what we came for. Most of it.' She strengthened the binding spell and eyed the chieftain. 'This binding will hold for an hour. It will not harm you further.'

She and Hakat moved to the door. Hakat peered out, making sure the way was clear. He nodded and stepped over the bound body there. Jelindel followed him.

'Good enemy,' Faruk said.

Jelindel looked back.

'Meet again.'

'Perhaps.'

'Kill you.'

'Perhaps.' She turned to go.

'Ask dragons.'

She stopped. 'Ask the dragons? Why?'

'Dragons taught first men. Gave them speech.' The laugh rumbled out again. 'This you should have known.'

Jelindel stared. 'The language of the first men came from the dragons?'

Even as she said it she knew it to be true. Some of the words for dragon meant 'shepherd' and 'father', even 'guardian'. How could she have been so stupid? The traces of the ancient relationship between dragons and men were still to be found in modern-day Q'zaran, like the impressions of bones sometimes found in ancient rocks, the fossils of the past.

Jelindel bowed to the Farvenu. 'Thank you,' she said.

'Hunt good,' Faruk bid her as she left.

Daretor stared in horror at the bloated figure lying on the straw pallet. 'Zimak?' he asked, incredulous.

Two podgy little eyes opened in the fat face, then blinked rapidly. The figure struggled into a sitting position, still staring.

'What have you done to my body?' Daretor demanded. He almost reeled with anger, but QeSu tugged his tunic.

'It's not his fault,' QeSu said, confused. Although her Q'zaran was poor, she was sure Daretor had claimed that Zimak was in *his* body.

'Nothing ever is,' Daretor said sourly. He shrugged off QeSu's hand.

'Daretor? Is it really you? Tell me it's you,' said the corpulent man on the floor.

'It's me, Zimak. And this is QeSu. We're getting you out of here.'

'Gah, they're going to eat me,' Zimak said in a high-pitched voice.

'Keep your voice down,' Daretor warned. 'We know. That's why we're here.' He handed Zimak a meat cleaver.

'I don't understand. How did you get to this paraworld?' Zimak asked, gripping the meat cleaver.

'Same way you did. On the *Sargasso*. Now, fewer questions and more listening. This is what we're going to do.' Daretor quickly outlined their plan.

Zimak blinked his sunken eyes. 'You call that a plan?'

'Fine, stay here and get eaten.'

'Hie, I never said I wasn't desperate enough to try it.'

Daretor and QeSu backed out of Zimak's cell, leaving it unlocked. Together the two returned the way they had come. They tossed the key back to the guardsman, then QeSu fainted. It was an ancient ploy but sometimes the old ones were the best.

QeSu was pretty and somehow, in the process of visiting Zimak and coming back, her tunic had miraculously opened part way. The swell of her breasts could be clearly seen as she lay on the floor. Three of the guardsmen jumped to their feet and crowded around her. They decided that she needed air and were of the opinion that her tunic should be opened further, especially as it was an emergency.

Daretor was behind them. It was a relatively simple matter to yank a sword from one of the guardsmen's scabbards and shove the guard forward so that he tripped over QeSu. In the same fluid movement, Daretor brought the pommel crashing down on the skull of the man straightening up. The third spun around, unsheathing his own sword, while the one sitting retrieved his pike. QeSu grabbed the nearest guardsman's ankles as he charged Daretor. He promptly fell flat on his face, and as he tried to gain his feet Daretor kicked him hard in the head. By this time, the tripped guard had also armed himself with a pike. QeSu rolled out of the way.

'Drop your weapons and I will spare you,' said Daretor. Their response was to charge him. The pikes were several feet longer than Daretor's sword but the tales of his swordsmanship were not myths. The guards, on the other hand, seldom had to do any real fighting, and merely used their weapons to intimidate prisoners. Daretor parried the two points and charged, smashing his elbow into the jaw of one guard, instead of running him through. The last guard turned and ran, rather than face Daretor alone.

Unfortunately for him his escape route led past Zimak's cell. Just as he must have felt he would live to fight another day, a somewhat bloated foot shot out of a cell door and tripped him. He went sprawling and came to a stop when his head encountered a wall.

Meanwhile, Daretor held the remaining guardsman at sword point, before marching him to the cell formerly occupied by Zimak and forcing him inside. Quickly they dragged in the other three and locked the door.

They retrieved the guards' swords and wheeled to leave when one man called to them, his voice piteous. 'Don't leave us here. When they learn you've escaped they'll eat us alive.'

Daretor glanced at QeSu. She nodded. 'He's right.'

Daretor did not know what to do. It was not in his nature to allow such a fate to befall anybody, especially men who were not his enemies. He compromised by placing the keys on the floor outside the cell, some twelve feet away. He then gave them the top half of the broken pike, noting that the guards wore leather belts.

'Tie your belts together. Using the pike as a hook you should be able to get the keys in a short time. I suggest you leave this place and don't come back.'

'It's more than they deserve,' Zimak grumbled, lumbering alongside his lithe companions.

'Charity has never become you,' Daretor allowed. 'But of more importance, I daresay the Farvenu will be more annoyed that their guards failed in their duties than their missed breakfast. It is they the daemons will be chasing, not us.'

It took less than ten minutes to exit the building and head for the fountain. There was no hue and cry behind them. So far so good. They could only hope that Jelindel's mission had gone as smoothly.

They reached the designated fountain without incident, but there was no sign of Jelindel and Hakat. QeSu was worried. They hung back in the shadows, watching the streets, nervous and apprehensive. Zimak wanted to know all that had happened since he had been abducted, but Daretor told him to keep quiet. There would be time enough later to fill him in, or there would be no time for anything.

'I do not like this delay,' whispered QeSu.

'Me neither,' Daretor admitted.

'Let us go to my room as planned.'

Daretor debated the suggestion with himself. What if the two groups passed each other on the way? Though that was less likely in this city where few thoroughfares had parallel streets. Still, there were alleyways and lanes – anything was possible.

He had just about decided to remain where they were when the decision was made for him. A siren blared high above and even in the dark they could see a swarm of Farvenu erupting from the pigeonhole windows.

'That's it,' said Daretor. 'Come on!'

They scrambled through the shadows, hugging the walls beneath overhanging eaves, moving as fast as possible. Whatever was watching from the air had not yet reached the area. QeSu assured Daretor that the other clans would join the chase, if not to aid the injured clan, then to be part of whatever sport was on offer. The Farvenu were a hunting species and they would not lose an opportunity to chase prey.

Daretor was tormented by possibilities of what might have happened. Had it not been for the keen night vision of the predators, he would have dashed from the shadows and run full pelt for QeSu's room. He had not yet seen Farvenu in action but Hakat had assured him that they were lethal.

It took some twenty minutes to reach the boarding house. They let themselves in by the back entrance. Jelindel and Hakat were waiting inside, but there was no time to even exchange greetings. The rear window exploded inwards as a screeching shape hurtled into the room, huge wings beating, talons raking. Jelindel flung a spell and the attacker rebounded from an invisible wall. Groggy, the Farvenu started to get up.

The house rocked as more of the creatures landed on the roof and began tearing away the shingles. Lath and plaster rained down.

'Hakat,' Jelindel shouted. 'The machine.'

Hakat didn't need to be told twice. He set it on the floor and worked the controls. A light came on and the machine hummed. 'It needs to work up its power,' he said.

'If there's a way to speed it up, do it,' Jelindel urged. 'Daretor, Zimak, back to back. QeSu, get behind us and stay with Hakat. No matter what, don't leave the circle. It's your only chance to escape.'

Jelindel faced the window while Daretor turned to the door. Zimak scanned the ceiling. They had barely taken up their positions when a ball of fury blasted in from each direction amidst a rain of broken glass and pulverised plaster.

Jelindel flung another impact spell even as Daretor wove a blur of lethal steel in front of him. The creature's reflexes were almost miraculously fast. Daretor parried frenzied blows and, through sheer luck, managed to chop off one of the creature's hands. She shrieked but did not break the fight; instead she pressed her attack even harder. Daretor slashed, jabbed, and ducked as talons raked the air where his head had been a second ago. Then one clawed fist ripped the sword from his fingers and he knew he was about to die.

Zimak spitted a falling Farvenu, then twisted laboriously to hack at the Farvenu attacking Daretor. Even as he threw his cleaver he knew he was too late. Then time slowed down. Daretor saw the scything talons arc towards him. He tried to jump back but stumbled on either QeSu or Hakat. Compared to the speed of the talons he might as well have been moving under water. He started to yell an instant before the talons made contact. He was staring at them and the part of his stomach they were on the verge of disembowelling. Then his scream died in his throat as the talons swept through him as if he were immaterial, a ghost.

The room dimmed and there was a brief period of numbness. All ceased to be. Daretor was cut off from not only his companions, but the rest of the universe. Abruptly the world of noise and colour crashed back into being.

They were standing on the side of a sandy hill. The sun was shining. It was early morning. And they were alive.

Chapter 8
THE DAMNED QUEEN

They were not on Q'zar, that was obvious.

Two blood-red suns hung in the sky and four moons sailed low on the horizon beneath a green and translucent sky.

'What went wrong?' Jelindel asked.

Hakat shrugged. 'There wasn't time. The settings are finicky.'

'Which explains why daemons appear throughout history but there's never any real proof,' Jelindel surmised. 'They zap somewhere by mistake, like taking a wrong turn . . .'

'At least I got us out of there,' Hakat pointed out.

Daretor clapped him on the back. 'And you'll have no complaint from me. The fact remains that we're lost.'

'Well, more like at sea without sails,' said Hakat, fiddling with the machine.

'How soon can we jump to Q'zar?' Zimak wanted to know.

'Not any time soon,' apologised Hakat. 'The machine must recharge. Makin' the jump uses a lot of power. We just gotta wait.'

'How long?' Daretor asked.

'Dunno,' said Hakat. 'Twenty-four hours, more than likely. Five people is a lot for one of these portable machines.'

Jelindel frowned. It was yet another snag in their plans, not to mention another day for the poison to spread further throughout their bodies. She shrugged off her unease. 'We need to find shelter and, if we can, food.'

'I don't think we should risk going near a town,' said Daretor. 'It won't hurt us to go without food for a day and a night.'

Zimak looked stricken. 'A day and a night? I'll starve!'

'You know what you need?' Daretor asked him. But they never found out what Daretor thought Zimak was lacking. There was a clopping, jingling tumult in the distance. It sounded all too familiar.

'Armed riders, a large squad,' said Daretor, drawing his conclusions from the sound alone. 'They're coming this way.'

'Nowhere to hide,' Zimak pointed out.

'Surely not everyone we meet wants to kill us?' said Jelindel, exasperation in her voice.

Presently a squad of perhaps a hundred armoured cavalry came into view over the crest of a nearby hill. The riders reined in their strange two-humped mounts and stared impassively at the group. What appeared to be the officers rode over. They wore loose linen turbans wrapped around their faces and flowing white cloaks.

As a professional soldier of fortune, Daretor assessed their strengths and weaknesses. The newcomers were skirmishers, fast, hit-and-run adversaries, not at their best in a prolonged battle. The Q'zarans separated reflexively, presenting dispersed targets.

One of the riders dismounted and strode towards Jelindel. Daretor moved to intercept him. With a wave of her hand Jelindel bade him stay where he was.

As the rider reached Jelindel he yanked free his scimitar. Before anyone could react he dropped to one knee and offered the sword to Jelindel.

He spoke formally in a language that was foreign to Jelindel. He then inclined his head. Unable to understand him, Jelindel looked to the others; they were similarly at a loss. The rituals of such meetings were often universal, so she gently took the sword from his grasp then handed it back to him hilt first. A soft sigh came from the mounted men. Jelindel judged that she had acted correctly.

She gestured that the man rise and he spoke to her in a melodious tongue that she once more could not understand. He seemed puzzled and tried another language. Hakat whispered to Jelindel that he knew the speech.

She waved him forward. 'What did he say?' she asked.

'My understanding isn't very good but it is one of the languages used in the great market place on Farvane.' He spoke haltingly to the officer for some moments. There was much waving of hands and bowing. Finally Hakat turned to Jelindel.

'He says they are the Kesparii. They are a desert people and this is the border of their realm, which lies to the west. The nearest settlement is a few hours from here and he wishes us to go there.'

'There is more, isn't there? Why did he single me out?' Jelindel asked.

'He says they were sent to get you. His people knew of your coming.'

Daretor frowned. 'How could anyone know that? We came here by sheer accident.'

Jelindel shook her head. 'There are no accidents,' she said. 'For them, or for us.'

'His name's Markul. He's an officer.'

'Tell Markul we will come.'

Markul listened to Hakat. Then he spoke rapidly, with more waving of hands, after which he issued curt orders to his men. Hakat translated. 'Some of his men will double up. He asks us to mount and ride with him, as walking would take too long and there are predators in these parts.'

The two-humped beasts with long necks and lantern-shaped heads kneeled. All mounted, except for QeSu who insisted in sitting behind Hakat. Markul shrugged. The command then split, the majority remaining to continue patrolling the region while the others, some fifty in all, made good time.

They rode through an area of sparse vegetation: scraggly bushes and thin spiky grass such as the suns permitted. The temperature did not seem high, but quite possibly it was winter. In any case deserts were created by lack of rain rather than excessive heat.

They rode for several hours. During that time what vegetation there was ceased entirely. They entered a region of sand dunes and baked-clay flats that glittered with vast white scarves of encrusted salt where lakes had once been.

Despite the temperate climate, the unending sunlight dried out the throats of the visitors, making them dizzy with fatigue. It had been some time since they had slept, and all had passed through danger and great stress. Jelindel knew they were at the end of their endurance. She had Hakat ask Markul for a rest and some water once she realised that the journey was not going to be over for some time to come.

Markul smote his forehead with two fingers and Jelindel smiled at the universal homeliness of this gesture. Water was given to the visitors and they rested for a short time. Markul assured them they were very close to their destination.

They continued. Coming over a sharp rise a sprawling city,

encircled by a stone wall, spread out below them. Pink-hued, the sandstone buildings were mostly square-shaped with narrow windows set at irregular intervals across each façade. Some buildings had minarets, whereas others were turreted. Pennants hung slack in the humid air. Even the towering palms clustered around a small oasis were picture still.

Militaristic, was Jelindel's first thought.

Immediately an alarm bell began clanging. Many figures swarmed the walls, but Markul had one of his men sound a signal on a horn. The distant bell began pealing slowly, signalling the end of the alert.

'They're well organised and alert,' Daretor said.

Jelindel nodded. 'Which means they have formidable enemies.'

'You trust them?'

'Yes, I do. I can't explain exactly why but I feel they mean us no harm. Further, I feel that we are supposed to be here. I'm not sure why.'

They rode down the slope towards the town. 'As long as they're not planning a long engagement,' Daretor said. 'They might consider it rude if we drop dead from poisoning in the middle of our visit.'

They reached the city wall and the iron-bound wooden gates, fully three feet thick, swung open. A cheer went up as they entered, and all eyes fell upon Jelindel.

'It's you they're interested in,' Zimak noted, spurring his horse close. 'I wonder why.'

'You don't think it's my natural charm?' Jelindel asked.

He opened his mouth to say something, but realised it was one of those questions that could only get him into trouble if he answered.

They were led into a quiet courtyard in the middle of which

a fountain carved of dazzling white marble bubbled. They dismounted, and stable hands led their mounts away. Markul escorted them into the cool stone interior of what appeared to be either a large mansion or a small palace. He spoke briefly to Hakat then disappeared.

'He's gone to get his chieftain. An' I think he said something about food.'

Zimak straightened. 'Food?'

'Unpalatable to Q'zarans,' Daretor quipped.

Markul reappeared, followed by a white-haired man, with an air of regal command. He bowed to Jelindel and she bowed back, which rather startled him. When the older man spoke his voice was a pleasant baritone that was oddly reassuring, even to those who could not understand a word he was saying.

Hakat explained that the chieftain was thanking them for coming, and inviting them to a meal after they refreshed themselves. He told them that in the desert all strangers, if they came in peace, were welcomed.

An hour later they were treated to a sumptuous meal that included more roasted meats than they could remember seeing in any one place: lamb, pork, fish, chicken, and duck, all done to perfection, with a scatter of dried fruits, including figs and apricots. From experience, Jelindel knew that such cooking would have taken some time to prepare – another indication that they had been expected.

As the meal progressed, the visitors relaxed. The good cheer of the desert folk and their deep respect for Jelindel assuaged their fears, but did not lessen Daretor's certainty that something was expected of them. Hakat whispered that he kept hearing the word 'prophecy', and it somehow seemed an integral part of their presence.

After the meal came sweet pastries, fruit and sherbet, then sweet wine. Dancers and tumblers entertained them. By the end of the evening everyone was drowsy with food and fatigue, and ready to sleep where they were. They were finally shown to their bed chambers and left alone.

As soon as she lay down, Jelindel began to doze. Daretor roused her with a touch. 'You seem to know what's going on,' he said. 'Can you not tell me?'

She placed a hand against his cheek. 'They have something that needs doing. I don't know what it is, but I do know that I am appointed by prophecy to the task.'

'Which prophecy?'

Jelindel shrugged and yawned. 'Who knows? By the universe perhaps. By White Quell. I don't know, and I can barely keep my eyes open. We can talk more in the morning . . .'

She drifted off to sleep, leaving Daretor disgruntled and puzzled. Despite his weariness he lay awake, staring at the shadows on the ceiling. Just before he closed his eyes he thought he saw shapes and images in the shadows, dark things that worried him. He dismissed them as the imaginings of a tired mind.

Next morning they woke early. There was a charged feeling in the air, a sense of expectancy. Breakfast was brought to their rooms. Courtiers appeared and led them to steam rooms built of marble and containing great baths of scented warm water. Jelindel and Daretor could have spent the whole day there, bathing and playing. But too soon the courtiers returned, bearing clean clothes resembling those of the desert soldiers. At the sight of the clothes Daretor felt a heaviness descend on him. Why dress them to fight?

The chieftain and Markul met them on a large sunny balcony. From here they could see the town. Sculpted from a white rock that reflected the sun, it sat on the edge of a huge basin that stretched to the horizon. Markul spoke. Hakat translated. The town had once been a port and the basin a vast inland sea. Long ago a war between sky gods destroyed the sea and dried out the land, leaving only desert and rock.

With Hakat's aid, the chieftain explained the prophecy.

'It was foretold,' he said, 'that a great mage would come from another paraworld. She would bring with her four companions.'

'Gah,' Zimak spat, 'we've been dragged to this godforsaken place to fulfil some god's whimsical prophecy.'

Sensing venom in Zimak's words, the chieftain glowered. Hakat prompted him to continue. 'The exact time and place of her coming was also known. That is why Markul and his men were waiting for you. Indeed, we have been waiting for you for two thousand years, and it is the great fortune of all those alive that you came at this time.'

He paused and slowly gestured to the great desert basin. 'It never rains in the desert, nor does anything grow there. It is a wasteland.' He turned to face them. 'In the basin there is a low hill of shingle. It is unremarkable to look upon yet inside there is a tomb, if such it can be called. She who lies there is dead yet not dead. Her name is Ortha. She was queen of this city when water lapped its piers and the sails of ships flew on the horizon. She ruled when the sky gods fought, and when the waters were sucked into the heavens and the winter clouds came no more. It is for her you have come. It is for her that you are here.'

Jelindel nodded. 'I am to awaken her,' she said.

Daretor stared from Jelindel to the chieftain. He wanted to add to Zimak's scepticism and to stop this nonsense, but he held back. They were stuck in this place until Hakat's machine recharged. Damn all magic to Black Quell's beard! he thought.

'If I understand this,' said the chieftain through Hakat, 'you are not solely here for our benefit. You have troubles of your own and a perilous journey ahead. Perhaps the queen, once awakened, may counsel you on what lies ahead.'

'Perhaps,' agreed Jelindel. 'When do we start?'

'Jelli,' warned Daretor.

She turned to Daretor and took his hands. 'It's all right, darling,' she said. 'Trust me.'

'Hie, why do I find that such a hard task?' Zimak said. No one was listening to him, and Hakat did not translate his words.

The chieftain gave a signal. Trumpets blared and Markul led Jelindel and the others to the courtyard. There, giant camel-like creatures awaited them. At Markul's urging they mounted and set off for the main gate. The road was lined by cheering people. The crowds gazed with bright, eager faces and eyes full of hope. Daretor felt the burden on them grow. What were these people to him and the others? Strangers. No more or less. They had their problems, but then so did his own group. This was madness. They had their own tasks to perform, their own lives to consider: even now the poison flowed in their veins and took its final course. Each minute they tarried shortened their chances of success in their quest, as well as their lives.

They rode out of the town under a sun so bright that the land shimmered and seemed to be made of shifting images rather than rock and sand. The sand was so dry that puffs of fine dust were thrown up by every footfall.

Daretor's misgivings grew, even without solid evidence or signs of threat. Like Jelindel, he found that he trusted Markul and his people. Unlike her, however, he did not share their faith in the ancient prophecy. It did not make sense to him, perhaps because he was a simple fighting man, and perhaps because he was tired and wished the adventure over. Hearing prophecies was one thing; being part of them was quite another. He simply wanted to go home.

They journeyed for several hours. How the locals found their way amongst the low wind-blown dunes or recognised one part of the desert from another, Daretor could not tell. To him the landscape was featureless, and as desolate as grief.

Perhaps sensing the unease of their riders, the camel creatures fretted and reared their long necks in an effort to dislodge the bits between their jaws. The drivers merely whipped their flanks with thin bamboo strips, and gave sharp, whistled commands.

They rested during the hottest part of the day. The Kesparii swiftly erected awnings of gaily coloured silk. Everyone, except those on watch, stretched out and drank a beverage made from cactus sap called *huppa,* and slept. The desert folk were experts at brief rests. Markul said they could even sleep for short periods whilst in the saddle. This gave them the ability to travel far and fast, and strike where they wished. Surrounded as they were by fierce enemies, all competing for the scarce resources of the land, such tactics were highly effective.

Sipping his *huppa* and gazing at the desert, Markul's weather-beaten face revealed little. When he spoke, his voice held a wistfulness that Daretor could not reconcile with the stern vis-age, or the harsh land that had shaped it.

'We dream of the ocean,' Markul said via Hakat. 'No one in this landlocked country, nor even his great-great-great-grand parents, has seen the great oceans that lie far to the south. Yet in our dreams we hear the waves on the shore and smell the salty spume. My son tells me that only a few days ago he woke from a vision to the sound of seagulls. I had to ask one of the elders what creature this was. He said it was a bird that lived on the shore and whose raucous cry was part of the song of the sea.' He looked at his companions. 'Do you think our dreams a strange thing?'

Jelindel shook her head. 'Not strange,' she said. 'A little sad, like the memory of someone we have lost. Yet I would hazard a guess that these dreams have increased of late.'

Markul looked at her sharply. 'How could you know that?'

'It fits the prophecy,' she said. 'And our coming here.'

'Are we to make an ocean here then?' Daretor asked. Markul shrugged and did not answer. Perhaps the subject was too hurtful for him. Daretor did not ask again; instead, he thought about the question he had asked. It seemed to him that in order to find the dragonsight they were destined to heal the ills of others, even as they remained unable to heal their own. He did not understand it, but he felt that the dragonsight had a hand in this. Maybe there was an even larger prophecy that they were a part of, one so vast and inexplicable that they could neither understand it, nor predict the outcome.

After the break, which refreshed the visitors far more than they would have thought possible, the squad moved on. The second part of the journey lasted some four hours. By the end Jelindel and the others were not only tired, but saddle sore. The ungainly rhythm of the camel creatures worked muscles in their thighs and backside that they did not realise they had, and set them blazing with pain.

'Gah, I'm aching all over,' Zimak complained, dismounting.

Daretor jumped down from his camel as lithely as he could. 'By all the gods it feels good to be this size,' he said. At Jelindel's slanting eyebrow, he added, 'Just making an observation.'

A hundred yards away stood the entrance to a dry gulch. They rested briefly, ate and drank, then Markul led Jelindel, her companions, and a select group of Kesparii into the gulch.

The walls were of dark rock, unlike most of the exposed and weathered rocks they had seen in the desert. The rift in the land twisted and turned like a crazy serpent, and wound its way for a mile or more before opening out into a vast basin.

In the middle of what appeared to be a dry lake bed stood a small hill composed of stones and bleached bones. Daretor did not like the look of the latter. He wondered if other would-be warriors had been coaxed into trying to fulfil the age-old dream.

Markul pointed at the hill. 'Queen Ortha sleeps within. "Free her and that which she has drained from this land will be set right",' he quoted through Hakat.

Jelindel took a deep breath. 'I guess that's my cue.' She kissed Daretor and looked at the others. Then she encouraged her mount toward the hill. Before it could take five lumbering steps, Markul whistled shrilly. The animal stopped abruptly. Hakat interpreted Markul. 'The prophecy says the queen is awakened by the five.'

Daretor shrugged. He had been outfitted with a sword and chain mail, as had Zimak and Hakat. QeSu was equipped with a short stabbing spear.

To the others Jelindel said, 'I was hoping you weren't involved. I can't speak for you, but I'm willing to do this. Somehow I think it will benefit our cause.'

Daretor urged his mount forward with his heels, not daring to imitate the Kesparii whistling command.

'The sooner we get this done and are gone the better,' said Zimak. Hakat and QeSu, though more uncertain, agreed. Together they set off for the hill. Markul bade them farewell and wished them luck.

They crossed the burning sands to the foot of the hill. It was little more than a high mound, not unlike the burial cairns found in parts of Q'zar. There was no sign of an entrance.

'Let's take a look,' Jelindel suggested. They skirted the base of the hill. Barely a third of the way around, Zimak called out.

'What's that?' He pointed.

Halfway up the side of the mound was a dark cavity. A crude set of steps carved in the side of the slate hill led up to it. With a sense of gloom, Daretor led the way. Pausing at the entrance, he looked at the others.

'Stay close,' he said simply.

'Gah, Daretor, afraid of the dark?' said Zimak, swatting at an annoying insect.

'After you,' Daretor replied, stepping aside.

'I guess I *am* the biggest,' Zimak said. He brushed past Daretor and stepped forward. Immediately, he realised that he was not inside a cavern. Indeed, he was not even underground. Above burned the same Kesparii sky, only it was painted a greener hue. Also time seemed to move at a different pace – it was earlier in the day and the moons burned brighter. He gaped at the water lapping his feet. 'Hie, Daretor, it's not dark in here at all,' he called, and then realised that the others had failed to appear behind him. 'Daretor? Jelindel?' Fear crept into his voice.

The foursome appeared behind him, seeming to step out of thin air.

'About time,' Zimak said, forcing a grin. 'Take a look at this place, will you? All we have to do is cut a channel through the walls and the ocean can flood back out where it belongs. All that queen and dummart prophecy stuff was nothing but horse dung.'

'Keep your voice down,' Jelindel warned. 'Sound travels far over water.'

They stood on the pinnacle of an island. In all directions, as far as the eye could see, moved a dark and restless ocean. Other islands broke the surface here and there, the shorelines marked by the white surf. Above their heads seagulls wheeled and cried, and fought each other for morsels.

'We have stepped back in time,' said Jelindel in wonder.

Zimak pointed. 'There's a light.' They craned their heads and stared. A pearly glow rose behind a sharp ridge several hundred yards away.

'I think we have to go there,' Jelindel said, pursing her lips.

The way was not easy. The seabed was covered in razor-sharp rocks and jagged stones that could slice open a calf muscle or amputate toes through hard leather soles. As they waded through the shallows, Jelindel suspected that this was part of a test.

She exhorted everyone to hurry. QeSu slipped and caught herself by thrusting out her hand. A sharp stone sliced deep into the palm. She cried out and Hakat rushed to her side. Tears stood in QeSu's eyes, but she did not complain. Jelindel took her hand and cast a spell. The wound closed over, though it remained tender.

It took them an hour to traverse the relatively small distance. When they finally reached the backlit ridge they gazed down into a natural bowl in the mountain side. The base was as smooth as glass and a milky opalescence filled the air. When they made their way into the bowl, the light gave the impression that they were deep beneath the ocean.

In the centre of the bowl was a raised dais with a stone sarcophagus, covered in strange hieroglyphs. Jelindel cautioned the others to remain behind her. Warily, she approached the coffin. Inside lay a naked woman whose bearing was regal and peaceful. Her dark hair was long and her milky white skin contrasted sharply with her full red lips. The others peered over Jelindel's shoulder. Zimak seemed particularly spellbound.

Then several things happened at once.

QeSu cried out and pointed, turning swiftly about. In each of the four cardinal points of the compass a vista impressed itself on the air, as if projected onto the pearly glow. Each vista showed a vast battlefield boiling with combatants of every shape and size and kind imaginable. Terrible engines of war were being dragged and pushed through the endless ranks, and brought to bear upon the enemy. In the vista opposite the same engines could be seen from the opponents' point of view. Similar vistas unfolded on the other two screens. It was as if two great battles were being fought and they could see each from both sides of the front line.

Before anyone could comment on the bizarre display, a warrior representing each of the armies appeared at the four cardinal points. Within seconds of gaining their new bearings, the warriors yelled ferociously and charged. At the same instant Jelindel's hand flew to her mouth. A jagged gash opened on the belly of the naked queen, as if a sword stroke had sliced her. Queen Ortha screamed, but did not wake. Blood spurted from the wound. Without a doubt it was mortal and she would quickly die if not helped.

'Stop them!' Jelindel said, leaning into the sarcophagus.

The others grasped their weapons and rushed forward to meet the charging figures. Even QeSu, whose hand was still sore, joined in the fray. Daretor met his foe head on and dispatched him with a single stroke. Zimak similarly wasted little time, although he was fighting somewhat clumsier due to his excess weight. Hakat had more trouble but he also managed to deal with his opponent. QeSu flung her spear with all her might and skewered her attacker through the chest. She rushed forward and extracted it just as another figure charged her.

Three more warriors appeared and attacked Zimak, Daretor and Hakat.

Meanwhile, Jelindel used her magic to heal the deep gouge

in the queen's stomach. No sooner had she repaired the damage than another wound appeared in the queen's chest, inches from her heart. No blade was visible, but the queen flinched and cried out in pain. Before Jelindel could even start healing the wound, two more appeared in the woman's chest, one stabbing right through her left breast.

Jelindel muttered spell after spell and drew her hands over the wounds, sealing them, and reattaching the flesh by magical means. She wiped away the blood with the hem of her robe. All the while she felt her own life ebbing, as she transferred more and more of herself to heal the patient.

The others were battling a bizarre variety of warriors. As soon as one died another appeared, just as the deadly wounds in the body of the queen did not stop. Jelindel realised that each time one of her companions killed an attacker, the queen experienced the warrior's death.

The conflict seemed endless, for time was not marked by the passage of any sun.

Zimak slashed down, felling his fifteenth victim. He realised that he had fought his way across the arena and was now facing his disoriented opponents the moment they appeared through their paraplane portal. He called out to the others and they followed his lead.

It was a long and wearying battle that often seemed to have no end; it instilled in each a weary despair. Hakat and QeSu had the hardest time, but Zimak's ruse saved them. As time wore on, the gaps between the attackers lengthened, as if the defenders were somehow winning and getting time on their side. Oddly enough, the exhaustion was not really physical; if it had been they would have died earlier at the hands of a fresh attacker. It was their minds and souls that seemed to slow and stumble, and fill with hopelessness. They continued to fight on and win, though oftentimes by chance and good luck rather than skill. It was as if the fighting was a ritual, or ceremony. Although their new opponents were felled the instant they entered the arena, the defenders grew more weary as the battle lengthened.

Jelindel also was tiring in the most crucial sense: her magic was drying up. She was now drained at the deepest level, and her power was becoming less effective. She felt the desert growing in her soul, a vast gritty ocean of aching intensity.

They knew that this punishing pace could not last. Despite the small respites that seemed to expand between attacks, there was no end in sight, nor could any of them think how to bring the nightmare to a close.

Daretor felt as if his limbs were made of lead. They still functioned normally; they still moved with deadly speed and accuracy, yet he felt empty, a husk.

'I'm exhausted,' he croaked, trying to raise his voice above the clash of arms. The others echoed his feelings, in words or grunts.

'I don't know how to stop it,' Jelindel said, a hysterical edge in her voice. If they stopped killing the attackers, the queen would suffer no more wounds. In turn they would be swamped and killed. Twice she had sought the entrance to this place, but it had been sealed. The wall of the amphitheatre was seamless.

'Yes, you do,' said Daretor. 'The prophecy.'

'I'm telling you, *I don't know.*'

Daretor stepped back from the shimmering portal as another warrior entered its field. The stones beneath his feet were slick with blood, and the bodies of the fallen had all but corralled him. He readied his sword for yet another blow.

Finally Jelindel had no more power. It was gone and would take hours to recharge. She slumped against the platform, gazing at the queen whose body was rapidly becoming insubstantial. At that moment the defenders were reeling from more attackers.

Hakat staggered back, suffering a shoulder wound. QeSu flung her spear and killed the attacker as he was about to slay her lover. There was no shortage of weapons lying about. She quickly hefted a short sword.

'Gah!' Zimak cried, stumbling over a corpse. He stayed down, clutching a dirk and staring at the portal as a man-shaped darkness gathered within.

The queen was the consistency of mist. Jelindel reached out and her hand passed through the monarch. An idea came to her. She pushed herself onto the sarcophagus and lay down in the space occupied by the dissipating woman.

'Jelli, no!' Daretor called out.

It was too late. Jelindel merged with the fading monarch. As she did so, the milky light blinked out. The vistas were next. The attackers disappeared and the queen sat up, her long hair hiding her nakedness.

Queen Ortha looked about, dazed. When she saw the defenders she smiled.

'You have done well,' she said. 'Many others have failed over the eons.'

Daretor walked to the dais. 'Where is Jelindel, the woman that saved you?' he demanded. He barely had the energy for the raging anger he felt.

The queen climbed slowly out of the sarcophagus and the others gathered about her. Still smiling she reached out and touched each in the middle of the forehead. Daretor was last. When her fingers came into contact with his skin he felt a profound sense of wellbeing and safety. The underworld vanished and he stood once again at the base of the hill in the lakebed.

Only it was no longer dry. An inch of water sloshed about Daretor's feet. Markul stood some yards away, staring first at Daretor then at the water. He was weeping for joy. His mouth gaped and he pointed as though entranced.

Queen Ortha stood still. She was literally seeping into the ground. Fluid ran from her fingers in impossible torrents, as though a huge dam had burst from within. All around the desert, sand darkened with moisture as Queen Ortha's lifeforce spread like a stain.

'Another curse,' exclaimed Zimak, drawing his sword.

Markul said something in his tongue.

'No, no, it has merely begun,' explained Hakat.

'What's begun? Who's doing that to her? Can it be done to us?'

'This is what I have always been,' said the queen dreamily. 'I was ripped out of the land many, many years ago and trapped in human form, cut off from the soil that is my home by the accursed sarcophagus.'

Daretor caught sight of Jelindel climbing down from the cave entrance. He rushed up and helped her down the path. The queen continued her rapid transformation. A weary Jelindel stood before her.

'When I merged with Her Royal Highness, I learned the truth,' panted Jelindel. 'The spirit of the land has great power. Ancient beings, more than mortals but less than gods, tore the queen from the soil and used her energies to open portals to the four worlds. That's where the armies came from.'

'They were powerful children. We were their pawns and this was their game,' added the queen. Her voice was increasingly thick and slurred. 'When they tired of their game, they abandoned it and moved on.'

'Moved on?' gasped Zimak. 'You mean they're still out there?'

'They no longer concern themselves with the likes of us,' the queen told them. 'They are in a time and place beyond reckoning. The sarcophagus, the portals, the armies, it was all like a sandcastle left by children on a beach. And I was as a beetle trapped within the walls of the sandcastle. Now the walls have been breached . . . I am free to become . . . myself . . . again. I thank you . . .'

The desert floor was sodden for as far as the eye could see. Queen Ortha's face melted into the ground. As it did so, the ground rumbled, shaking the mortals standing there. Where she had been there now stood a column of water. Even as they watched, it collapsed and merged with the sand.

'By the odd gods, I hate magic,' grumbled Daretor.

'How could you hate something so beautiful?' asked Jelindel, who managed to dredge up the energy to be annoyed.

'Any problem that cannot be solved with a sword is not to my taste,' he said tersely.

'When you marry your sword don't bother sending me a wedding invitation,' muttered Jelindel, climbing wearily between the humps of a camel.

The return journey was fast. Dark and heavily burdened clouds appeared overhead. A downpour began and did not abate. Every ancient waterway, etched out of the desert during the centuries of desiccation, ran with water. Flash floods filled the gulches and canyons.

Toward the end of the journey the only thing that prevented the riders from drowning were the gently sloping basin sides, which had once been the 'shallows' of the sea. As they galloped through the sucking sand, and made for the town that was now within sight, there came a vast roaring noise. None dared look back lest the smallest delay hastened their doom.

The town gates opened and a great cheer went up from the citizens. The chieftain walked out to greet them, his fine shoes splattered with sand and his robes bedraggled by the rain. He did not seem to care.

'The ocean is coming back, as foretold,' he announced. People danced in the rain, like children.

Everyone watched from the ramparts as the tsunami exhausted itself against the lower shoreline. None cared that structures built outside the city walls were reduced to rubble, or taken out to sea. Each new demolition dazzled the crowd.

Jelindel, Daretor and the others stayed as guests of the chieftain for three days. Though their mission was urgent, they felt profoundly exhausted. More than that, they had a deep desire to witness the results of their strange battle in the desert.

A day after the battle, the great basin was beneath a sheet of water as far as the eye could see, though it had not yet risen to its full depth. Small waves broke upon the shore several hundred yards below the city wall. Eager townsfolk continued rebuilding the ancient piers and docks. Although fallen into disrepair, the docklands were quickly readied for this auspicious moment. A fleet of boats was prepared for launching, and ancient tales of great fishing expeditions were retold to eager children.

Thicker garments replaced the thin linen robes that had been the fashion for centuries. Little work went on in the city. From dawn till dark most of the folk gathered on the town ramparts, or on what they were calling, not without a sense of awe, the shore. Festivities and celebrations were held day and night. Jelindel and her companions were feted as saviours. Musicians crowded the five, reciting poetry and singing songs in their honour.

As the third night approached, Jelindel announced their departure. The chieftain thanked them profusely for the miracle they had wrought. Markul, with a kind of warrior's shyness, presented Jelindel with a necklace on which hung a solitary pearl.

'This was made,' Hakat translated, 'on this very shoreline two thousand years ago. It has been in Markul's family ever since.'

'I cannot accept it,' Jelindel said. The flawless pearl was beautiful and had to be worth a king's ransom.

Markul closed her hand around the relic. 'Soon we will have others, thanks to you. May this become an heirloom for your family as it has been in mine.'

Jelindel donned the necklace and everyone cheered.

Hakat set up the machine and turned it on. It hummed and lit up. The Kesparii looked in amazement. Machines were unknown in their world.

'It's a kind of magic,' Jelindel explained.

'I think the contraption's ready,' Hakat said when a row of lights began flicking.

The Kesparii kept a respectful distance from the otherworld machine. A silence descended as a shimmering light encompassed the travellers.

Jelindel waved and then they were gone, but they were not forgotten. A thousand years later the story of the witch woman and her companions who, with their own hands, remade the ocean was still being told. Even Zimak's girth became a thing of impossible myth.

◈

They materialised close to a hamlet. The Q'zaran villagers welcomed the group as they would any travellers – with suspicion. This suited them. A farmer allowed them to use his barn for the night, and Jelindel paid in kind by tending the man's sickly cow.

The next morning, as they prepared to set out for D'loom, the sky was darkened by the huge form of S'cressling. She settled on a nearby knoll, much to the astonishment of the villagers. Hakat and QeSu stood gaping.

Jelindel and Daretor rushed forward to greet Osric. They pulled up short when they saw he had one arm in a sling. Zimak waddled after them, puffing. The force-feeding given him by the Farvenu had been too successful.

'I thought you were dead,' Jelindel called.

'And I you,' Osric shouted back.

'But how did you escape Fa'red back in D'loom?' Jelindel asked.

'Fa'red knocked you two out. I tried to fight and got this for my trouble.' He indicated his broken arm. 'After that, you were bound and taken away. As for me, I was imprisoned for several days then sold into slavery. When my new owners sought to transport me across the Marisa River they got a rather nasty shock. S'cressling has that effect on people. After that, they were only too happy to free me and all the other slaves. I came back to D'loom as quickly as I could but you were nowhere to be found. S'cressling circled the area for days. It was as if you had disappeared off the face of Q'zar.'

'We had,' Jelindel said sombrely.

'Then last night S'cressling picked up your scent from the Sacred One's blood mark and we came here as fast as we could. We are only a few hours south of D'loom. Tell me, where have you been?' His mouth gaped when he saw Zimak. 'And you, Zimak, what happened to you in Yuledan?'

Zimak told them how he had been attacked by the deadmoon warriors and woke up on the *Sargasso*. Daretor brought the story up to date and introduced Osric to Hakat and QeSu. They both regarded Osric and S'cressling with apprehension.

'Now what?' Osric asked, ignoring Hakat and QeSu's stares. 'Are we any nearer reaching our goal?'

'With luck,' said Jelindel. 'Let's ask S'cressling.'

Osric frowned. 'S'cressling?'

'I'll explain on the way,' Jelindel said. They climbed the knoll and stood before the dragon. S'cressling, in turn, observed them with great unblinking eyes that seemed immeasurably old.

'S'cressling,' Jelindel said, 'do you know the language of the first men of Q'zar?'

The mind speech of the dragon was like the sound of boulders moving deep in the earth, or like far-off thunder. It was hard to understand but not impossible. When necessary, Osric translated verbally.

'I know it,' replied the dragon, in their minds. 'The dragons gave mankind the gift of speech and taught them language. Before that they had only the speech of wild animals.'

Osric's brow knitted in confusion. It appeared that the dragons were universal; their magic and knowledge spanning the paraworlds.

'What is Q'zar?' Jelindel asked.

'Not what, but who,' the mind speech rumbled.

'Who was Q'zar?'

'The first dragon born of the Original Egg. All dragons are descended from Q'zar.'

The Q'zarans lapsed into silence. This was a history so ancient that not even myths and fairy tales hinted at the truth anymore.

'Do you know what the word Hadirr means?' Jelindel asked the dragon.

S'cressling stared down her long snout. It was impossible to read an expression in that majestic face. Perhaps she smiled. 'Hadirr means "abode of the clouds" in the Old Speech,' she told the humans.

Osric scratched his head. 'She knew all the time,' he said. 'Why didn't you tell us before?'

'You did not ask,' said the dragon. There was a trace of mockery in her tone, good-natured though it might have been. 'Would you spoil the games of children?'

To that they had no answer.

'I should have known,' Osric said. 'We say, "Out of the minds of dragons". And I call myself a dragonrider. I should be flayed alive.'

Daretor and Zimak were still frowning. 'That still doesn't solve our problem,' Daretor pointed out. 'Where on Q'zar is the "abode of the clouds"?'

Jelindel stared at him in surprise. 'Come on, Daretor. Think about it.' Exasperated, she said, 'Think "valley".'

'The Valley of Clouds is in Dremari,' he said slowly. 'The Stone People's realm is somewhere beneath Fa'red's keep. No doubt he thought that a rich joke at our expense.'

'Gah, he won't be laughing when I get my hands on him,' Zimak cursed. 'Look what he's done to me.' He grabbed a hold of his flabby stomach.

'You were well on the way to obesity without Fa'red's help,' Daretor seethed.

'Right you two,' Jelindel said pointedly. She noticed that Hakat and QeSu looked confused. 'S'cressling, if you would be so kind?' she said.

The dragon rested on her haunches to enable them to climb her flanks. When the group was safely secure in their harnesses, S'cressling launched into the air and began the journey back to Dremari, beyond the Valley of Clouds.

Chapter 9
ABOVE AND BELOW GROUND

They landed in the same spot as before, a mist-enshrouded mountain top invisible to prying eyes and inaccessible to any but the most determined. Osric, Hakat and QeSu remained with S'cressling. Even though Jelindel healed Osric's broken arm, it remained weak and there was little he could do in a fight. Zimak did not get the same consideration. Climbing up and down steep mountain sides and quite possibly running from an assortment of enemies seemed the perfect recipe for losing weight, and strengthening a fat, force-fed body.

'Gah, Jelindel. This isn't fair,' he wailed, not for the first time. 'I suffered as well. Do you think I enjoyed eating that food? They stuck a tube into me and poured it in. I couldn't even taste it!'

'As allegory, Zimak, that takes a lot of beating,' said Jelindel, putting a hand to her head.

'What's an allegory?'

'Never mind,' she said, patting his bulging stomach. 'Just don't name it after me.'

'Am I being insulted?'

'Definitely. Meantime a little exercise and you'll be fine.' She stared at him and frowned. 'Actually, quite a lot of exercise. There's nothing magical about building muscles. I daresay the body you stole from Daretor was made by blood, sweat and tears.'

Zimak appealed to Daretor. 'It's your body. How can you sit there smirking?'

'*You* need to sweat it off,' Daretor said. 'You will go and eat like a pig.'

'It wasn't my fault. They *made* me eat!'

'Nobody can make you eat,' Daretor said, pretending he did not know the truth. 'Either way, it's time you went on a diet. This little adventure will be good for you.'

'There's nothing "little" about any adventure with you two,' Zimak growled. Having established that neither Jelindel nor Daretor would indulge him, he distanced himself from both.

Later that evening they came to the main gate of Dremari. This time, instead of presenting papers that they no longer had, Jelindel cast a cloaking spell. When a gap in the foot traffic opened up they joined the flow of pedestrians, carts and wagons, careful to avoid contact with anyone else.

'I don't see why you can't do this everywhere we go,' Zimak grumbled. 'It's a lot easier than risking being seen.'

Jelindel closed her eyes momentarily. 'For the hundredth time, Zimak. Magic use leaves an aura. A signature visible to other sorcerers and adepts, showing that it's being used and by whom.'

'Then why use it?' Zimak said.

Jelindel said to Daretor, 'I'd ask you to hit him if I thought it would knock sense into him.'

Daretor smirked. 'I'm loath to knock my own body about. But White Quell it's tempting at times. Perhaps it's not all Zimak's fault. They say those who eat too much think less.'

Dremari was crowded. The city was in the middle of the Solstice Festival and the streets were clogged with locals and visitors. There were merchants, street vendors and entertainers of every kind. Circus acts, fire-breathers, jugglers, dancers, musicians, food sellers, trinket vendors, herbalists, refreshment stands, and outdoor cafes jostled among processions and horse-drawn floats. Moving through the city was difficult and Jelindel doubted they would find accommodation.

Yet the packed crowds also helped hide them, and what they were about.

After numerous enquiries they found an innkeeper who, in exchange for two gold oriels, allowed them to sleep in the upper section of his stable. The fact that it was filthy and stank of horse dung made no difference to the price he charged.

'If you want to haggle,' said the man, 'go some place else. There's plenty will think the stable a fine place to rest their heads this night.'

Jelindel paid, but they did not retire immediately. They found a booth in the corner of the taproom, not far from the warmth of a welcoming fire, and ordered drinks. They also managed to secure what food the scullery maid was willing to serve at this late hour. It was little enough, but after fighting the crowds for several hours they were ravenous.

They ate, drank and relaxed like all the others around them, then in furtive whispers they discussed plans.

'There has to be some path or portal down to the realm of the Stone People,' Daretor insisted.

'Obviously, but is the path open to mere mortals?' Zimak

asked, looking pointedly at Jelindel. 'Besides, Fa'red isn't going to hang a sign on a door somewhere, that says, "This way to Stone People".'

'White Quell forbid anything should be easy,' Jelindel murmured. 'Nor do we know how far their domain is beneath Dremari. It might be a hundred yards or ten miles. I can work a portal charm, like those which lead to paraworlds, but it would have to carry me to the right place. I would hate to end up inside a block of granite.'

'Then there's only one thing to do,' Daretor said.

Jelindel nodded. 'We must pay Fa'red a visit.'

Zimak snorted. 'Gah, that's a great plan. You don't seriously believe for one minute that he's going to tell you anything useful? You could chop him up into tiny pieces and torture them individually, yet he still wouldn't admit anything. Look what happened the last time you trusted him.'

Jelindel cocked a weary eyebrow. 'Well, what do you suggest?'

Zimak was about to say he had no idea when a slow wide grin broke across his bulbous cheeks. 'I'm glad you asked,' he said.

'Look, I'm the brains behind this. So I shouldn't have to actually *do* anything,' Zimak said in a hurt tone. 'That's what generals have captains for.'

Jelindel glared at him icily.

'No, you can forget it,' he insisted.

Her eyes bored into his.

'Oh, fine then,' he snapped. 'Have it your way. You always do.'

'You're a sweetheart,' said Jelindel.

'I'm an idiot.'

'Finally, a confession,' said Daretor.

Jelindel became sombre. 'This is still very dangerous. So take it seriously.'

'My middle name,' Zimak said gloomily.

'Zimak Danger Chubby,' Daretor said. 'If it weren't my body, I would propose a toast to your ill health.'

'But it *is* your body,' Zimak said. 'You'd do well to remember that. I might just let it go further, so much so that not even your fanaticism will get it back into shape.'

'Why you little snake rat –'

Jelindel stepped deftly between them. 'If you want to fight, do it against an enemy.'

Daretor dropped his clenched hands. 'Then find a way to switch our bodies so I need no longer look at him,' he seethed.

'One thing at a time, Daretor,' she said. 'We're going to need Osric's help. If I can trust you two alone for five minutes, I'll fetch him.'

Daretor thumped Zimak on the shoulder. 'Send Lord Chubby here. He needs the exercise.'

'I could squash you like a fly,' Zimak threatened.

Jelindel left them to their bickering, hoping that neither would mangle each other's body. Not permanently, at any rate.

They left the stable after dark. This was more by habit than necessity since the streets were brightly lit for the benefit of the festival revellers and were, in any case, packed. The sheer numbers afforded better camouflage than any amount of darkness could have provided.

They moved slowly, going with the ebb and flow of the crowd. They stopped now and then to sample wares on stalls, to watch street performers, or listen to diatribes by incensed citizens that stood on soap boxes at street corners, all with missions to save the world.

Despite the gravity of the situation and the days inexorably passing, they enjoyed the festive spirit that gripped the streets. Jelindel walked hand in hand with Daretor, and Zimak kept a moody silence.

In this way they crossed several city blocks and came close to the castle, which was, uncharacteristically, open to the public. This was a rare event, only occurring three times a year. Along with dozens of sightseers they strolled into the castle grounds where more tents and side shows had been set up, along with a long tent displaying a visual history of Dremari and its illustrious royal family. It was, most knew, pure fabrication. But it was also standard procedure for new would-be dynasties replacing overthrown houses.

As they wandered amongst the tents and hawkers, Jelindel suddenly nudged Zimak, indicating a portcullis with her eyes. In a low whisper she said, 'The inner courtyard lies through there.'

Zimak scowled. 'And how am I to get to it? Fly? Why, there must be two dozen guards that I can count, and more inside maybe.'

'One day, Zimak, you will hopefully learn to look for the silver lining instead of perpetually seeking the rain,' Jelindel said.

'I had a rotten childhood. *You* spent little enough time in the D'loom marketplace, and if it hadn't been for me you'd have rotted there.'

'Maybe,' said Jelindel. 'Although I'm sure our poor scribe friend, Bebia Ral'Vey, would have something to say about that. He did provide us with security and shelter, after all.'

'Tch,' Zimak scoffed. 'You call his table shelter? It was me who kept the bully boys away from you. And Daretor who led you to the mailshirt that released the magic in you.' He wagged a finger. 'You owe us, Jelindel.'

'Enough!' Daretor growled. 'Is there a way for Zimak to get in there?'

'Let's keep wandering. Some method may present itself.'

They continued their apparently aimless wanderings around the outer courtyard. As Zimak had pointed out, the portcullis, thick, heavy, and presently lowered, was well guarded. No entry could be hoped for there.

Jelindel looked up at the inner wall. It rose at least twenty-five feet and what embrasures it possessed were narrow. It was designed for shooting fire arrows and scrutinising the enemy, not wriggling through.

Half an hour later they were in a large brightly coloured tent in the shape of a tower. It was some eighteen feet tall and bedecked with pennants and ribbons. The three paid the huckster, who ushered them inside. Madame Mooska sat at a small table, ready to divine their futures.

The soothsayer smiled when she saw her customers. They were perfect. Just the sort of country bumpkins she liked. She waved them to chairs. A lamp of milky crystal sat on the table – the fabled Crystal of Hegiza'a, or so she claimed. Madame Mooska had no idea where Hegiza'a was or even if it existed, but it impressed people.

'Welcome, welcome,' she said huskily. 'I am Madame Mooska. Now, which one of you wants to go first?'

'I will,' said Jelindel gravely.

'Place your hands on the table so that the Crystal of Hegiza'a can pick up your vibrations.'

'Vibrations?' Zimak asked frowning.

Daretor nudged Zimak in the ribs and he lapsed into silence, looking bored.

'I am going to foretell your future, dear,' said Madame Mooska dramatically.

Jelindel shook her head. 'Actually, I came here to foretell yours.'

Madame Mooska looked at her, confused. Then she jumped in alarm. The Crystal of Hegiza'a was glowing. She stared at it. 'It's never done that before.' She looked up at Jelindel, suddenly suspicious. 'What do you mean you've come to tell my fortune?'

'You are going to meet a very powerful adept, who is going to put you to sleep,' Jelindel said. 'When you wake up you won't remember any of this.'

'Now just one moment –' Before Madame Mooska could remonstrate further, Jelindel waved her hand and the woman froze, her mouth open, the spittle still gleaming on her lower lip. Then she collapsed slowly and gracefully.

Jelindel stood up, businesslike. 'Right,' she said. 'Let's get to work.'

Zimak swallowed. 'Is it going to hurt?'

'Hopefully not not much, anyway. I mean, not a lot.'

'Oh, you're the Archmage of Reassurance, you are.'

'Get on with it,' Daretor said impatiently. He opened a pack and removed a series of poles that fitted into one another, each containing several holes. He then poked smaller rods through the holes, forming a crude ladder.

Meanwhile, Jelindel murmured a charm. Zimak started to feel queasy. Suddenly he went limp, as if he had no bones in his body. His flesh distorted, losing shape.

Zimak wailed softly. 'I don't like this . . .'

'Shhh. It's only for a few minutes. Besides, it was you who gave me the idea back in Ishluk. Does "Dissolving bones and leaving behind one big pile of useless human sludge" ring a bell?' she asked merrily.

Speechless with fright, Zimak watched as Daretor positioned the ladder against the back of the tent, which abutted the castle wall. He scrambled up and felt about till he found a narrow slit window. He quickly cut a hole in the tent then scrambled back down and picked up Zimak as if he weighed only a quarter of his normal weight.

With Jelindel steadying the ladder, Daretor climbed back up and pushed Zimak, now rubbery and flexible, through the embrasure. Zimak moaned, feeling his body contort and compress. It was not a pleasant sensation, but in a moment he was through the aperture. He dropped with an odd, heavy plop onto the stone flags. And there he lay for some time.

'Are you all right?' Daretor hissed.

'If you can call this all right, yes.'

'Take care,' Daretor said, and disappeared.

Zimak was on his own. He moved his head slightly and surveyed the passageway. It was clear for the moment.

Some time later he felt his bones knitting together. If he thought the earlier sensation was strange, it was nothing compared with the itch that wracked his body as it healed.

It was part of the plan that Zimak be discovered. Later that evening he was found inside the highly secure and strictly off-limits inner courtyard. He was immediately surrounded by a dozen guardsmen. As they rushed him he raised his hands. Blue shafts of light rippled from his fingertips, sending the guardsmen sprawling. Zimak had no sooner congratulated himself than a mesh net dropped from above, entangling him so thoroughly that he fell headlong to the ground. The more he thrashed, the tighter it became.

Zimak managed to twist his head far enough around to look up into Fa'red's face.

'We meet again,' said Fa'red, smiling. 'Guards, you know what to do with him.'

They dragged Zimak to an interrogation cell. He was left unbound, with the door wide open. He did not even get up off the bunk. He was sure that the door had some manner of trap spell.

After several minutes, Fa'red came in. 'You seem to have gained some wisdom in your travels, Zimak,' he observed. 'Along with a taste for lots of food, by the look of you.'

'Is this the reception I get?' Zimak asked, trying to sound incredulous. 'I was under your protection when those dragonriders captured me, poisoned me, and forced me to do their bidding. I escape, return to Dremari as would a loyal devotee, and *this* is how I get treated. Like a common thief!'

Fa'red's brows came together. 'Don't try my patience, boy. I can flick you out of existence with the merest thought.'

'Do it,' Zimak challenged.

Fa'red stared at him. A muscle in his neck flexed once then relaxed. 'I see. You are warded against the lesser forms of magic. Interesting. I don't think I've ever quite seen that configuration before. But you are not immune to cold steel, I feel.' He whipped out a dagger and held it to Zimak's throat.

'Hie, Fa'red,' Zimak said, tensing his neck. 'I returned by my own free will and this is the thanks I get.'

Fa'red whispered in his ear, 'Where is she?'

'You should know. You sent her there.'

'Do not play games with me, you little miscreant. *Where is she?*'

'Right now, she's here in Dremari. In a few hours, however,

she will be in the domain of the Stone People. I came to warn you, but –'

Fa'red laughed in a forced manner. 'She doesn't know where they are.' The blade nicked Zimak's throat, and he squealed.

Zimak slowly raised his hand, palm up. Fa'red watched it as a rat would watch a snake. The hand flipped over and his index finger pointed down at the floor. Then it came back up and waggled at Fa'red.

'The Stone People's realm is beneath Dremari. She knows. The blade, Fa'red. You're cutting me.'

Fa'red eased the blade from Zimak's neck. Blood trickled down the steel. 'Well, wonders will never cease. You may yet prove of value to me.'

'Praise indeed,' said Zimak, dabbing his neck.

Fa'red regarded him. 'I confess that I am somewhat confused by your presence.'

'I imagine you are,' said Zimak, scowling at the blood on his fingers. 'The Farvenu are your friends. Hospitable bunch.'

'Invited you to dinner, did they?' Fa'red laughed.

'Breakfast actually.'

'They do love their food.'

'The feeling wasn't mutual.'

'Shall we get down to business?'

'As you like.'

'What are you doing here? And please don't tell me you returned here voluntarily.'

'I don't see why not.' Zimak tried to looked hurt.

'Really? You expect me to believe that you're suddenly willing to betray your friends?'

'Who said they're my friends? And who said anything about betrayal?'

Fa'red stared at him, his mottled face expressionless. 'Continue.'

'You want the dragonsight.'

'I've renounced it, as you know. I too am bound by . . . certain rules.'

'By subterfuge, yes,' said Zimak. 'But what if the dragonsight were given to you freely?'

Fa'red thought about this. He could not conceal his excitement. Nevertheless he scowled.

'And why would you give such a precious relic to me?'

'Money, riches, power, why else? I might add that I was set to become the Dremarian princess's consort, a king in waiting if you like.' He looked about the cell as though he could see beyond the thick grey stones. 'If not for that vixen Jelindel, I would be ruling Dremari right now as its rightful king.'

'Had the Preceptor not swept through and slaughtered everyone in sight,' Fa'red commented dryly. 'That aside, you seek power. Is that all?'

'Is that all? No, that's just a start. There's also the little matter of an antidote.'

Fa'red waved a hand dismissively. 'That can be arranged. I am not yet convinced.'

'What's there to be convinced of? We're not seeking the dragonsight for our personal gain. And I have no doubt, unlike my colleagues, that as soon as we hand it over to that wretch Rakeem, he will either have us murdered on the spot or let the poison do its work. Either way, our futures seem rather predictable right now.'

'So you wish to make an alliance?'

'Hie, Fa'red, it's as easy at that. The dragonsight for the antidote and some trifling remuneration.'

'Where is the witch?'

'I can't tell you that.'

'Can't or won't?'

Zimak considered. 'Won't.'

'I could extract the information.'

'You could, but by then she'll be gone. She might even have the dragonsight.'

'Unlikely,' said Fa'red. 'Getting to the realm of the Stone People would only be the first step. There would be further hazards.'

'As you know, Jelindel's very resourceful.'

Fa'red sighed heavily. 'At best she's an extremely talented Adept 9. Even now I suspect her luck is due to run out.'

Zimak pursed his lips. 'She knows more than she shows.'

'And from whom did she obtain this knowledge?' Fa'red leaned forward ever so slightly.

'A dragon,' Zimak said and was surprised at Fa'red's reaction. Indeed, the archmage appeared positively unsettled. 'Do we have a deal?' he added, pushing a little. Fa'red scowled and paced about the cell, tugging his beard.

'Well?' Zimak pushed.

'Let me think!' Fa'red almost shouted.

'I –' Zimak began, but Fa'red waved him peremptorily to silence and strode for the door.

'You're free to go,' he said. 'But Zimak, if you have uttered one lie to me, I shall seek you out and you will wish never to have been born.'

Zimak rose from the bunk, satisfied with his performance. His plan, embellished by Jelindel and Daretor, was going as smoothly as he had hoped. He carefully considered what he had said. Had he actually told a lie?

◇

Fa'red stalked through the hallways, heading for his private quarters. He was housed in sumptuous luxury in the section of the castle normally reserved for visiting royalty, a fact not lost on the mage. In accordance with custom, he was given an honorary guard, although attack by ordinary mortals was unlikely. The real protection surrounding his rooms was less substantial yet far more powerful. They could not be seen or smelt or touched, yet they could strike like lightning when needed.

He strode past the guardsmen, hardly noticing them. As he stepped through the main entrance to his quarters he made a small, subtle sign beneath his robes, so that no prying eyes might see, and muttered a single ancient watch-word. The forces that guarded his rooms were barely constrained and were as inimical to him as to anyone, yet it was he who had summoned them to this world and it was he who held them in check by the sheer power of his magic.

Once inside, he went to his workroom and unlocked a stone cabinet, removing a silvered scrying mirror in a gilt frame. He waved his hand across it. The surface became milky. A face appeared – stern, hard, with a button nose and small glinting eyes.

'Master?'

'Come quickly. Meet me in the antechamber.'

Jelindel sat perfectly still. Indeed, she hardly seemed to breathe. Daretor watched with concern. She was pale, and there was a slight sheen of sweat across her brow. She was in another place, exploring the paraplane as she had done many times before, most notably when they were searching for the dragonlinks.

Daretor felt helpless. Frustrated, he began to pace. It bothered him that Jelindel was somewhere he could not follow. He was not jealous, just worried for her safety. If something happened he could not protect her. His sword and his fighting skill could not prevail in the insubstantial realm.

Jelindel's eyes suddenly blinked. She sucked in a long noisy breath before slumping over. Daretor caught her and held her tight. She finally looked into his face, smiling wanly.

'It's done,' she said. 'He took the bait.'

'He went to the Stone People's domain?'

Jelindel shook her head. 'No, he sent a lackey and I managed to track him.'

'So you know where it is?'

'I know, but there is a problem. It's sort of . . .'

Daretor looked at her sternly. 'Just tell me.'

'Fa'red has constructed some kind of magical shield around the Stone People's domain.'

Daretor sat back. 'Then that's it. He's won.'

Jelindel shook her head. 'I didn't say I couldn't get through it. I'll just need help. I know the spell he used, and there's a configuration key for it.'

'So he'll be expecting you to work it out?'

'If he's still not underestimating me.'

'Then what are you waiting for?'

'Apart from rest, inspiration,' Jelindel said, closing her eyes.

Chapter 10
RESCUING MELYAR

Rested, Jelindel called Daretor over. 'It's possible that Fa'red's power, even his surveillance abilities, are being drained by the exhausting magic he's employed against us.'

'And?' Zimak prompted.

'I've worked out a key to unlock Fa'red's configuration.' She thought for a moment. 'Think of picking a lock with a hair pin. Use too much force and it breaks or bends.'

'So if Fa'red's spell isn't too strong, your key will unlock it?' Daretor deduced.

'That's the theory,' Jelindel said.

'And if your key breaks?'

'Then we could be in for a rough time.' Jelindel smiled quickly. 'Life's dangerous and horrible, and then you die.'

They returned to the stable. Hakat and QeSu joined them. They had had an interesting time amid the festivities, and both were exhilarated to be in such a beautiful city, in the middle of a festival, without the constant worry that something dark and dreadful might swoop out of the sky and carry them off. The only news they had gathered was that Fa'red, according to the rumour they had picked up in the taverns near the castle, had collapsed and even now was bedridden. They had not been able to confirm it.

They moved the discussion to the inn, and Jelindel ordered food while they debated their next move. Jelindel made it clear that she could open a gap in the shield that Fa'red had constructed around the Stone People's domain, but she would have to go alone.

Daretor wanted to know why she had to go alone. She explained that the Stone People lived *four miles* beneath the city. Her powers could not transport anyone other than herself such a great distance through solid rock. Even then there was some chance she might miscalculate and end up inside the rock itself, an interesting fossil for future generations to unearth.

Daretor was adamant. 'You're not going alone,' he said again.

'Be reasonable, Daretor,' Jelindel said, spreading her hands. 'This is the only way to retrieve the dragonsight. Without it we're going to die.'

Daretor grumbled and muttered, but there was little he could say. Hakat stared at them both. This was the first the young couple knew of Jelindel's plans. Jelindel had not told them much, partly because they had endured enough already and deserved some semblance of normality in their lives, and partly because it was not wise to have too many people privy to a secret.

'I don't know why you got to go to this stone place,' Hakat said, 'but am I right in sayin' it's underground and hard to get to?'

Jelindel sighed. 'My magical powers are limited,' she said. 'Nor are they all equal in strength. I am stronger in some areas than others, just as Daretor is a better swordsman than an archer.'

'There has to be a way,' said QeSu.

'There is a way,' Hakat said. 'There's the paraworld machine.'

They all looked at him. Jelindel frowned. 'But it's for travel *between* paraworlds.'

'So it is.'

'It can be used to move from one place to another within the same world?' Daretor asked eagerly.

Hakat shook his head. 'No, it can't do that.'

Daretor scowled. 'Then what good is it?'

Hakat was grinning, as if he saw a joke the others did not. Jelindel stared at him. Then she too grinned.

Daretor looked at them. 'What?' said Daretor. 'What is it?'

Jelindel took his hand. 'Hakat is right. The machine cannot transport us *within* the bounds of a paraworld, but it can take us to another paraworld and bring us back to a *different* location from the one we left.'

'Zimak, you stay here with Hakat and QeSu.' She beckoned Daretor. 'Looks like you can come after all.'

Zimak smiled. 'For once I agree with your plan,' he said.

Whatever Jelindel was expecting, the reality was far more over-whelming. That was partly because she knew, within two seconds, that they were not in a paraworld that she had remotely heard of. A moment later she knew that they were probably not leaving any time soon.

Hakat had been quite emphatic. They would be there for the blink of an eye. Everything would be a blur, then they would be on their way again. After they had prodded him, he had admitted that glitches occasionally developed.

'So if it's not the blink of an eye, then how long?' Jelindel had asked.

'Twenty-four hours,' he had said. 'Or forty-eight. But you must be back on the same spot.'

The 'spot' was a cobblestone alleyway filled with rotting refuse and a dank smell of decay. Almost as soon as Jelindel and Daretor materialised a thunderous noise boomed overhead. They covered their ears, looking about in great alarm. An enormous metal creature lumbered across the gap of sky above the alleyway. It had long wings that did not flap and wheels fixed beneath them. Even as they watched, the wheels folded up into the underbelly and disappeared, as if they had never been.

The thing was gone as quickly as it had appeared, but its roar lingered in the air. Jelindel and Daretor edged closer to one another.

'Some kind of bird?' Daretor asked hesitantly.

Jelindel shook her head. 'It was made of metal and there was no magic in it.'

'Well, what of it? We'll be out of here soon enough.' He gazed around him in repugnance. 'It smells worse than the D'loom fish market,' he said.

'Hakat may still make the transfer,' she said. 'Let's give him some time.'

Daretor gripped his sword. 'Hakat's *machine* is unreliable,' he said. 'Such things will never catch on.'

'I wonder. I think the metal bird was a machine.'

'What would be the good of such a thing?'

'Maybe there were people in it.'

He stared at her. 'You think it eats people? Then it's some kind of dragon.'

'I meant that maybe people get inside it to travel from one

place to another, the way we rode in Fa'red's airliner, and on S'cressling's back across Q'zar.'

Daretor was not much cheered. The concept seemed crazy to him.

They waited another twenty minutes, but clearly nothing was going to happen. They would have to return to the alley twenty-four hours from now.

'We must mark this spot,' said Daretor.

Jelindel spoke a spell and a tiny flicker of blue light leapt into the cobblestones. 'Done,' she said. 'I could find this place blind-folded now.'

'What do we do in the meantime?'

'Lay low. Get something to eat. Try not to attract attention.'

'I've had some experience at that these past few years.'

'And?'

'It frequently doesn't work.'

'Maybe you were trying too hard.'

The injustice of that left him speechless so he followed Jelindel to the end of the alleyway. Opposite was a large building, some forty or fifty floors high, seemingly made of panes of glass that reflected the scene behind them. It was an awesome sight but also a puzzling one.

'Why build something so high?' Daretor wondered.

Jelindel pursed her lips. 'Maybe they don't have much land.'

'These paraworlds are usually reflections of Q'zar, are they not? Which means they must have about the same land surface.'

'But perhaps more people,' Jelindel guessed.

She stared at the road. It was strange enough in itself, being surfaced with some kind of unbroken black substance. Even from here it smelled of tar. If the road was strange then the creatures travelling on it were bizarre in the extreme. Except they weren't creatures, unless the humans inside them had been swallowed alive or had willingly stepped into the jaws of the creatures.

Metallic-looking wagons of an endless variety of shape and colour raced along the tar-surfaced track. Their speed was frightening. Just as odd was the orderliness with which they raced. Jelindel suspected that it *was* a race of some kind. Maybe whoever reached those strange, changing coloured lights at the end of the street won. If so, what was the prize? And why did they not stop long enough to collect it? Perhaps it was a symbolic triumph, pride being taken in the accomplishment itself.

If so, that suggested a high order of social development. A paraworld of evolved human beings, thought Jelindel. How wonderful. Imagine the learned discourse one could have with them.

'Are the animals dangerous?' Daretor asked, his hand gripping the pommel of his sword.

'I don't think so. I think the humans inside are controlling them.'

Daretor spat. 'Machines again. This must be a cold science paraworld. Let us hope there are no Farvenu here.' His eyes raked the sky, looking for the beasts.

'If I'm not much mistaken that looks like a tavern over there,' Jelindel said. 'Let's see if our gold is acceptable here. And if we can speak the language.'

It turned out that the language was similar to one spoken in Lycellia, confirming a long-accepted theory that the paraworlds – being slightly flawed duplicates of Q'zar – often duplicated species, languages and customs, though usually with bizarre twists.

The language spoken here – called English – was hard to understand, mainly because it contained much slang and many odd words. But with hand gestures, lots of pointing, and good will, they made themselves understood.

As for whether gold was acceptable, it was, though it took the proprietor some time to believe that their coins really were gold. In the end his wife decided the matter, apparently knowing something of the value and nature of gold coins. She appeared from a back room with her hair ornamented with small cylinders made of some kind of mesh.

After that they were served drink and food, though the looks they received were many. Obviously, their manner of dress was outlandish, just as the bland clothing of the people here seemed lacking in personal style. The clothing of the women was another matter. As such Daretor enjoyed watching them, especially the ones with short dresses. He had cause to ponder how much Zimak would kick himself for missing this.

A middle-aged woman appeared with some kind of contraption and asked them if they wanted their picture taken.

Jelindel apologised, mistaking the word. 'I'm sorry, we have no pitcher for you to take.'

The woman stared at her a moment, then spoke very slowly, over-enunciating each word: 'No, dearie. I. Take. *Your*. Picture.'

Daretor whispered to Jelindel, 'Is she a thief?'

'I don't think so. It must be some local custom. Let's humour her.' They both nodded, smiling. The woman whipped up her black box, aimed, and apparently pulled a trigger, for it clicked.

Daretor's hand went to his sword. But Jelindel's stayed him. 'It's similar to Hakat's machine. Only that drew "photographs".'

A flash of light dazzled the pair, and a piece of paper slid out of the base of the machine.

The woman pulled out the paper and waved it in the air for awhile. Then she handed it to the bewildered Q'zarans. They stared at it with fascination. It was an instantaneous painting of them. It showed Jelindel and Daretor, smiling hesitantly.

Daretor let his sword slide back into its scabbard. They had, of course, seen something similar back on Farvane, although this parchment sketch was uncannily lifelike, considering it was drawn so quickly and didn't have to be 'developed' like Hakat's.

The woman said, 'Oh, you want another one? This time with your sword out, dearie?'

'No,' said Jelindel, nudging Daretor.

The woman said, 'Used to be a Doctor Who fan meself. Went to all the conventions and masquerade parties.'

'Doctor who?' Jelindel asked.

'We won't go down that road, deary me,' the woman chortled. When Jelindel and Daretor looked bemused, she said, 'That'll be five quid, love.'

The proprietor called out, 'They got gold coins, Mabel. Best take one. Trust me.'

She took one, frowning suspiciously. The proprietor reassured her a second time and she went away grumbling.

'This is a strange place,' Daretor said. 'When they say *take*, they mean *give*. If someone offers to help us we must be very careful.'

Jelindel nodded. 'They seem a fairly peaceful lot though.'

Jelindel settled for water, while Daretor drank beer out of a glass tankard. They ate what was called a steak and kidney pie with a thick red sauce. It was not unlike pies of their own world. Jelindel thought she would like the recipe for the Heinz Tomato Sauce. It would be a big seller in the D'loom market stalls.

When they finished eating, they left the establishment, intending to look for somewhere to sleep. The proprietor told them to keep their eyes peeled for a hotel. The image of peeled eyes was horrific but it was said in an offhand manner that made them think the suggestion was purely metaphoric. Possibly it indicated a grim and cruel history, now long behind them.

After nearly being run over by a large two-tiered vehicle with 'Covent Garden' written on a faceplate, they found a hotel and trouble.

They entered a large square, full of fountains and pigeons and strolling couples. On the far side was a sign. In large glowing letters it said, Ritz Hotel. They struck out for it. Halfway across the square, which was dark in this spot, two men stepped out from bushes. One of them had a metallic device in his hand and was pointing it at them. His manner made it clear it was a weapon.

'Hand it over. Everything you got!' he snarled.

Daretor smiled. 'I think I'm beginning to get it,' he said. 'He means he wants to *take* all our money.'

The two men looked at each other. 'You're winding me up.' He stepped forward menacingly. 'What are you?'

'I'm a warrior,' Daretor said, stating the obvious. 'Do you wish to fight?'

'No, pal, I wanna swap recipes.'

'Really? Do you know the recipe for tomato sauce?' Jelindel asked.

One of the men said to the other, 'They're friggin' retards.'

The one with the gun cocked it, pointing it at Daretor. 'Give me all your money, retard, or I'm gonna blow your friggin' brains all over the park. *Comprende, retardo?*'

His finger tightened on the trigger. Daretor whipped out his sword. Jelindel spoke a word of magic. Blue light leapt to the gun. The bullet rolled out of the barrel and dropped to the ground. Then the weapon turned red hot.

The mugger holding the gun screamed. He dropped it, and clutched his burnt hand, staring at Jelindel accusingly. He staggered backwards and fell over a bush. The pair had seen enough. The fallen mugger scrambled to his feet and both men ran for the trees.

'Nothing really changes,' said Jelindel. 'There are those who give and those who take.'

'Except here, the givers take and the takers give,' said Daretor. He picked up the bullet. 'I fail to see how he thought this was going to hurt us. It's not even pointed. In fact, it's blunt.' He tossed it over his shoulder.

'Well, let's get some rest.'

'Can I help you, ma'am? Is this man bothering you?'

They turned to see a man in uniform. When he saw Daretor holding the sword, he pulled out a gun and pointed it at them.

'Don't move,' he said. He spoke into a device attached to his shoulder. An invisible man's voice answered. A moment later two more uniformed men joined him, also pointing guns. They wore badges on their tunics and soft peaked caps. Daretor couldn't imagine those things protecting their heads from a thrown rock, much less an arrow or a sword strike.

'Use your magic again,' Daretor urged.

'I think these are like watchmen and guards. See the uniforms?'

'Put down your weapon. Do it now. Then make like an aeroplane!' one of the men demanded.

Jelindel told Daretor to comply. He lay down his sword.

'What's an aeroplane?' he asked.

He didn't have time to find out. The three men tackled him to the ground. They twisted his arms behind his back, knelt on him, then shackled his wrists together.

'Jelli,' Daretor shouted.

'We need somewhere to stay the night and I think these people will accommodate us. Excuse the pun,' she said, crossing her hands behind her back. She whispered a quick cloaking spell, hiding her valuables. It was too late to do anything about Daretor's sword.

One of their captors was picking it up gingerly, as though he had never seen the like before.

One of the men shackled her wrists. She relaxed. She did not feel that the men intended to harm them; they were simply being neutralised. It seemed that life in this city was more precarious than they had imagined.

One of their captors then found the gun lying on the grass.

'Is this yours?' he asked.

'No,' said Daretor. 'A man pointed it at us and told us to give him all our money.'

'I didn't see anyone,' the constable said, squinting into the darkness.

'He ran away.' Jelindel pointed to a copse of trees.

'He pointed a loaded gun at you, then he dropped it, and ran away? Is that your story?'

'That's what happened, yes.' Jelindel wondered whether she was missing something.

'Are you a retard?'

'The man with the "gun" thought so,' Daretor confessed.

The policeman stared at him. 'You think a judge is gonna buy that story? Take some advice. Get yourself a real good lawyer. You're gonna need one.'

'You're apprehending us?' Jelindel asked.

'No, ma'am, I'm inviting you to a party down at the station.'

'A party of what?'

'Shut up and listen. You have the right to remain silent, you have the right to a lawyer . . . '

An hour later they were in a strange building getting their fingers pressed onto an ink pad. The inky tips were then pressed onto a strip of white parchment. Then they were made to stand against a wall and someone took their photograph. Daretor smiled for his. This was the one part of the process where he knew what was expected of him.

'What are you, some kind of clown? Zip the lips!' drawled the photographer.

Daretor was placed in a holding cell in the basement of the building. He was with a dozen others. Jelindel was on the next floor up. Apparently they would go before a judge in the morning and have an arraignment, whatever that was. In the meantime, the cell was noisy and full of mostly aggressive and moody people that reminded Daretor of the alley denizens in D'loom.

He was still confused but tried to make light of it. 'We needed somewhere to stay for the night anyway,' he told a derelict who was fingering his leather tunic.

Finding a corner, Daretor settled down to rest. Before he could fully succumb to sleep he was viciously kicked wide awake.

Two large inmates stood over him. 'What do we have here then? A right freak show. Smells freakish, too,' said one of them. 'Take your top off. I'm cold.'

Daretor started to get up but the man kicked his arm out from under him. Falling to one side, Daretor rolled away from the man's boot. The inmate's foot slammed into the wall. He yelped, but his exclamation was cut short when Daretor leg-swept him.

His companion swore and rushed Daretor, who promptly bent into the man, then fell backwards, using the man's impetus to throw him into the cell door. The inmate slammed to the ground and lay still.

A cheer went up from the others in the cell. After that Daretor was left alone until morning, when he was taken out for his arraignment. Jelindel was already in the courtroom.

He was about to join her when two policemen stopped him. 'Isn't it time we left?' Daretor called.

Jelindel stood up. 'How was your room?'

'A little crowded, and filled with vermin,' Daretor said. 'I've an itch, and it's not just to get out of here.'

'All part of life's rich tapestry,' Jelindel said. 'I learnt a lot of slang and –'

There was a loud bang. Turning, Daretor saw a man in a ridiculous white wig, glaring down at him from a high bench.

'You'll excuse me for interrupting you,' the man said, 'but it is MY COURTROOM AND I'LL HAVE SILENCE!'

Jelindel said, 'I think that's the judge.'

'What does he judge?' Daretor asked.

'Us, I think.'

The gavel pounded the bench again. 'You will address the court, or I will have you removed from this courtroom. Do you understand me?'

Jelindel frowned, unravelling the man's speech. 'We don't really. You see, we're not from around here. I think you're right, Daretor. It's time we left.' She addressed the bench. 'My companion here and I would both like to thank you for your hospitality and for breakfast. It was our first time in a hotel.'

Jelindel took a step towards Daretor. A policewoman tried to restrain her. Jelindel murmured the freezing spell she had used on Madame Mooska, and the officer froze in mid action.

'Watch out,' someone screamed, 'she's armed.'

Jelindel crossed to Daretor while everybody in the courtroom scurried for cover.

'We're going now,' Jelindel said. She inscribed a character in the air and spoke two words.

'You wait right –' the judge roared. Then he, like everybody else, froze. Jelindel and Daretor left by the front door. A few moments later, life came back into the courtroom.

'. . . there until I –' The judge gulped and closed his mouth. The prisoners had vanished. People began screaming. Officers rushed into the corridor, guns drawn.

The judge sat back and wiped his brow. To no one in particular, and in a voice barely audible, he said, 'I think I'll take the rest of the day off.'

Jelindel and Daretor wandered about the city.

By mid-afternoon they happened on the square where they had been arrested. From there they found the cobblestone alleyway. Judging by the sun, they had at least two hours before Hakat's machine could transfer them out.

Till then, they decided to remain close to the point of transfer and keep out of trouble. Daretor had lost his sword, which had, Jelindel surmised, been the cause of their arrest. Weapons in public were strictly taboo. Unless you were a 'mugger' or the 'bill'. It was just as well the Preceptor had not thought of such a concept. Imagine only his army being armed! Everyone on Q'zar would have been at his complete mercy.

Their clothing still drew attention wherever they went. Even sitting at an outdoor café caused a minor commotion. Jelindel could not tell if people were simply curious or if they were afraid. To put them at ease she made a point of smiling whenever people looked her way. Some, from sheer reflex perhaps, smiled back sheepishly. Others retaliated by either glaring, or promptly looking away.

This paraworld was without a doubt a wondrous place of cold science, but there was something missing. For a long time Jelindel could not put her finger on it and then it sprang to mind. There was little connection between people. Strangers rarely spoke and everyone seemed in a hurry. They even ate quickly. When they conversed it was in short, sharp sentences.

Daretor nudged her, breaking her reverie. 'We're being watched.'

The woman was old, and dressed in a dowdy manner. Her hair was unkempt and she carried many shiny, crumpled bags. When she noticed their eyes on her, her own eyes lit up. She approached their table by leaning on her trolley and tottering forward.

'You're from Q'zar,' she accused. She spoke in the halting street dialect heard on the streets of D'loom.

Jelindel stood up and answered in the same tongue. 'We are.'

The woman swayed and would have fallen had Daretor not helped her to a seat. She looked emaciated. They ordered food and drink that she ate with her fingers the moment it arrived.

The waiter blanched. When Daretor narrowed his eyes he stepped back from the table and retreated. Through the windows, Daretor saw him conversing with an officious looking man in a white tunic. For some unfathomable reason, the man also wore a girl's black ribbon tied in a bow around his neck. Daretor wondered about its significance.

'How did you travel here?' Jelindel asked. She also wondered why the woman was in such poor condition.

'My name is Melyar,' she said. 'I was a neophyte in the Temple of Verity in Hamaria, though I was born in D'loom. In the first few weeks of my training a novice dared me to show her my strongest spell.'

Bemused, Jelindel thought back to her first meeting with Onala, when she too had been a neophyte.

'Well, I was a fool, wasn't I?' the woman continued. 'And all of fourteen. What did I know? I stole into the library that night, opened one of the forbidden books and learnt a spell for paraworld travel. I thought I would make the journey and bring something back to boast about. What a terrible mistake that was. And I've paid dearly for it.'

'How long have you been here?' Daretor asked.

'Forty years, give or take. You see, the spell was just for travel one way. Like a fool I kept using it, popping from one paraworld to another, hoping to get back. Eventually I arrived here but not till I'd gone to a daemon-ridden paraworld that scared me so much I never dared use the spell again.'

Jelindel eyed her rags. 'You have indeed fallen on hard times.'

'That I have,' said Melyar. 'I was locked up for years in a place for crazy people. Then I stopped trying to tell them the truth and told them what they wanted to hear. Finally, they let me go. This is a hard paraworld, even though it looks so bright and prosperous. It isn't prosperous for everyone, and I don't like the cold science that permeates every aspect of their lives. I don't trust it in my heart. Then I saw you sitting here, as plain as day, dressed in the garb of Q'zar. I couldn't believe it. I didn't dare to believe it. At first, I thought I really *had* gone crazy and that I should end up back in that horrid place where they tie you to beds and force you to swallow potions they call pills.' She blinked back tears. 'It's so lovely to hear the old words again . . .'

Jelindel took her gnarled hands in hers. 'Do you wish to go back to Q'zar?'

Melyar's eyes opened wider than before. For a moment she was too choked to speak. She nodded vigorously, as if not trusting her voice. 'Can I come with you?' she said finally.

Jelindel shook her head. 'We are on a mission that could well prove fatal. I wouldn't take you into danger. But I will attempt to send you back.'

Awe came to Melyar's face. 'You can really do that?'

'She is the Archmage Jelindel dek Mediesar,' said Daretor.

Jelindel registered Daretor's doubt. 'I can try to send Melyar back to Q'zar, but not us through deep rock.' She shrugged. 'It's hard to explain. Trust me.' To Melyar she said, 'I cannot return you to any particular place on Q'zar. You might land in the Passendof Mountains.'

'Anywhere on Q'zar would have to be an improvement on this paraworld,' Melyar said fervently.

It was nearly time for their own transfer. They led Melyar to the cobblestone alleyway and gave her most of their coins, as well as a message for Zimak and the others, if ever she found them. 'In all probability, this laneway is a gateway to many paraworlds. Since we arrived at this exact spot from Q'zar, you could well return to our departure spot,' Jelindel reasoned.

'Then why can't *we* go back? Daretor asked.

'Because if I'm wrong, and we miss Hakat's machine calling us back at a given time, we too could wind up somewhere days away from them. And we don't have days to waste.'

Melyar was shaking with excitement. 'I feel as though I've wasted my life,' she said, clasping Jelindel's hands tightly. 'I will never be able to repay you.'

'Repay me by helping someone else,' Jelindel said. She gently unclasped Melyar's hands and bade her stand back. Then she murmured a long intricate spell and conjured an intense coruscation of blue light that shot out and engulfed Melyar in a whirling funnel. Melyar let out a frightened squeak, and then she was gone.

Jelindel stood transfixed.

'Are you ill?' Daretor asked. He had to shake Jelindel for a response.

'I think it worked,' she said. 'I'm getting pretty good at this, aren't I?' She poked her tongue through her lips in thought. 'Then again, I can't guarantee where precisely Melyar went to on Q'zar, and that troubles me.'

'As she said, anywhere is better than here,' Daretor said, pulling her to the designated spot. His inner time sense told him that they had less than a minute till the transfer.

'Let's hope it works this time for us,' he said. 'I don't fancy ending up like Melyar. Did you see the look on her face? I've never seen someone so happy.'

'Now we need to concentrate,' Jelindel said. 'We could well be stepping into instant danger.'

'I look forward to the time we step *out* of it,' Daretor mumbled. The appointed time came. And went. Daretor groaned inwardly.

'Well, it looks as if we're here for another –'

They entered the paraplane just as a door opened and a man in a white apron came out carrying a garbage can. He stared at their twinkling afterimage as they dematerialised then dropped the can and bolted back inside, yelling.

Jelindel and Daretor materialised back in the same alleyway. '– day,' Jelindel finished, then looked around. 'Or maybe not.'

'Did we –?' Daretor asked.

'I'm afraid so. Look.' It was true. The walls enclosing the alleyway were different, more damaged and definitely more weathered, though the smell of decay still hung in the air.

More obvious still was the view from the alleyway, which was in a section of streets that quartered the side of a fairly steep hill. On the previous paraworld – the paraworld of the metal bird – a large building with many glass windows had stood opposite, blocking their view. Now it was gone. From where they stood they could see that they were in a ruined city. The buildings were crumbled and many had collapsed. All were covered with the stain of time, and silver-grey lichens that lent the ruins an air of dubious respectability. The streets were filled with debris and dirt. Plants and small trees grew everywhere, even from the walls of buildings and from rooftops. It looked like the city had been abandoned for many decades.

A bloodcurdling howl broke the strange silence and raised the hair on the nape of Jelindel's neck. It was a sound humankind knew in its infancy and would fear for as long as it existed. *Wolves.*

Another howl answered the first, then another and another. They seemed to be all around and each howl was closer than the one preceding it.

'Remind me to wring Hakat's neck when I see him,' said Daretor, preparing to defend himself.

They still had not moved from the point on which they had materialised. It had already been several long minutes since they had arrived. It appeared that Hakat had been unable to transfer them out of this paraworld.

'We need to get off the street,' Jelindel said. 'Maybe high up in one of these ruins.'

Daretor jumped up to a window ledge and leaned down to pull up Jelindel. Dark shapes moved lithely into the mouth of the alleyway. Although they were clearly of the wolf family, they were like no wolf either of them had ever seen. The creatures were the size of bulls and with something of their ferocious physique. Bunched rippling muscles swelled their forequarters, sloping down to smaller legs at the back. They had a single small horn on the snout, like a rhinoceros, and huge canines protruded from their upper jaw even when their mouths were closed. Their glinting red eyes reflected rage and hunger.

'Maybe it's time we –' Daretor never finished the sentence. The wolves uttered a low gurgling noise then sped towards them. At the same moment they entered yet another paraworld.

Chapter 11
THE STONE PEOPLE

Jelindel and Daretor reappeared on a narrow ledge halfway up the wall of an underground cavern. Its vastness took their breath away. The cavern was easily several leagues across and a league high. It was lit by a strange pearly light that diminished shadows.

Enormous stalactites and stalagmites of myriad colours reached down from the ceiling and up from the floor like gnarled dragons' teeth, shining with a hypnotic iridescence.

In the space around the stalagmites, the floor of the cavern was cut by fissures and pocked with deep pits in which lava bubbled with a harsh light. It reminded Jelindel and Daretor of the lair of the Sacred One in the Tower Inviolate.

A rough and precarious track led down from the ledge to the cavern floor.

'Hooray for Hakat. I think he's done it.'

Daretor looked into the shadows as though expecting the wolves to materialise. Without his sword, he felt particularly vulnerable.

Jelindel started downwards immediately. After one more glance at the sheer beauty of the cavern, Daretor followed. They had to watch where they put their feet; one step, if miscalculated, could plunge them instantly to their deaths on the sharp stalagmites far below. As it was, pebbles cascaded down the ragged edges and created larger landslides further down the sheer drop.

It was an exhausting journey and they had little breath or concentration to spare for conversation. Only once did they speak on the way down. Jelindel had nearly fallen and had stopped to catch her breath and calm her nerves. If Daretor was uneasy with closed-in spaces, she was less than happy with heights.

'I should have let S'cressling fry Fa'red when I had the chance,' Jelindel swore under her breath.

'You had him more or less disarmed,' Daretor pointed out. 'It wouldn't have been honourable to kill him – though I could be persuaded otherwise now.'

'Trust me, Daretor. An Adept 12 is never "disarmed". I learned that much from Lady Forturian and Madame Dione.'

They continued in silence. A little over an hour later they reached the ground and stopped to rest. Jelindel gazed about. 'I need to go into the paraplane. The dragonsight should be visible from there.'

Jelindel sat cross-legged on the ground and her gaze turned inward. From the outside, Daretor noticed little except that she sat still as stone. It was almost as if Jelindel had stopped breathing. Though Daretor would never admit it, he was frightened. He wondered what would happen if she did not find her way back. Would her body stay like that, growing weaker and weaker? Would it die and yet continue to sit there, unaware that it was dead? He shivered. Such thoughts were not worthy of a warrior.

Jelindel was aware of his fears and almost smiled to herself.

Normal human emotions became attenuated and strange in this place of shifting dimension and thought. In some ways it was like hiding in the ceiling of a building and gazing down through air vents into particular rooms. But it was also like being in the rooms looking up at the unseen watcher in the ceiling. In a sense she was watching herself watching herself.

She pried her awareness away from this self-replicating process. The paraplane was notorious for its capacity to ensnare the untrained mind within its endless spider web of thought within thought, of sight inside seeing, of a maze of perception in which one could be lost forever.

The secret was in the negation of the ego, the putting aside of self, and embracing all of creation. In this way her awareness moved out from herself, spun through the manifold dimensions that was the paraplane, and found what she was seeking.

The dragonsight pulsed with an unearthly vitality. It possessed a signature that was utterly alien, yet not frighteningly so. It was not like most talismanic objects that harboured magic so black and corrosive that they could annihilate a mind that even casually brushed by them.

The dragonsight was simply different. Not bad, not good. Just different and very powerful. She saw that it was, indeed, with a group of Stone People and that they were trying to hide it. It was some distance from where they were, and the path was unclear.

'Jelindel!' She vaguely heard Daretor's cry and swept her awareness back in his direction. They were no longer alone. The newcomers' intention was not clear to her, nor was their true nature in the physical realm she occupied with Daretor. She saw, branching off from herself and Daretor, all the past choices that had led them here and all the future ones that stemmed from this moment. In some of these, she and her lover lay dead.

She brought herself back to her body and opened her eyes.

'We have company,' Daretor said.

Standing silently some twenty yards away were a dozen Stone People.

Jelindel nodded slowly, realising she had made a novice's mistake. She had thought the name was somehow ornamental, but she had been wrong. These creatures appeared to be made of stone; they stood some four to five feet in height and their limbs and bodies were composed of slabs of crumbling rust-brown rock, though their eyes were as black as basalt.

When their presence was acknowledged, the creatures moved forward a little. Despite their obvious great weight and solidity they moved with surprising agility.

Jelindel had a vision of what it might be like to have one of these creatures come after her: a single-minded and inexorable boulder that never rested, never slept, till it squashed its prey.

Jelindel held up her hand, palm outwards, in what she hoped was a common gesture. 'I am Jelindel dek Mediesar from Skelt, a coastal realm of the upper world. This is my companion, Daretor.'

'Why are you here?' asked one, his voice like the grinding of stone on stone. Surrounded as they were by a sheer granite face, it felt as though the entire cavern had spoken.

'We seek that which was stolen.'

'Do you accuse us?' rumbled the speaker.

'No. This thing was stolen by a magician called Fa'red.'

'You seek the dragonsight.'

'Yes, we do.'

'We do not have it.'

She could not tell from his voice if he intended ill or not. The inflections were too strange, too guttural, to translate into human experience. She flicked a look at the walls of the cavern and saw no escape path. Fa'red had chosen well.

'That does not mean we cannot retrieve it,' the speaker added. Now there was a hint of menace in his words.

She gazed at the phalanx of Stone People with some uncertainty and took a deep breath. 'You must know that this artefact is of great importance.'

'It is of great importance to you. It is nothing to us. We do not concern ourselves with the doings of the upper world. Nor do we favour trespassers in our realm.'

The creatures moved closer and there was now definite menace in how they regarded the trespassers. 'You must go back to your world,' said the one who had spoken first. 'You are not welcome here.'

'We cannot return until our quest is complete.'

'Then perhaps you will never return.' There was a rumble of agreement from the other Stone People and they began to edge forward. Jelindel and Daretor took a step back. Daretor laid his hand on his scabbard, forgetting he no longer had a sword. In any case, it would have been useless against the granite hides of these creatures.

'Wait.'

The others stopped as one of their own pushed forward. He came close to Jelindel and Daretor and almost seemed to be sniffing.

Then he turned back to his kin. 'We must help these soft skins,' he said.

The first speaker rumbled in what the Q'zarans took to be dissent. 'We do not meddle, Olag. You know this. If they cannot leave as they have come, then their lives are forfeit.'

'You do not understand, Taroc,' Olag hissed. 'They have been inside the Stone of Temis!'

The Stone People stared at Jelindel and Daretor in awe. Finally Taroc said, 'Is this true? You have been inside the Ark of the People?'

Jelindel returned the stare. To Daretor, she said, 'He refers to the Tower Inviolate . . .'

The swordsman nodded cautiously. A great sigh escaped the mass of Stone People, and the tension eased.

'We will help you.'

'Why is the . . . Stone of Temis so important to you?' Jelindel asked gently, not wishing to offend.

'That is a story as long as the universe and twice as wide,' said the speaker. 'Suffice to say that it is the vessel that brought my people to this world, that gave us this great rock as home and harbour, after a journey lasting many long ages. It is the holy place of my people. The Ark. The New Beginning. By some miscalculation, or evil, the Stone of Temis vanished, leaving a wasteland in its wake, the one you call Dragonfrost. With it went the dragons.'

'You don't mind that we have violated your fabled ark?'

'Mind? How could we mind? If we should forbid others to gaze upon the greatest jewel of this or any other paraworld, we would know no end to our shame.'

'Even villains?' Daretor asked.

The Stone Man shook. A shroud of dust and pebbles tumbled from him. 'How may bad people become good, unless they come to know ultimate goodness?'

There seemed no answer to this and the Q'zarans made no effort to find one.

Jelindel returned to the quest at hand. 'About the dragonsight,' she said. 'You should know that the dragons have come back to Q'zar, and the talisman we seek is –'

The Stone People suddenly erupted into a clamour that

sounded like an avalanche. They ignored the Q'zarans for several long minutes. Finally the grinding hubbub subsided and Taroc addressed them.

'I apologise for our inattention. We are overjoyed by this news. Of old, my people knew the dragons. We were allies. They were of the sky, but their bones were as old as the earth, and we forged a kinship that was rare in those ancient times.

'When they went away we mourned for centuries, never expecting to see them again. Tell me, soft one, have they returned to Dragonfrost from whence they departed?'

Jelindel nodded cautiously.

'What has the dragonsight to do with all this?' the grinding voice asked.

Jelindel explained that she deduced the dragonsight was the heart of the old dragon itself, the Sacred One, and that with its aid the rulers of the Tower Inviolate had enslaved the dragons for a thousand years. The gem had to be returned to the dragons to set them free.

'You go then to set them free?' a Stone Man asked. 'Not to enslave, not to destroy?'

'We go to liberate, even if we lose our lives in the doing,' Jelindel said. Beside her, Daretor nodded his support.

The Stone People held a low grinding conference. After a time they turned to Jelindel and Daretor. 'We will help. There is a small band of our people that have been led astray by the magician you named. He poisoned their hearts and ruined their minds, and now they do not know the difference between good rock and bad, between day and night. We have left them to themselves for too long perhaps. We will now rectify this matter. They have the dragonsight.'

◇

Moving through rough-hewn tunnels that reached deep within the earth, an army of Stone People tromped the ground with barely more than a tremor. Jelindel and Daretor had difficulty accepting their situation. They had been startled to discover that the Stone People could literally walk through walls, melting into the rock and passing through it, albeit slowly, as if they moved through thick treacle. Just as easily, they could sink into the ground, and create fissures through which their guests could squeeze. The Stone People were to the rocky earth what fish, or perhaps sharks, were to the great oceans.

How far they travelled, Jelindel did not know, but the journey took several hours. By the end, Jelindel and Daretor were bruised, cut and exhausted. Taroc came to them at the stopping place.

'You must sleep,' he said. 'Our people will see to the preparations. We will wake you.'

With that he stepped backwards and melted into the wall. Jelindel and Daretor threw themselves down, too tired to care. Within moments they were asleep.

They woke to a low rumbling that seemed to come up from the depths of the earth.

Taroc appeared. 'War has begun,' he said. 'Our former brethren are stronger than we thought, for they use dark magic. Can you destroy such arts?'

'I'll try,' said Jelindel.

'Come with me quickly then. I will guard you as best I can.'

They hurried after the Stone Man, darting down tunnels, pushing and pulling one another through fissures, some of which had been newly fractured.

They arrived at a different and, if possible, larger cavern. The geology of this one was more grim: it had been formed by a convulsion of the earth, and scoured by gushing lava flows and volcanic activity. The rocky floor had been wrenched into contorted shapes, and great gouges cut through the ground as though a giant sword had slashed at it.

'It's hard to breathe,' Jelindel shouted to the Stone Man.

Sulphurous gases were choking them, but Taroc nudged them forward. 'We must hurry.'

Then a hail of rocks rose high in the air and arced towards them, as if launched from unseen catapults. 'Behind me,' rumbled the Stone Man.

Jelindel did not move; instead, she spoke words of magic. Blue light gushed from her lips and formed a spinning vortex in the air. The rocky projectiles slammed into the tornado of light, spun several times, then were flung back on perfect reverse paths.

The Stone Man gazed at her in apparent approval. Then rocky hands shot out from the ground and grabbed his rock-sized ankles. He tottered sideways, and suddenly he was being pulled under. He struggled, but more granite hands seized him.

'Go. That way,' he boomed, pointing. 'Destroy the dark magic!' He vanished into the earth; a slight bubbling of the cavern floor the only sign that he had been; then it too subsided and the rock was rock once more.

Jelindel and Daretor hurried in the direction Taroc had indicated and clambered over the scree. From the top of the slope they had a good view of the fighting. It was a battle like nothing they had ever seen before.

The field was jammed with Stone People, tearing off chunks of rock and stone and hurling them with deadly accuracy and mind-numbing speed at their adversaries. The missiles flew through the air and impacted loudly, shattering heads and chests, and amputating limbs. The dead and dying slowly sank into the earth from whence they had come eons past.

The two sides surged against each other, making headway, then losing it again. They were well matched in sheer brute strength, though the opposing side was small in numbers. In the rear ranks of the opposition, Jelindel could see a clump of Stone People surrounding something that emitted a flickering light.

'The fools,' she cursed. 'They're using some kind of magecraft. They'll bring down the roof if they're not careful.'

'That might not matter to them,' Daretor opined.

'Perhaps, but it will be decidedly uncomfortable for us.'

A wave of darkness rushed forward like a small tidal wave and slammed into the front ranks of the Stone People, shattering them into pebbles. The wave dissipated and was then followed by another that hurled itself outwards. Jelindel reacted immediately, muttering a spell, and flinging it away.

The two forces impacted with a sound like great metal drums colliding. There was furious struggle between the two magical forces for a moment, then both vanished.

The battle continued unabated. Projectiles shot back and forth, Stone People clashed face to face with awesome results, their stone fists literally hammering each other to pieces. At the same time, others emerged from the ground or from walls and boulders, or melted into them to appear somewhere else in a surprise attack.

'Can you help them?' Daretor said, steadying himself with outflung hands as the ground twisted and rolled.

Jelindel too spread her hands for balance. 'I have no way of knowing who are Taroc's people and who aren't,' she said. 'The best I can do is ward off the magic used by the other side.'

Jelindel turned her attention to the group at the back. 'Of course.' She looked at the ceiling, where an extrusion of basalt showed. Almost without thinking, she hurled a massive spell at the dark basalt. An instant later it wrenched free of the roof and plunged straight down upon the group using the dark magic. The rest were discouraged and within moments the battle was over, the Stone People under Fa'red's control having retreated into the rocky rampart at the rear of the cavern.

Daretor caught Jelindel as she collapsed from the strain of maintaining her magic. Rocks were still raining down, so he heaved and dragged her to safety. No sooner had he crouched over her, than a figure rose slowly from the stone at their feet. Daretor jumped back in alarm. But it was Taroc. He appeared unhurt.

'We thought you were dead,' said Daretor.

'Stone People are hard to kill. You can shatter us into pieces sometimes and we will reform, though it might take a hundred of your years.'

He held out a lumpy gem of reddish jade, bound by a short leather thong.

'The dragonsight,' Jelindel whispered. 'You found it.'

'It was with those you crushed, as we knew it would be.' He handed the artefact to her. 'Now that we have kept our part of the bargain, you must free the dragons.' And he told her what to do with the dragonsight when they reached the Tower Inviolate.

'We will do this,' said Jelindel. 'I promise you.'

'I am known to the Sacred One. When you see him, tell him that the Stone People have not forgotten the kinship between our races.'

The Stone People led Daretor and Jelindel to the surface, where they discovered they were in a mountain range west of Bravenhurst, barely two hundred miles from Dremari. They bid Taroc and his people farewell.

Jelindel looked out across the plain. 'With luck S'cressling will scent that we're above ground.'

'Give me the ground to walk on anytime,' Daretor began, then thought twice about that statement. After what they had just experienced, the ground would never be the same again.

They climbed wearily down a steep gorge to a wide valley. Here, they tarried only a short time before S'cressling alighted beside them. A grinning Osric leapt off the dragon's back to greet them, followed by Zimak.

'Nothing like a dragon to stage a jailbreak,' said Zimak. 'How have you two been faring?'

Jelindel gave Zimak and Osric a hurried account of all that had happened.

'So you were caught between a rock and a hard place?' Zimak said, but the pun was not even sneered at.

'You have the relic?' Osric said.

Jelindel showed them the dragonsight. Zimak was curious in a professional, thieving manner, but it was Osric's reaction that startled them. He almost swooned, and S'cressling lumbered closer to observe the relic. Thin tendrils of smoke wafted from her nostrils.

'We've wasted enough time,' Jelindel said. 'It's a long flight to the Tower Inviolate.'

'Let's hope it isn't too long,' Daretor said grimly. 'I feel the poison like meltwater in my blood.'

Zimak patted his body. 'Now that you mention it, I too have a chill. Only I thought I got it riding S'cressling. While you two were cosy down below, Osric and I have been freezing our orchids off.'

Daretor had no strength to dispute Zimak's statement. They climbed aboard the dragon, and a moment later they were aloft. S'cressling banked sharply, swooping southwards.

Chapter 12

INTO THE SPIDER KINGDOM

S'cressling's huge wings beat the air like thunder, and the noise of their passage echoed through the mountains. Wandering shepherds, leagues away, looked up, fearing some nameless threat.

Jelindel and Daretor drowsed on the cramped deck, glad to be in the open air and beneath the sun again, despite the cold. Osric was overjoyed that they had recovered the dragonsight. S'cressling too seemed happy in an inscrutable, dragonish sort of way.

Despite her exhaustion, Jelindel roused herself enough to ask Osric and Zimak about Melyar. 'She made it back all right?'

'Don't sound so surprised,' said Zimak. 'The woman wouldn't stop crying. She kept going around touching everything and she pinched me at least four times. She said she couldn't believe her good fortune. And she had these flimsy bags that broke the moment you put anything in them. Gah, it's no wonder the woman's gone mad, living in such a weak paraworld.'

Osric took over. 'By then, the festival was ending, so we were able to find her a place to stay. We also purchased her passage with a camel train back to D'loom. She had been very happy till then. I asked her why her mood changed so suddenly. She said all her family and friends must be dead or gone by now. I told her that that did not need to be the case and that the Temple of Verity was still a strong order. She looked more hopeful after that.'

Jelindel only wished she could have been there when Melyar arrived. More to the point, it raised her belief in her own abilities. She had somehow magicked Melyar straight back to her original anchor on Q'zar. That had involved a degree of precision that she had never dared hope for.

'Hakat and QeSu, what of them?' asked Daretor.

'Gone forever, thanks to Jelindel,' said Zimak. 'And the thieving scoundrel's taken the machine, too.'

'What?' exclaimed Jelindel. 'The machine he can keep. And I did nothing to them.'

'Yes you did. They have been so inspired by your powers and scholarship that they want to be just like you. Melyar promised to get them into the Temple of Verity. Hakat as a lackey, of course, not a neophyte.'

'You're making this up,' said Jelindel, her eyes narrowing.

'Not at all. In order to repay you Melyar said she had to do something for someone else. For once the truth is funnier than a joke. You seem to have an inspiring effect on weak minds. Fortunately I'm thick-skinned, and am proofed against you.'

'Zimak, your skin is so thick that an arrow would go all the way through without encountering anything else but skin.'

Zimak patted his paunch. He looked at Daretor's glaring face. 'You're right. There does seem to be a fair bit of it.'

◈

Zimak was rankled by Jelindel's earlier comment about him being thick-skinned. So much so he could not help goading her. Sitting opposite them and stuffing dried beef strips into his mouth, he said, 'If you two don't wake up I'm not keeping any of this for you.'

Without opening his eyes Daretor grunted a reply: 'Good. More chance you'll choke to death.'

'That's a fine thing to say to somebody who's occupying your body and who's saved your life several times over.'

'And I yours,' Daretor grumbled, sleepily elevating one eyebrow. 'As for the body, you're welcome to it. I have this one more or less how I want it and I've decided that size and brawn doesn't matter.'

A gamin of a smile touched Jelindel's cheeks, but she kept her eyes closed. A shout from the mane drowned Zimak's attempt at a scornful reply.

'I've been looking over the maps and our path to the Tower Inviolate will not be easy,' Osric said.

'Is nothing easy these days?' Daretor grumbled, pushing himself up on one elbow.

'As long as I can sleep,' Jelindel murmured. 'Finding the dragonsight despite Fa'red's interference wasn't the easiest heist I've been involved in.'

Osric sat down near Jelindel. Sensing his unease, she struggled back to alertness. 'Is everything all right?'

'I believe so, although all is not what it appears.'

'Aha.' She rubbed her chin thoughtfully. 'Something troubles you?'

'Not me,' said Osric. 'S'cressling is the troubled one. Her dragonsense has her restless.'

Daretor sat up. 'I judge we have five days before the poison takes effect. Is there a safe way to the citadel? Any more of these delays will put an end to us.'

'I don't know as yet,' Osric said. 'But I was thinking . . . you have the dragonsight and it is said that the jewel can sometimes see the future. Perhaps it would be wise to consult it.'

Jelindel frowned, fishing out the crimson gemstone from where it hung inside her tunic. It pulsed a dull red, with a rhythm that had an odd familiarity, as if it were telling her something that she should know.

Osric eyed it with awe and reverence. It was a talisman of great power that meant far more to him and his people than to the wayfarers who were his friends.

Jelindel gazed at the dragonsight. 'Despite all my skills, Osric, I still have no idea how to use it. That it has immense power, I know. I can sense it. My heart seems to have fallen into rhythm with its beat. But the key to its power is beyond me, at least for now. Still, I will keep prying at it; perhaps I'll get lucky.'

S'cressling suddenly banked sharply. A sound like a plague of locusts filled the air even as the dragon bellowed in anger and defiance.

Fighting to keep their footing, the four scrambled about the deck and gazed in horror at the sight before them. The air was alive with fearsome creatures that manoeuvred to and fro in an insane dance, as if engaged in an aerial dogfight. S'cressling had blundered into the middle of a lethal battle by dropping out of the clouds above.

'By all my odd gods these are not of Q'zar,' Daretor swore.

'Just where are we?' Zimak demanded of Osric.

Jelindel turned to the dragonrider. 'Could the Tower Inviolate have brought these things in with it?' And other creatures too, she wondered.

Osric held on tight as S'cressling jerked to one side. 'We're within the citadel's realm.' He shook his head wildly. 'I'll try to explain later. Hold on.'

The creatures were giant spiders, covered in sharp steel-like bristles and chitinous armour. They had long vivid orange and black legs that whipped and sliced like scimitars. Their fangs, trailling thick ropy threads of saliva, worked hungrily, snapping open and shut like bolt-cutters, while two rows of ruby eyes glinted.

Vast plumes of liquid silk trailed from their finger-like spinnerets, knitting into broad webs, with which they trapped and worked the invisible air currents, steering first one way and then another with astonishing and frightening speed. Although there were many species that travelled thus upon Q'zar's air currents, none was the size of these monstrosities.

'What in Black Quell's beard?' Zimak said, barely above a whisper.

'Look out!' warned Jelindel as a spider came sailing low across the deck, its fangs slashing at Daretor. He threw himself down, narrowly avoiding the lethal sword-length teeth.

Osric rushed forward to command S'cressling. The ponderous dragon flat-planed its membranous wings and sailed swiftly past two spiders plummeting in a deadly embrace.

Zimak gripped a safety rope and pulled himself toward his fallen companion. Holding the rope with one hand, he unsheathed his sword and stood guard over Daretor until he found his footing. 'Here,' Zimak said, throwing Daretor a sword. 'Don't get my body damaged.' He threw a short sword to Jelindel, who caught it deftly.

Jelindel kept her head down but watched the aerial combat carefully. 'I think there are two sides fighting one another, and that we have flown into the middle of it,' she said as S'cressling ducked and wove her way through the melee.

'That'll be a comfort when we're diced and sliced, and in their bellies,' Daretor ventured.

'Osric, can we get away by diving?' Jelindel called.

Osric nodded and shouted something that was ripped away by the wind. S'cressling went into a steep dive.

'I think he said, "Hang on",' cried Zimak, as the deck tilted alarmingly. The tactic didn't work. Whatever battle the spiders were engaged in had come to its conclusion, and while a number ballooned away into a nearby cloud, others twisted and dropped in pursuit of the dragon.

Clearly, S'cressling was far too large a target for the spiders, but her puny riders were not. The spiders made several low-flying swoops across the deck, snatching at them. Their ability to manoeuvre was daunting.

S'cressling's jaws snapped open and a jet of fire shot out, roasting a spider in midair and catching the webbed plume of another. The spider web flamed and dissolved instantly. With a hideous screech, the spider clutched its abdomen with its legs and dropped like a stone.

Zimak and Osric cheered, but S'cressling's attack did nothing to deter the other spiders, except to give them a deep respect for the front end of a dragon. Consequently, the Q'zarans were taken completely by surprise when the spiders attacked from behind.

Jelindel slashed at one attacker but her sword merely glanced off the spider's fangs as they snapped about her. She felt two sharp pricks in her shoulders and a moment later two hairy legs swept her up. Within seconds its bristles pinioned her like living vices. Fighting a creeping drowsiness she muttered a spell. Tiny guttering blue light formed about her lips then lashed out at the closest spider, binding it instantly in a coruscating shell of electric light. Just as quickly the spell dissipated on the wind. Jelindel finally succumbed to semi-paralysis. The spider crouched, then launched itself into the air.

Unbalanced by S'cressling's attempts to escape, Daretor and Zimak also fell easy prey to the attackers.

Only Osric was spared as he was too far forward and therefore close to S'cressling's deadly furnace.

Moments later, the triumphant spiders rose at great speed into the upper air currents, far beyond S'cressling's ability to follow or retaliate.

Osric's small voice rose up from below. 'I will find you!'

The spiders flew so high that it was difficult to breathe. The bitter cold froze their limbs and further dulled their minds. Jelindel expected to die and thought that this was probably a far more pleasant end than what their captors had in store for them.

So it was that after many hours Jelindel became dully aware that it was getting warmer. From this she deduced that either the venom was fading or they were descending. Both proved to be the case as she glimpsed a vast forest below. Soon she could smell pollen and resin on the air, and hear ululating voices and the thrumming of many feet. She glanced at the others. Zimak was either unconscious or dead; Daretor was hanging slack against the spider's legs but his eyes flicked open and met hers. He gave her a wan smile.

'We're not yet dead?' he croaked.

She could barely make out the words. 'We may wish we were,' she managed to say.

'Aye,' he said, and relaxed into his tormented slumber.

The warmth was a profound luxury, like discovering an oasis in the desert. Jelindel felt her limbs revive and her mind become fully alert.

It was clear that the spiders were dropping toward the thick forest canopy. As they did so, Jelindel noted that their captors were gradually changing colour to blend in with the new environment.

Skylines were deployed in great cone-shaped fans that slowed their descent. One by one they dropped into the thick foliage and vanished from view.

As Jelindel's captor plunged in amongst the trees she shut her eyes for an instant then forced herself to watch; she needed to stay alert, to learn all she could, in case there was the slightest possibility of escape.

She was amazed to discover a city set high in the trees many hundreds of feet above the ground. The spiders detached themselves from the skylines and dropped onto broad spider webs set amongst the trees; nearby were the dwellings of humans, each linked by wide wooden thoroughfares that spanned the lofty gaps between trees, and on which a respectable volume of foot traffic could be seen. However, the humans that Jelindel could make out were clearly slaves; each wore nothing but a leather loin cloth, and some kind of silver torc-like jewellery around their necks.

White baubles the size of horse trays hung from the tree trunks. With a start Jelindel realised that these were silken egg sacs.

The arrival of the spiders caused the nearest humans to stop what they were doing and fall upon their knees; each bowed low to the nearest spider, and a chant sprang up. The humans weren't just slaves, they were *worshippers*.

Daretor's spider had landed nearby, though there was no sign of Zimak. Daretor and Jelindel looked at each other.

'Seems we've been captured by Black Quell's minions,' said Daretor sourly. 'And no better place for them to breed,' he added, looking around.

Jelindel worked warmth into her shoulders and legs. 'We're alive, Daretor. That in itself proves these monstrosities can make mistakes.'

The spiders dumped Jelindel and Daretor on a nearby pathway and hissed several commands that sounded intelligent, despite the sibilant speech. The two were immediately surrounded by human slaves and bundled away to a cage high in a tree. They were given wooden bowls filled with gruel and water. Setting the bowls aside they gazed at the aerial city from a small barred window. A short time later Zimak was thrown in.

Some hours passed. Finally the door opened and a tall man in rustic hessian robes entered. Acolytes or guards flanked him; it was hard to tell.

He introduced himself as Usel and claimed to be a priest who ministered to the souls of the damned, by which he clearly meant his own people. He explained that the spiders had descended upon the forest city three generations ago. They had killed many and enslaved the rest. There were several different tribes of privateer spiders that only ate other arachnids; they were also in conflict with a kingdom to the north, which the spiders raided mercilessly. However, the spiders were almost useless in any kind of orthodox warfare on the ground. Something had happened recently though. The sky had tumbled in on them and changed colour, as had the planets. It was as though a powerful magic had descended upon them.

'You're no longer where you think you are,' Jelindel said. It was useless trying to explain paraworld travel to these people.

How could she explain that a huge mountain and everything within its circumference had been sucked through the paraplane to Q'zar? 'And your priesthood. The spiders let you be?'

Usel shrugged. 'We have a certain amount of freedom. The spiders are . . . pragmatic. Anything that keeps their slaves docile seems a good thing to them.'

Daretor scowled. 'So you collaborate in the enslavement of your own people?'

Usel's face flashed with anger. 'I collaborate in keeping as many of my people as possible alive. If you would like to keep breathing, I suggest you learn from our example.'

Daretor snorted but said nothing.

Zimak spoke instead. 'How do we get out of here?' he asked.

'Get out?' Usel repeated, enunciating the words as if they were from a dead language. 'There is no getting out. You are here, and here you will stay, at the mercy of the Kindred.'

'What kind of mercy is that?' Daretor growled.

Usel was philosophic. 'It will be what it will be. No man knows his lot.'

'Great,' said Zimak. 'Slave today, food tomorrow.'

Usel grunted. 'The spiders do not eat as we do. They wrap their food in cocoons and hang them for several days. Then they suck their victims dry so that only the husks remain. It is a lingering, painful death.'

'This just gets worse,' Zimak said. 'What manner of people are you to let yourselves get slaughtered like that?'

Usel looked at each of them in turn. 'Several Samaritans made the mistake of killing the cocooned prisoners to end their torture. But the Kindred descend to massacre ten for every one thus put out of their misery. They only enjoy fresh, live fare.'

'Even I would rather go out fighting,' Zimak said.

Usel smiled as though enjoying a private joke, then beckoned one of the acolytes forward. He held three of the silvery torcs, which turned out to be a kind of special web. The acolyte went to fit one about Daretor's neck but the swordsman knocked him to the ground.

Usel stared pityingly at him. 'One word from me and the Kindred will come for you, and you will fight to join the ranks of the Undying.'

'Undying?' Zimak said. 'Immortals?'

Usel glanced at the giant thief, but returned his attention to Daretor. 'Immortality yes, but at the price of pain and suffering unlike anything you have ever experienced.'

Jelindel put a hand on Daretor's arm. 'We must bide our time for now,' she said mildly.

Daretor considered. 'For now,' he said. An acolyte fastened the circlets around each of their throats, pressing the ends together. Within moments the necklaces were seamless; they were also as tough as hardened steel.

'By these,' said Usel, 'the Kindred can find you anywhere you go.' To the acolytes he snapped, 'Take them to the Place of Testing.'

They sat in a wooden cage as the contraption was lowered by a dragline several hundred feet to a huge wooden platform. Beside them sat two sullen-faced slaves. As they descended one of the slaves struck up a conversation.

'You are the newcomers?' he asked. He must have been handsome in his time. His silvery thatch of wild hair was pulled back into a ponytail and tied with a leather thong. Jelindel noted that he was also lame in one leg.

'We were captured this morning,' she answered. 'And you?'

'Some years ago. I was a mercenary. I was ambushed along with my entire squad. I am all that is left, and now I am useless because of my leg. My name is Retok.'

Daretor rattled the cage. Two slaves were at once by his side, their swords pricking his skin.

'Where are they taking us?' he asked, ignoring twin trickles of blood coursing his arms.

'Are you skilled fighters?'

'We give a good account of ourselves.'

'You are to be tested,' said Retok. 'If you pass, you will live in a manner of speaking.'

'And if we fail?' Zimak asked.

'The spiders are ravenous at this time of year, made all the more so by these strange events.' Retok waited for a response. When he received none, he continued. 'Yet there are worse things than becoming fodder. Sometimes those who win, lose, and sometimes those who lose, win.'

'What is that supposed to mean? Does everyone here speak in riddles?' Daretor demanded.

Retok grinned. 'I see you have met our high priest. No doubt he made you think you would be kept alive if you acquiesced. Unfortunately, since travelling to this place, the Kindred have need of ground fighters. Much is happening that is beyond their understanding.'

Retok's shoulders slumped. 'For a year I have planned an escape, but for naught.' He indicated the southern approach to the forest. 'One thing I did learn. The Kindred have covered that approach with sheets of silk. Attached to them are signal threads. Put one step on their trap and they spray digestive juices.'

Zimak's face paled when he noticed Retok's scarred and inflamed leg.

'All other paths are otherwise fortified,' Retok added. 'Our overseers have left nothing to chance.'

Jelindel felt the man's despair. 'There is something you aren't telling us.'

Retok thought about his reply. 'Forewarned is not always forearmed, my lady,' he said. 'Sometimes it is better not to know one's fate.'

'Well that's great,' said Zimak sourly. 'That's just great. As if poison in our veins isn't enough . . .' He snapped his fingers and grinned fleetingly. 'Hie, if the spiders eat us, they might get a good dose of poison.'

'I have a feeling we're not heading for the fodder cocoons,' Jelindel said.

The bamboo cage grounded abruptly and the gate was yanked open. The occupants stepped out on to a wooden platform that was a hundred yards across. On the other side a dozen warriors stood to attention. Their eerily still poise seemed almost inhuman, as if they had dispensed with breathing altogether.

Following their gaze, Retok said, 'The Undying. Pray you do not join their ranks.'

'Hie, they don't look so tough,' Zimak said. 'Do we have to fight them one at a time or all at once?'

Retok's lips curled into a tight smile.

One of the Undying stepped forward. The other man that had been in the cage with them was handed a sword and shoved onto the battle quadrant, a cordoned off forty foot square area in the middle of the platform. The man went immediately into a fighting stance but it did him little good. The Undying moved with reflexes that were unbelievably fast. In seconds, he was so much twitching meat on the platform, gushing blood.

'They move pretty fast,' Zimak said clinically.

'The Kindred have a power that is not unlike that of the dragon's magic. It binds the Undying together.' Retok would say no more. He was given a sword and pushed into the square by two slaves. The same Undying soldier met him and the warriors launched into a fierce sword battle. Retok proved to be a master swordsman, but with his withered leg he could barely hold his own against the phenomenal speed of his opponent.

Suddenly, he flung away his sword and stood panting before the Undying. The other paused, as if noting this. He saluted Retok then decapitated him cleanly and swiftly.

Jelindel looked away, disheartened. Then it was Daretor's turn. He took the sword given him and weighed it in his hand, judging its balance. He flashed Jelindel a quick smile. Few, if any, ordinary mortals could best Daretor at the sword. Or, for that matter, Jelindel and Zimak. Yet Retok's words of caution and his bloody demise had unnerved them.

Daretor stepped into the square. A new Undying broke ranks and marched forward to face him. Daretor tensed as his opponent drew near, for what approached was clearly a corpse; one animated by the uncanny magic of the Kindred. Instead of muscle and sinew, the body before him was knit together by hundreds, perhaps thousands, of spiderlings linked together like a living mailshirt. It emitted a low, insect-like keening.

Daretor stared at the crawling, shifting monstrosity, noting that the eyes were human enough.

'Are you alive?' he asked.

'I am alive in a sense,' said the Undying in a rasping voice. 'You are new?'

Daretor nodded. The other almost shrugged its spider-controlled shoulders. The gesture was grotesquely human. 'If you equal or defeat me, you will be colonised. The Kindred will lay their eggs in you and the newborn Kindred will devour you slowly from within, replacing your muscles and sinews. You will become as me. An elite warrior.'

'Can you be killed?' asked Daretor.

'To die forever? That is what I pray for.' He raised his sword in a gladiatorial salute. Daretor did likewise, although revulsion shivered through him.

The Undying slashed with lightning speed. Daretor nearly lost all in that first second but he managed to block the deadly cut, and immediately moved in under the other's guard to thrust him through the chest. The Undying staggered back as a collective gasp went up from the assembled onlookers. It seemed that few ever managed to make contact with an Undying.

The thrust had little lasting effect. The Undying soldier recovered and came back like a charging bull, slashing hard. Daretor blocked, parried, drove forward again. The blades flashed with blurring speed, almost invisible to the human eye.

Jelindel anxiously bit her lower lip. Even Zimak became uneasy as the duel continued. The moves were so fast it was difficult to make out what was happening. Only the rapid clanging sound of steel on steel told the full story.

'Do something,' Zimak urged Jelindel.

She shook her head. 'Not yet. Wait.'

The Undying, barely breathing, stood back. Through slightly parted lips he said, 'You fight well. Do not fight *too* well.'

'Can you be defeated?' Daretor reiterated, panting heavily.

'I can, but no more than that can I say.'

Daretor swung suddenly, severing the Undying's sword arm. The Undying snap-rolled aside and snatched up the sword with his other hand. He was once again on his feet, closing for battle. The technique happened in an eye blink.

Spiderlings scuttled across the platform and returned to their host, seemingly revitalising him.

Daretor feinted, fell back, switched sword arms, and in one clean move sliced off the head of the Undying.

A ripple of disbelief ran through the gathered Undying.

Zimak winced.

The body went into a crouch, swung wildly at Daretor, then against all reason shed its living skin as it collapsed.

Thousands of spiderlings dropped from the corpse like a spilt bag of marbles and scuttled across to the ranks of the other Undying, where they swarmed into other bodies, taking up residence within.

Meanwhile, Daretor's opponent sagged into a carcass of parchment-dry flesh and bone.

At that moment the throaty notes of a shell horn sounded. All heads snapped up. Spiders scrambled for the trees, crashing upward through foliage and branches, scrabbling for the canopy. A sickening stench floated down, making everyone cough.

Jelindel grabbed a slave by the arm. 'What's happening?'

'We are being attacked. We must go to our battle stations at once,' the slave screeched, clearly terrified.

Zimak took over from Jelindel and held the slave in a wrist lock. 'By Black Quell's beard what is that awful stench?'

The slave nearly swooned such was his fear.

'The smell?' Zimak asked patiently.

'The Kindred are secreting their plumes and taking flight. They will not stay among the trees during an attack. To your battle stations!' the slave screamed.

Zimak pushed the slave from him. In the scant moments it took Zimak to interrogate the slave, the platform had emptied, save an Undying who had silently crept up on them and stood guard.

'I never did like heights,' Jelindel said. 'Daretor?'

The swordsman threw his sword to her. She caught it, and in the same motion, sliced upwards. The Undying guard brought his own sword around and met her attack with a resounding clash. The moment that Jelindel staggered back, Zimak swept up Retok's fallen sword and swung with all his might.

The Undying's head hung in the air for a split second as though in shock, then fell. Its body followed seconds later. Within seconds the spiderlings abandoned their host and, with no ready host available, milled around in confusion.

The trio made for the edge of the platform and peered over. The ground, though clad in murky shifting shadows, was only a hundred feet below. They quickly located three draglines hanging from the platform. Tying them together gave them a reach short of the forest floor.

Jelindel pulled the knots taut, testing their strength. 'It will have to do.'

Already they could hear the battle sounds approaching. Daretor tied off the makeshift rope and dropped the end over the side. One by one they climbed down, hand over hand, and looping the hardened silk between their ankles and feet. It was tiring and dangerous work; their sweaty palms made their grip slippery. Had it not been for the stickiness of the draglines they would have lost their hold and plummeted to their deaths. Once, Jelindel started to fall but Daretor snagged her wrist and held on till she regained her grip on the rope.

Shortly they were on the ground, breathing heavily, and listening to the battle noise. The air was alive with the sound of frenzied chittering. Without a word, they moved in the opposite direction, ploughing through deep leaf mould that slowed their passage on the one hand, and dampened the noise of their passing on the other.

Before long they entered a section of the forest where the trees were knitted together by impenetrable spiny gorse. They stood more than twenty feet high and seemed to form walls through which rough paths ran.

The three made use of the paths and picked up the pace, but it wasn't long before the reality dawned on them.

'It's a maze,' said Jelindel, plucking a brownish swatch from one of the thorns. The kid leather clearly came from her own tunic.

'We're going in circles,' Daretor confirmed. 'Retok warned us of ground defences.'

Zimak glanced apprehensively at the dark thorn maze. 'What do we do now?' A sudden noise made them stop and listen. It was the sound of a creature breathing, along with something else . . . like a large body being dragged through the mulch.

'If we're going to be lost,' Zimak answered himself, 'I think I'd rather be in another part of the maze.'

'For once we agree on something,' said Daretor, keeping his voice down.

'You don't suppose the Kindred have some ground-dwelling cousins, do you?' asked Jelindel.

Zimak scowled. 'You can keep your imagination to yourself.'

'Let's move, then,' she said. 'Whatever happens, Osric will be looking for us. S'cressling might also sense the dragonsight if she's close.'

'Let's hope she senses it in time,' said Daretor.

'Can't you *use* that thing? Maybe it could show us the way out,' Zimak said.

'Zimak is right,' said Daretor.

'I can try,' Jelindel said, 'but right now I think we should stay on the move, and try to keep a straight line. We need to find a hill or a clearing.'

With Daretor leading, they pushed on cautiously. Zimak picked up the rear, while Jelindel carefully examined the dragonsight, running her fingers across its multifaceted surface and murmuring soft spells that sounded like prayers.

The trio had been moving for almost an hour when they heard the noise again, startlingly close. They were moving through rank brambles and weeds when the noise burst on them. Something charged from the other side of a thorn wall. It nearly broke through, and they glimpsed a vicious set of mandibles and the front part of a spider that was the size of a cow. It tore frenziedly at the wall, trying to gore them.

Daretor struck down with his sword, cleaving the creature's skull. They didn't wait to see if there were any more. Heedless of the thorns snatching them, they hurried on, putting as much distance behind them as possible.

Breathless, they eventually stumbled to a halt, hands on knees, trying to get their breath.

Jelindel gasped a few words. 'I *felt* it!' she said. When she had her breathing under control, she explained that moments before the attack she had felt a kind of *tug* inside the dragonsight, as if it were indicating the direction from which the attack was about to come. And before that, she had noticed that every time they reached a crossing or a fork in the way she had felt a similar, but fainter, tug that she had dismissed as some quirk of the gemstone.

'What are you saying?' asked Daretor.

'I think it's trying to tell us how to get out of here.'

'Why would it do that?' asked Zimak. 'It's done nothing for us so far.'

Jelindel had thought about that. 'Maybe it wants to go home as much as we do. I say we try it. We have nothing to lose.'

From that point on whenever they came to an intersection of

gorse corridors or a fork, Jelindel gestured either left or right, or straight ahead. Daretor forged down the path indicated.

Shortly they had left the maze and re-entered the forest proper. The dark walls loomed behind. Exiting the maze, however, must have triggered an alarm.

Suddenly the ground quivered on all sides, then bulged upward; arms appeared, then bodies. With a rasping sound half a dozen figures rose out of the ground like salmon bursting from water.

The creatures seemed to be made of the earth itself except that they were accoutred with scimitars and sharp curving daggers. The Q'zarans dropped into fighting stances, back to back, as the golems closed in with unsheathed swords.

Jelindel muttered a binding spell and sent it arcing toward the vanguard. Nothing happened.

'They're using the spider magic. I can't stop them,' she said helplessly.

The two sides clashed, broadsword upon scimitar. The sound echoed hollowly beneath the boughs of the forest. Daretor quickly sliced one of the creatures in half. Just as quickly it reformed, the dirt from which it was made flowing back in to fill the cut and rejoin the severed halves.

Battling for their lives, Jelindel and Zimak were discovering the same thing. The three Q'zarans were far better fighters than their adversaries. Only humans bleed when cut, and eventually tire. There could be only one outcome to a fight such as this. It would just take time.

As they hacked and hewed and slashed and parried, Jelindel tried every kind of spell she could call to mind, but nothing came to their rescue. Zimak chopped the legs out from under one of the golems. Though it grunted as if in pain, and toppled to the ground, it was back on its feet within seconds, sword swinging viciously.

'We can't keep this up,' wheezed Daretor.

'The dragonsight, Jelindel,' Zimak cried. 'It's built on dragon magic. Try *something!*'

Jelindel pulled out the talisman. At the very sight of it, the earthen creatures fell back, recognising its innate power. At the same time they seemed to know, intuitively perhaps, that it could not be used against them . . . at least not by the mortals. They renewed their attack.

'It won't work,' Jelindel said. 'I don't know how to use it.' She stumbled, rolling to one side as a sword pierced the ground beside her head.

'Then in White Quell's name, let's get out of here,' said Zimak. Like the others, he had just heard distant sounds high in the trees; that of large bodies moving at speed through the upper canopy.

An idea occurred to Jelindel. 'Zimak is right. Follow me.'

They broke out of the encirclement and fought a rear-guard action beneath the trees, always maintaining as steady a pace as the relentless onslaught from behind allowed. In this fashion they progressed several hundred yards.

Suddenly Zimak tripped and went down. Instantly, his two attackers leapt towards him. He scrambled away furiously, tossing up so much mulch in his fright that it nearly obscured all sight. Then he hit a fallen log and came to a groaning stop.

His two pursuers raised their swords high for the kill, barrelling towards him. Jelindel cried out and even Daretor winced at the imminent and unpreventable kill. Just as the two earth creatures reached Zimak they started to come apart, ploughing back into the earth. Seconds later, they were all gone.

Daretor and Zimak stared in amazement.

'What just happened?' asked Daretor. He noted that Jelindel did not seem surprised. 'You expected this?'

She nodded, trying to get back her breath.

'Zimak gave me the idea,' she said. 'When the dragonsight failed, I realised that this kind of protective magic operates within boundaries. Once you cross the boundary line it no longer works. I just didn't know how far we'd have to go.'

Daretor picked up a stick and drew a line in the ground a few inches from his feet. Hacking a piece of vine from a tree he collected another stick and made a cross.

Zimak frowned. 'What are you doing?'

Daretor rammed the inverted cross into the ground. 'Leaving a signpost. This is one line unsuspecting wayfarers shouldn't cross and one that escaping slaves *should*.'

At that point the circlets around their necks lost their shimmer and unthreaded.

Daretor ripped the circlet from around his neck and threw it across the clearing. 'That's one piece of jewellery that I'll never miss.'

Two days later they found a hill that rose out of the endless trees and broke free of the forest canopy. There they sat and waited, hungry and cold. Each had vomited bile mixed with blood. Jelindel observed that their eyesight had deteriorated and their blood had thinned, no doubt due to the nature of the poison. The slightest cut sluiced blood, further weakening them. Their various wounds were easily fixed with the laying of the hands, but even this drained Jelindel. Daretor insisted she leave the minor scratches to heal of their own accord.

On the third day Zimak, whose sight had deteriorated the least, spotted a dark speck in the horizon.

They hid, fearing it might be a patrolling spider. As the flying creature neared, fire gushed from its jaws and S'cressling settled on the hilltop. The Q'zarans left their cover and embraced Osric, filling him in on their adventures. He had had trouble locating them, and the Kindred had driven them off several times.

Jelindel really didn't care. 'As long as I can sleep,' she said, speaking for all of them.

Chapter 13
TO STORM A CITADEL

Jelindel stirred some hours later. Daretor and Zimak lay snoring to either side of her. Osric alone stood guard at the mane.

She reached over the side of the platform and spat a wad of bloodied phlegm. They appeared to be climbing still, for they were barely clearing the lower jagged buttresses of the Algon Mountains. S'cressling was battling icy air currents, striving to maintain an even keel. The wind bit at Jelindel's face, numbing it. She hunched her shoulders and rubbed her skin brusquely, working life into it.

To the right the mountain range rose, a solid wall. Jelindel saw herds of skittish goats scampering across the rocks, some leaping down impossibly steep slopes that funnelled into a caldera. Noticing she was awake, Osric pointed below.

Their shadow was see-sawing across the rugged terrain like a paraplane anomaly. Any living creature it touched or passed fled in a frenzy. S'cressling hung her head and screeched hungrily, adding impetus to the scurrying creatures.

Jelindel squeezed in beside Osric at the mane.

'At least S'cressling seems to be enjoying herself,' she called, raising her voice to be heard above the shrill wind.

Osric nodded. 'Hunting is in her blood, although she was never a predator.' He pulled a shawl from beneath the mane and handed it to her.

'And you?' Jelindel asked, tucking the shawl around her neck. 'You were raised in slavery, but now you're an adventurer.'

'I'm having a good time,' he replied honestly. He waved at the sun as though it in itself was all he desired. 'The hours are somewhat erratic, but my employers are not slave drivers. And I would swap all that I had as a slave for the freedom I now enjoy.'

For a moment his humour reminded her of Zimak. 'I'm glad to hear it,' she said. 'I haven't yet figured out why you're coming back to the Tower Inviolate of your own free will.'

Osric's youthful features became serious. 'There is a simple matter of the poison,' he said. 'By Zimak's reckoning your time is running short. He was sick before. Just blood came up.' When Jelindel said nothing, he added, 'You seem little concerned about death.'

Jelindel stared into the distance. 'Far from it. I'm the happiest I've ever been, yet my life is about to end. I gather Zimak has been discussing it with you – he doesn't share much with us.' She turned her gaze to Osric. 'It eats at Daretor's very core. He's fixated on honour, and dying from poison has no honour in it at all. Yet he doesn't speak of it. Nor do I, really. There's nothing to be gained by complaining. We must consider success our only future.'

'You Q'zarans are strange,' Osric said. 'It seems I am more concerned about your dilemma than you are.'

'Our lives mean that much to you?'

Osric looked at Daretor and Zimak. 'Your companions are

heroes back on my world. They rescued me from the Tower Inviolate. If not for them my people would still be living in fear and subjugation, and I would still be a slave.'

Jelindel followed his gaze. Daretor and Zimak *were* heroes, even here on Q'zar. Yet they were mere mortals, too, prone to human failings. 'You know that Rakeem will never keep his promise. His type never does. You could have just abandoned us and fled.'

'There are few places on Q'zar where S'cressling and I would be welcome. And I strongly suspect that my future has many paths. Pray that I choose wisely.'

'What do you see as *your* future, Osric?'

'One path is that my people will follow us here and topple King Amida and his people. Another sees the dragonsight in the hands of the Sacred One, and again the fall of King Amida. Yet a third sees the Tower Inviolate travelling back to our own world where my people will be waiting to avenge themselves. In any event, you three are intertwined in my future. That much is certain. You *have* to survive the poison.'

'And if Rakeem manages to keep the dragonsight?'

Osric stroked S'cressling's flowing mane, as though soothing her. 'That is not a path that I see,' he said simply.

Jelindel slapped Osric on the back. 'I feel better already.'

The journey back was faster than they had hoped. S'cressling seemed galvanised and managed to pick up an airstream that swept them across the Algon Mountains, to the Tower Inviolate.

It was night when they arrived. On the mountain side they found a hiding place, overlooking the massif. There was a cave here; inside they found the remnants of a hermit's camp. Discarded food, clothing, a pair of broken sandals, and ashes of a long-dead fire. Whoever had been here had fled in a hurry.

Osric built a fire. Over a light meal they discussed their plans.

'There's no point trying to storm the place,' Zimak said.

'Not with one dragon,' Osric agreed.

'We know that Rakeem will not honour the agreement,' Jelindel mused. 'That one knows little except treachery.'

'But you have the dragonsight,' said Osric. 'Can you not use it to bargain with him?'

'Perhaps. Whatever ploy we can think of, I'm sure Rakeem has thought of the counterstroke.'

'Well, all I can say is, we'd better get this right the first time,' said Zimak. 'I don't fancy dying an agonising death.'

'Perhaps Rakeem will take pity on you and cut your throat,' said Daretor.

'It's still your body,' Zimak reminded him.

'Not as I knew it!' Daretor said.

'Hie, Daretor, it bleeds pretty easily . . .'

Jelindel tried to block out their tedious bickering. To Osric she said, 'You lived in the Tower Inviolate for many years. You must know it like the back of your hand.'

Osric nodded.

'And you have friends there?'

Again he nodded.

'By my count, we have two days at most before the poison takes over completely,' Jelindel said, gazing sombrely around. 'Two days . . .'

'What are you thinking?' Daretor asked.

'I've had a thought,' she replied.

The plan was incredibly dangerous. Then again they had been living with danger for so long that it ceased to be anything but normal.

'I once swore that I would never again trust a woman. For you I shall make an exception,' said Osric.

Zimak retched. 'Gah,' he groaned, 'see what having to trust you does to me, Jelindel?'

They set off at dawn. Not long after, S'cressling caught sight of something beyond human vision. Osric saw nothing at first, then he called to the others and pointed.

'All that I can see is a dot,' said Daretor.

'Can S'cressling see something that we cannot?' asked Jelindel.

'Yes,' replied Osric. 'Her eyes are like the objective lens of a farsight. They gather more light than our small eyes. That dot is sure to be more than an eagle, trust me.'

'Then what?' asked Daretor. 'A dragon?'

'Something the size of a dragon, but not a dragon.'

'But nothing else of that size can fly,' said Daretor.

'I know, and S'cressling cannot believe her eyes,' said Osric.

Jelindel thought for a moment, then frowned. 'By any chance would S'cressling have caught sight of a giant, headless chicken growing out of a cottage?'

'Well, now that you mention it, yes,' said Osric, looking relieved. 'I mean, there are strict regulations about flying a dragon while under the influence of alcohol –'

'It's diving,' exclaimed Daretor. 'Diving almost straight down.'

'The chickenrider has seen us, but does not want to be seen,' said Jelindel.

'Chickenrider,' said Daretor, staring at the distant dot as it vanished into a cloud bank. 'The term lacks a certain epic quality.'

'How much do you know about that thing?' asked Osric.

'I've flown one,' said Jelindel.

'You've flown a giant chicken?' Osric said flatly.

'Well, sort of stoked one, and steered it.'

'Stoked? Steered?' responded Osric.

'It burned fruit peelings, rotten vegetables, all that sort of thing,' said Daretor. 'You shovel some in every half hour or so.'

'Burned?' asked Osric. 'Don't giant chickens eat?'

'There was a funnel, and a shovel was provided,' said Daretor. 'If you stopped shovelling, the thing stopped flying and you were in big trouble.'

'Fa'red,' said Jelindel. 'All sorts of pieces from a very difficult puzzle suddenly fall into place.'

'Fa'red grows giant chicken dragons in flying cottages?' asked Osric.

'Those things are not dragons,' explained Jelindel. 'They are like the cabin of a fishing boat mounted on a chicken without a head, a chicken grown to the size of a dragon. Unlike dragons, they are totally controllable. They have no brain, eyes, or anything. They do precisely what the chickenrider wants. They are fearless, and need a steersman and shoveller to fly. They can also carry perhaps a dozen archers, or magicians, or a load of clay pots full of lamp oil that can set half a city on fire.'

'Still vastly inferior to a dragon,' said Osric with a trace of a sneer.

'Not if there are no dragons to compete with,' said Jelindel. 'Fa'red only had to keep the dragonsight from King Amida's hands until the thousand years expired. Then the dragons would be free of their enslavement – that is, according to myth.'

'It is no myth,' Osric asserted. 'The Sacred One had his power stolen a thousand years ago by a potent wizard. He bound the dragonsight for a thousand years so that dragons would learn humility before humankind. If, once that time has elapsed, the dragonsight is still in the hands of a human, the dragons will still be enslaved. And another thousand years of slavery will follow. It's imperative the Sacred One lays claim to that which is rightfully his.'

Jelindel thought back to what Fa'red had told her earlier. 'If Fa'red fails to unlock the power of the dragonsight, he might simply return it to the Sacred One, making peace with the dragons. Once he's achieved that, he might help them return to their paraworld.'

'That's presuming the dragons want to abandon their birthplace for another paraworld,' put in Osric.

Daretor cut in. 'With no dragons, the giant chickens – Fa'red calls them airliners, by the way – will have only the flying spiders to compete with for mastery of the skies, and the spiders have limitations, as we discovered. If Fa'red returns the entire mountain to the other paraworld, in all likelihood the spiders will go with it.'

'I wonder how many of the airliners Fa'red has grown?' asked Osric.

'Probably a dozen or so,' said Jelindel. 'That number in skilled hands could sink a war fleet, either on the high seas or in port. You see, they just need to stay higher than bowshot or catapult range; they only have to drop pots of burning oil.'

'It will be a very one-sided fight,' said Daretor. 'Totally without honour.'

'But militarily very effective,' said Jelindel. 'Osric, can you ask S'cressling to fly through the cloud down there, so that we can look around for the airline base.'

'I really thought I had seen the last of this sort of undignified fighting,' protested Daretor.

S'cressling changed course and began a long, shallow dive for the place where the distant dot had vanished into the clouds. The sky was a brilliant blue above, while the cloud base was a flat, grey carpet that stretched from horizon to horizon.

'How does she know where to go?' asked Zimak, looking past Osric. 'All that cloud looks the same.'

'How do you know what to do with a sword in a fight?' replied Osric. 'If you have been doing something all your life you tend to do it without thinking, and be good at it. The position of the sun, the patterns in the clouds that we cannot see, the feel of the wind, the pressure of the air, it all adds up.'

'How do you know all that?' Zimak wondered.

'I don't. S'cressling does.'

They entered the layer of cloud. Immediately they were blinded and chilled by mist so thick that they could not even see S'cressling's head. They seemed to be flying blind for a very long time.

'What if this fog is close to the ground, rather than fog really high up?' Zimak asked.

'S'cressling can feel the pressure of the air around her,' said Osric. 'The pressure tells her that we are ten thousand feet above the ground. Two miles high.'

'Ah, that's comforting – gah!' Zimak exclaimed. 'Mountains can be higher than ten thousand feet. What about if these clouds are hiding mountains?'

'S'cressling cheeps every few moments, then listens for an echo. If she hears an echo from dead ahead, then there is a mountain there.'

Zimak scowled. 'Then what?'

'She starts flapping, gains height, and flies over. Or she might do a few more cheeps to work out the mountain's outline, and fly around it.'

'I don't hear any cheeping,' Zimak said dourly.

'She is cheeping, only it is too shrill for you to hear.'

'Gah, what's the point of that?' asked Zimak

'Cattle, sheep, other prey like that cannot hear the dragon coming, so the dragon does not give away its location. That is why they can strike in total darkness, mist, and smoke, and why they approach in silence.'

'Then how can you tell she's cheeping?' Zimak wanted to know.

'Zimak!' Jelindel snapped.

'It is all right,' said Osric. 'I can't tell if she is cheeping, but I am fairly sure that she is not feeling depressed and contemplating suicide, so I doubt that she is likely to forget the cheeping, fly straight into a solid wall of rock, then plunge in a mangled heap to rocks thousands of feet below.'

'But –'

By now even Osric was becoming annoyed. 'Look, Zimak, next time you have your sword out and are fighting for your life, do you really think you would need me there yelling at you to keep your eyes open?'

'Enough, Zimak,' Jelindel said. Something in her tone made Zimak clamp his mouth.

The mist began to lighten. Moments later they were a little below the cloud base. They were high over farmland.

'Now are you convinced?' asked Osric. 'We are a mile and a half up, and there are no mountains.'

'I can see some hills,' muttered Zimak.

'No more than two hundred feet high,' estimated Osric.

'And I see a town,' said Jelindel.

'They are pretty common,' replied Osric.

'This one is running.'

'What?' gasped Osric and Daretor together, as Jelindel brought her farsight to bear on the dark patch far below.

'The giant chicken-cottage things, hundreds of them, all running along in formation.'

'Hundreds?' exclaimed Daretor. 'Did you say hundreds?'

'That I did,' said Jelindel, looking elsewhere. 'I also see that Fa'red's growing many more airliners. So many, hundreds, perhaps a thousand.'

'I've heard of a face that launched a thousand ships, but a thousand giant chickens?' said Osric.

'How could Fa'red have found the money for so many?' asked Daretor.

'Well, they live on chickenfeed,' said Jelindel. 'Admittedly, an awful lot of chickenfeed, but then chickens eat just about anything: grass, leaves, garbage scraps. An army of five thousand could do the work of tending them, and most kingdoms have armies that size, or larger. Fa'red must have convinced some ambitious monarch to provide the manpower, in return for invincible steeds for his army.'

'That's totally and absolutely without honour!' spat Daretor. 'Imagine a warrior being killed in battle, then having to explain to the gods of the afterlife that he was trampled to death by a giant chicken. I mean if he fronted up to the Warrior's Circle in paradise with a story like that they'd slam the dummart door in his face.'

'Hie,' Zimak said. 'That two-timing rat Hargrellien.'

'You're right,' Daretor admitted grudgingly. 'Last time we saw her, she said she was going to build something called a squadron. She must have done so, and joined forces with Fa'red.'

'For all her faults, she did save our lives,' Jelindel reminded them. Her voice caught. 'There,' she cried. 'Look down there.'

'Fires,' observed Daretor. 'Someone is fighting back.'

'Not so,' said Jelindel, squinting through her farsight again. 'There's . . . four no, five airliners dropping fire pots on a stone bridge. The airliners are about as long and wide as a ship. I think they're just in training.'

'Still not as good as a dragon,' boasted Osric.

'True, but still vastly better than no dragon at all,' Jelindel repeated. 'A thousand airliners could move an army of ten thousand at a hundred times the speed of marching men. Such mobility would win most battles before they began.'

'. . . a hundred times the speed of a marching man,' muttered Osric. 'Hold a moment. That's as fast as S'cressling.'

'Yes,' said Jelindel. 'We must be sure to stay clear of them.'

Daretor leaned over the side of the palanquin. 'Remember that town that was running along the ground? Well now it's taken off and flying.'

'Osric, we're still descending,' said Jelindel. 'You were meant to keep S'cressling near the clouds so we could hide quickly.'

'Well you could have told me.'

'Flock of two or three hundred airliners about to intercept,' reported Zimak.

'Climb!' shouted Jelindel. 'Tell S'cressling to climb for the clouds.'

For the next few minutes nothing more was said. S'cressling beat her wings, gaining dozens of feet in height with every stroke. The squadron of airliners spread out like a vast net in the sky.

'They climb faster than we do,' said Osric. 'How can that be?'

'They are bred to do nothing except fly and run,' explained Jelindel. 'Nor do they have the weight of a head and neck.'

'No head,' said Osric. 'That means they will not have echo location like S'cressling does. Once we are in the clouds they will be blind yet she can still locate them.'

'All very nice as long as we can reach the clouds,' said Daretor, stringing the only bow on board. 'We have two dozen arrows.'

'Three hundred airliners, ten archers on each, that's odds of three thousand to one,' said Jelindel. 'Sufficiently bad odds for a gloriously heroic battle, Daretor.'

'Is that meant to cheer me up?'

'I'd not dream of it.'

The first of the arrows began to whiz past. The cloud base was still hundreds of feet above. S'cressling was beginning to tire after the frantic climb, for most dragon flight is achieved by riding air currents. Only occasionally do they flap their wings to gain a little height, change direction, or find a better air current. Daretor was certainly no match for the best of the enemy archers. Most of his shots fell short of their target, and would probably not have hit even if they had made the distance.

Occasional arrows were hitting S'cressling, but all bounced off her scales.

'Can't you ask S'cressling to spray them with fire?' demanded an exasperated Daretor.

'That takes energy, and she needs all she has to out-distance our foe. If they get any closer, we will be shot full of arrows in a thrice,' replied Osric. 'Besides, they could – argh!'

An arrow had struck the youth's arm, pinning it to the wooden saddle frame. Jelindel was beside him in an instant, cutting through the shaft and pulling it out.

'Are you all right?' she asked.

'Just winged me,' gasped Osric. 'Why is it always me who gets it in the arm?'

'Just lucky I guess,' Jelindel said, smiling. 'Hold still, I'll need to staunch the blood.'

'Make it quick, please.' He winced. 'We need to take evasive action.'

No sooner had the wound stopped bleeding than S'cressling

banked sharply. A grotesquely large chicken, wearing a stream-lined cabin nearly collided head-on. But for S'cressling's exhalation of fire, which incinerated the airliner, they would surely have crashed into one another.

'That is what I feared. Suicide attempts,' shouted Osric. 'A collision with something as large as that will kill even a dragon. They're not invulnerable, after all.'

'But the riders would be killed too,' said Daretor.

'They only have to jump clear, and other airliners could swoop down to catch them.'

They ascended into the mists of the cloud base. S'cressling was suddenly the only one not flying blind. Damp, chilly, but concealing mists swept past.

'S'cressling says that the airliners are already far behind,' Osric reported.

'So, at least we saw the foundation of Fa'red's plans and survived to tell of it,' said Daretor.

'All the more reason to keep the dragonsight out of his hands,' said Jelindel.

'Never thought I'd be so happy to fly in clouds,' said Zimak. 'Osric, she is cheeping, isn't she?'

'Indeed she is.'

'One matter still puzzles me,' Jelindel admitted. 'Why didn't Fa'red take control of the dragons when he had the dragonsight?'

'Because the dragonsight is only half of it,' explained Osric. 'One also needs to control the Sacred One. Fa'red could not do that; the Sacred One is too big to carry away. When the dragons are free, they could take the Sacred One back home. Or they might stay – it is all conjecture. If they go, I suspect Fa'red will be unstoppable.'

Jelindel and Daretor hung on grimly as the night air whistled around their heads. The turbulence was the worst they had encountered. Zimak looked morbidly into the darkness on either side. The dizzy rush of wind, the sense of something massive just off in the darkness, was profoundly unsettling. All three were close to collapsing. Although Jelindel was as spent as her companions, she secretly syphoned off some energy to them.

S'cressling was navigating through the canyons of the massif. It was a feat dangerous by day and almost suicidal by night, even by the light of three moons. Osric had insisted S'cressling knew the canyons like his tongue knew the roof of his mouth, and that she could fly them blindfolded. At which point Zimak had asked, 'So how many times has she flown them *blindfolded*?'

'Zimak, shut up,' Jelindel chided.

Thus they were shooting along narrow canyons. Walls rose sheer on either side for thousands of feet, blocking out what little starlight there was, for the moons, unfamiliar to S'cressling, were casting multiple shadows. The canyon was only a few yards wider than the dragon's wingtips. The sense of rushing speed between the formidable and unforgiving barriers was breathtaking and frightening. One wrong move and they would be dashed to pieces in midair, their pulverised bodies falling through inky blackness to the jagged rocks below.

The Q'zarans were never entirely comfortable flying on the back of the dragon even in daylight. Despite the chill night air they sweated, sitting rigidly on the deck, clutching guy ropes and stanchions.

'If we get through this,' Zimak said, 'I'll never fly again.'

'Then you'll have a long walk home,' said Daretor.

'Fine. Dragonfrost exists no more.'

'There are other dangers now, though,' Daretor replied. 'Nevertheless, I'll be with you.'

'You sound like a couple of nagging spinsters,' said Jelindel, without trace of conviction.

The massive slabs of darkness continued to rush past. Those on the deck did not dare to move as the dragon banked first one way and then the other, the sickening aerobatics wracking their stomachs with nausea. The nightmare continued for what seemed an eternity.

In the pilot's saddle, Osric grinned to himself. He had not bothered to tell his companions that the flight was not quite as dangerous as they thought. Although dragons had astonishing farsight, they were often almost blind in close quarters, and would peer at objects, especially people, first with one large unblinking eye and then the other, trying to bring them into focus. Thus, even in day time, S'cressling would not have used her eyesight for such delicate and dangerous manoeuvres to any great extent. She used a combination of innate knowledge of the canyon layout and her wingtips, which acted like a cat's whiskers. S'cressling's speed was more apparent than real. In the confined space, she flew at a leisurely pace, which was exaggerated by the wind and darkness.

Several times she deliberately let her wingtips brush the canyon sides, as though familiarising herself with the walls due to the unfamiliar shadows now cast by Q'zar's moons. In addition, she used a process not unlike that used by bats; sounding distances by echoes. This was Osric's 'cheeping'; the sound S'cressling bounced off the canyon walls was at too high a frequency for mortal ears to hear.

The truth was that there was far less danger than the Q'zarans imagined, but S'cressling was unaware that she could have put their minds at rest. After all, they did not ask her.

She flew like this for some time before, finally, turning into a canyon that ended in a cul-de-sac. She flew for another fifteen minutes, enjoying the sense of coming home. Ahead lay a place that she had not visited in some time. There was a great joy in her heart at the thought of returning.

At the mane, Osric knew they were almost at their destination. He called back to the others and told them the news. Zimak grunted in relief even as he coughed up blood into a rag. The poison had been acting on his system severely.

Moments later S'cressling banked hard, dropped some three hundred feet, and flared her wings to kill speed. Then they were on firm ground again.

The three Q'zarans rose unsteadily to their feet. It was still too dark to see much, and they knew they were somewhere halfway up the side of a canyon wall. They could just make out round blobs of deeper blackness where the mouths of great tunnels gaped in the stone walls.

'Well, we're here,' said Osric from the darkness nearby.

S'cressling moved deeper into the tunnel at whose entrance she had landed. The tunnel went straight for two hundred yards then turned at right angles. They saw a glimmering of light. When they rounded the bend, an enormous cavern opened before them. It was almost a dragon city, and contained over a hundred nesting dragons, all of whom turned to scrutinise the newcomers.

Recognising S'cressling, several called out greetings in deep-throated trumpeting sounds. S'cressling answered.

'So this is a dragon nursery,' Zimak murmured to himself.

'Remember what I said,' Osric reminded them. 'Do not leave S'cressling even for a second. Dragons are lethal when protecting their young.' He looked at his bandaged arm. 'And they smell blood,' he added, keeping a straight face.

'Are we safe here?' Jelindel asked, picking up on Zimak's unease.

'We're safe for as long as S'cressling keeps us safe.'

'Good old S'cressling,' said Zimak, uncharacteristically patting the dragon on the flank. He nervously eyed the horde of dragons that diligently eyed him back. 'I've always said, you can't beat S'cressling, a dragon among dragons, honest, friendly, *loyal . . .'*

'Zimak?'

'Yeah, yeah. I'm shutting up, okay? See? I've shut up.'

S'cressling made her way through the vast cavern, wending her way between the great rocky nests, all the time heading for the mouth of another tunnel that opened in the far wall.

Sometimes she stopped to exchange greetings with a dragon sitting on a clutch of eggs. The long-vowelled sonorous tongue of the dragons was hypnotic to the ear, even oddly reassuring. It made Jelindel feel strangely safe, as a child might in the dark night, when she suddenly hears the familiar tones of her father's voice. She wondered why this should be. It was apparent that Daretor and Zimak felt the same way.

Only once did Jelindel glimpse a dragon egg. She was not surprised to see that it was like a polished stone, something made from the bones of the earth and shaped into a smooth, gleaming ovoid by a trick of nature. She could hardly believe that such a solid-looking object could house new life, or indeed that it could even be hollow.

Osric later told her that she was lucky to see an egg. The dragons jealously guard them from view, even from dragonkeepers, with whom they generally have a good relationship. 'It is probably because they sense magic in you,' he said. 'In some way, they see you as a kindred spirit.'

Before long they left behind the great nesting cavern and entered the tunnel that led to a vast rookery in which dragons sheltered with their young. The young dragons were actually far more dangerous than their elders, though not by design. They were not malicious, just big and strong.

'They could bite you in half, though not mean to,' said Osric.

After a while they came to a series of smaller tunnels, clearly intended for men. After brief farewells, Jelindel, Daretor and Zimak lit smoky torches and entered the tunnels. Osric returned with S'cressling to the canyons.

Jelindel and the others had not gone far when a dreadful odour washed over them.

'By all the gods, what is that foul smell?' Zimak asked, gagging.

'Perhaps if you listened when things were explained to you, you would know,' said Daretor, whose own nose was screwed up in disgust.

'You mean Osric's little speech before we landed? For your information, I was trying valiantly not to throw up on everyone, so I was a little busy.'

Jelindel, breathing through her mouth, waved them to silence. 'Creatures live here,' she said. 'Scavengers that keep the dragon caves clean.'

'And I suppose they're huge, with great teeth and unpleasant dispositions?' Zimak said.

'Not at all,' said Daretor. 'They're blubberous and irritating and they talk too much.'

They came to a wide cavern studded with stalactites and sta-lagmites. The stream running in the middle was ink-black. Even when a torch was held above its surface, its depth could not be guessed.

But that was not what held their attention.

'I'm not walking through that,' said Zimak. 'I'm not.'

'Fine. Go back and say hello to the dragons for me,' Daretor said, despite the fact that he himself looked ill at the thought of crossing the cavern.

They stared in dismay at the cavern floor. It was covered in pools of seeping, pulpy matter that heaved and pulsed and smelled like putrefying flesh. Whole segments seemed to be dissolving slowly into ropy threads of saliva-like liquid that glistened noisomely in the torch light.

'I'm not crossing that,' Zimak said again.

Jelindel was squinting. 'Maybe you won't have to,' she said. 'If we climb that rock we can reach the stream. Assuming it's not too deep we should be able to follow it to the other side.'

'Gah, assuming it's not packed with nasty things just lying in wait for the unwary.'

Jelindel looked at Zimak. 'Can you stop being so negative?'

Zimak shrugged. 'Just pointing out the obvious dangers.'

Jelindel did not reply. Instead, she clambered onto the rock and crawled along to a point where she could, with some difficulty and a badly skinned knee, lower herself into the water.

Daretor stood on the rock looking down at her. His face was grim. 'Zimak could be right,' he said. 'We should test the water first.'

'We have nothing to test it with,' said Jelindel. 'Except me.'

She started splashing with her feet. 'Jelli!' cried Daretor, suddenly alarmed. 'Have you gone mad?'

The dark waters lay still all around. 'I'm here,' she said. 'Come on, let's get moving.'

With many sideways glances at the dark stream, Daretor and Zimak climbed down and followed Jelindel along the shore, about six feet out from the bank. Here the water was up to their hips. They moved quietly and said little. It was hard enough to breathe the stinking air without trying to talk as well.

They were almost within reach of the exit tunnel when the things attacked. They appeared to be giant water rats with thin, elongated snouts, almost like a species of alligator, and armed with many lethal teeth. The creatures came surging up from the inky depths, water cascading from their furry backs, jaws snapping. Jelindel would have been pulled under at once if Zimak's reflexes had not been faster. Finding it difficult to walk he was using his sword as a staff. In one quick move he thrust it deep into the mouth of the animal as it lunged at Jelindel.

A great thrashing began in the water as dozens of the creatures surged forward. There were so many they got in each other's way. Zimak and Daretor's swords flashed and thrust. Blood added a deeper flush to the dark stream. Jelindel spat weak binding spells, adding one that tripled a creature's weight so that it sank to the bottom.

'This way,' yelled Daretor, scrambling onto a rocky outcrop. With the last of his energy he dragged Jelindel out of the water, then they covered for Zimak. In seconds, they were several feet above the stream. Below them was a frothing sea of snapping jaws.

'It doesn't look as if they are much into climbing,' Jelindel said, trying to regain her composure. She gulped in air to stay conscious. An indefatigable fatigue was sweeping through her.

Zimak hawked some bloodied bile down at the slavering creatures. 'If blood's what they want, they can have it.'

Daretor forced himself to stand. 'Give them all you want,' he said. 'I'm saving mine.'

They climbed over more rocks, putting as much distance between themselves and the maniacal animals as they could. Oddly enough, the creatures did not pursue them into the pulpy mass. The humans understood why soon enough. Daretor had spotted a tunnel in the wall and made for it. It led for a moment toward the stream. An over-eager creature surged partly out of the water and onto the bank, its forepaws sinking into the putre-fying mass. With a speed that was frightening, knotted tentacles whipped out of the mass and dragged the creature into the sodden depths. The amphibian squealed once and was gone.

'What in Black Quell's pit was that?' Zimak demanded shakily.

'Let's not find out,' said Jelindel. They hurried towards the tunnel mouth, taking extra care not to come within reach of the morass.

Behind them, the water creatures were enjoying a feeding frenzy.

'They're eating their dead,' Zimak gulped.

The three climbed wearily into the tunnel. Here a faint breeze blew in their faces and brought a warm earthy smell free of taint. They breathed easy for the first time in a while. The tunnel bore them quickly and effortlessly through the remainder of the barrier wall into a narrow ravine on the floor of the inner crater. Some miles away, across the crater, could be seen the single tall pinnacle of rock, atop which sat the Tower Inviolate. They stopped for a rest.

The path ahead looked dry, but forbidding and long. Nor was danger far off. Dragons patrolled the airways, circling the tower, while single dragons looped around the crater. Osric had explained that the only way to reach the tower unseen and uninvited was via the network of narrow ravines on the crater floor. These ravines were often no more than six or seven feet across and as much as forty feet deep. No dragon, Osric had said, flying normal patrol, could see to the bottom. Nevertheless, he had cautioned them not to look up, in case their pale faces became visible. He'd also cautioned them to hide all shiny gems and buckles. This done, they set off.

If it was hot in the crater, it was sweltering in the ravines. Within minutes sweat was pouring off them, and their clothes hung dank and heavy, weighing them down. Their packs chaffed and added to the burden. Before long they trudged along the snaking maze-like ravines feeling so fatigued that they could not imagine fighting off any attacker.

'Our water won't last at this rate,' said Daretor, panting.

'We shall see,' Jelindel replied, somewhat cryptically.

Then they both looked at Zimak.

'What?' he asked. 'What did I do now?'

'Nothing,' said Jelindel.

'Which is the point,' said Daretor. 'You haven't complained once since setting foot in these canyons.'

Zimak, who still carried quite a bit of fat, shrugged. 'No one ever listens anyway. Besides, I've come up with a whole new philosophy of life.'

Daretor raised an eyebrow. 'Really?'

'Yes, really.'

Daretor gazed at him for a moment. 'Well, are you going to share this wondrous revelation, or keep it to yourself?'

'I'm going to live in the "now".'

'The now what?'

'Just the now. The moment. The present. I'm going with the flow of events.'

'What flow? What are you talking about?'

'The flow. Life is like a stream. It flows along. You can either go with the current or you can fight against it and try to swim upstream, or you can get out of the water entirely. It's your choice. Me, I'm going with the flow. And right now, this is the flow. Trudging along, sweating like a pig, about to die horribly in all likelihood.'

'I've heard of something like this,' Jelindel said. 'The monks of the Nerrissi Plateau have a similar faith.'

'They do?' Zimak said, surprised.

Daretor groaned. 'You're only encouraging him,' he said. 'The poison has driven him mad, and you're making it worse. Going with the dummart "now". Being in the "flow". The babblings of a deranged brain, if you ask me. Next thing you know he'll be talking to common stones.'

'Well, the Nerrissi monks do –' Jelindel began.

'I don't want to hear it,' Daretor said. The others shrugged and they continued. For the next several hours they moved wearily, but they covered a lot of ground. At various junctures they were reassured to see that they were closing in on the tower.

They were probably half-way across the crater floor, when they spotted several high-flying dragons soaring overhead. It was at this point that their water ran out.

Jelindel called a stop and they rested for several minutes. They knew that they had little chance of reaching the tower without water. Even if they did, they would be in no condition to carry out the plan.

'What are we going to do?' Zimak asked, his eyes glazed.

'Isn't that a question about the future?' asked Daretor. 'I thought you were the fellow who lived in the now?'

Zimak waved him away, too drained to waste words. 'Jelindel?' he asked again.

'There is something I can do but I am loath to do it. It may give us away.'

'We may be dead either way then,' Daretor pointed out.

'Perhaps. In any case it's too soon. Let's move on.'

They trudged on, putting one weary foot in front of the other. In this manner, they covered half the remaining distance, but then could go no further. All three were stumbling, their mouths gaping, their breath coming in dry gasps.

They finally staggered to a stop. Zimak sat down, unable to get up again. Daretor lowered himself to the ground with as much dignity as he could manage and looked to Jelindel. She swam in and out of focus before his eyes.

'Whatever you're going to do,' he said, 'now would be a good time.'

Zimak smiled through cracked lips. 'See? *Now* would be a good time.'

'Imbecile,' said Daretor.

Without speaking Jelindel slid to her knees and began to rub her palms across a section of the ravine wall. As she did so she murmured an incantation. Very slowly, as if reluctant, a flickering blue light gathered on her lips. Instead of leaping out, it slid across her cheek, down her neck and arm and into the rock, where it sparkled and foamed.

A moment later the rock darkened and began to sweat. Water started oozing from the very pores of the stone until a small trickle formed.

'Quickly,' Jelindel said. 'Fill the canteens, drink as much as you can, then fill them again. I can't maintain this for long.'

Rakeem's head whipped up. A puzzled look flashed across his face, cutting him off in mid sentence. The guard captain he was speaking to raised his eyebrows.

'Vizier? Something troubles you?'

Rakeem silenced him with a motion and frowned. 'I sense

something . . .' he said, 'not far away but not close either . . . an unfamiliar magic . . .'

The captain looked troubled.

'Double the guard,' Rakeem snapped. 'It may be nothing but . . . something . . .'

They made it to the base of the tower. As Osric had promised they found an ancient fissure through which they squeezed. Inside was a natural chamber that seemed to have no ceiling. The walls were perfectly smooth and there appeared to be no way to scale them.

'What now?' Daretor asked.

'I can use the last of my magic,' Jelindel said. 'We're inside the pinnacle itself. Some magic must be practised within the tower from time to time, and that might cloak mine.'

'What kind of magic?' Zimak began, stifling a yelp as he suddenly rose in the air. On either side of him Jelindel and Daretor also levitated. Jelindel spoke a spell, and a sphere of ethereal light burst from her hand. Their rapid ascent caused it to flicker.

Osric and S'cressling put their plan into practice. The intention was to create a diversion. They swept from the canyon into the inner crater. The great crimson dragon soared quickly across the surface, drawing no more attention than any other dragon. The hour was late in any case, and there were few dragons about, except for far-off sentinels that paid S'cressling no heed. If the tower were to be attacked they believed it could not possibly come from a dragon.

S'cressling swooped into the landing bay, folding her wings

and coming to a feather-light stop. There was almost no one about. Bored engineers shuffled out to remove the dragon's harness and lead her to the feeding troughs. But that was as far as the routine went.

S'cressling bellowed angrily and reared up on her back legs. Gouts of greenish flame sprang from her snout and swept back and forth across the walls and tunnel entrances of the bay. A sheet of flame licked across every surface and thick smoke filled the air. Sulphur fumes made everyone choke.

Osric leapt to the ground and raced for the loading bay doors. He had to stop them from being closed. S'cressling turned her attention to the barracks at the far end of the bay, before heading back to the entrance and taking flight again. Outside, she flew up around the tower, spraying it with gouts of fire. Meantime, Osric ran along a winding corridor, grabbing weapons from an armoury table set up for emergencies.

Jelindel, Daretor and Zimak continued to rise for several hundred yards. Eventually they reached a roughly hewn, domed 'ceiling' containing a trapdoor. Daretor managed to wrench it open. They levitated through, and stood once more on a rocky floor.

Zimak swallowed. 'I still hate flying,' he moaned.

'Osric said it's the safest way to travel,' Daretor said.

'Osric sticks his head between the jaws of a dragon, too. You call that sane?'

Before Daretor could respond, Jelindel fell against his shoulder. 'Jelli?'

Jelindel's face was pasty-white. Blood congealed around her mouth like smeared lip paint. 'Keep moving,' she wheezed. 'We've still got a way to go.' She stopped to gain her breath. 'According to Osric, sane or not, we can't reach the Sacred One except by the elevator box thing on ropes. It's on the upper levels.'

Daretor signalled for Zimak to help him. Together they supported Jelindel. 'Let's hope our "diversion" is working,' Daretor said.

'Pray it is,' Jelindel agreed. She was starting to feel a little better.

An ancient spiral staircase, hewn from the rock, led upwards. They hurried up the steps. After what seemed like an eternity they found themselves in the back of what was once some kind of large chamber. Now, mildewed tapestries hung on the walls and dozens of crates were stacked about. Jelindel went to the door, opened it a crack, and listened. All was quiet.

They crept out. Suddenly, Zimak stumbled and collapsed. He was gasping for breath and the colour had drained from his face.

Jelindel felt his forehead and took his pulse. 'The poison's finishing its work,' she said grimly.

Zimak breathed with effort. 'Help me up,' he ordered. They assisted him to his feet. 'We've come too far to let it win. Gah, Daretor. I don't suppose you want to swap bodies?'

'Not right now, no,' Daretor replied.

'Whatever happens,' Jelindel said, 'we must return the dragonsight to its rightful owner.'

'Easier said than done,' Zimak wheezed.

With an arm around Jelindel and Daretor's shoulders, Zimak managed to make good time. They realised that they were on the lower levels. With directions from a terrified page, they soon found the staircase used by the workers. The page was left tied up in an unused chamber. As they had hoped, there was little traffic on the stairs. The diversion had to be working.

Osric had been seen, but eluded capture in the maze of passages that formed the middle levels. Finally, he was cornered. Fortunately, the strength of the guard facing him was not great, and the narrow corridor that led to where he stood could be held against many. It was a standoff, and that was as he wished it.

The captain of the guard held off. He saw no reason why he or his men should die. There was a simpler solution. 'Send for the vizier,' he ordered. 'Tell him the traitor Osric has returned.'

A guard ran off. Osric unsteadily released pressure on the long bow that he had readied to fire. Although his arm had only sustained a flesh wound, it was nonetheless throbbing.

Meanwhile, outside the tower, S'cressling was wreaking havoc. She had managed to set fire to several towers and even the palace itself. Soon she would have to withdraw. Already half a dozen dragons with half-dressed riders were issuing from the launch bays. The distraction had worked admirably.

Then something unexpected happened.

As the dragonriders closed in for the attack, S'cressling bellowed. The other dragons suddenly swooped away. What she had told them in the ancient tongue of the dragons was that they could be free if they would join her. The dragonsight was no longer with King Amida. Even now it was on its way to the Sacred One.

Her brethren were puzzled. Clearly, S'cressling was not being controlled from the tower. The king and his vizier would never brook such behaviour. Indeed, the penalty for S'cressling's actions was death. The fact that she was unharmed told the dragons all they needed to know: the binding magic was unravelling. The dragons that had loyally melded to their riders now disobeyed their frantic commands, and withdrew to consult one another. Others flipped over, shaking riders from their seats.

With terrified screams, the dragonriders plummeted to the crater far below. Seven dragons belched a torrent of flame against the bulwarks of the Tower Inviolate.

Inside, Osric's heart leapt. Their time had finally arrived.

Bells rang throughout the tower and trumpets blared. Several guardsmen raced past, not realising that Jelindel, Daretor and Zimak were intruders. This gave the trio the confidence to act with less hostility when encountering the defenders. Several times they passed unnoticed and unremarked. But such luck could not hold out for long. Nor could their pace last – all were clearly ill. They walked with great difficulty and spoke haltingly. The poison's effect was consuming them.

They had reached the upper levels and were staggering down a corridor that opened into a wider hallway when they met their first serious opposition. A small squad of dragonriders was hurrying to the outer ramparts to determine the cause of the clamour. When they saw the Q'zarans, they paused, then charged, swords drawn.

The fight took a terrible toll on the trio. Jelindel falteringly cast binding spells on several of the attackers and Daretor killed one who rushed precipitously upon his sword. Zimak managed to dispatch another, who had tripped over a fallen comrade. The remaining dragonriders fled along the corridor.

'Gah,' Zimak spat. 'These people have no taste for Q'zaran blood.' He almost swooned, but the wall stopped him from falling.

Jelindel bent over double, then straightened, inhaling mightily. Perspiration beaded her forehead. 'I doubt they're too worried about us,' she said. 'Time's on their side – why risk their lives to shorten ours?'

Daretor nudged them forward. 'We're not done yet. If it's the last thing I do I intend taking Rakeem with us.'

'Keep that thought,' Jelindel said, forcing her legs to move.

They found the elevator and tugged on the rope, then waited an agonising few minutes as the box ground up to their level. When it finally arrived, they flung back the doors and piled in. Jelindel stopped Zimak.

'I need you here, if you're able. Make sure nobody interferes with this contraption,' she said.

Zimak's face was wracked with pain, yet he said, 'Jelindel, you two have all the fun.'

The elevator cabin dropped. Jelindel had an uncomfortable sensation in the pit of the stomach and her ears blocked.

The journey to the lowermost level seemed like it would be uneventful. Suddenly they heard, far above and muffled by distance, the clash of arms, and the curses of injured men. There was little they could do. Fate had taken them in its grasp and they must follow where it led.

There was a distant scream that grew swiftly louder, followed by an almighty impact on the roof of the elevator box.

Jelindel offered a brief prayer to White Quell that the fallen body hadn't been Zimak's.

The entire cabin shuddered as though in response to Jelindel's muttered prayer. It banged against the walls of the vertical tunnel, and then they were falling.

The cabin bucked and lurched as it gained speed.

Jelindel called out a spell that emerged from her lips as blue light. Nothing happened.

Daretor braced himself for the afterlife.

◇

Zimak leaned on his sword in front of the elevator doors. He was thinking that lately he was always being left behind or mislaid, and that his place was really at the centre of things. Only in such places could glory be acquired – not that he particularly wanted glory. But after riding with Daretor for such a long time, some of the warrior's principles and ideals had begun to rub off on him. Certainly glory was very good for getting girls into haylofts. Scars worked well too, but were often painful in the getting.

By White Quell, next time he would *insist* on going along. He might be the biggest of the three, but that was all the more reason why he should be with them.

He was just succeeding in working himself up into a black mood when he was attacked. Two dragonriders had been sent with a group of lackeys. They led the charge down the ill-lit corridor.

Zimak staggered forward to meet them. His annoyance had pepped him up to some extent, though he was also pale and shaky. He met the first man with a deft parry and riposte. His hand shook with the effort of withstanding the dragonrider's onslaught.

He managed to wound his opponent with a complicated feint that had worked many times before. Seconds later he left a deep cut in the sword arm of the second man, forcing him to step back from the battle. The lackeys, most of whom were holding pikes and meat cleavers, hung back indecisively.

'FLEE!' Zimak screamed, and the lackeys fled. Zimak smiled. He was struggling to keep his eyes focused, and the ground seemed to be coming up to greet him.

The wounded dragonrider took this moment to hurl himself at the Q'zaran.

Sensing rather than seeing the dragonrider rush him, Zimak

stumbled back, barely parried the blow, then shoved the man hard in the back as his momentum swept him past. The man crashed headlong into the elevator door, smashing through the guard rail, and disappeared from view. His scream faded into the depths of the elevator shaft.

Zimak turned to face the remaining dragonrider. The man stared back nervously.

'Your job is done here,' Zimak slurred, summoning up enough strength to sound like he could enforce the implied threat. It worked. The man nodded in a kind of awkward salute, then fled. Few, it seemed, wanted to combat the mantid gladiator, as Daretor and Zimak had become known.

Zimak almost felt good. If it hadn't been for the fever that was even now spilling blood from his mouth, he would have danced a little jig. Then the ropes holding the elevator snapped with an audible crack that whipped Zimak's head around. With a sense of impending horror, he dragged himself to the broken door and peered down the shaft.

Jelindel's spell had not failed. It had simply taken time to gather power from her depleted body. Just as Daretor expected the elevator's crushing impact, the cabin lurched and began to slow. Not by much at first, but the retarding force increased. Within a few seconds the cabin was descending at its normal speed.

Daretor sighed and slid down the wall to rest on his haunches. He had barely enough energy to keep his eyes open.

The elevator came to a halt with a thump that threw Jelindel to the floor. Daretor dragged open the doors, then stepped back into a weak fighting stance. Before them stood the vizier, Rakeem, and a dozen bodyguards, all with drawn swords.

Rakeem marvelled at their endurance. 'You have done well, for barbarians,' he said. 'But I will take the dragonsight now.' He stepped forward, hand outstretched.

Over their shoulders, Jelindel could see the dark shape of the Sacred One. When Rakeem mentioned the dragonsight it stirred and sighed.

Jelindel held up a leather pouch. Rakeem eyed it hungrily. 'Give it to me willingly,' he said, 'and I shall spare your lives.'

Jelindel muttered something and blue flickerings engulfed the pouch. 'One word from me, a thought even, and my magic will consume the dragonsight.'

Rakeem bristled. He forced himself to use an even tone. 'You're bluffing. No power on your puny world could best the dragonsight, much less yours.'

Jelindel forced a smile. 'Luckily, I'm ever underestimated. Such a spell would consume me, granted. But I'm dead anyway.' She tightened her grip on the dragonsight and bared her teeth. 'What's it to be?'

'Name your price,' Rakeem grated.

'The antidote.'

'Why, of course. You only had to ask.' He gestured and a man stepped forward with a vial. 'Take one mouthful only,' he said as he handed it over. He reached for the dragonsight but Jelindel held back her hand.

Jelindel sniffed the vial cautiously then took a mouthful. When Daretor had taken a sip, she handed the vial back. 'Have this taken to our comrade who guards the elevator on the upper level.'

Rakeem glanced at the shattered elevator. 'As you wish, but doubtless he is already dead.'

'Do it!'

Rakeem gestured to two of his men. 'Do as she says. If he is unconscious, pour it down his throat.' The men hurried off to a concealed door that opened on to a stairway. 'There. It is done. Now let me have the dragonsight.'

'In a moment,' said Jelindel. 'Let us see if the antidote works, or is itself another poison.'

They waited several minutes in an effective standoff. Shortly Jelindel felt her strength returning and the fever retreating from her limbs and brow. Daretor also looked much healthier. Part of Jelindel's mind told her the antidote had been laced with a magic potion, hence its rapid effectiveness.

'Enough,' said Rakeem suddenly. He raised his hand and his men tightened their sword grips. 'I have waited long enough. Give it to me.'

Jelindel threw Rakeem the pouch. Daretor stared at her in horror as Rakeem caught it and eagerly looked inside. For a moment his attention was taken. Jelindel drew Daretor to one side, away from Rakeem and closer to the Sacred One.

Then Rakeem looked up. 'Guards. Kill them!'

The battle that followed was as swift as it was deadly. Jelindel managed to bind three of the fighters, but Rakeem's magic blocked further use of that spell. She then used one she had tried once before, to great effect, and managed to temporarily blind several men. The odds were still against them, however. Daretor drove forward, toppling two guards and forcing the others into confusion. Jelindel fought off several attackers, but the outcome was never really in doubt. They were weakened and vastly outnumbered. Jelindel barely managed to deflect Rakeem's spells; that merely distracted her from the battle. In one of these moments she lost her sword.

Reinforcements arrived, and they were surrounded by more

than fifty fighting men. Rakeem stepped forward only when Jelindel and Daretor had their backs to the wall, and sword points at their throats. Daretor glowered, throwing down his weapon.

'I salute you,' Rakeem said. 'You are great warriors, but I'm afraid the day goes to me. Now you shall die.'

Jelindel had noticed what the others, in their fighting fervour, had not. The Sacred One, old and feeble as he was, had crawled from his rocky island and dragged himself, with painful slowness, onto the narrow rocky bridge joining the island to the main chamber floor. But he could go no farther, the bridge being too narrow for his bulk, and too flimsy for his weight.

'Well then, what if I should hand over the real dragonsight?' Jelindel asked.

'You bluff,' said Rakeem, waving back the guards.

She reached inside her tunic and drew out the authentic relic. Rakeem gasped. He pulled an exact replica from the pouch, performed a quick exploratory piece of magic on it, then threw it away.

'You bought very little time for the effort,' Rakeem sneered. 'Kill them!'

Jelindel held the dragonsight up high. Just like Osric, all the fighters reacted in awe; many fell to their feet in an attitude of prayer or penance. Others took on a glassy look. Even Rakeem seemed momentarily cowed, but recovered all too quickly. He threw a spell at Jelindel even as she flicked the dragonsight high into the air. Rakeem's spell altered its trajectory. It arced over the heads of the fighters and flew towards the glowing fissure.

Rakeem screamed and tried to grasp it with magic. Jelindel deflected his charm with her own.

The dragonsight was falling into the fiery chasm. Jelindel cried out, as much in disbelief as horror. For all their efforts and risks to end like this seemed harsh indeed, as if the gods themselves had turned against them.

She started to slump, as if giving up finally, but something was rising in her, words of an ancient charm that came unbidden from another mouth. The unfamiliar words jumped from her mouth of their own accord: Thaddeus Pike's voice boomed: '*Illorn ahn aksar!*'

Energy flooded into her, sang through her limbs. Before she knew what she was doing, she broke into a run, dashing between Rakeem's fighters. Many swung at her but their movements were slow and sluggish, as if they were moving underwater. Long slow oaths erupted around her like tiny muffled explosions as Rakeem's fighters realised what was happening. Thaddeus's charm had speeded her up to several times the normal rate. Now she moved like a blur, avoiding the sword strokes as easily as an adult outmanoeuvres a child.

The charm, Jelindel knew, would come at a great cost. For a few moments of heightened speed and reflexes, she would expend enormous amounts of energy and afterwards collapse, helpless.

Meanwhile, the dragonsight was still flying through the air. To Jelindel it moved with eerie slowness as it curved down towards the chasm. She saw that the Sacred One had dragged himself to the very brink of the ugly gash in the chamber floor, his one remaining eye fixed on the amulet, as if willing it to himself. Jelindel knew that dragon magic did not work like that.

She burst from the ranks of Rakeem's defenders and sped across the chamber floor. Even with her increased reflexes it would be a very near thing. The dragonsight was falling, falling to its annihilation. Jelindel put on an even greater burst of speed. To Daretor and the others it seemed almost that, for a moment, she vanished from human sight, so swiftly did she move. Then in a blink she was at the edge of the chasm. But something was wrong. She was teetering. Her face was grey and drawn. Yet she managed to lean out, one arm outstretched, and pluck the dragonsight from the air.

With a roar, Rakeem leapt towards her. He was followed by his faithful. Daretor was ignored, but he sped along with the others, cursing that he was too far away to help Jelindel.

Jelindel had never felt so tired in all her life. Even thinking was an effort. All she wanted to do was sink to the floor and sleep. Peaceful sleep. Oh, how she wanted that! But the noise behind her pricked her mind back to some semblance of sharpness.

She glanced behind. Rakeem and his men bellowed towards her. Despite the fog in her mind she knew they must not reach her. It had something to do with the amulet now clutched in her hand. The amulet! She must give it to the dragon crouched on the other side of the bridge in quivering alertness, watching her.

She turned and staggered towards the bridge. Behind her Rakeem closed the distance between them.

Jelindel reached the bridge, stumbled on to it. It was arched, rising by some seven or eight feet as it towered over the fiery chasm below. She felt the hot breath of magma on her face, scorching her skin. The heat stabbed into her throat and lungs as she breathed the sulphur-laden air. She did not falter. Somehow she kept going, though her tiredness made every step a labour.

She tripped on something and stumbled, falling to her knees. A howl of triumph rose behind her. *'Get up. Get up, Jelindel,'* she said through gritted teeth.

But she could not rise. Lifting her head she looked across the crest of the bridge into the eye of the dragon. It seemed to beckon her. With a weary oath she started crawling towards it on hands and knees, oblivious to the jagged surface of the bridge tearing her flesh.

She reached the very top of the arch and there she slumped, unable to go any further. Raising the hand holding the amulet, she made to throw it to the dragon. As she did so the Sacred One lunged onto the bridge. There was a terrible cracking noise. The bridge shook, then started to crumble. Jelindel cried out in fear and grief, though not for herself; for all the things that would now not be undone . . . This was her last thought as she and the Sacred One plunged into the chasm.

On the chamber floor, Rakeem and his followers skidded to a stop and gazed at the spot where the dragonsight and the Sacred One had been moments before. Daretor let out a single sobbing gasp, not believing that he had lost Jelindel.

Then a great gout of flame shot up from the chasm and all groaned. Some fell to their knees, knowing that the Sacred One and the amulet had struck the magma far below. In the silence that followed there was a new noise, hard to place. A soughing, like wind in trees.

Something rocketed out of the chasm and swooped about the chamber, before coming to a stop above Rakeem. It was the Sacred One, its left eye socket no longer empty. Jelindel slumped on the dragon's neck, barely able to hang on.

Rakeem screeched in anger.

As they watched, all realised that the Sacred One was no longer old and feeble, nor partly blind. The gaunt frame filled out with youthful flesh; his wings stretched and flapped power-fully, and a deep crimson hue appeared on his leathery skin. It spread and deepened, until it was an iridescent glow such as no one had ever seen on a dragon.

Fire gushed from the old lungs; it was no feeble spray of sparks, but a furnace.

Zimak arrived via the stairs and joined Daretor, who was still facing off a squad of Rakeem's men.

'Put down your weapons and yield!' Jelindel called out, her voice harsh with exhaustion.

Rakeem snarled angrily. 'Yield? Yield! I do not yield to scum or to mindless beasts of the air!'

Jelindel was too weary to reply.

The Sacred One was not. A great gout of flame shot out and consumed Rakeem where he stood. The dragon's head swivelled towards the fighters and all but a few threw down their weapons and abased themselves in supplication. Those left standing were turned to char from the knees upwards.

Thus the enslavement of the dragons of Q'zar came to an end. Nor, as Fa'red had thought, did they return to their paraworld at once. Fa'red had not realised that the dragons had dreamed of returning to their fabled home. Besides, three gallant Q'zarans had freed the dragons and returned the dragonsight. Dragons knew honour and gratitude. They also took very badly to being treated as pawns.

'Pawns?' asked Jelindel as she stood in audience with the Sacred One. 'How can beings as powerful and wise as dragons be pawns?'

'If you have been enslaved, anything is possible,' the rejuvenated dragon replied via mind thought. 'Fa'red stole the dragonsight to bring us here, I am fairly sure of that. He knew that Rakeem would move the kingdom. Using the dragons he would have conducted a campaign of terror to get the dragonsight back.

If he had failed, we would have been freed, and therefore turned on our masters; then returned to our paraworld. The question is who would want a campaign of terror?'

Jelindel thought for some moments. Only one man stood to profit from frightening the entire continent witless.

'Someone who wished to unify the kingdoms of Q'zar under his rule,' she responded. 'Fa'red. It is my feeling that he visited every monarch within hundreds of miles, demonstrated his air-liner power, then told them that it was their only hope against an invasion of dragons that was soon to come. He then stole the dragonsight, knowing that Rakeem would follow, bringing the dragons with him. When the nobility of the lands hereabouts learned of their coming, they fell over themselves to provide Fa'red with enough soldiers to grow and tend his squadrons, along with thousands of tons of chickenfeed. He would have insisted that the combined squadrons be placed under his direct command. When the dragons vanished, he would have said that he managed to vanquish them by magic alone, and still have the most powerful military force in history at his disposal.'

'And if the dragons leave, he will still be able to achieve his ends,' said the Sacred One. 'I believe that you will need some help.'

'Until we bring Fa'red to book, no one will be safe, that's true,' Jelindel mused.

For several days after that, no dragons were to be seen on or over Dragonfrost. Humans still went about their business in the tower, and guards were visible building defensive walls. Huge flying objects were certainly in evidence above the plain, however. Through her farsight Jelindel could see the chickenriders scrutinising the castle with their own farsights.

The attack came out of a clear blue sky the next day. Alarm bells began to ring as sentries reported several great V-formations flying over the mountains in the distance. Everyone immediately ran for the shelter of secure rooms deep inside the castle. Jelindel, Daretor, Zimak and Osric were watching from the mouth of a cave some distance away as the first wave of airliners came in, diving fast. Dark pots fell from their cabins as they passed over the castle. They burst into flames as they struck the roofs and battlements.

'BUK BUK BUK-CAW!' the airliners crowed.

'Those things could make sieges a thing of the past,' said Zimak. 'Even the very best of castles couldn't withstand such an attack for more than a few hours.'

'What worries me is that there must be two hundred of those things,' said Jelindel.

'Hie, Fa'red and Hargrellien must have sent their entire force.'

'Arithmetic has never been your strong point, has it Zimak?' said Jelindel. 'Two hundred airliners is a mere fifth of the force that we saw in Fa'red's staging grounds.'

The castle burnt fiercely after no more than fifty of the living battle machines had attacked. It was at this point that the surprise was sprung. All around the castle, from peaks, rocky outcrops, and ruined towers, boulders unfolded to become dragons, hiding within their own folded wings. Of a sudden, it was a hundred dragons against the two hundred war galleys of the air.

To be fair, this wave of airliners was not equipped for what came next. They were loaded with firepots filled with soap and lamp oil, and had only a few archers aboard. The dragons attacked by flying up under the vulnerable airliners, where arrows could not reach them. The dragons set the huge feathered wings aflame, so that the airliners dropped from the sky, trailing smoke.

The crews leaped for their lives and unfurled simple wicker and canvas wings to slow their descent. Still, it was not all one-sided. Many of the airliners flew in a staggered formation, so that they could cover each other and to allow their archers to fire at anything attacking from below. Not many arrows penetrated the dragons' scales, but those that did sent the great creatures plummeting to their deaths.

'Why do they fall prey to mere arrows?' asked Daretor, staring in disbelief.

'Probably poison on the tips,' Jelindel said worriedly.

'But I was hit, and suffered no ill effects,' said Osric.

'You are a creature of the natural paraworlds. Dragons are partially magical. Poisons that affect you or me do not affect them, and the reverse is true as well. It reeks of Fa'red's cunning.'

'Still the dragons are winning three to one – oh no, look over there!' Osric exclaimed.

They gazed in dismay at the hundreds of airliners that were now visible in the distance.

'Gah,' Zimak snorted. 'A thousand more of them.'

'Eight hundred,' said Daretor, who had a talent for estimating ranks of warriors, ships, or anything military at a distance.

'With such numbers involved, is the difference important?'

'Two hundred less to kill,' said the pragmatic Daretor.

As the newcomers joined the battle, it became evident that they were loaded with archers instead of firepots. Fa'red had not only built his squadron to bomb castles, bridges and warships. They really were equipped to kill dragons. More and more dragons plummeted out of the air, plunging thousands of feet to be smashed to bloody flesh and splintered bone on the rocky highlands. Fiery wreckage rained from the sky.

'BUK BUK BUK-CAW!' thundered a giant airliner.

'Look, that huge airliner, the one that looks like a battle galley of the air,' said Jelindel. 'That has to be Fa'red's flagship.'

'Why so?' asked Osric.

'His crest has been painted on the side of the structure,' said Daretor. 'He must be here to savour his triumph. With one dragon killed for every three of his airliners, Fa'red will win and still have more than half of his force left over.'

'Dragons are being brought down by mere arrows,' pondered Jelindel.

'Such a humiliating defeat,' said Daretor. 'It's not honourable for something so big to be brought down by something so puny.'

'So puny,' said Jelindel thoughtfully. 'Too puny to kill a dragon, and poison would not paralyse them instantly. There is some sort of magic cast into those arrows.'

'Well once they hit the ground after falling three or four thousand feet it hardly matters, the result is still a dead dragon,' Zimak observed.

Jelindel snapped her fingers. 'We're fighting the wrong way!' she cried. 'The arrows aren't killing the dragons. Hitting the ground at high speed is doing it.'

'We need a giant net to scoop them up,' responded Zimak.

'Osric, call S'cressling!' Jelindel said.

Osric was aghast. 'She's in the battle. To flee a battle is highly dishonourable for a dragon.'

'Nothing is as dishonourable as dying needlessly. She has to organise rescue squads for her brothers and sisters. The fastest, most elite dragon fighters must skirt the battle, diving after stricken dragons to pluck the arrows out of them and break the paralysing magic.'

S'cressling was some minutes in responding to Osric's call. By the tossing of her head and the glare that she gave Jelindel, it was clear that she was not happy to be dragged out of the fight. After a minute or so S'cressling took Osric onto her back and sprang into the air, beating her mighty wings.

Jelindel and Daretor watched as the huge creature banked to skirt the great sphere of whirling, plunging creatures and airliners.

'The dragon wasn't convinced,' said Daretor. 'You brought her dishonour.'

'She doesn't have to be convinced. She just has to carry the message,' replied Jelindel.

A huge, multi-hued dragon was hit by an arrow. It spiralled slowly out of the battle. S'cressling went after him at once, catching up to him after he had dropped about half a mile. With a snap of her jaws and a twist of her head she tore the arrow from the dragon's flank and tossed it aside. Immediately the larger dragon came back to life, beating his wings, striving to regain height. S'cressling stayed with him, apparently communicating in the way of dragons.

'Why doesn't he rejoin the battle?' asked Daretor.

'Because I told Osric that rescued dragons would probably make the best recruits – there. He's going after another paralysed dragon.'

Before more than a handful of minutes had passed, there were a dozen rescued dragons patrolling the base of the battle. The dragons that they in turn rescued were ascending right back into the fight. In no time, the dragons were losing very few of their number. Burning houses with charred wings and kicking legs fell from the sky, trailing smoke. Some of the human operators chose to ram the dragons, and leap to safety on their wicker and cloth wings. Dragons with broken wings or twisted necks spiralled out of the fight, to plunge to their deaths. Archers fell from their stricken mounts like nuts shaken from a tree. Operators glided out of the battle, only to be flamed by dragons that were currently idle, and all the while dragons belched flames, while arrows fell like a dark, sinister rain.

Nearly an hour into the battle, Jelindel and Daretor noticed that Fa'red's living machines were falling out of the sky almost continuously, sometimes trailing smoke, and occasionally breaking in pieces. The battle had become just a prolonged slaughter of the living battle machines, and those of their riders whose wicker and cloth wings did not function properly.

The Sacred One drew most of their attention now. Finally he had fought his way to Fa'red's flagship. Golden flashes of magic spewed between the combatants. The dragon's fiery breath mushroomed against an invisible barrier about Fa'red's airliner. The next moment it vaporised and Fa'red retaliated with a broadside of red tendrils that struck out to lasso the Sacred One. He writhed for a moment like a fish in a net, but snapped through the magical bindings with his scythe-like teeth.

'Can't you help him?' Daretor asked Jelindel.

'Not now, Daretor. I'm assisting the others. This showdown has to be between the two champions.'

'Fa'red's flag-chicken is on fire!' said Zimak. 'The old guy's going for it now.'

'There. Look! A wing's collapsed. Everyone aboard's jumping for their lives with those wicker wings.'

The Sacred One dived after Fa'red's airliner. His breath flamed many of those who bailed out while others escaped on fast air currents.

The defenders did not know it at the time, but this marked the end of the battle. Osric reported that several of the escapees from Fa'red's flagship were picked up in midair by others of the hybrid bird-forts. These, in turn, fled rather than rejoin the battle.

Robbed of their leadership, and seeing their numbers steadily decline in the face of the onslaught, the morale of the remaining operators collapsed. Some surrendered, some scattered, and others had to cope with mutinies between their crews and the archers. Although the last of the fighting was to be a long time trailing off, the battle was over. Victory was with the dragons.

In the days that followed, great changes came to the Tower Inviolate. King Amida was overthrown, and all his supporters imprisoned or banished. Those who wished it were sent back to their own paraworld. Osric's people and their dragons were brought through to Q'zar, using the dragon magic.

One particularly important ceremony was performed as soon as people and dragons stopped fighting each other. Osric was escorted by a squad of nervous warriors between the ranks of an honour guard made up of enormous, battle-scarred dragons. Upon reaching the pavilion at the end, Osric was officially crowned temporary Regent of Dragonfrost with a circlet of office. His new subjects cheered as the selected dragons puffed a twenty-one fireball salute into the air.

Osric began his reign by sending ambassadors to all the nearby realms, and making reparations for the depredations of the dragons under Rakeem and King Amida. His neighbours were pleased merely to have some peace. Nobody felt inclined to say that what was on offer was not enough.

Fa'red was sought amid the mountains, but he was not found. The wily sorcerer was assumed to have escaped on one of the battle machines that fled the fighting just after his flagship was destroyed. Like the Preceptor before him, most assumed that he had gone to ground and would never be heard from again.

'The likes of Fa'red are never truly defeated,' Jelindel warned as she stood in Osric's chambers, watching him sign the decree ending the search.

'I am aware of that. I am also aware that we have done everything possible to find him, yet failed,' replied Osric.

'Daretor has declared a quest. He has dedicated his life to tracking down Fa'red and Hargrellien,' said Jelindel. 'Zimak's going with him for some unfathomable reason. Although I suspect it will be to talk him out of it.'

'I have heard such rumours. Why are you not going with them?'

'Because right now I can probably do more good here. Have you thought about my suggestion?'

'You mean organising some dragon folk as a type of special constabulary to ride the dragons? Yes. Patrols like that will bring back peace, and it will be very welcome.'

'So you agree, just like that? Whatever happened to all your suspicions about women?'

'With one woman in particular . . . With you, I don't think they apply.'

Jelindel laughed.

'What is funny?' exclaimed Osric, suddenly embarrassed.

'Oh, I'm just thinking how nice it is to be wrong,' replied Jelindel. 'The thousand years of darkness that I once foresaw is giving way to a new dawn. It makes me happy . . . for lots of reasons.'

'The ancient prophecy said that when the dragons came back to Q'zar, so too would peace and justice fill the land for all the days to come. Can it really last forever?'

'As with all such prophecies, only time will tell,' said Jelindel. 'The indications thus far are very promising . . .'